A Pair of
Silver Wings

James Holland was born in Salisbury, Wiltshire, and studied history at Durham University. He has worked for several London publishing houses and has written for a number of national newspapers and magazines. He is also the author of three works of history and three previous novels, including *The Burning Blue*. Married with a son, he lives near Salisbury. His website address is www.secondworldwarforum.com

Praise for James Holland

'Holland skilfully turns the screw of tension as the last months of peace slip away . . . When the war comes the book roars into life, demonstrating the author's love of and knowledge in the flying sequences. *The Burning Blue* is traditional fiction, saved from Boy's Own Paper sentimentality not only by the swearing and sex, but also by Holland's total immersion in the period. He has joined the few who can bring history to life'
Guardian

'Holland is a master at evoking time and place, with haunting descriptions'
Daily Telegraph

'Vividly, intelligently, movingly, Holland's monumental chronicle tells it like it was'
Mail on Sunday

Also by James Holland

FICTION
The Burning Blue

NON-FICTION
Fortress Malta: An Island Under Siege 1940–1943
Together We Stand: North Africa 1942–1943:
Turning The Tide In The West
Twenty-One: Coming of age in World War II

A Pair of
Silver Wings

JAMES HOLLAND

arrow books

Published by Arrow Books 2007

2 4 6 8 10 9 7 5 3

First published in the United Kingdom in 2006 by
William Heinemann
Random House, 20 Vauxhall Bridge Road
London, SW1V 2SA

www.randomhouse.co.uk

Addresses for companies within The Random House Group Limited can be
found at: www.randomhouse.co.uk/offices.htm

The Random House Group Limited Reg. No. 954009

A CIP catalogue record for this book
is available from the British Library

ISBN 9780099436461

The Random House Group Limited makes every effort to ensure that the papers
used in its books are made from trees that have been legally sourced from well-
managed and credibly certified forests. Our paper procurement policy can be
found at: www.randomhouse.co.uk/paper.htm

Mixed Sources
Product group from well-managed
forests and other controlled sources
www.fsc.org   Cert no. TT-COC-2139
© 1996 Forest Stewardship Council
FSC

Typeset by SX Composing DTP, Rayleigh, Essex
Printed and bound in Great Britain by CPI Cox & Wyman, Reading, RG1 8EX

For my Parents

A Pair of Silver Wings

PART I

England

Somerset – May, 1995

The sun burned down on his face. Although his eyes were closed, the world was not dark; rather, it seemed to be diffused by a gentle orange glow. A soothing, warm, orange glow. He was lying down, stretched out and almost hidden by the long grass that surrounded him. A shadow passed across his face and he opened his eyes: she was looking at him, just inches away, the sun lighting the back of her head and giving her flaxen hair an unreal glow, like a halo. She was something good, angelic even; something unsullied, incorruptible. Her mouth was moving, the lips moist, and her eyes smiling, but the words were invisible and unheard. Every feature of her face was so clear: the small nick in her eyebrow where the dark hairs refused to grow; the small mole on the end of her left earlobe; the deep-brown eyes that searched his own face. So clear, as though he were staring at her through a magnifying glass. As though her face filling his view was somehow protecting him.

The sun vanished and in its stead came rain, and he was no longer lying down gazing at her, but rather, crouching, in a corner of a dark building. She had gone. There was straw at his feet and other people nearby. Men, crouching with rifles. He was looking through some kind of opening and watching soldiers walking steadily up the hill towards him. They looked inhuman, more like machines, because they were indistinct, faceless. He was turning towards someone near him, someone yelling at him, his mouth screaming, the veins on his neck pulsing with panic and terror. He still couldn't hear the words but now he was running, his heart beating loudly and increasingly fast. A muddy track, a wall and thick undergrowth, scratching, tearing his skin, and a voice that was telling him that no matter how much pain he felt, or how much his face and hands were running with blood, he must not stop until he reached the summit. And then he was there, on the bald patch of ground, looking down, his world beneath him. He could see all around him but his eyes were fixed on a line of people standing against the wall and the soldiers opposite. He had to do something. Panic welled within him – panic born from helplessness. 'No!' he was screaming, 'Don't do this!' But no matter how hard he shouted, no noise came from his straining mouth, his pleading lost to anyone but him.

*

Edward Enderby woke with a start, and for a moment felt quite disorientated and short of breath. It was a dark night, but even in a small town like Brampton Cary the streetlights ensured there was a faint filter of neon, and soon the features of the familiar room began to focus. Edward turned, still half expecting to find the door side of the bed filled with the warm and gently breathing figure of his wife, and was dismayed to see that the sheets and blankets had been wrenched from the sides and into a state of disorder. His pyjamas were clammy, too, and when he put his fingers to his brow, he touched beads of sweat.

His alarm clock had long since lost its luminosity, so he reached over and turned on the side light, his eyes smarting with the sudden brightness. Squinting, he cursed – *only half-past four* – then got up, took off his pyjama top, straightened the sheets and tucked in the sides, and eased himself back into the window side of his bed.

Having turned off the light again, Edward lay back, staring up at the ceiling. It was the second time in a week he'd had the same dream, and the third time in ten days. *Three times too many.* He'd thought such dreams had gone away a long time ago, but suddenly the past was rushing back again, refusing to let him alone. Refusing him the peace he desired. Cynthia used to make allowances; invariably, after a particularly disturbed night he'd be irascible and short-tempered the following day. 'It's all right, I understand,' she'd tell him, discreetly keeping out of his way, and protecting Simon from his father's bark. One time, soon after they had been married, he'd even hit her. He hadn't meant to, but he had been crying in his sleep – a little *upset*, Cynthia had said – and so she had woken him. For a moment he'd not seen his wife, but someone quite different, and so had angrily struck out, shouting 'Don't touch them!' He'd hit her quite hard too – the bruise on her cheek had kept her indoors for the best part of a week. He'd been horrified by what he had done – it had upset him more than he'd been able to express. Of course, he had apologised profusely, assured her it was just his dream and that he had been confused – he'd even offered to sleep in a separate bed. But as always, she had been understanding, even suggesting it had been her fault for having roused him. He had not moved into a different bed, and neither of them had ever spoken of it again.

Edward sighed. *Why now?* he wondered. He'd spent the past fifty years trying to forget, but it seemed old ghosts were not going to let him go yet. He continued staring at the ceiling for some time, the ticking clock the only sound. He tried to think about other things: about the cricket later that day – the first match of the term. But his mind would not let him. No matter how hard he tried, those ghosts wanted to haunt him and there was nothing he could do about it.

He leaned over and turned on the light once more. Then he picked up his book, put on his glasses, and began to read.

When Edward Enderby had first come to Myddleton College as a twenty-seven-year-old history teacher in the autumn of 1949, there were only a couple of other masters who had been in the war – the younger ones like himself – but rather more who'd served in the Great War thirty years before. Both conflicts were rarely mentioned, and then usually in the form of an admonishment to one or other of the boys – 'To think I fought the war for you lot!' or, 'If you think that's hard, Baker,' (or whoever), 'then try spending three years in the trenches!' Even at Edward's interview, the headmaster had not mentioned his war record, except to mutter, 'So, could put you down to help with the Corps?' In the staff room, both the First and the Second World Wars were understood to be as out-of-bounds as the pubs in Brampton Cary were to the boys. It was simply not the form. To brag about one's exploits would be to 'shoot a line' (in old RAF parlance), while to dwell on the hardships was considered whingeing. Besides, it was the next generation they needed to worry about – the boys now at the school.

For Edward, who wished to put the matter out of mind as far as possible, this unwritten rule was most welcome. As far as he was concerned – and he felt sure the other new masters felt the same – it was a relief to be able to channel his attention towards teaching and to whether the first eleven were going to beat King's Taunton for the first time in a quarter of a century.

Thirty-eight years later, when Edward finally retired, he was one of only four members of staff old enough to know what war was like. Mr Cowley, the art master, had been in a tank regiment in Germany when the war had ended; the chaplain, Reverend Troughton, had spent two years in the Royal Navy and had served under Mountbatten. Neither advertised the fact, but it was known amongst the boys. Sometimes their achievements were underplayed; sometimes they were exaggerated. The school rumour mill rarely got it right. Mr Wilkinson, on the other hand, the head of classics, made no secret at all about his time in Burma. Mr Wilkinson positively loved talking about it, and would regale the boys with tales of jungle warfare and his time as a Chindit, sneaking up behind Japanese strongholds and blasting them to smithereens. He'd always been popular, Mr Wilkinson, with both the boys and the rest of the staff. He was an enthusiast, passionate about his subject, passionate about everything, it seemed. Passionate even about the war.

By contrast, Edward had never spoken a word about his war years. If Cynthia knew little about it, then he was certainly not going to go blabbering to his colleagues and to the boys. There had been times when one or other of the boys, and even the masters, had directly asked him, but he'd either brushed it aside with an 'Oh, nothing very exciting,' or told them not to be impertinent and to mind their own business, depending on his mood and who had asked the question. On Remembrance Sunday, he'd never worn any medals, nor had he ever had either photographs or pictures from his war years in any part of his house. Whenever it became known that he'd once been a Spitfire pilot – and somehow, some way, these rumours did evolve periodically – such talk soon evaporated. Mr Enderby? Surely not! Fighter pilots were supposed to be flamboyant, romantic figures; larger than life. That wasn't Mr Enderby at all.

The school had saved him, as he'd known it would. A cocooned environment, where, in those grim post-war years, the depressing effects of rationing, war damage and economic hardship were felt less keenly. A place where he could attempt to forget the past. He'd felt that the moment he'd arrived for his interview in the summer of 1949. Even its situation, nestling in a hollow, surrounded by rolling Somerset hills, had given the impression that both the school and the town were somehow sealed off from the rest of the world. It was why he'd never left. At Myddleton he'd always felt secure, settled. And it was why he was still there, even though his teaching days were over. 'Don't you want to *do* something with your retirement?' Simon had asked him. *I am,* Edward had thought:

he still ran the history society for the sixth-formers, still watched most of the home games. And he read, and continued to build his train set in the attic. He had no desire to 'travel the world' as Simon had suggested he might when Cynthia died, as though constant global travel was a Utopian existence to which all men should aspire. Occasional forays to Spain and France or a week's fishing in Scotland were quite enough.

More than enough, really. He couldn't see himself even making it that far afield too often again in the future. The small town house he and Cynthia had bought on his retirement was the ideal place to see out his days. One of a number of new properties built around a redeveloped mill house, they'd been lucky to get it. Neither too large, nor too small, it had decent and cost-effective central heating, a garage and small garden, and all the fittings worked beautifully. He supposed the stairs might get a bit much later, but now, when he was thankfully free of arthritis and other signs of advancing old age, he felt unconcerned by the potential hazards of the future.

And until a few weeks before, he'd been comparatively content, if content was the right word. His existence was, he knew, fairly banal, and had become more so since his retirement, revolving as it did around daily and weekly routines that altered slightly with the changing seasons. For most of his adult life, habit and routine had proved a great defence against unnecessary brooding; a certain amount of readjusting had been required when he had retired, and again when Cynthia had passed away, but for the last six months a sense of calm had returned. Anyway, he always tended to feel brighter at the beginning of April, when once again the cricket season began, and there was the prospect of summer and long days of light stretching before him.

But then the dreams had started again, unsettling him and shattering his peace of mind. They'd never gone entirely, but he'd not had as many so close together for some time. It had left him not only short of sleep, but irritable. Throughout the day, he'd suddenly find himself thinking about it, the images of his dreams re-entering his mind, but now only clearer. It was like having a bad shadow following him around, prodding him in the ribs the moment he settled down to do something.

*

This latest dream had shaken him further, and although reading for a while usually helped him back to sleep, he was still wide awake at 7.30 a.m. when his alarm clock began ringing furiously. For much of his life, the shrill sound of the hammer pounding against the bells had been his signal to get up and start his day. When he had been teaching, he had always, without fail, risen at 6.30 a.m., then during the holidays had allowed himself a lie-in and moved it forward an hour. Since his retirement, it was set at 7.30 a.m. permanently. For some reason that he had never articulated in his mind, he felt unable to rise until the alarm rang, no matter how awake he might be before that time, and so it was not until then that he pulled back the sheets, swung his legs over the edge of the bed, and got up.

In the bathroom, Edward looked at himself in the mirror. *Tired,* he thought, and with his fingers pulled at the skin beneath his eyes, before running a basin of hot water in which to wash and shave. The steaming water refreshed him. *Didn't have much of that then,* he thought to himself, then cursed silently. *Think of something else, damn you.* His face had aged well. It was lean, without much loose skin, and despite the dark smudges at his eyes, they were still as clear as they had been all his life; he looked good for seventy-two. His hair was thinner than once it had been, but he was not really balding – just receding a little, perhaps. And although it was mostly white, there were still streaks of dark. This made him appear younger than he really was.

Having completed his ablutions by trimming his moustache, Edward went downstairs, still in his pyjamas, to make tea. This was another old habit. When Cynthia had been alive, he'd always brought it back upstairs on a tray, so that his wife could have a cup in bed before starting the day. Now, he simply boiled the kettle, poured out a pot, and then went back upstairs to dress while the tea brewed. 'Four-and-a-half minutes is the perfect length to brew a decent pot of tea,' his father had been fond of saying – and he should have known, having spent many years in the tea business before the war. Edward followed his father's rule almost to the second. It took him almost precisely that time to dress: plain drill trousers, fresh socks, check shirt and tie. Lambswool pullover. Brogues, polished before bed the night before.

Sitting at the pine kitchen table, eating a breakfast of toast and cereal, Edward read the newspaper, the radio burbling softly in the background. The daily copy of the *The Times* had been a retirement luxury he had awarded himself. When he had still been teaching, he had always read the copies delivered to the staff room; he liked to keep up with the latest news and political wranglings, and to read the sports reports. Although it was expensive to have the paper delivered to his door, Edward felt it was something he could afford. He scanned over the front page, then flicked through until he saw, on page thirteen, a large feature about the plans around the country for the forthcoming VE Day fiftieth anniversary celebrations. Edward sighed again, hurriedly turning the page, but then suddenly the radio distracted him. The reporter was at Hyde Park in London, describing the preparations for the coming weekend's events. With him was a former paratrooper who had been dropped over Arnhem, and who had been freed just a couple of days before the end of the war. '*Yes, I'm looking forward to it enormously,*' said the man. '*It should be quite an occasion.*' He was, he told the reporter, hoping to catch up with some of his former comrades in arms through the Veterans' Link that had been established. He'd already spoken to a few. '*One of my old mates, he lives in Spain now,*' he continued, '*but he's coming over this weekend and we've planned to meet in the tent on Saturday afternoon.*' Another reporter then came on air from a village in Suffolk. The village was expecting a number of Americans who had been based on a nearby airfield during the war. A street party was being prepared in their honour. '*We've always had a soft spot for the Yanks,*' said one villager. '*It's going to be a wonderful reunion this weekend.*'

Edward got up and switched off the radio. No wonder he was having bad dreams. Everywhere he turned, there was the war. 'I wish everyone would just stop going on about it,' he muttered. *It was a long time ago.*

The morning seemed to pass slowly. Edward had felt irritated and restless. He'd walked into the town to buy a few provisions, only to see Union Jack bunting being put up along the high street. Back at his house, he tried to read the newspaper, then his book, but his mind kept wandering, thinking and *remembering*. One cause for cheer, though: at least it was a nice day, warm and sunny, with only a slight breeze. He left the house early and walked up to the first eleven pitch nearly an hour before play was due to start.

A few of the players were already there and had changed into their whites, so Edward paused by the pavilion steps to watch them practise, then, when the cricket master arrived and called them in, Edward ambled off again, heading over to one of the benches in front of a row of horse chestnuts bordering the far side of the ground. The trees were dense with fresh, dark green leaves and sprinkled with white and pink blossom. Beneath, heavy shadows from the boughs danced softly in the breeze. Edward eased himself down onto the bench, the sun high above him, and adjusted the brim of his panama.

Few of the boys, or the staff for that matter, stopped to talk to Mr Enderby, and he rarely made any attempt to speak to them. He considered it was no longer his place, and in any case, he was aware that he had not been especially popular with the boys during his time at the school. They had respected him, he'd felt, as a teacher, but he had never gained their affection. He'd been too remote, too strict. 'Icy' had been his nickname – not the worst, but hardly a term of endearment.

His relationship with his fellow members of staff had been much the same. Over the years, some had been friends – even good friends – but towards the end he had become conscious that amongst the younger members of staff he was considered something of a relic. He'd once overheard a new teacher talking about him to another in the staff kitchen. 'Old Icy's a bit of a dinosaur, isn't he?' the new man had said.

'He terrifies me,' admitted the other, 'so no wonder the kids are scared of him.' This had hurt Edward more than he had been prepared to admit. Discipline was, he believed, important, and no pupil had ever disrupted one of his classes. But he had not meant to intimidate his colleagues. Following that incident, he had made a concerted effort to try and appear more friendly, but had struggled to think of anything to say to them; he could talk forever about Plantagenets or the French Wars of Religion, but when faced by two teachers in their twenties, his mind went blank beyond mild pleasantries about the state of the rugby fifteen. He'd always been a bit shy, though, even as a boy. Even as a young man.

It was halfway through the opposition's innings that Edward spotted Neil Watkins ambling slowly towards him. A mild wave of irritation swept over him, because he knew Neil would stop and talk. He had always liked Neil well enough – they'd been colleagues for a dozen years; Neil was due to retire himself in a couple of years' time – but Edward wasn't in the mood for conversation. He felt tired and wanted to be left alone.

'Hello, Edward,' said Neil as he approached the bench. 'A promising start to the season.'

'Yes,' said Edward. 'I like the look of the bowling this year.'

Neil sat down beside him and talked about the team's prospects, then suddenly said, 'Do you miss it?'

'What?'

'The teaching. The school. I mean, you're still living in the town.'

'That doesn't mean I'd rather be standing up in class every day.'

'No, I suppose not –'

'I miss the cricket on days like this. May always used to be my favourite month in the school year.'

'My last summer term,' said Neil.

Edward smiled at him – *you'll be all right.* They were silent for a moment, then Neil said, 'How long did you have the first eleven? You were still in charge when I first came here.'

'Nineteen years.'

Neil nodded thoughtfully, then said, 'Don't think much of this new chap.'

'Elkins?'

'Yes. He's not what you'd call "liked" in the staff room. Too full of himself by half.'

'He's young.'

'Maybe, but he has his favourites. I can't stand that. One should always try and be fair. Of course, there are always some boys one likes more than others, but . . .' He let the sentence trail off. Edward said nothing. A minute or so passed, the batsman played and missed, and then Neil said, 'How's Simon, by the way?'

'Fine, thank you. Busy doing his thing in London.'

Neil nodded. 'Accountant?'

'Lawyer.'

'Of course – yes. Made it through the recession all right?'

'Yes. Seems to be doing fine.'

'Oh good – yes, my brother-in-law's managed to keep his job, too. Lots of his colleagues were given the boot, though. You going to come along this weekend, by the way?'

Edward turned and looked at him.

'For VE Day?' added Neil.

'No, I don't think so,' said Edward. He began turning his signet ring, then said, 'Who's this bowling now?' It was, he knew, a boy called Chilcott. He'd watched him several times the year before.

'Oh, er, Chilcott. He's only fifteen. Personally, I think he's been brought into the firsts far too soon, but that's Dave Elkins for you. Anyway, it sounds like it might be quite fun. There's going to be a street party in the high street, you know.' Edward nodded. 'The CCF band are doing their parade through the town. Hope they sound better than they did last Remembrance Day – bloody awful, weren't they?'

Edward stared ahead at the cricket. 'Lovely shot,' he muttered, and began clapping gently.

By the time he arrived back at home later that evening, the headache that had begun earlier was still throbbing dully. He felt exhausted, but the prospect of sleep gave him a sinking feeling he could not shake. *This time next week,* he thought, *it'll be old news.* The world would have moved on again. Perhaps then his life would get back to normal. Sitting down in his armchair in the living room, he paused a moment. His house, he reflected, looked as ordered as ever, unaffected by the turmoil running through the mind of its owner. Tidy and *still* – a new house that suffered neither draughts nor noise. Cynthia had always kept a tidy house, and since she'd died, Edward had made sure it remained that way, hoovering and dusting regularly. The cream carpet had barely a stain. The cushions on the sofa were plumped up and fresh, although, in truth, they were rarely used now. Cynthia had always sat on the right-hand side of the sofa, Edward in his armchair. With no Cynthia, the sofa had become an ornament, purely a feature of the room. He looked at his wife's engagement photograph on the side table by his chair. She had been a striking young woman, tall and poised; he'd been lucky to marry her. It had been her mother who had insisted on the photographs being taken – at a small studio in Ripon. He could remember it perfectly. He'd been reluctant, but Cynthia had said, 'Please, darling, do it for me,' and now he was glad he had – not for the pictures of himself, but for this one of Cynthia, the one he had looked at almost every day since 1948 when his future mother-in-law had given it to him.

Her fine black-and-white features eyed him now, as placidly as they had ever done. What would she say to him? Probably very little; she had never tried to penetrate the deep recesses of his mind, always accepting that whatever had happened to Edward had occurred before she had met him. 'I'm marrying you for what you are now,' she'd once said after they became engaged. If she'd wanted to know more, she had never asked, and Edward had never told her; nothing but the barest outline. He was no different from millions of others. They'd all suffered. She had, however, always been there for him, her companionship and her kindness a comfort. He missed her.

The silence in the house enveloped him completely, so that when the telephone next to him on the side table rang, the sudden shrillness made him jolt in his seat.

'Hello?' he said, after fumbling a moment with the receiver.

'Dad, it's Simon.'

'Simon. Just talking about you earlier. How are you?'

'Fine. Good, thanks.'

'Glad to hear it. Yes, Neil Watkins was asking after you.'

'Watty? He still there, then?'

'Yes. This is his last term.'

'Good Lord. So you're not the only one wedded to the place, then.' He chuckled, then said, 'So what have you been up to?'

'Oh – this and that. You know. Watched the first eleven today.' He heard Simon sigh.

'Who won?'

'We won. Or rather, I should say they won – Myddleton, that is. Got some good players this year.' He cleared his throat then said, 'And how's Katie? And Nicky and Lucy?'

'Yes, they're all fine, thanks. We're all on, um, pretty good form, I think.'

'And work all right?'

'Fine. Busy. It always is . . . But – listen, Dad, I want to ask you something.'

'Yes?'

'Well, actually, it's Nick, really. He's asked me to ask you. And – well, I want to ask you as well.'

'Ask me what?'

Simon paused, then said, 'We wondered whether we could persuade you to come up this weekend? There's a big do going on at Hyde Park – for VE Day. Nick's studying it at school at the moment and was really hoping you might celebrate the anniversary with us.' Edward said nothing, so Simon continued. 'There's lots going on: stalls and shows, and a fly-past in the afternoon. There's going to be a Spitfire, Dad. And there's – I've got it here – there's a tent for veterans. The 'Veterans' Link', it says.' He began reading, ' "The Veterans' Link has been set up to help former servicemen who fought in the Second World War reunite with their wartime comrades." You might meet some of your old friends from the squadron. Dad?'

'I don't know, Simon,' said Edward.

'Please, Dad. It would really mean a great deal.'

It was Edward's turn to sigh. 'It was a long time ago. I'm not sure I . . .'

'Fine. Well don't, then. I clearly shouldn't have asked.'

Edward winced as he heard the anger and frustration in Simon's voice. 'Simon, look, thank you. Really. And please thank Nick – I mean it. Just let me think about it, will you? I – I – well, this is stirring up things, you see, things . . . well, anyway.' He cleared his throat again, then said, 'I'll ring you in the morning, I promise.'

'Well, I won't be in, so speak to Katie. But Dad, you know, maybe it's about time you did confront all this stuff. Maybe it would do you good. Think about that.'

'I'll ring tomorrow.'

'Bye, Dad.'

'Goodbye.'

Having replaced the receiver, Edward got up and went into the kitchen to prepare his supper. He had barely cooked a meal in all the years he had been married to Cynthia, and had still not become used to feeding himself. It seemed so pointless to go to all the bother of dirtying pans and grills just for one. His solution was to eat as simply as possible, and food that made a minimum amount of mess and clutter. Earlier, he had bought a piece of cod, and now he placed the fillet on a tray in the oven, and put on a few potatoes to boil. He rested his hands on the faux-marble counter. He wished things might have been different with Simon. They had barely spoken since Christmas. And when they did, it was always the same: a stilted conversation, or rising irritation on the part of his son. 'You're too hard on him,' Cynthia used to say, but what had Edward been supposed to do? He couldn't have shown favouritism to his son – not in front of the other boys. And what was the alternative? Simon at the state school in Wincanton, while he taught at Myddleton College? While he was a housemaster and they were living in the school itself? He wished they had been able to afford to send him to one of the other schools nearby, but it had not been possible. But rather than thanking him for a good education and leg-up in life, Simon had shown him nothing but resentment. It had been ever thus, ever since Simon had gone to Myddleton, and the grudge had continued after school, and was, it seemed, as strong as ever, even now that his son was in his forties. He loved Simon, of course he did, but sometimes he felt as though he were talking to a stranger. Sometimes it seemed impossible to think that Simon was his own flesh and blood. Edward sighed. His headache had not gone away.

However tired he may have felt, sleep eluded him. Lying in bed, the same thoughts ran round and round his mind. For so long he had kept a tight rein on his life, but now, suddenly, it was as though forces beyond his control had swept down upon him, destroying his peace of mind: at night, the ghosts of his past; during the day, the newspapers and radio; and now Simon and Nick – they had come together, pushing him into a corner from which he seemed unable to escape. He turned over, but couldn't settle, then turned again, staring straight up at the dark ceiling. Whatever peace he had established in his life had been built on somewhat flimsy foundations; but he did not know how he could shore them up once more.

Edward groaned out loud, and then the first chinks in his resolve began seeping into his mind. Perhaps, he wondered, if he went to London, he might then be left alone.

The first eleven often started their Saturday matches at eleven o'clock, and so it was this first Saturday in May. Moreover, it was another home fixture, which had given Edward a chance to watch a couple of hours of cricket before setting off on the long drive to London. He had never used to mind driving, but in recent years he had found the motorways so busy it had become a more arduous exercise. Still, it meant he could arrive and leave when he wanted; trains to Brampton Cary were infrequent, and he wanted to be able to make a quick escape back home should the need arise.

He turned into Simon and Katie's street off the Fulham Road just after five that afternoon. After parking and taking out his case, he walked through the gate and for a moment paused in front of the heavy wooden door with its stained glass panels, then lifted his finger and rang the bell. 'He's here!' came Katie's muffled voice from within, and then the thunder of running footsteps down the hallway. It was his grandson, Nick, who opened the door. Smiles and welcomes: overexcited hopping from Nick, a bashful grin from the nine-year-old Lucy; a peck on the cheek and a hug from Katie; a pause then a hand on the shoulder from Simon, and Edward was directed into the living room, with its toys and clutter and half drunk cups of coffee.

'Sit down, please,' said Katie, as Edward hovered by one of the sofas. She stretched behind him and moved a newspaper and one of Nick's sweatshirts out of the way. Nick immediately launched into a long list of the events that were taking place: what was happening in Hyde Park, what was happening in the Mall. He reeled off a list of exhibitions and then told his grandfather about the fly-past that would take place on Monday. This, he had clearly decided, was the highlight, not just for himself but for his grandfather too. *Why did I come?* thought Edward.

'Nick's very excited,' said Simon unnecessarily, and ruffled his son's hair. 'He's been on a school trip to the Imperial War Museum, haven't you?'

Nick nodded. 'It was brilliant, Grandpa.'

17

'And you saw the Spitfire, didn't you?' said Simon.

Nick nodded again, a big-toothed grin across his face. 'No-one could believe it when I told them you'd flown one!' he said.

Both Nick and Lucy soon disappeared. Only later, when they were all sat down for supper in the kitchen, did Edward's interrogation really begin. 'Grandpa, what was the first plane you flew?' asked Nick, as Katie began serving the food.

Edward looked at Simon, but immediately realised he would get no help from his son. Inhaling deeply, he said, 'A Tiger Moth.' Nick looked blank.

'It was a biplane,' he explained. 'Open cockpit, too. A marvellous thing to fly. There wasn't much air traffic back then. You simply took off and whizzed around the sky. It was as though a completely different world had opened up. The sense of freedom was exhilarating.'

'What next?'

Edward thought for a moment. 'A Harvard. A two-seater, but single-engine. Built as a trainer. And I flew a Miles Magister as well.'

'So when did you get to fly a Spitfire?'

'That came later, when I joined my squadron. I went operational on a Hurricane.'

'A Hurricane? Really?' Nick said. 'I didn't realise you'd flown one of those as well.'

'I flew all sorts of planes. Even jets after the war.'

'Did you?' said Simon. 'I had no idea.'

Edward shrugged. 'New planes were being developed all the time.'

And so it continued, with Simon, Katie and Lucy listening as Edward tackled his quizzing as deftly as he could. He'd never been asked so much about flying, not by Simon, not by anyone. But then, when Simon had been a young boy, it wasn't something anyone had done. The shadow of five-and-a-half long years had hung too heavily over the entire country. But there was no collective stonewalling now, however. As a child, Simon might have known better than to try asking his father about his war experiences, but Nick had no such inhibitions. 'Oh, you don't want to know about all that,' Edward had said. But with absolute ingenuousness, Nick had replied, 'Yes, I do.'

As Nick peppered away, so Edward found it harder to maintain his normally flawless armour plating. After all, he did not want to snap at the boy – a grandson he saw far too infrequently. Fortunately, Nick seemed more interested in the aircraft his grandfather had flown than the circumstances in which he had flown them.

The grilling only stopped with the children's bedtime. As Katie took them upstairs, Edward pushed back his chair and began helping Simon clear away the table.

'Leave that Dad, honestly,' said Simon. 'Can I get you anything else? A glass of wine? Coffee?'

'A cup of tea would be nice,' Edward replied. The kitchen had been extended from the back of house; the table stood under a glass roof. It was a light room – and large too. Brightly coloured plastic numbers covered the fridge. A battered dresser stood against one wall, its shelves crammed with cookery and dog-eared children's books. Against the opposite wall was a food-stained sofa with crushed cushions and an inside-out sweater slung over its arm. Edward could remember when the children had been much younger and the kitchen – the whole house – had been in a far worse state: toys everywhere. It had been impossible to sit down without planting his backside on a piece of jigsaw or cobbled toy car.

A sudden roar of jet engines made him look up. Overhead, a large airliner passed over west London.

'How do you like it?' said Simon. Edward looked up and watched his son stirring a tea bag into a mug.

'Milk no sugar, please.' Simon added milk, stirred the tea bag a bit more, then took it out, dripping, and dropped it into the bin.

'There you are,' he said, passing the mug.

'Thanks,' said Edward. He peered at the dark orange liquid.

'Let's go next door,' said Simon, pouring himself a glass of wine. 'It'll be more comfortable.' Edward followed obediently, sitting himself down stiffly against one end of another flat-cushioned sofa.

'Relax, Dad, for God's sake!' said Simon, exasperation creeping into his voice once more.

'I am, perfectly, thank you,' said Edward.

'You don't look it. Honestly, I want you to feel at home here. We're not a bloody hotel.' But Edward didn't feel at home. He couldn't, not here. There was nothing *familiar* about Simon's house. And he disliked sharing a bathroom with Nick and Lucy – more garish plastic and a lock that didn't work. He dreaded having a shower in case one of them walked in on him. Sitting with his orange tea, he already wished he could be back at home, drinking proper tea, sitting on his own familiar chair and avoiding this current awkwardness with Simon.

'Anyway,' said Simon. 'We thought just you, Nick and I would go tomorrow, and then Katie and Lucy would come with us to the Mall the following day. Sound OK?' Edward nodded. 'Really, Dad,' Simon continued, 'it'll be fun. Nick's terribly excited, you know.'

'Yes, I can see that.'

They were silent a moment, and then Simon said, 'Perhaps you'll see some of your old friends from the squadron.'

'I doubt it.'

'Oh, I don't know. There's a large veterans' tent, you know. That's where they've set up the Veterans' Link to try and reunite old war comrades. You'd like to see some of them wouldn't you?'

Edward looked down at his tea. A scum was forming at the top. 'Hmm,' was all he said.

'But I thought the best bit about war was the camaraderie. I know you don't like talking about it, Dad, but surely you'd like to see some of your friends, if you could?'

Edward sighed. 'Simon, please,' he said. 'Drop it, will you? I'm happy to go along with you tomorrow because Nick wants me to, but don't push it.' *Damn it*, he thought. 'Look, sorry Simon. I didn't mean to snap. Really – it's just . . .' He let the sentence hang.

Simon shook his head. 'I want to understand, Dad, I really do. But you just won't let me. Christ, what on earth happened to you back then? You survived, didn't you? You were one of the lucky ones, for God's sake. Why won't you ever talk about it? Why won't you ever tell me about what happened?'

'It was a long time ago.'

'Not really.'

'I can't really remember all that much, anyway.'

'Rubbish. It was a huge part of your life – a huge part that I know nothing about. And I'm *still* none the wiser. If I knew just something, Dad, then maybe I could understand why you're like you are – the closed book you've always been.'

'Oh, Simon, now you're just being melodramatic.'

'Am I? Am I, Dad? Well, I'm very sorry, but I'm just not like you. I don't want to bury my head in the sand, living my life with this bloody great shell around me that no-one can penetrate.'

'It's nothing to do with you, Simon.'

'Of course it is – you're my father, for Christ's sake. It's affected me as well, you know. I've had to live my life with this shadow hanging over us all.'

Edward was reprieved by the sound of Katie coming back downstairs. He'd known what was coming next – *and Mum had to, as well.* They both fell silent until she walked in. 'That's that done for another night,' she said. 'Will you go up and say goodnight to them, Edward?'

'Of course.' He stood up, smiling at Katie and deliberately avoiding his son's eye. Taking the stairs slowly, anger burned within him. How dare Simon talk to him like that? Lecturing him about something he knew nothing about – the bloody nerve! *I should never have come,* he thought, then wondered whether he could feign some illness during the night and drive back to Somerset first thing the following morning.

He went in to see Lucy first, then Nick. His grandson was lying on the floor reading a book. A large poster of a Spitfire was Blu-Tacked to the wall above his bed.

'Just come in to say goodnight,' said Edward. 'What's that you're reading?'

'Just a book about planes,' he said. 'Grandpa?'

'Yes?'

'I'm really glad you've come.'

Edward smiled. 'See you in the morning, Nick.'

Of course there had been no question of leaving. Simon had even apologised – no doubt, Edward thought, at Katie's insistence. Over breakfast it was as though the conversation of the previous evening had never happened, any residual tension diffused by the children and by Nick's mounting excitement. So it was that by just after ten o'clock, they were on the Underground and pulling into Hyde Park

Corner station. With a screech the train came to a halt. As the doors of the train opened, a mass of people burst out and Edward almost lost his footing, stumbling onto the platform.

'You all right, Dad?' said Simon, offering a cramped arm of support.

Edward nodded. Nick was ahead, but momentarily out of reach as the mass pushed towards the steps leading off the platform. Edward was amazed. Around him were other veterans, berets on their heads, their blazers jangling with rows of medals. But they were only part of the crowd; there were vast numbers of people of all ages swarming towards Hyde Park. Another mass of people had formed at the base of the escalator. Edward inched forward. He could feel a knot of pressure building up in his stomach. For a moment, he closed his eyes, and allowed the throng to lead him. *This is ridiculous,* he thought. *Calm down.*

Nick was waiting at the top of the escalator and the three of them then pushed through the opened gates and out into the warm sunshine. They followed the stream of people through the gates of the park and towards the Serpentine Road. The sound of military bands playing their marches gradually increased the closer they got, and was joined by the reedy sounds of wartime songs. Through the trees, Edward glimpsed marquees, olive green vehicles, and flags – countless flags. Every other person appeared to be clutching a plastic Union Jack.

Nick was almost skipping with anticipation. He pointed towards the display of modern tanks and military vehicles. 'Can we have a look at those, Dad?' he said, turning and tugging at Simon's sleeve.

'Of course we can,' said Edward, before Simon had answered. He smiled at his grandson. In appearance, Nick was so much like Katie: blond, tousled hair and the same deep brown eyes – but in character exactly as he remembered Simon had been at twelve. It was uncanny.

Disinterested soldiers stood by the display of modern tanks and armoured personnel carriers. While Nick gawped at the tanks, Edward watched two old men walk over to one of the young soldiers. 'We could have done with a few of these in Africa,' one of them told him. The soldier nodded and smiled politely. 'Reckon we could have seen off those bloody 88s all right with these, hey, Reg?'

'Cor, I should say,' said his friend.

The sun was warming. Edward took out his handkerchief and wiping his brow, looked around. *All these people*, he thought. Fifty years on, the war had become a pantomime, a kind of travelling circus of tents and big band dances, of costumed women in ATS uniforms and bright red lipstick. There was little connection with the real war in this temporary theme park. *And thank God for that.* He smoothed his moustache. He felt the heaviness in his stomach ease.

Simon and Nick rejoined him and together they walked past more stalls and more marquees. The smell of fried onions filled the air. Generators hummed above the beat of big bass drums. Ahead of them stood the largest tent of all, some two hundred yards long.

'What's in there?' said Nick. 'Can we go and look?'

'I think it must be the Veterans' Centre,' said Simon. 'Dad – do you want to go in?'

Edward looked at him for a moment, then found himself saying, 'Yes – just a quick look.' *What are you thinking?* he told himself. The feeling of nausea returned, yet despite his fears, despite his determination not to have his life turned on its head, there was an even stronger force that was tugging at him, urging him to look back. *Like Orpheus,* he thought, as he signed the register at the entrance.

'RAF on the left,' said the official, pointing vaguely.

Inside the tent was teeming with veterans and their families. He watched three men hug one another, their medals chinking together as they embraced. They had been so young then, Edward reflected. Boys, really. And now look at them: white-haired, and sallow-skinned, with bony knuckles and enlarged ears. Old men. What had they got in common with the men they had once been? Nothing but memories, memories it seemed they now wanted to share, after years of keeping them bottled in a long-forgotten trunk. Laughter rang out above the low murmur. It was hot in the marquee, the smell of grass and the plastic tenting cloying. It added to Edward's renewed sense of mounting unease.

'Did *you* win any medals, Grandpa?' asked Nick, walking close beside him.

'What? Yes, one or two,' Edward told him as his eyes darted around the vast white pavilion.

'What were they?'

'Oh, I don't know,' said Edward.

'Come on, Dad,' said Simon. 'What did you get?'

Edward sighed. 'It was a long time ago – I barely remember.'

'But you *do* remember.'

Edward said nothing.

'Come on, Dad.'

Edward began toying with his signet ring, then glanced at Nick, looking up at him expectantly.

'Well, if you must know, they gave me the DFC twice over. But they're meaningless. Plenty of people more deserving than me got nothing at all.'

'What's a DFC?' Nick asked him.

'A Distinguished Flying Cross,' Simon told him, then said, 'Dad, I had no idea. Jesus.'

'Really it's nothing,' Edward said more sharply than he'd intended. 'As I said. Just a bit of bronze and silk. Anyway,' he added, 'I've seen what they do to people's jackets. They weigh a ton.'

Notice boards stretched for hundreds of yards around the inside of the tent. They found the RAF area, the crest and number of each squadron heading a section. Every one included notes from former members trying to make contact once again.

'Here's 324 Squadron,' said Nick. He had hurried on ahead and was now standing in front of the board, his finger pointing to the emblem. Edward breathed in heavily, then began looking at the messages. Most were from ground crew, although there were a couple from former pilots.

'Recognise anyone?' asked Simon.

'No, not yet,' said Edward, 'but I was only in the squadron six months in nearly six years. People came and went throughout the war, you know.'

Suddenly he froze. Near the bottom of the board was a simple typed message. 'BARCLAY' was the heading, bold and underlined. Underneath was a neat and succinct note: 'I am trying to find out about my uncle Harry Barclay, and would love to hear from anyone who knew him. Many thanks. Andrew Fisher.' Finally, at the bottom of the card was an address and telephone number in Beaconsfield.

'No, nothing here,' said Edward, moving quickly on. He could feel his heart pounding. Nick was following behind him, oblivious to his grandfather's turmoil, calling out numbers of squadrons as they passed along the wall of messages. He hurried past, running ahead. 'Six hundred,' called out Nick eventually, 'Six-oh-nine, six-twenty, six-thirty, six-three-six. Here we are, Grandpa.'

Breathlessly, Edward scanned the board – a couple of names he remembered: Michael Lindsay, a pilot, and Pete Summersby, one of the erks, as the ground crew were known; yes, he remembered them all right. Then he saw it again: the same notice, in the same neat type. 'BARCLAY'.

'My God,' muttered Edward.

'Dad? You all right?' It was Simon, standing beside him. 'Dad?'

'What? Oh yes – yes, thank you. Fine. Just, um –' He took out his handkerchief, dabbed his brow, and stroked his chin for a moment. Then, forcing a smile, turned to Simon, and said, 'Yes, I remember these two.' He pointed at the names. 'Mike Lindsay. A good pilot. Not what I'd call a close friend, but a friend all the same. Well, I suppose we all were on Malta. You had to get on, or else you'd go mad.' Simon looked at the board and nodded slowly. 'Look,' Edward continued. 'It's stifling in here. Why don't we go back out for a bit? Have a drink. You could do with a Coke or something, couldn't you, Nick?'

'All right,' said Simon. 'But are you going to try and find these two? I mean, they must be here if they left their names.'

'Let's just get a drink first,' said Edward.

They found a table near the dance floor and bandstand. The military band was now playing the themes from a number of war movies, and Simon began whistling along as he piled up the debris of gnawed chicken bones, smeared ketchup, cold chips and cardboard plates, and pushed it to one side. Then he disappeared to join one of the many queues snaking from the food and drink stalls. Edward closed his eyes for a moment, feeling the bright sun gently warm his face. A vision came into his mind and he immediately opened them again and sat bolt upright. Nick seemed not to have noticed because he said, 'Grandpa, do you think we could go to an air show one day? At Duxford they actually fly Spitfires.'

'We'll have to see,' said Edward.

'Can you remember the last time you flew a Spitfire?'

He could. Distinctly. 'In 1946,' he said. 'After the war. It was a Mk 24 – an almost completely different aircraft to the early models. Very quick. Really, it had unbelievable power – for a piston engine, at any rate.' He was finding talking to his grandson about the various types of Spitfire – in particular – easier than he'd expected. And *safer* too; he was still explaining the difference between the Griffon and Merlin engines when Simon returned with the drinks.

Since his discovery in the Veterans' Centre, Edward had been wondering how he could get back inside the tent without Simon and Nick. Now it dawned on him. Nick had soon finished his drink and was beginning to get restless. Glimpses of various sites were catching his attention. It was all too obvious that he wanted to be off again, and so when he suggested they look at the displays put on by the re-enactors, Edward said, 'You two go. I could do with another ten minutes' pause.'

'We can wait,' said Simon.

Edward waved his hand at them. 'No, no. Nick's itching to be off again. You two go and I'll meet you back here by the bandstand.'

'Well, if you're sure.'

'Go on, off you go.'

He watched them disappear amongst the crowds of people, then hurried off himself, back into the Veterans' Centre. Briskly, he walked back to the 324 Squadron message board and carefully, in block capital letters, wrote down Andrew Fisher's name and address, then slid the paper back into his inside jacket pocket. He looked furtively about him, then headed for the exit once more.

'Squadron Leader Enderby!' said a small man with slicked-back greying hair. Edward stopped and looked at him. The man wore an RAF blazer and tie, and was holding out his hand. Edward took it and shook it vigorously. 'Hello,' he said. 'How are you?'

'You don't remember me. Pete Summersby,' said the man.

'Pete Summersby – of course I do,' said Edward. 'Good Lord! How *are* you?'

'Oh, can't complain. How about you, sir?'

'You can drop the "sir" now, Pete, for goodness sake. Edward, please. But very well, thank you. Very well. Keeping busy, you know.'

'I remember looking after your Spit many times,' said Pete.

'Mine and others,' said Edward. 'You were quite brilliant – you and all the ground crew on Malta. Wouldn't have done it without you.'

Pete smiled appreciatively. 'Good of you to say so.' He looked around him, and said, 'This is quite a carry-on, isn't it?' then added, 'Have you seen the message board?'

'What, for 636 Squadron? Yes, I have. Noticed Mike Lindsay's been here. Haven't seen him since the war.'

'Yes, Mike's here somewhere. He's just the same – amazing, really. Actually, I'm meeting him later. Will you come along?'

'Well, I'm rather in the hands of my son and grandson, to be honest. But tell me where and when, and I'll try.'

'Three-thirty in the bar here. It would be good if you could make it. Good to catch up on old times.'

Edward nodded, then looked at his watch. 'Gosh, I must be going – my son will be wondering where I've got to.'

'Did you, er, see the notice about Harry Barclay?'

'Yes.'

'Are you going to get in touch?'

'Look, Pete, I've really got to go. Let's hopefully talk about it later. Three-thirty, you say?' Pete nodded. 'See you then. Really good to see you again, Pete.' Edward shook his hand, and hurried on out of the tent. When he reached the bandstand, to his relief, neither Simon nor Nick was there. Finding another table, he sat down. The band was playing 'Lili Marlene'. He began humming, softly, along to the tune. *The Snakepit*. He and Harry had brought the house down that day.

His explanation, when Simon asked why he was at a different table, was that he'd gone 'for a pee' and on his return had found their table gone. If Simon had doubted him, he'd not said.

'So, you want to go back to the Veterans' Centre?' he asked his father.

'I don't think so. Perhaps later on.'

'But you're going to add your name to the message board?'

'Oh, I don't know, Simon.'

'Why not?' Then he stopped, held up his hands and said, 'All right, fine. Whatever.'

Edward turned to Nick. 'What would you like to see?' he asked. 'After all, it's your day.' He caught Simon's disapproving eye. *Well, sod him,* thought Edward. *I'm not going to be bullied by my son.* And as it happened, there were a host of sites Nick wanted to look at. They stopped for lunch, but otherwise the hours passed as they wandered back and forth across the vast site. Three o'clock came and went; so did three-thirty. They finally left just after four, both Edward and even Simon declaring their exhaustion. And while Nick refused to admit his tiredness, he had by then noticeably begun to drag his feet.

Simon hailed a cab. ('I can't be bothered with the tube,' he said, having seen the crowds pushing their way towards the Underground at Marble Arch.) In minutes, as they bumped their way down the Bayswater Road, Nick was asleep.

'Well,' said Simon, patting his knees, 'that wasn't so bad, was it?'

'No,' said Edward. 'And Nick seemed to enjoy it. He wants me to take him to Duxford.'

'And will you? I'd like to come too, you know.'

Edward smiled at his son. 'As long as the questions are about aeroplanes and nothing more.'

Simon laughed. 'It's a deal.'

Later, much later, Edward lay in bed, but despite his exhaustion, sleep once more eluded him. Even that afternoon, he'd managed to put Andrew Fisher's notice out of mind; he'd kept his run-in with Pete Summersby to a bare minimum; and when he could have been churning over those blighted days on Malta with Pete and Mike Lindsay, he had been wandering around some exhibition about modern European unity.

But at night it was not so easy. At night, lying in bed – especially an unfamiliar and, frankly, uncomfortable bed – there were fewer distractions. His mind began to brood, to bring unwanted memories back to the forefront of his consciousness. And even when unconscious, having finally dropped off to sleep, his addled brain mixed those images, scrambling them into a series of indelible sequences that were once again so horribly familiar.

Edward finally set off for home on Monday afternoon, satisfied that any duty owed to his son and grandson had been more than honoured. Earlier in the day they had all gone to the Mall, Katie and Lucy included. Edward had not enjoyed the experience. To begin with, he had not slept well and so had woken feeling tired and irritable; over breakfast, he had found it trying to have to pretend to be even-tempered when really he wanted to snap at both Nick and Lucy and tell them to stop making so much noise. The Mall had also been far too crowded for his liking. Thousands upon thousands of people had turned up to wave flags and cheer, but although he was a supporter of the monarchy, the sight of the far-off members of the Royal Family appearing on the balcony of the palace stirred no feelings of patriotic fervour within him. They were simply too far away. In any case, his view was spoilt by a large man standing directly in front of him with a young girl perched on the man's shoulders.

The fly-past – the supposed highlight of the weekend – was over all too quickly and was marred by the absence of the promised Spitfire, the one plane Nick had wanted to see above all others. He was distraught – not even the sight of the Hurricane could make up for it. Later, it transpired that the plane had suffered some mechanical hitch and been forced to remain on the ground. Only Edward's assurance that he would accompany his grandson to Duxford in the summer lifted Nick's spirits.

'Really? Is that a promise?' Nick had said, his face brightening somewhat.

'A promise,' Edward replied, conscious he was succumbing to a mild form of emotional blackmail. His mood worsened, however, when Simon took him into the garden and spoke to him in hushed tones about the noise Edward had made the previous night. 'Nick and Lucy heard you, Dad.'

'What are you talking about, Simon?' Edward had snapped.

'Dad, you were shouting in your sleep last night. They were worried, but didn't like to say anything.'

'I'm sorry – must have been a bad dream or something.'

'Dad – please. I want to help, really I do. You shouldn't be having bad dreams.'

'Not dreams – a dream, Simon. I can't even remember having had it,' he lied.

'But it must have been pretty bad if you woke the kids up shouting.'

'I really don't remember.'

Simon had put his hands in the air – *I despair* – and then they had sat in silence for a moment, until Edward had looked at his watch and said, 'I should think about getting going.'

He made his escape shortly after, just before four o'clock. Simon's family all gathered at the doorway to see him off, but his son had walked with him to the car, parked a short way further down the street.

'Thanks for coming, Dad,' he said in a conciliatory tone, his hands on his hips. The two of them had never quite known what to do at departures: an embrace was out of the question, but a handshake seemed too formal. So they tended to do neither.

'That's all right. I enjoyed myself,' he lied. 'Thank you for looking after me so well.'

'And we'll see you soon?'

'I'd like that.'

Edward eased himself into the driving seat, Simon closing the door for him. 'Drive carefully,' he said, as Edward wound down the window. 'And Dad?' he added. Edward looked at him. 'No – nothing. We'll talk soon.'

With a final wave, Edward drove off at last, relief flooding over him. *Penance done,* he thought. *Now home.*

But he did not go straight home. He had thought he had always known his own mind, but his brain was beginning to play strange tricks on him. For the most part, it still told him what he knew to be right: that he should put the war out of mind, and that he should concentrate on the present, not the past. But a quite different part of his mind was sending quite opposite signals: telling him to go to London, to take Nick to Duxford. Now it was urging him to make a pointless detour from his route home. It had come upon him quite suddenly, as he was at last free of the capital and making good progress along the motorway; and although he had tried to banish the thought, a short while later he was exiting the motorway and heading towards Woking instead.

Turn around, he told himself. *It's not too late.* But he did no such thing, driving on through countless sets of traffic lights and over roundabouts, all of which were desperately unfamiliar. How long had it been? Years. Decades, even. What had once been a quiet commuter town was now a sprawling conurbation, linked, it appeared, quite seamlessly with Aldershot, Farnborough and several other old Surrey towns. It was more by luck than anything that he eventually found himself in the centre of old Woking. There he stopped, examined his road map, and then continued on, until he found himself passing a signpost that told him he had reached Chilton. At first he could not understand how this could be – he remembered Woking had been much further away and the village far smaller; there had been no cluster of modern red-brick houses built up along the edge of the village when he'd been a boy. But the heart of the village, with its myriad of different houses and the 'The Chequers' pub, was unmistakably the same place. He drove on, past what had once been the village shop, (he was glad to see the Victorian postbox was still there), then almost at the village's edge, turned left, following a white sign to the '13th Century Church'. The road had hardly been a road at all before the war; rather, just a gravelled lane, its high hedges rich in blackberries by the end of summer. He smiled to himself, thinking of the purple-stained fingers he and his mother would get after an afternoon's picking. Edward crawled along at barely more than walking pace. There, ahead, was the familiar bend to the left, and then after, a turning on the right. There seemed to be more trees than he could recall, but, with a quickening heart, he saw the house through the now dense foliage. He paused for a moment, looking, remembering, then drove on, until the church came into view, its steeple rising above the hedgerow, and as the road straightened, so its silvery grey body emerged too. He parked at what had once been a turning circle for carriages and traps in days gone by. This at least was still gravel and stone, and largely unchanged from the place of his memory. Freshly cut grass and nettles lay along the verge at the foot of the brick and flint church wall, giving the late afternoon air a heavy scent.

The lych-gate handle clacked loudly as he turned it and walked through into the churchyard. There was no-one about, although faintly, from across the field behind the church, he could hear the distant sound of music – wartime music yet again – coming from The Chequers. Everyone, it seemed, was using this VE Day bank holiday to have a party. He noticed no new graves, no freshly turned soil, and only on a few of the graves were there some tired-looking flowers. Turning left along the path that ran away from the church door, he soon found the headstone he was looking for. A simple grey stone, now so covered in lichen it was hard to pick out the chiselled writing. He bent down, put out a finger and traced the words along the warm, roughened stone. His father had been a good man, he thought. They had always been close – far closer than Edward had ever been to Simon. 'We'll always be proud of you,' he had said to his son as Edward had left to join the air force. 'Be strong and always try to do the right thing by yourself and by others.' Edward had never forgotten those words. He could very clearly picture his father saying it, on the platform at Woking, holding his son's arms, and framed by the steam from the engine behind him.

A bee lazily buzzed nearby. Edward left the churchyard and walked the hundred yards or so back up the road to the driveway. Looking around him, there seemed to be no sign of life, so checking once more behind, he gingerly started towards the house. It looked familiar, although different. Smaller than he remembered – it had always seemed vast to him as a boy – yet he supposed that was inevitable; the combination of his increased age and the trees along the driveway, now grown so much, had helped to shrink it. Even so, it was still a fair-sized house: a Regency vicarage that had been palatial for a family of three. He paused for a moment and chuckled to himself. Could it *really* be fifty-odd years? Those had been happy days – carefree, certainly. A time *before*, to be cherished. In his mind the house had remained as it had been then, sealed in an airtight room, preserved just as it was forever. How strange it was to be looking at it now, and for it to have aged sixty years in a trice. A conservatory had been added; the house was now pale yellow, not white. And where there had once been his father's black Wolseley Twelve, there was now a large estate car parked in the drive.

He stopped, then walked on slowly, his heart beating faster. He wasn't sure what he would do if someone saw him, or suddenly emerged from the house. What was once his to wander over freely now belonged to some nameless, faceless people; he had no right to be there, and yet his curiosity was urging him on. The gravel crunched underfoot. Small clouds of insects stood out in the late evening sun. He smiled remembering how his mother always complained that the midges seemed to single her out. 'I don't know what it is about me,' she had said on numerous occasions, 'but they find me particularly succulent.' And then she would wildly whisk her arms around her head.

Reaching the end of the drive, he now stood directly opposite the front of the house. He waited a moment, paralysed with indecision. Should he go on and knock at the door, or peer through the windows? Or turn around now, and walk back to his car? More memories stirred within him. A birthday party on the lawn; playing French cricket with his father. Building a snowman with a friend who stayed with him one Christmas – a friend whose name he had forgotten but whose face he could picture vividly. He could hear no sound of life from either the garden or within the house. Surely, he thought, they would have seen me by now? And so he stepped forward again, towards the front door, unmistakably the *same* front door, with its much-polished door knocker and handle and half crescent of glass above it, glass that helped light the hallway. Reaching the portico, he lifted his hand, touched the cool brass of the knocker, then let go again. What would he say? What was he hoping to find? He turned his signet ring, then stepped back. He looked around once more, but there was no-one. No sign that the current incumbents were about. *Must be out celebrating*, he thought wryly. A long-forgotten memory suddenly returned, and briskly he walked to the side of the house, to one of two large windows. Yes, it was still the drawing room – different furniture, no eclectic *objects* that his parents had collected during their time in East Africa and Asia, but the same room nonetheless. Then he peered closely at the second pane from the bottom on the right. 'Good Lord,' he muttered. There, scratched into the glass was the inscription he remembered: 'Tom Isaac'. The very same pane of glass that had been there since 1850-something, the pane of glass Mr Hopcroft, the gardener, had shown him as a boy. 'Our secret,' Mr Hopcroft had said with a wink.

'Who was he?' Edward had asked him.

'A real hero he was,' Mr Hopcroft had told him. 'Married my grandfather's eldest sister and won a Victoria Cross in the Crimea. One of the very first.' What had become of him, this hero from a long-ago war, Edward could not recall, but he knew the story had fired his childhood imagination. And he, too, had decided he should leave his mark. Edward stood up straight again, his heart quickening. It would mean walking behind the house, to a part of the garden dangerously far from the front drive. He knew it was madness, knew that it was wrong to venture into someone's house without their consent, but he also knew that he *had* to look. With a final backward glance he hurried around the house and across the lawn to a large copper beech that stood high over the far end of the garden. One of the main branches had been neatly lopped off, but it still appeared to be in good health, a still tall and proud tree. He put his hand to the bark, and allowed it to slide over the trunk as he walked around it. And then he smiled. 'Here it is,' he said aloud. Admittedly, the bark had almost healed over the raw wood where his penknife had once cut, but the letters, 'EE', and the date, '1935', were unmistakable, clearer, he realised than the chiselled letters on his father's gravestone.

Another furtive glance and Edward hurried back across the lawn, round to the front of the house, down the driveway, and back out onto the road. In just a few minutes he was back inside the safety of his car. He waited a moment, closing his eyes, and breathing out deeply. Really, he thought, he was too old to be sneaking about like a burglar. *But it was still there.* Edward looked at the church once more, silent and indefatigable, then started the engine and slowly drove off. But as he passed by the entrance to the drive once more, he braked and looked down the drive for one last time. It was, he reflected, quite extraordinary what the brain could keep locked away. It had been a long, long time since he'd thought of the house – a place of happiness and innocence, of security and of simple pleasures; yet seeing it once more, rediscovering those simple links to a life he had supposed had been lost forever, he was aware a door had been unbolted and flung wide open.

A short, sharp blast of a car horn jolted him from his reverie and made him look up. A car faced him, and its driver, a middle-aged man wearing an expression of profound irritation, was agitatedly waving his arm in the direction of the driveway. The indicator, Edward noticed, was also flashing. Beside the man, a smartly dressed woman was mouthing, 'We want to turn in there!' Edward held up his hand in apology, and reversed. *The current custodians.* Shaking their heads, they thundered down the drive, dust clouds rising in their wake. 'Got away in the nick of time,' he said out loud to himself.

But it was too late, as he had known it would be the moment he had seen the house again. He had crossed an invisible threshold from which there could be no going back. The force that had pressed him to find Chilton once more was, he realised, stronger than his will to resist. Sights and smells; such necessary prompts to memory. As he rejoined the motorway, his thoughts were not on the heavy holiday weekend traffic, but on events that had occurred many years before. The beginning of the war; *his* war at any rate: September, 1940, the start of his flying career. *At Cambridge, of all places.* Edward shook his head. He barely recognised that man – man! He'd still been a boy! A boy who'd known nothing; just nineteen years old and keen as anything. What a grand adventure it had seemed. What a thrill. *What a thrill.*

Cambridge – September, 1940

It was not the start to his flying career that Edward had expected: nearly three weeks into the course at the Initial Training Wing and he still had not been in an aeroplane. Instead it had been marching up and down the parade ground, carrying out the kind of PT he'd done at school, and endless hours in the classroom: law and admin, hygiene and gas, elementary aircraft maintenance and the correct signal procedure when using an Aldis Lamp. Edward had scored 100 per cent on that particular test, but this did little to ease the frustration he felt. He had joined to fly, to see some action. He worried it might all be over before he had had his chance.

And he'd forgotten his mother's birthday. He felt bad about this, but fortunately had managed to escape during a study period and had found her a photograph frame from a camera shop on King's Parade. '*I'm sorry this is so late,*' he wrote to her later that evening in his high-looped scrawl, '*but we've been working like demons and never finish until at least 6.30 p.m. – which leaves little time for shopping. I could have managed it yesterday, but there's a church parade this Sunday and the CO said I had to get a haircut beforehand. He said my hair was "disgracefully long"! So, sorry mother, but those wavy blond locks you always liked so much have been unceremoniously lopped off.*'

'Are you nearly done, Eddie?' Harry Barclay was lounging on his bed, flicking through a magazine. 'What a load of rubbish this is,' he said slapping the magazine down on the floor. 'Come on, I want to get to the pub.'

'Five minutes,' said Edward. He had stopped writing and was tapping his fingers on the table. 'I'm sure I meant to ask her for something. My mind's gone blank.'

'Money?' suggested Harry. 'Someone needs to supplement our paltry pay from the Air Ministry.'

'No,' he said, then took up his pen again, speaking slowly as he wrote. 'Sorry – to – be – a – nuisance, but – could – you – please – send – my – cricket – whites, boots – and – socks, plus – one – or – two – white – shirts?'

'Of course,' said Harry, 'can't have you letting the side down.

Now tell her you love her, and let's get going.' He got up off the bed, lit a cigarette and put on his jacket, then held out Edward's for him to take. 'Ready now?' he said.

'Ready,' said Edward.

Many from the course were already there; it had become something of a ritual. And there was news, too – that they would soon be going to Canada. It was unclear precisely where this rumour had sprung from, but most of the recruits gathered round the bar seemed to accept the veracity of the news. 'The girls out there love English accents,' said one. 'And they're all gorgeous,' said another. Everyone laughed; they were all quick to do so after a long day of study. There was also a palpable sense of shared excitement amongst them. Edward was proud – and relieved – to be finally wearing uniform, especially the uniform of a would-be pilot. He sensed the others felt much the same way. Pilots, particularly fighter pilots, were held in high esteem; he just prayed he would become one too. Any other course of action – from joining Bomber Command, to Coastal Command (widely perceived to be the bottom of the heap) – was simply unimaginable, and it was why he was determined not to let himself down at any point in his training. He knew Harry was of the same mind – they had talked about it; and it was why, after just two pints, that they nodded at one another, finished their drinks, and headed back to their room in St John's.

'I'm not sure I want to go to Canada,' Edward told Harry as they wandered along the deserted streets, 'even if the girls are stunning.'

'Why not?'

'Well, it'll take us even further away from the war, won't it?'

'Hardly,' said Harry. 'We've got to cross the Atlantic, don't forget. Lots of nasty U-boats to dodge.'

'That just makes it worse. I'm not sure I like the idea of a long sea voyage. I just want to get in an aeroplane.'

'But think of all the flying in Canada. Vast empty blue skies. We'll get far more flying there than we would stuck over here. And think of all those Canadian girls, as well.'

'I hadn't thought of that. Perhaps I don't mind so much, then. I just don't want the war to be over before I get my chance.'

Harry laughed. 'Eddie, believe me, I don't think there's much chance of that. My old man says this is going to take years, and I tell you, he's right.' He slapped Edward on the back. 'Come on, Canada will be fun.'

Away, far beyond the colleges on their left, the last faint streaks of light were disappearing. Their footsteps sounded loud on the pavement; Cambridge was still that night, and dark too. Not a single light twinkled. The roofs and minarets of the colleges stood out against the embers of the day, but the town seemed to be covered by a heavy shroud that still, after a year of war, felt unnatural. And although many of the colleges were once more filled with young men, albeit in military uniform rather than gowns, there was no sense of the vibrancy and buzz normally to be found during term-time before the war.

The porter nodded to them as they passed through the gatehouse of St John's. 'I wouldn't mind coming here after the war,' said Harry as they trotted up the wooden staircase to their room.

'Perhaps,' said Edward, 'although I think after this I might have had enough of studying.'

'Maybe you're right,' said Harry as they reached their room. 'It's funny: you're worried it'll all be over too soon, but I can't really think of what it will be like when it's all over. Normal life seems to have vanished so quickly.'

As Edward washed in the bathroom along the corridor and got ready for bed, it occurred to him that despite the lack of flying, he had much to be thankful for. Harry was right. Canada *would* be marvellous: long days swirling high in the sky and in a country untouched by war. After all, the Luftwaffe could hardly reach across the Atlantic. And he would be going in good company. Already he had made a number of new friends, not least Harry. Could it really be only three weeks since his mother and father had seen him off at the station in Woking? He felt he'd known his new friend a lifetime already. Initially, Edward had been rather in awe of Harry. He was older – twenty-four! – a sports writer for the *Evening Standard*, someone who had even played cricket for Kent. But then they soon discovered they had much in common: although Harry was several years older, he, too, had been born in India, and had spent his early life roaming from one colonial outpost to another. His father worked not for a tea merchant, but for the Shell Oil Company, but the Barclays had also moved back to England when Harry had been still young. They lived not in Surrey, but Kent, and from what Harry had told him, their house was not dissimilar to the Old Rectory in Chilton. And although Harry was not an only child, his sister was a number of years older and had been away at boarding school during those early years abroad. She was now married. Harry said he barely knew her.

But it was not just similar interests and backgrounds that had drawn them together. It was shared experiences as much as anything that cemented friendships, and Edward had met Harry not at the Initial Training Wing, but on a tumultuous day in London a day before the course began. Edward had been having a coffee in a café at Liverpool Street whilst waiting for the Cambridge train. It was around four o'clock on a beautiful late summer's afternoon. London had spent the day bathed in sunshine beneath a deep and cloudless blue sky. The sun was bearing down on the great ceiling of vaulted glass, so that the station concourse shimmered and flickered with brightness. Edward had been absent-mindedly glancing over a newspaper, when he noticed a man breathlessly walk in wearing the same brand new blue uniform, and clutching a battered suitcase that had clearly survived many long voyages around the globe. Immediately, Edward knew he had seen him somewhere before. As he struggled to remember where, the man had also noticed Edward, and grinning, waved to him like an old friend and headed over.

'Harry Barclay,' he said, holding out a hand. 'Mind if I join you?'

'Harry Barclay, my God!' said Edward. 'I saw you get a hundred against Surrey at Guildford two years ago.' Edward stood up and shook his hand.

'We still lost, though,' grinned Harry. 'Play much yourself?'

'Whenever I can. I only wish I could bat as well as you.'

'Oh, I'm pretty rusty these days, you know.' He grinned again, and as they sat down, Edward signalled to a waitress in what he hoped seemed a nonchalant manner.

'Tea, I think, thanks.'

Harry took off his cap, and ran his hands through thick, wavy dark – almost black – hair, then pulled out a packet of crumpled cigarettes from his pocket and offered one to Edward. 'God, it's a hot one today. I'm boiled. Smoke?' he said, tapping an end of the packet so that a single cigarette stood out from the rest.

'Thanks,' said Edward. The waitress came over and hovered expectantly with her notepad. 'What'll you have?' asked Edward.

Harry grinned again, said, 'What are you on? Coffee?' then smiling at the waitress, said, 'I'll have a cold drink, please. Squash or something? Thank you.' He looked at his watch. 'What've we got? Twenty minutes. Plenty of time.'

'I suppose you haven't had much chance to play cricket this summer.'

'No, not a lot. Still managed a few games, though. Actually, I haven't played that much for Kent since the game you saw.'

'Why not? I thought you played superbly.'

Harry rubbed his fingers together. 'I had to get a job – if only Kent would pay me. I was lucky, though. I was doing a few pieces for the local paper and then got a letter from the *Standard* offering me a job. And since I was living in a flat in London and travelling about a bit covering cricket and even tennis, I didn't really have the time to play any more.'

'Surely your editor would have given you the time off.'

'Maybe. But it's very competitive on the paper. If I'd continually taken time off, someone else might have taken my place and done a far better job than me. I was very fortunate to be given the chance to make a living from what I love doing. I didn't want to blow it.'

Edward said, 'I can't think of anything I'd rather do. It must be a wonderful job.'

Harry chuckled. 'Yes, it's not bad. But then I reckon flying will be a lot of fun too.'

Quarter of an hour later, they were making their way through a blast of steam towards a carriage on the King's Lynn train. It was busy, but they found places in a compartment already occupied by an older man with a lined face and two middle-aged women. On schedule, a whistle blew and the train lurched and then began to steadily pull away.

'Ah, that breeze is good,' said Harry, lifting his face towards the open vent at the top of the window. Edward followed likewise, momentarily closing his eyes as the draught buffeted his face. He was glad to be on his way again. There was a knot in his stomach – excitement and a sense of anticipation.

They had only been gone a few minutes when they heard air-raid sirens wailing mournfully across the city, their drone sounding loudly through the open window. Edward looked up at Harry, then at the other passengers. All looked anxious, their heads turned to the view of the city.

'Probably nothing,' said the older man, taking his pipe out of his mouth.

'It usually is,' said one of the women, tutting at her companion, who nodded in agreement.

'Nuisance raids, they call them,' said the first woman. 'A couple of bombs then off they go again.'

'Usually not even that,' said the man. 'Just reconnaissance planes.'

'Well, hopefully we'll soon be able to ensure there's even fewer of them coming over,' said Edward. He smiled at them, then at Harry.

'That's the spirit,' said the man, just as they heard explosions, distant at first but then immediately closer.

'Oh my God,' said the first woman suddenly, 'Jesus, would you look at that.' Edward glanced at her now ashen face, then followed her gaze, peering up at the sky. Away to the east, almost as far as the horizon, the deep blue sky was now covered with a rash of black shapes. Harry had stood up and now all of them – normal decorum evaporated – were crowded around the window, staring aghast at the scene unfolding before them. Vast black plumes of smoke were already pitching into the sky, whilst above were puffs of dark smudges where anti-aircraft shells had exploded. The train continued, falteringly, slowly. Outside the noise of explosions was constant. It reminded Edward of the finale of a Guy Fawkes' Night firework display, except that this was louder and its effects so devastating. Overhead, aircraft droned like a massed swarm of insects, their engines audible over the din of explosions as they finished their bomb run and headed on over London.

'It's the docks,' said Harry. 'They're hitting the docks.'

'Oh my God,' said the second woman, holding a hand to her face, 'my sister and her family are down there.'

The train stuttered into Tottenham Hale then jolted to a halt. In the compartment, they all looked at each other. Edward wondered what they were supposed to do. On the platform, a guard in a tin hat was hurrying down the platform ordering everyone to disembark and to shelter at the entrance to the Underground station.

The man and the two women bustled out. Harry and Edward waited to let them go, then followed. On the platform, a woman was screaming hysterically, but most seemed shocked into mute silence. From the streets nearby were the sounds of fire engines, their bells ringing shrilly. 'Come on,' said Harry, leading Edward to one end of the platform and away from the mass of people. 'Just look at that.'

What had begun as single plumes of smoke had now become one vast dark cloud, rising high into the deep blue until it passed across the sun. Even from several miles' distance, they clearly saw flames angrily swirling into the sky.

'Just imagine the poor bastards caught under that lot,' said Harry.

'Come along, lads,' said an elderly guard. 'Best be getting into the shelter.' Obediently they did as they were told, heading down the stairs and joining the huddle waiting anxiously in the Underground entrance. More bells clanged nearby, and a further two fire engines sped past.

A stick of bombs erupted not far away. Smoke and dust billowed into the sky, followed by a deafening crash as a building collapsed. Edward jolted; he was not the only one.

'A bit close,' said Harry. 'It would be cruelly ironic, don't you think, if we were bombed out before even setting foot in an aeroplane.'

'The bastards. Just wait till I get my hands on them.'

A woman standing next to them was clutching a young girl, and swaying back and forth, trying to soothe her daughter. She looked terrified, but catching Edward's eye said, 'You make sure you get them for this. Who the hell do they think they are, coming over and bombing our city?'

'We'll do our best,' said Harry, 'just as soon as we can,' and touched his cap.

'Don't worry,' added Edward, 'we'll soon send 'em packing. You'll see.' It was bravura he felt absolutely to be true, even though he was aware that neither of them were yet qualified to say it. Standing there, smoking once more with Harry, Edward felt a sense of relief sweep over him. To his surprise, he did not really feel scared, not even when he'd seen the dark mass of bombers for the first time. His heart was drumming in his chest, but from a sense of excitement. Already, he felt himself to be taller even than his five foot ten inches, and older than his nineteen years. It was as though he had already come of age: not only was he now in uniform, but in the middle of an actual raid. At last he had a proper part to play in this war. He thought of the long months since leaving school the year before. He'd been so bored. Three terms teaching at a prep school in Surrey had been purgatory. He'd felt so impotent, so *wasted*. And in the holidays he'd had to watch the mounting numbers of young men his age proudly parading their uniforms. With every week – every day – that passed, so his impatience had grown. When were the RAF going to send for him? Why was it taking so long? Sometimes he wondered whether he'd dreamt the whole thing; that he'd never been interviewed at Kingsway at all.

Now, however, the moment had come. There was, at long last, something useful for him to do. Something worthwhile. Soon *he* would be the hero in the many adventure books he had devoured as a child.

As the sound of bombs and firing at last petered out, so people began moving out of the cramped Underground entrance. Edward and Harry followed, climbing the steps to the main platform just as the all clear sounded. It was a little after six o'clock. Even in Tottenham, several miles from the main infernos, the air was heavy and acrid, the stench of burnt rubber, dust and other fumes cloying and more choking than the worst London smog.

'I can't believe it,' said a man behind Edward and Harry, his face drained and sallow. 'I can't bloody believe it.' Most looked pale, too, stunned to say anything at all.

Guards ushered them back onto the train. 'Departing in five minutes!' shouted one of them, as he marched up and down the length of the platform. Edward and Harry returned to the same compartment but there was no sign of their fellow travellers. In their place was a man in his thirties wearing army uniform.

'Something else, eh?' he said to them as he sat down. 'Quite a bloody show.'

Edward, sitting opposite him, nodded. He wanted to ask him

what he thought this meant, this sudden large-scale bombing of London, but kept his thoughts to himself.

'You chaps started training yet?' he continued.

'On our way now,' said Harry.

'Well, good for you. Make sure you give them what for when the time comes.'

It still gave Edward a sense of satisfaction when he thought about the officer saying that, and in the passing weeks his sense of purpose, his hopes for glory and honour, had not diminished in any way. 7th September had already been dubbed 'Black Saturday'; the bombers had returned again that night and had continued to pulverise the docks long after Edward and Harry had finally reached Cambridge. The attacks on London and other cities around the country had continued every day since without respite. Throughout the country, shock had given way to outrage, a feeling shared by Edward, and fuelling his determination to exact his own revenge. So it was with some relief to him when it was confirmed that they would indeed be going to Canada for their flying training – and without delay; their course was being accelerated and cut short by a week.

'I've been thinking,' Edward said to Harry as they returned to their room in St John's later that night. 'The time taken from the course more than compensates for the length of the journey to Canada, so we'll be flying just as soon as if we'd stayed in England.'

'If not sooner,' said Harry.

Later, Edward wrote again to his parents. His mother had been worried about him; another letter had arrived that morning, in which she had fretted about Cambridge being bombed. '*We have had a few warnings, but no raids, so please do not concern yourselves on that account,*' he scrawled. '*I may not be able to write again for a while because our course has now been shortened and we have to cram all our exams in before we finish. I shall barely be able to think straight let alone write letters.*' He was itching to tell them about Canada, but instead added, '*Also, we might not be getting our promised leave. The CO's trying to get us 48 hours, so fingers crossed. More than that I can't say – you know how it is. Everything's very hush-hush. I'll send a telegram when I know more.*'

Forty-eight hours it was – two days that had to include the time it took to reach Chilton from Cambridge and then to get to Liverpool. It did not worry Edward; as far as he was concerned, the sooner they set sail the better. And in any case, he knew he would quickly tire of his mother's fussing. Even so, in order to add a sense of drama to the occasion, he decided not to forewarn them with any telegram, but to arrive in Chilton unannounced. The ploy worked, as he knew it would. 'But why didn't you warn us?' exclaimed his mother, embracing him tightly. 'You poor thing! Come in, give me your bag, let me get you a drink.' Edward almost believed he'd been one of the pilots fighting to save Britain, rather than an RAF trainee with only a few weeks at an Initial Training Wing to his name.

As soon as they had sat down he told them about Canada. 'No bombs there, Mum.'

'Yes, well that's something,' she said. She still looked pinched and anxious. They were in the drawing room, with its familiar and comforting furniture, pictures and smell; a smell of wax polish and the faint scent of late summer roses from the garden. The grandfather clock ticking imperturbably, unobtrusively making itself heard whenever there was a pause in the conversation.

'Fancy a stretch in the garden?' said his father suddenly. Edward glanced at his mother – *sounds serious* – then said, 'Yes, all right.'

'I'll see how cook's getting on,' said his mother, rising.

It had been raining during his journey down, but had now cleared. It was early evening, the light already drawing in, but the air was fresh and clean.

'I'm glad nothing's dropped near here,' said Edward as they walked across the damp lawn. 'I've far more reason to feel anxious about you two being here, so close to London.'

'Oh, we're all right. I hardly think the Germans are going to try and bomb Chilton, or even Woking for that matter,' he said.

'And what about you, during the day? London's changed in the last month.' He'd seen some of the damage for himself, having decided to walk across the river from the Embankment to Waterloo. Bombed-out buildings had been vomited onto the road. Edward had watched teams of men and ARP wardens busily trying to clear up the mess; and as he walked over the Thames, a heavy, acrid stench wafted on the breeze of the river – a smell like the embers of a bonfire after a heavy downpour of rain.

His father nodded. 'Most of the raids seem to be at night. But you're right. It's looking a bit of a mess. Don't worry, though, we've a very strong basement that could withstand most things.' He smiled then added, 'and I promised solemnly to your mother that I would always take cover in case of a raid.'

'She does like to worry.'

'We're lucky she cares.' They had reached the copper beech at the end of the garden. There was an old bench there, left by the previous owners. Edward's father sat down. 'I've always liked this spot,' he said. 'Hard to think there's a war on when you're sitting here.' The leaves rustled gently in the breeze. From somewhere safe in the foliage above, a wood pigeon was cooing. Edward looked at the carving he had made six years before, and ran a finger over the letters etched into the bark.

'Still there,' said his father.

'Yes. It seems a lifetime ago that I did that.' Edward sat down beside his father. 'You were furious, do you remember?'

'Well,' he said, 'it's wrong to go around carving on trees. Blatant vandalism. You had to be taught a lesson.'

'A painful one if I remember rightly.'

'Did you ever do it again?'

'No.'

'Well, then. An entirely justified course of action.' They both laughed. In truth, Edward had found his father George a remote figure when he'd been young; someone who was away for much of the time, and all too often meting out some punishment or other whenever he was home. They had become closer, however, as Edward had grown and his father had spent more time in London and less overseas. His father, he realised, had punished him only because his mother would so rarely do so. He had invariably deserved it. Edward glanced at him now: greyer, much greyer in recent years, but in his fifties still fit and healthy, and the cornerstone of their small family. And no matter how distant he had once seemed, he had always been the person Edward looked up to above all others; the person he trusted the most; the person he relied on to guide him through life.

'Ah, you were always a headstrong young boy,' said his father, stretching. 'It's a good thing, you know. You stand up for what you believe in and you've determination too. But Edward, you must promise me something.'

'Of course.'

'Promise me you won't be reckless. There's a fine line between the two. One is a positive, the other quite the opposite.'

'I won't, I –'

His father held up a hand to quiet him. 'I saw what happened to reckless young men in the last war. Few ever made it home again. You're a grown man now, and no doubt you feel immortal and untouchable. I know you're itching to do your bit, and I'm very proud of you for that. But you're also still my boy. War is very dangerous. Aeroplanes are dangerous. Be careful, that's all I'm saying. Be determined, but don't be reckless. Come home for your mother – and for me.'

Edward felt emotion welling within him. He wanted to speak, but for a few moments he was worried that if he did so, he might cry. So instead he just nodded, and when the moment had passed, said, 'All right, Dad.'

'Good boy,' said his father, gripping his son's knee. Then he shivered and said, 'It's getting cold. Shall we go in?'

Thirty-six hours later, as the sun rose pinkly in the east, he was on board ship, bound for the New World, the Liverpool shoreline inching further and further away, until it was completely enveloped by the morning haze.

'Gone,' said Edward, exhaling a cloud of smoke.

Standing beside him, Harry Barclay was also smoking pensively. 'Next time we see England,' he said, 'we'll be qualified pilots.'

Edward grinned. 'I can't wait,' he told his friend.

Somerset – May, 1995

Edward had been right about one thing: interest in the war had quietened considerably in the days and weeks that followed the fiftieth anniversary celebrations. There had been no more documentaries, no more features, and no more interviews with veterans. In Brampton Cary the bunting had come down, as it had elsewhere around the country. Edward's life continued as before: his daily routines and rituals, watching the school's increasingly successful season. Occasionally seeing former colleagues and friends. A night at the theatre in Bath.

But his life was not the same. The rest of the world might have put the war to the back of their minds once more, but he had been unable to do so. The dreams had become an almost nightly recurrence. Moreover, for the first time in many years, the nightmares had begun to vary. The old one still plagued him, relentlessly the same in every detail, but other images haunted his sleep. There was one in which he was flying through towers of white cloud, all sense of time and speed halted, as though he were motionless. Below, the earth seemed distant. He was so high that it was impossible to see any distinct features. Nothing to suggest the turmoil being waged below. He felt at peace, drifting there amongst the heavens. But a deafening noise shattered this calm. The screaming roar of aero-engines, and then two Messerschmitts were bearing down upon him. Edward swivelled his head frantically from one side to the other, but although they sounded loud enough to be almost on top of him, he could only see them fleetingly, a glint of metal, the smiling faces of the goggled pilots, and cannon tracer hurtling over the wing of his own machine. He was screaming, trying to block out the noise, whilst clutching the control column and desperately thrusting the aircraft back and forth in an effort to shake off his attackers. But the controls became heavier, the response more sluggish. Panic overtook him; he knew what he must do, but he could not, no matter how hard he tried. The aircraft was slowing, and its movement lessening, until it was flying in an almost straight and level line. And this time when he glanced behind him, he could see one of the Messerschmitts just yards from his. Could see the pilot grinning, his lips curled in satisfaction. A moment later he was not in the cockpit but watching, listening to the screams of another man: 'Oh Jesus no . . . Mother, save me . . . Jesus Christ . . . Mother, please!' And then just as the aircraft blew up, Edward was jolted awake, writhing and clutching his ears until he came to, and he realised he was no longer eighteen thousand feet high, but only in his bedroom with its double-glazed windows and warm cream walls.

Nor was it only at night that his mind had become dominated by war. During the day he repeatedly found his thoughts returning to those events, remembering incidents, snapshots of conversation, and thinking about the people he had known. Thinking about certain people in particular. How incredible the mind was. More than fifty years had passed and yet he found he could recall so much with absolute clarity. More than that: he could picture where the conversation took place, and the circumstances in which it had done so, and yet he'd not been aware that these memories had been stored away all these years, like folders in an old filing cabinet, brought out now, shaken free of dust and reread once more.

Harry, Harry. Edward had taken out his diary on a number of occasions, had looked at the address and telephone number of Andrew Fisher. Once he had even gone so far as to lift the receiver of the telephone. But, no. A letter would be better. *Tomorrow,* he had told himself. *I'll write tomorrow.* Tomorrow became the next day. A fortnight after returning from London, he still hadn't written to Andrew Fisher.

Sometimes his memories were prompted by chance references. One day he was reading his *Times* when he came across a small article about Uplands, Ontario. 'Well, I never,' he muttered to himself. He could certainly remember that place all right. Harry had been right about the flying in Canada. It had been cold, certainly, and there had been much snow on the ground for much of the time, but for almost the entire ten weeks of the course, the skies had been clear and blue. They'd all heard of trainee pilots getting lost in low cloud in Britain and hurling themselves into the side of a hill. There had been no such danger in Canada – the greatest risk to begin with had been landing on compressed snow – the brakes had been difficult to control, but to begin they had flown with experienced instructors and no-one had come to any serious harm.

It had been the ideal place to train: the nearest town was some miles away, and in what little free time they were given, there was not much they could do. Instead, he and Harry had decided to continue to work as hard as they could, helping each other through the large theoretical part of the course and giving one another encouragement with the flying. Once again, their dedication had paid off. Halfway through the ten-week course, when the Initial Training School was complete, both Edward and Harry had been assigned to continue their training on single-engine aircraft, while half their number were to immediately convert to twin-engines. He remembered scanning down the list put up in the mess, and the overwhelming sense of relief when he saw his name in the left-hand column.

His instructor throughout his time in Canada had been a huge, burly Canadian called Rex Miller. 'Flying will feel awkward and unnatural to begin with,' Miller had told him at the beginning of the course, 'but the day will come when suddenly it will feel as natural as riding a bike. The aircraft will feel like an extension of your own self. When that time comes, then we can really start getting down to business.' He could picture Miller saying that as though it had been last week: walking towards one of the line of Tiger Moths, feet crunching the snow. Edward had patted and rubbed his gloved hands together, and nodded; he had believed Miller, but at that moment, just a week into the course, was feeling twitchy about the flight they were about to make. Edward smiled to himself. He was sitting on his favoured bench under the horse chestnuts, and barely watching the cricket at all. Miller *had* been right: he could remember the flight when everything clicked; could remember it better than his first solo, or even his wings test. January, 1942, a week or two before his wings. From the moment he'd clambered into the front cockpit of the Harvard, turned on the magnetos and fired the engine, he'd felt a sense of empowerment and control. Climbing to nine thousand feet, he'd seen the vast flatness of the Ontario plains spread out beneath him, disappearing into an infinite blur on the horizon. The sun streaked across the wings, and then he began to twist and pirouette, dancing through the sky, the sky and ground rolling around him. And he was doing it without thinking, just as Miller had said; the aircraft had become a part of him, and he had whooped and laughed for joy at the sheer thrill of flying, and had thought how lucky he was to have the chance to do something so utterly exciting and wonderful.

The wings test had been a formality after that – both he and Harry had passed with 'above average' marks, and although both had behaved with restraint as the announcement had gone up on the notice board, back in their room he and Harry had laughed and clasped one another. 'We did it! We bloody well did it!' Harry had said, jumping up and down with glee. Both had laughed again at their shaking fingers as they'd tried to sew on their wings badge. 'Too excited to stitch anything,' Harry had said, then cursed as he pricked himself with the needle.

That had been in February, 1942, but it was not until the middle of May that they had finally made it back to England. For five weeks, they had been stranded at the embarkation depot in Nova Scotia, waiting for a passage home. Others from the course had already gone, but a half dozen, including Edward and Harry, had not been drafted for departure. Edward had thought teaching at a prep school had been frustrating, but it was nothing to the disappointment he had felt in Nova Scotia. 'We're standing still,' Edward had complained. 'Why is there so much waiting in the RAF?' Even Harry, so much more even-tempered, had been champing at the bit.

At last, at long, long last, they were told they would be shipping out. They were packed and ready to go – due to board the ship the following morning – when someone at the camp developed scarlet fever. Everyone was immediately ordered to the sick bay to be tested for immunity. Of the six due to sail that day, three were immune; Harry, Edward and a Canadian pilot were not. They would not be getting on the ship after all. Edward had thought he would explode. He had shouted and railed, bemoaned the unfairness of life, expressed his utter contempt for the doctors at the camp, but it was no use. He and Harry had come to loathe Nova Scotia. 'Brilliant if bird watching's your thing,' Harry had said, 'otherwise pretty pointless.' The camp was surrounded by wild country, wooded and rugged. It was, they agreed, probably a beautiful place in summer and in peacetime, but hellish if you were desperate to fly and do your bit to win the war; and made considerably worse by the fact that it was now spring and the snow had turned to rain, and the rows of wooden huts in which they were housed were surrounded by thick, glutinous mud. The mud! It got everywhere: into their huts, splattered around their trousers, into the deepest crevices of their boots. And there was nothing to do. The nearest town was Debird – renamed 'Deadbird' – a half-hour walk away through the mud, and consisting of four shops and a collection of windswept houses. 'A trip to the seething metropolis?' Harry would say most days, and Edward would nod sullenly and off they'd trudge.

To while away the time, they played endless games of cards – Edward's poker skills improved enormously – and spent hours discussing their perfect day should they ever make it back. This would see them spending lavishly. The amount of pay they were saving was the only consolation of this enforced confinement; with nothing to spend it on, both there accruing more than they had ever had in their lives. The details varied from day to day, but the essence was this: they would book themselves into a smart hotel – the Ritz, for example – have long, hot baths followed by a shave at the barber's in Victoria Arcade. The afternoon would be spent in a leisurely tour around Lord's Cricket Ground, then, with the sightseeing over, it would be back to the hotel for cocktails, where, through the combination of their great charm and pilots' uniforms, they would persuade two beautiful girls to go out to dinner with them at one of the finest restaurants in town. This was to be followed by a long night of dancing and further drinking.

They never did have the Perfect Day, however – at least, not as they'd imagined. There'd been no time. Having spent the best part of three months doing nothing, it appeared the RAF needed them urgently after all. From Liverpool, they had reported right away to the officers' mess at Uxbridge. From there they would be posted to their Operational Training Units. Edward could remember very clearly the sense of mounting anxiety both he and Harry had felt. They still desperately wanted to fly fighters, but this was far from certain: they could easily end up flying twin-engine aircraft after all, or be posted to Army Reconnaissance or Coastal Command. Nor did they want to be separated, although they knew it was very likely; the RAF had little time for the personal wishes of its junior officers.

Yet having trained together, and remained in Nova Scotia for so long together, they had come to depend on one another enormously. Edward had made good friends at school, but had never had a friendship as close as the one he now shared with Harry.

But after the frustrations of the past few months, their good fortune returned. Their anxieties had been for nothing: both were assigned to fighters, both were sent to the same Operational Training Unit, and, four weeks later, their training complete, both were posted to the same squadron.

For the fourth night in a row, Edward woke up sweating and shaking. Once his brain had recovered and he realised he was in his bedroom after all, he felt so upset he thought he might even cry. He couldn't understand it. Why now? Why, after keeping it all consigned to the vaults of his mind for so long, was it flooding back, tormenting him and refusing to give him any peace? And yet, later, as he ate his breakfast and his eyes absently skimmed the front page of *The Times*, it occurred to him that looking back on some of those days, remembering the excitement and the funny times he had had with Harry, had been comforting in a way; cathartic even, for want of a better word.

After breakfast he made himself a cup of coffee, then took himself into the sitting room and sat down on his usual chair. He glanced at the photograph of Cynthia. 'All this was before I even knew you,' he mumbled. For some time he sat staring out at some undefined spot, his newspaper folded on his lap. Several minutes later, he stood up suddenly, slammed his newspaper onto the chair and stomped upstairs. He took a pole from behind the spare-room door, hooked it into the hatch in the ceiling and pulled down the retracting aluminium steps. Somewhat shakily, he climbed up into the roof space. Even up there, where eyes seldom preyed, the impression was one of neatness. Cardboard packing boxes and old suitcases were piled carefully and clearly labelled. He knew exactly where to look: a black metal money tin, not much bigger than a large shoebox. It stood on top of a couple of boxes labelled, 'Edward – Old Files etc.' He had not kept many mementos from his life, and hardly any from the war. He lifted the tin. It was not heavy. Carefully he descended the ladder, one arm clutching the tin, the other steadying himself on the ladder. Then he hoisted the ladder again and shut the hatch. For a moment, he paused on the landing, then went into his bedroom. Downstairs, with its windows and glass doors leading into the small garden, was too exposed; he wanted privacy, complete privacy.

Laying the tin on the bed, he undid the catch and opened the lid. A wave of mustiness leapt out from the long-sealed contents. He fingered the strip of ribbon that had denoted his medals – that had once been sewed to the breast of his RAF tunic. The tin contained a collection of other things he had forgotten about: his birth certificate, a small Bible given to him at his christening – 'With love from John, 16th July, 1923' inscribed on the inside. Who was John? He had no idea. A menu from a Christmas lunch in 1942, cuttings from the *London Gazette* with his citations. There were a few letters, too – letters he had found after his mother had died. They had been written during the early part of the war – the last was from June, 1942. He had wondered at the time why she had kept only those; he'd written regularly, whenever he had been able. One was stamped '10th September, 1940', and he picked it out, carefully taking the paper from the envelope. '*Dearest Mother, Sorry to make another request but could you send my cricket whites? It looks like we might be playing cricket every weekend that we're here. I'm sharing a room with Harry Barclay, the sports writer of the* Evening Standard. *He's a terrific fellow and a fine batsman. Dad and I saw him score a hundred for Kent a couple of years ago. Isn't it funny to think we are now going to be flying together?*' Another was stamped '9th July, 1941'. It was to his father, written whilst at his Operational Training Unit at Debden. '*We should finish here next Monday – have no idea where I'll get posted, but I hope it's still with Harry. It really is essential that we stick together as we get on very well indeed and that makes a lot of difference when going to a new station.*' Then he smiled. '*As regards your last warning about liquor: apart from three or four shandies, I haven't had any sort of alcohol at all since coming here. I never believe in drinking too much too often, but just occasionally when I'm not flying the next day.*'

Ah yes! thought Edward. He remembered he had shown both his father's letter and his reply to Harry – they'd thought it hilarious. A few days later they had been told they were both going to 57 Squadron to fly Spitfires. To celebrate, they'd all taken the train into London – he and Harry and most of the pilots from the course – and had headed first to the White Horse pub in Mayfair and then to a string of clubs. And every time they'd bought another round, Harry had said, 'Of course, Eddie only drinks shandies and only when he's not flying the next day.' It had seemed more and more funny as the night wore on. My God, but they had been drunk that night; and if not quite the Perfect Day of their imaginations, it had certainly been a very memorable – and happy – one nonetheless.

They had all drunk a lot back then. More than he ever would again. Even when they'd joined 57 Squadron in Cornwall – they'd gone to the pub most nights. Edward had thought nothing of waking up still half drunk. A blast of oxygen soon cleared the head.

He placed the letters next to the medals and other bits of paper, then took out the blue silk scarf folded there. His heart was quickening, a shot of nausea rose from his stomach, and he felt his throat tighten. Hastily, he put it down again. *Not now,* and for a moment he had to look away completely. He sighed heavily, shuddering as he breathed out again, closed his eyes briefly, then turned back to the box. At the bottom of the tin lay what he was after. The blue cloth binding of his logbook was faded and stained, and the paper yellowed with ageing. Putting it to one side, he placed everything else back, shut the lid and carefully lodged the tin in the bottom drawer of his chest of drawers, next to his folded pullovers; there was plenty of space there now that it housed only his clothes.

He noticed his hands were shaking slightly as he opened it and began flicking through. People from the past leapt from the pages: commanding officers and flight commanders, signing off his monthly tallies of flights. His own handwriting, scrawled in the fountain pen his father had given him when he'd been sent off to school – he'd kept it with him for much of the war. Some people used their logbooks as a record of flying only, but Edward, like others, liked to add comments and small notes along the way. Here and there were the details of various dogfights: '*had a squirt, but he disappeared into cloud*' and occasionally a swastika when he had shot an aircraft down. '*We were the second English course to be trained under the Joint Air Training Programme in Canada – the flying discipline was very strict, but the flying was most enjoyable,*' he had written at the end of his time in Ontario, then added, '*We hope the*

Canadians will be coming to England with us – gee, they're swell guys (to put it in Canadian).'

How young he seemed then. He felt suddenly overwhelmed by sadness, and his throat tightened once more. He ran his hand across his eyes. The loss of youth, the loss of innocence; it was so tragic. But most of all he felt a sense of despair for what he knew now faced this young man; a young man so full of exuberance and striking vitality.

He was being drawn back, and he felt powerless to do anything about it. He hadn't asked for the fiftieth anniversary; he hadn't wanted to go to London. But he recognised that opening that tin box from his past had been his choice. It was something he had sworn he would never do. A line had been crossed; a point of no return. The broken nights would continue, the daydreams too. Sitting on the edge of the bed, he rubbed his forehead, his anger rising. He didn't want this; he wanted to be left alone – to watch his cricket, to potter about, to finish his life with some kind of peace of mind.

Edward stood up, sighed, then retrieved a small suitcase from the cupboard in the spare room. He had thought the past had been swept away by the life he had created at Myddleton College: the school and his family had ensured his great deception had worked for nearly fifty years. But now the game was up. There was nothing else for it: he had to continue what he had already unwittingly begun. If the past was erupting like a dormant volcano, then he had to let it run its course. A journey faced him; a journey into his past. He would be methodical about it. Cornwall first, then he supposed, Malta; and then, and only then, Italy. It was, he now realised, something he simply had to do. Only then would he rediscover the peace of mind he so badly craved. *But my God,* he thought, *I hope I have the strength for this.*

Edward glanced around, checking the clear blue sky for what seemed like the hundredth time. Once again there was nothing: no black specks on the horizon, just the other three Spitfires of Blue Section, Jimmy Farrell ahead of him, and behind and several thousand feet below, Eric Norton and Harry. Jimmy banked and turned, and Edward followed, weaving back in a wide sweep, the sun crossing over his wings and glinting blindingly as it glanced over the Perspex canopy of Jimmy's aircraft.

From sixteen thousand feet, Edward could see the whole of Cornwall and beyond stretching away from him, its familiar elongated shape and jagged coastline dozing peacefully in the late afternoon sun. Despite the beauty of such a sight, Edward was bored. Three days they'd been escorting the little convoy below – three days, and it was only now rounding Land's End! He had already discovered how tedious convoy patrols could be – most of the enemy fighter stations were further north in the Pas de Calais – but escorting a floating dry dock from Avonmouth on its way to Southampton was proving excruciating; since the tugs towing this cumbersome piece of equipment could manage no more than two knots, the Spitfires were forced to constantly weave back and forth, and at pitifully slow speeds. They'd taken it in turns, one section at a time, but even so, Edward had flown once already that morning, once the previous day, and twice the day before that. And the same every time: weaving back and forth, the Merlin engine barely ticking over and not even the faintest whiff of the enemy.

He looked at his fuel gauge: it was getting low. *Come on, Jimmy,* he thought, *let's head for home.* After two more sweeps back and forth, his earphones crackled and Jimmy's voice came through his headset. 'All right, let's go,' said Jimmy. *At last,* thought Edward, as they turned north-east, back towards Perranporth.

A little over ten minutes later, Edward landed and taxied his aircraft into one of the many blast pens hastily built along the station perimeter.

'Everything all right, sir?' asked Hewitson, as Edward jumped down from the wing root.

'Perfectly, thanks,' he said stroking the wing with one hand. The engine was clicking noisily as it began to cool.

'See anything?' said Parker.

'What do you think?'

'I take it that's a "no" then, sir.'

'Not a bloody thing.'

'Same old, same old,' said Parker.

'You said it.' Thanking them, he began walking back to the crew room, a large khaki marquee pegged in besides a number of small wooden huts scattered around the edge of the airfield. The last of the flight had landed and was closing in to one of the blast pens just ahead of him. Edward waved and seeing Harry wave back, hurried over.

'I can't believe we've got another two days of this,' said Edward, as Harry leapt off the wing to join him.

'I know what you mean.'

'Do you think we'll ever see any enemy planes? I'm beginning to think they don't exist – that it's really just a figment of our imagination that the Luftwaffe's out there.'

Harry laughed. 'I could think of worse ways of spending my time, though.' He put an arm on Edward's shoulder. 'After all, we're alive and improving our flying hours. That's got to be a good thing. And it's another beautiful day. I'm very happy to be alive right now.' He pulled out a packet of cigarettes from the top pocket of his tunic, gave one to Edward, then paused to light both. Now that 'B' Flight was in, the airfield had become quiet, as though it were dozing gently in the afternoon sun.

'Twenty past five,' said Harry aloud, glancing at his watch. He squinted and rubbed the back of his neck. 'Still warm,' he said. 'This weather's amazing.' Only the slightest of breezes was blowing off the sea. Gulls were calling from the cliffs.

'You're right,' said Edward, 'this *is* pretty good. I shall never complain again.'

Most of the other pilots from 'A' Flight were sitting outside the crew room on an assortment of striped deckchairs and old armchairs dragged out of the hut. The rest of 'B' Flight had already taken off to continue the escort work, while Jimmy and Eric were smoking and talking to Scotty, the Intelligence Officer. Edward and Harry joined them. Scotty raised an eyebrow in acknowledgement, but otherwise continued stroking his moustache and nodding earnestly at Jimmy.

'Oh, hullo, you two,' said Jimmy. 'Anyway, Scotty, I'm going to bloody well talk to Sam about this as it's a total waste of our time. Our poor Spits are dying flying at that speed. It's an insult to them. I tell you, they should send us to Warmwell and get us skipping over the Channel. Much better use of our time and our aircraft.'

'Hm,' said Scotty. 'I think it's no secret that some of the bigwigs are pretty clueless, Jimmy. But ours not to reason why.'

'Balls,' said Jimmy. 'Someone needs to stick their neck out. Perhaps I should call on them – in fact, I'd love to.'

'I'm sure that would go down well,' said Dougie from the comfort of his armchair.

'I don't care,' said Jimmy, flicking his cigarette away. 'I hardly think they're going to sack an experienced fighter pilot for speaking his mind.'

Dougie grinned. Scotty said, 'Oh, I wouldn't be so sure.'

Edward looked up as Sam stepped out of his hut and strode over.

'Jimmy wants to politely express his views about convoy patrols to the bigwigs,' said Dougie.

'Really?' said Sam. 'Excellent idea.'

'Sorry, Sam,' said Jimmy, 'but this is beyond a joke. If I have to weave back and forth over that bloody barge one more time I think I'll go mad.'

'Hear, hear,' muttered Edward.

The CO turned sharply and eyed him, an amused expression on his face. 'Well, here's something a bit more exciting for you. It seems Naval Intelligence are getting fed up with seeing German reconnaissance planes far out into the Atlantic. They're sending their Condors out from Brest and feeding information back to the U-boats. They want us to try and pick them off. Apparently, they usually swing by the Scillies at first light.' He turned to Jimmy. 'You can take Eddie here with you since you're both so keen for something different.'

'All right,' said Jimmy. 'You're up for that, aren't you, Eddie?'

'Of course.'

Sam clapped Edward on the arm. 'Good. And as soon as Green Section come back, "B" Flight can stand down.'

Edward was woken at 3.30 the following morning by an orderly shaking him. 'Sir, sir. Time to get up, sir.'

Edward opened his eyes immediately. It was still dark, but the door was open and light from the corridor was pouring into the room.

'All right, thanks,' he said, squinting sleepily. Across the room, Harry continued sleeping, his breathing heavy. Edward cursed his eagerness of the day before. He'd sworn to Harry that he was going straight to bed after dinner, but Harry had said, 'You can't possibly go to bed just yet,' and so Harry had agreed to have just one beer. But while they had been drinking their first pint, two girls had joined them. On holiday from London, they had arrived that afternoon; the RAF may have requisitioned the top floor, but the rest of the Droskyn Castle Hotel was still open to paying guests. Most were retired couples, but from time to time – increasingly it seemed – younger, female holidaymakers appeared, as anxious to find some male company as the pilots were to drool over them. And so Edward had stayed: they had been good-looking and flirtatious; he'd not wanted to miss out, especially as Harry seemed to be making good progress with the one called Dorothy. Occasionally, he had joined in the conversation too. Conversation with strangers – especially girls – did not come as easily to him as it did Harry, whose abundance of charm he had recognised the moment they had met at Liverpool Street station, but he had still felt a sense of excitement – a frisson of sexuality – as they'd sat there regaling Dorothy with their stories and listening to her ready laughter.

Ten minutes later, after a perfunctory wash and shave, (in which he managed to nick himself in three places), Edward stumbled downstairs and out of the front door of the hotel. His head throbbed and his mouth felt acidic and dry. A wind was blowing – it cut across him and he nearly lost his cap. He could hear the rollers crashing into the foot of the cliffs below. Patting his sides with his hands to keep warm, he wondered where Jimmy was. Clouds were racing across the sky, but it was impossible to tell what kind of day it would become; perhaps not as golden and warm as the previous few days, but it often blew along the north Cornish coast. To his amazement, they had even strapped their Spitfires to the ground on occasion, using guy ropes and large corkscrew pieces of metal. On one of his first flights, he had been greeted at the end of the runway by his fitter and rigger, who had signalled to him frantically to stop, then had jumped on either side of the tail fin. Edward had wondered what the hell was going on. 'The wind, sir,' Parker had explained once they had finally pulled into the blast pen. 'You're all right when you're landing into a headwind, but when it crosses you, the Spit's liable to tip over. We've discovered sitting on the elevators makes all the difference.' The blast pens, Edward quickly discovered, were more use in protecting the precious machines from the wind than they were against bombs. St Eval, up the road, had been targeted repeatedly by the enemy bombers, but so far little windswept, Perranporth had been spared.

It was all such a far cry from Debden and Uxbridge. Those had been large, busy fighter stations. At Debden, Edward and Harry had regularly watched squadrons taking off on offensive sweeps over France; had watched them coming back too, oil-streaked and with the canvas that normally covered the gun ports torn away by the firing of the guns. The war had stepped a little closer then; *that'll be us soon,* he had thought. From this first taste of life at Debden, and from what he had seen at Uxbridge, he had assumed all fighter stations would be the same: with proper facilities, solid buildings, hangars and decent crew rooms and messes. Perranporth had been a shock. The airfield was still severely lacking the most basic permanent structures. A couple of blister hangars had sprung up, but most of the maintenance work was carried out in drab green marquees. The poor aircrew were expected to live in hastily built wooden huts, while the crew room for the pilots was another large tent, and one that all too often flapped unnervingly in the wind and threatened to be whisked into the sea at any moment. Perched precariously above three-hundred-foot cliffs, the airfield had just a single runway and a perimeter track. Two more runways were being planned – according to Sam and Scotty at any rate – but the ground had still not been properly surveyed; and every morning the ground crew had to check the field thoroughly in case any old mine shafts had suddenly appeared overnight. Edward had thought he was having his leg pulled when this practice was first explained to him. 'No, seriously,' Jimmy Farrell had told him. 'I was driving round the perimeter one morning just after we moved here and I found one.' Edward had looked at him disbelievingly. 'I promise,' continued Jimmy. 'A bloody great thing – wide enough for you or I to fall down it. I picked up a stone and dropped it down, but I never heard it land. Literally, a bottomless pit.'

It was strange to think he and Harry had only been with the squadron a month; it felt longer. He remembered the sense of excitement they had felt on the train down: wondering what to expect, hoping the others in the squadron would be friendly and welcoming; but most of all the feeling of anticipation, of apprehension about finally flying operational in combat. He knew Harry was as eager to shoot down his first enemy plane as he was. They wondered what it would be like, *hoped* they had the necessary skill.

They'd not been disappointed by the other members of the squadron. An RAF station wagon had been sent to Truro to meet them and then they had been driven straight to the airfield. Spitfires were lined up haphazardly around the perimeter, but as they drove towards a cluster of huts, two aircraft took off, roaring past them. Harry had turned to him and grinned. *We're going to be a part of this.*

The station wagon had stopped outside one of the huts, close by the large khaki marquee. A thin man with a moustache stepped out of the hut and opened the door for them.

'Welcome, welcome,' he said, smiling. 'Pilot Officers Barclay and Enderby? Good to meet you.' He was, he told them, Flight Lieutenant John Scott, but they should call him Scotty. 'Everyone does. We're a pretty informal bunch around here, as you'll soon discover.' He was in his late thirties – 'way too old to fly'; rather, he was the squadron intelligence officer. 'I'll be the one grilling you every time you land. Anyway, put your bags down, then let me take you to meet the CO.' Then he looked at Harry and said, 'By the way, you're not the Barclay that opened the batting for Kent, are you?'

'Yes, at least, I did on a few occasions,' Harry told him.

'Well, well,' said Scotty. 'Always supported Kent. I've seen you bat once or twice. Thought you looked the part.'

'Thank you.'

'Don't suppose you've played much recently, though.'

'No, haven't picked up a bat in ages.'

They followed Scotty into another hut of bare, slatted wooden boards. On the wall hung a round clock, but otherwise the only furniture was a simple table used as a desk and an old wooden filing cabinet. 'Sam, these are your new pilots,' Scotty said. 'Barclay, Enderby – Squadron Leader Ben Sampson.'

Sampson stood up, and shook hands. Like Scotty, he was tall, and older – perhaps as much as thirty, with a large slightly beaked nose and dark, bright eyes and equally dark oiled hair. His handshake was firm. Edward felt as though he were back at school, summoned before one of the masters. 'Good to meet you,' said the Commanding Officer. 'Glad to have you on board.' Edward glanced at the purple-and-silver-striped ribbon above his breast pocket: a Distinguished Flying Cross. He imagined himself wearing the same ribbon one day. Lifting a couple of sheets of paper, Sampson scanned them quickly then, glancing up, said, 'So you've come from 52 Operational Training Unit, before that Canada. You've both been rated "above average".' He nodded approvingly. 'Very good. Bet training in Canada was fun.'

'Yes it was,' said Harry. 'Blue skies almost every day.'

Sampson smiled. 'And at Debden? You trained on Hurricanes. How many hours?'

'Forty-seven,' said Harry.

'Forty-seven and a half,' added Edward.

'A slender advantage,' he smiled, looking at Edward. 'Well, you'll be on Spits here. Not much difference. A bit more power – bit more of a lady, but you'll quickly get the hang of it.' He sat down, brought his fingers together, eyed them carefully, and said, 'We're a fairly quiet sector here, down in the toe of Cornwall. Convoy patrols, a few long-range sweeps. Occasionally we get called up to chase after some intruder, but for the most part we don't get too much excitement.' Edward felt his spirits drop. 'But believe me,' the CO continued, 'that's a good thing for men like yourselves. You may not know this, but 324 was in the thick of it for much of last summer. New pilots would come and go before you had time to blink. Here, it's a bit less frenetic. There's a few of us still here from those days, and we've learnt a few things about fighter combat. We'll try and help you, train you up a bit.' He smiled again, and as though suddenly remembering something he had meant to do earlier, reached for a small wooden cigarette box. 'Smoke?' Edward and Harry took one each, and Scotty, who had been leaning against the wall stroking his moustache, suddenly stood up and produced a match. 'Look, I know what it's like,' Sampson continued. 'You're straight out of OTU and you're itching to have a crack at some Germans. But just because you can fly fighters doesn't mean you've become a fighter pilot. There's a whole load of stuff you need to know that you'll never learn during training. Lots that *none* of us knew before last summer. So we'll take it a bit steady to begin with – nothing too strenuous. We'll get you up in a Spit, and some of us more senior chaps will show you a few of the ropes. You know, there was a saying during the Battle of Brit that if you survived your first three weeks, your chances of surviving much longer were greatly improved. I happen to still believe that's true. So listen to what you're told, watch out for the old wind here – it can blow a bit I'm afraid – and concentrate all the time when you're flying. Then in a month's time you'll be old hands.'

And four weeks later we're still here, thought Edward. Sam had been right, they *were* better pilots; and as Harry had pointed out, with every flight so their number of flying hours was improving; that had to be a good thing. Yet he still could not help his feeling of disappointment: with the airfield, with the almost total lack of action. In his imagination, he'd pictured it differently.

Now, perhaps, his luck was about to turn – that is, if Jimmy ever turned up. He glanced at his watch. It was now ten to four. He wondered whether he should go in and knock on his room. *Give it another five minutes.* Jimmy was one of the Battle of Britain veterans Sam had mentioned on their arrival. So too was Dougie Ross, and both were now flight commanders. Edward and Harry had been placed in Jimmy's 'B' Flight, along with an assortment of pilots from around the world. Eric was a Canadian, Jean-Hilaire was French; Stan Wheeler was from Australia, while Mickey McDonald was a New Zealander. Others were from England and Scotland, but there was no common thread. A true mishmash, as Scotty was fond of reminding them.

He liked Jimmy, though, and knew that he was lucky to have him as a flight commander – lucky to have Dougie and Sam as well. Experienced men; men he respected greatly. Only a couple of years older, Jimmy was still just twenty-one but looked younger, despite his long career with the squadron. Short, with dishevelled, strawberry blond hair, and a square, open face, he barely needed to shave. And he wore his experience lightly; there was none of Sam's gravitas about Jimmy. Moreover, he looked after his flight – always stuck up for them and made sure they all worked together. As a flight, they tended to stick together socially as well. Edward was eternally grateful that he had Harry there with him, but Jimmy had made it easier to get to know the others. He was grateful for that.

'All set?' said Jimmy, suddenly bounding down the steps. Edward nodded. 'Those girls were fun last night,' Jimmy continued. 'Wonder whether they'll be around tonight. Old Harry seemed to have booked his ticket with Dorothy – crafty dog.' He walked briskly round to the side of the hotel, whistling slightly. The very first streaks of dawn were lighting the sky away across Perranporth. They reached the Humber station wagon, Jimmy stepping into the driver's side. 'Let's hope it starts okay,' he said. It did, almost immediately, and then they were off, streaking through the narrow lanes at an alarming speed, the narrow beams from the headlamps offering no more than a few yards of light ahead.

At the airfield, the ground crew were already there. Faint lights glowed through some of the maintenance tents, while occasionally clangs and shouts were carried on the wind. The crew-room tent was flapping loudly. 'Quite a breeze,' said Jimmy, looking up at the sky. 'At least it's coming at us and not across us.' Edward followed Jimmy into the dispersal tent, where a bleary-eyed telephone orderly was waiting.

'Put me through to Portreath, would you?' Jimmy told the corporal. Edward waited, listening. 'Hello,' said Jimmy. 'We're all set. Any news of our Condor?' He paused. 'I see . . . all right . . . no, of course.' Handing the receiver to the orderly, he looked at Edward, said 'Come on,' and ran out of the tent. 'Slight change of plan – we need to get cracking.'

Seeing the two pilots running from the tent, their crews immediately fired up the waiting Spitfires, the roar of the engines carried by the wind. His heart racing, Edward snatched the parachute and helmet from the wing, and struggled to put his legs through the right straps. 'All right, sir?' said Hewitson. Edward nodded, then leapt up onto the wing root and hoisted himself into the cockpit. Jimmy was already beginning to move out – *how had he managed so quickly?* – and with fumbling fingers Edward frantically clicked the Sutton harness into its catch, and attached the R/T and oxygen leads. He breathed out heavily, waved at his ground crew, then moved off.

A crackle of static in his ears, then Jimmy's voice. 'Eddie, Portreath have reported perhaps a dozen bandits fifty miles south-west of Lizard. We're to forget the Condor today and go after this bunch instead. Follow me closely.'

'All right,' said Edward. He hoped he had sounded calm. The cockpit felt suddenly close and cramped, his breathing heavy. A strong gust of wind buffeted the plane and Edward felt it rock. 'Christ,' he muttered. It was only shortly after 4 a.m., and as they turned at the far end of the runway and faced west, Edward prayed he would not lose sight of Jimmy once they were in the air. From short distances he could make him out reasonably clearly, but it would be a short while yet until the sky was bright enough to see much beyond a hundred yards or so. He saw that Jimmy had his navigation lights turned on – *good. Keep sight of those.* Jimmy thundered down the runway. Edward followed, opening his throttle so that the whole aircraft shook vigorously. Moments later he was in the air, watching Jimmy's wing lights bank gently and turn south.

'Bison, this is Clover,' Edward heard Jimmy say. 'Heading 180 degrees. What's our vector, over?'

'Maintain course, 180,' came the measured voice of the controller from the sector station at Portreath. They headed out over a blacked-out Cornwall, climbing through swathes of hurrying cloud banks, then the land receded and they were out, high over the sea, climbing through heavy turbulence to twelve thousand feet. Edward heard Jimmy call the controller once more. 'Now twenty miles south of Lizard,' he said.

'Clover, this is Bison. Head 160 degrees,' replied the controller. 'I'm afraid the screen is blurring, so it's simply going to be up to you to find them. But they're only about twenty miles away, heading south-west towards Brest, doing no more than two hundred knots.

Your R/T signal is fading. Good luck. Over.' *We're on our own,* thought Edward. Looking down towards the Channel, he saw it was almost entirely covered in thick cloud. But at twelve thousand feet, the sky was wide and clear, and waking to the new day. Away to the east, the pale horizon was rising, with the first peak of sun, a golden tip, rapidly lighting the sky. A sudden break in the cloud, and as high as they were, Edward saw the white tips of the waves below.

'Keep scanning the skies,' came Jimmy's voice through his headset. 'We should come into range soon.' Edward did so, sweeping his eyes slowly, back and forth, up and down, as Sam had told him during their first flight together. 'No sudden movements,' the CO had warned, 'or you won't be able to focus properly. Keep it measured at all times.' But he could see nothing; it was like the escort duty. Once again they were alone in this vast sky.

'OK, there they are,' reported Jimmy. 'Eleven o'clock, slightly below.'

Edward strained his eyes, squinting into the early morning light. He could see nothing. 'Message received and understood,' he replied, his heart quickening once more. He scanned the sky again. *Too fast – calm down,* he told himself. Then suddenly there they were, tiny black dots, buzzing together. 'I see them!' Edward exclaimed.

'All right, good,' said Jimmy. 'Follow me closely, switch your gun button to "fire" and when I give the word apply emergency boost. Clear?'

'Clear.' Hurtling towards the enemy planes at over three hundred miles per hour, the distance was rapidly closing.

'Buster,' called Jimmy, so Edward applied the boost and saw thick black smoke puff from the exhaust stubs. The engine roared angrily and the airframe shook, but the Spitfire lurched forward with a marked increase in power. Time seemed to have speeded up. Edward recognised three Dornier bombers and five, then six, Messerschmitt 109s, three of which had split from the group and were turning to attack them.

'Don't go for the bombers,' Jimmy told him, his voice still steady and calm. 'Just aim for the fighters and watch those two turning wide. If it gets too hairy, get out of there and head for home.'

Edward followed. He realised he had no idea what to do. They'd fired at towed targets during training and he and Harry had practised dogfighting on numerous occasions, but it had been nothing like this. For a brief moment, his brain seemed to seize, and he was simply a spectator, watching with numbed fascination as the enemy aircraft – their shapes familiar but somehow more menacing now that they were real – manoeuvred to open fire. Then he heard gunfire and saw Jimmy attacking one of the 109s, which flipped over and fell away, white smoke following in its wake. A loud crack shook him and tracer hurtled over his canopy. 'Jesus!' he shouted, and then the underside of a Messerschmitt, pale grey and streaked with oil, roared just a few feet above him. And as it passed, Edward saw that his mirror had been torn clean off. A bullet had ripped it clean away. His heart pounded in his chest, and he felt short of breath. He could hear his laboured gasps into the rubber oxygen mask. *Christ, Christ!* he thought, then swivelled his head frantically around him. The bombers were already far away – *how did that happen so fast?* – but another 109 was turning again, preparing for another attack. Then he saw a further Messerschmitt diving away from him, so he turned the Spitfire on its back and followed it down. A thin line of vapour – or was it smoke? – trailed behind the diving fighter. It was still some way off, but with a large bank of cloud approaching, Edward pressed his thumb down on the small, round gun button, and felt the shudder as he opened fire. The Messerschmitt disappeared, and seconds later Edward, too, was plunging into thick cloud. *Five hundred miles an hour!* He could scarcely believe it. The engine was screaming from the strain of the dive. A glance at the altimeter – *three thousand feet already. Time to pull out.* He grimaced, clutching the control column, praying he could climb out of the dive in time. A second later he burst through the cloud, the breakers on the sea clearly visible, now just over a thousand feet below. But there was the Messerschmitt, almost straight ahead, now pouring smoke and gliding uncertainly towards the water. With both hands, and with clenched teeth, Edward held the stick towards him, his Spitfire shaking and groaning, but at last it began to level out, the horizon rising once more. *Thank God,* he thought. Speeding over the crippled 109, he quickly banked and turned back, but as he began lining up to attack, the Messerschmitt crashed into the waves with a fountain of white spray. When he looked again, the sea had closed and there was no sign at all that the aircraft had ever existed at all.

Had *he* shot him down? He wasn't sure, but it occurred to him that he had witnessed the death of another man for the first time in his life.

He was now heading south, and glancing at his fuel gauges, noticed with a sense of alarm that he had already used half. That brief engagement with the extra boost had swallowed up more than he'd expected. Circling, he guessed he was some sixty miles south of the Devon coast. There was no sign of Jimmy. Edward called him on the R/T, but heard nothing but a deafening roar of static. Setting himself a course for the Cornish coast, he hoped he would soon reach land once more. But what height should he fly? The cloud base was lowering rapidly, but if he tried to stay below, he risked not having enough height to bale out should anything go wrong, so he began climbing again, steadily, conserving fuel as much as possible. Perhaps in the clear he would spot Jimmy.

He broke through the cloud again at a little over seven thousand feet, the sudden bright sunshine dazzling. This time he swept the skies steadily, as he'd been told, but he could see nothing. He looked at his watch. Twenty to five. In another quarter of an hour he should be over land. Perhaps there would be a gap in the cloud. With any luck, then he would be able to spot a landmark he recognised. The roar of the engine had become a kind of constant silence. Glancing at the dials in front of him, everything seemed to be working perfectly, but then he thought he heard a catch in the engine. His body stiffened; straining his ears, he hardly dared move, but the whirr of the Merlin sounded constant and smooth. *You're imagining things,* he told himself, but he couldn't help wondering what he would do if the engine seized. Even if he could bale out, there was little chance of him surviving long in that swell – not if nobody saw him do so. He switched on the R/T once more. Nothing. He'd never realised how lonely flying could be.

The sun had now risen, the day awash with brightness. He glanced at his compass again and then froze, aghast: he'd set the compass red on black. *Shit, shit!* He was not travelling north, but south, on a completely opposite course. How had he been so stupid? Banking tightly, he checked his fuel gauges – now only a third full, and he was probably nearly eighty miles south of the coast. For a moment, he felt panic overwhelm him. If he baled out and ditched into the sea he would have no chance – not with the cloud and wind as it was, and with no radio contact. Cursing, he cut the throttle to conserve his precious fuel. There was little he could do but agonise over every passing minute.

Five o'clock. Edward looked at his fuel gauges again – they were all but empty. Below him there was nothing but cloud, a soft, undulating eiderdown of cloud. *Shit,* he thought. Breathing deeply, he pulled off his oxygen mask, and pushed down the stick, hoping the cloud base would be high enough for him to gain his bearings. He had soon dropped out of the clear and into the cloud once more. It was a strange experience, flying through cloud. All sense of movement disappeared. His dials told him he was travelling at three hundred miles per hour, but the cloud was so dense, he might easily have been standing still. He watched the altimeter fall: four thousand, three thousand, two thousand, fifteen hundred, hoping he was not flying over Bodmin Moor. It had happened to one of the pilots at OTU – they'd flown straight into the side of a hill. His fuel gauges now read empty.

'Come on, come on,' he said out loud. 'Where's the bloody land?' Any moment the engine would splutter and die. Less than a thousand feet above sea level. Perranporth was three hundred above – and the land to the south was higher than that. *Christ.* He glanced at the fuel gauge again, hoping the needle had miraculously risen but it had not. The cloud now suddenly began to thin – and yes! There below were glimpses of land, frighteningly close. Perhaps, he thought, he should look for somewhere to land right away – while the propeller still whirred in front of him. Losing a bit more height, he levelled out at just five hundred feet, but his relief was brief: moments later he disappeared into another bank of fog. *Don't think about crashing,* he told himself, just as the cloud thinned again. He thought he could see Truro. Was it? The view had been too brief, but he was sure he'd seen the cathedral. *Yes, it must have been.* He straightened his course, banking slightly northwards. Any moment he would be over Perranporth. He would try and make it home.

'Bison, this is Clover,' he called on the R/T, 'permission to land.'

'Clover this is Bison,' came the immediate reply; Edward sighed with relief. 'Permission granted. Where are you?'

'Not sure. Ten-tenths cloud. I'm out of fuel and hoping for a gap in the cloud.'

He circled, dropped a bit more height and prayed. His Spitfire was running on nothing but fumes. Now far too low to bale out, he would have to hope for the best if the engine cut; hope he could find a suitable field. He strained his eyes: he could see the faint outline of hedgerows but it was impossible to see exactly where he was. *Come on, come on – please God.* He banked again, then the fog momentarily cleared and there, like a vision from above, there was the airfield, unmistakably the airfield. 'Yes!' shouted Edward.

Gently banking the Spitfire, he watched more cloud race across the airfield, almost completely obscuring it once more. 'Bison, this is Clover,' he called again on the R/T. 'I can see the airfield and am landing now.' Ahead, just visible through the rapidly thickening fog, was the faint line of the runway. Below, a patchwork of damp fields, all differing hues of dark green and beige.

He pulled back gently on the throttle, then moving his left hand onto the control column, he raised his right to pull back the canopy, ducking as he did so to avoid knocking his head with the handle. The blast of fresh air buffeted his face, and he lowered his goggles as he felt his eyes begin to smart. He was now almost over the airfield. Edward glanced at the altimeter: *good, six hundred feet.* Cutting back the throttle further, he felt the great roar of the Merlin soften until it was merely throbbing gently, and banking, turned in a wide loop, his weight falling against the side of the cockpit. He felt his harness cut into his shoulders, and looked down at the faintly emerging airfield below. He eased the stick upright and the aircraft gently levelled, lined up perfectly into the wind, the single runway directly ahead of him. Lowering the undercarriage, he heard the wheels drone down from their position in the wings until they had locked tight. And at that moment the engine died and the propeller snapped to a halt. But the Spitfire was still gliding towards the ground.

With the huge nose slanting upwards, his view ahead was completely blocked, but he could see the grass either side of the runway rushing up to meet him. He glanced at the air speed indicator: eighty miles per hour, seventy, then a slight jolt as the wheels touched the ground. *Thank God.* The Spitfire rolled, rushing past the hastily erected blister hangars, the array of parked aircraft, and rows of wooden huts and tents. Only as he approached the end of the runway did he finally apply a bit of pressure on his brakes. Rumbling onto the perimeter track, he turned a couple of hundred yards then came to a halt. Edward sighed, closed his eyes and rested his head against the back of the bucket seat. Then, with shaking hands, he unbuckled his flying helmet, and ran his fingers through his hair. Some men were running towards him, but for a moment he sat still, in the calm, quiet, space of the cockpit, breathing deeply. Then he shakily hoisted his feet onto the seat, and clambered out.

Edward began walking slowly towards the crew tent. Minutes before, he'd wondered whether he would set foot on the ground again; on landing he'd felt suddenly listless and drained of all energy. But now his spirits were rising once more. He'd made it back; the fear he'd experienced had already been consigned to the past. And so as he walked into the tent and saw the other pilots sitting there, he grinned sheepishly. He could not help himself. Harry waved, and Edward was about to walk over to him when Jimmy walked in with Scotty.

'Eddie!' said Jimmy, clapping him on the back. 'Glad you got back all right. I was a bit worried when I lost you. What happened? Last thing I saw you were diving after a 109.'

'I think I got him, too,' he said, then noticed Jimmy raise an eyebrow at Scotty. 'At least, I fired a fairly long burst at him,' he continued, 'and then I lost him in cloud, but when I came out again, there he was, streaming smoke. I was just about to attack him again when he went into the sea.'

'Give him a half?' said Scotty, turning to Jimmy.

'Absolutely,' said Jimmy. 'He certainly wasn't smoking much when I hit him. Well done!' he said, clapping Eddie on the shoulder once more. 'Off the mark. *And* you made it back, despite the atrocious weather.'

Edward smiled. 'Only just – I ran out of fuel the moment I landed.' No point in telling him about the mistake with the compass.

'Sounds like perfect timing to me,' said Scotty.

'Absolutely,' agreed Jimmy, then said, 'Come outside just a moment, will you?' Edward followed. The wind cut across the airfield. Jimmy rubbed his chin, then said, 'Look, you did really well – *really* well – but there's a couple of things. Firstly, you need to keep a slightly better lookout. It'll come, I promise you, but you didn't even see that 109 come at you. If his shooting had been a bit better, you could have been in serious trouble.'

Eddie nodded. 'He did catch me off guard a bit.'

'You can't afford to let that happen again, Eddie.'

'No – no, I won't.'

'And never, ever, follow a plane down. You were lucky – I managed to get the guy who was about to hit you.'

'Which one . . .?' Eddie let the question trail. Jimmy looked at him. 'Exactly, Eddie.' He tapped his eyes. 'Use these a bit more. If you follow aircraft down, especially when you're outnumbered like we were, someone will do the same to you, and Bam! Before you know it, they're coming down on top of you and you've lost height, speed, and any advantage. And finally, you need to get a bit closer before you open fire. See the whites of their eyes – that means at least two hundred and fifty yards. I'm not saying you didn't hit him – maybe you did – but you'll struggle to knock anything much at the kind of range you were firing from.'

Eddie felt his cheeks burning. 'Sorry, Jimmy.'

'Don't apologise,' said Jimmy. 'I was just the same – honestly. That's how we learn. Now you know what to expect. It's just that you can't afford too many mistakes. The one you went after was probably even more new to it than you – and now he's not going to have another chance, is he, because he's sitting at the bottom of the Channel.'

Harry was sympathetic. 'At least it's only your pride that's been hurt.' He smiled, then passing him his mug of half-drunk tea, said, 'Here, have some of this and stop worrying.'

Edward took the mug gratefully. He hadn't realised how thirsty he was. Next to them, the canvas marquee sides flapped noisily in the wind.

'And you've got half a kill,' added Harry after a short pause. '*And* you've seen some action at long last. I'm very glad you're back, though. I don't mind telling you I felt a bit worried. Jimmy was back way before you and what with this weather . . .'

'I was a bit worried too, to be honest,' admitted Edward. 'Bloody scared, actually.' He looked around, then leant in closer towards his friend. 'Truth is, I set the compass wrong and started flying in the opposite direction.'

'Bloody hell, Eddie – no wonder you took your time getting back.'

'When I realised – well, it was a horrible feeling. I kept thinking I was going to end up in the sea. I thought: after all that training, I'm going to drown before I've had a chance to do anything. And then I started to feel angry. Nothing I could do, of course. Just had to hope for the best. Fortunately, luck was on my side.'

'You won't do it again, though.'

'No – I don't think I will.'

Harry put his hand on Edward's leg and patted it gently. 'Well, I'm jealous that you've seen an enemy plane before me, but I'm extremely glad it wasn't me trying to find Perranporth in the fog and with no fuel.' Another heavy gust of wind shook the marquee. 'Still,' he added, 'unless this cloud lifts, I don't think there'll be any more flying today. Spared for a day from escorting that bloody barge. I never thought I'd be grateful for bad weather.'

The wind worsened during the morning, so that the pilots were all ordered to help the ground crews pin down the aircraft. Slinging guy ropes over the fuselages, they were then pinned to the ground using what looked like outsize metal corkscrews. One man was knocked out cold as the wing of a Spitfire rocked with a violent gust and smashed him on the top of his head. 'Who's bright idea was it to build an airfield on the top of a North Cornwall cliff, anyway?' muttered Hewitson as they restrained Edward's own aircraft.

But the winds dropped later in the day, and the sky cleared – enough, at any rate, and by late afternoon, 'A' Flight was called upon to continue escort duties. 'B' Flight, however, were spared and stood down just before seven.

'A night out, I think, don't you?' suggested Jimmy as they clambered into the truck to take them back to the Droskyn Castle Hotel.

'What about the girls?' asked Harry.

'Well, perhaps they'd like to come too,' replied Jimmy. 'I know just the place in Truro. A lovely spot where they've still got plenty of beer and whisky.'

Nearly midnight, and the Humber was bouncing along the narrow, high-hedged roads of Cornwall. Everyone was singing, raucously and with varying degrees of tunefulness. '*When somebody thinks you're wonderful, what a difference in your day! Seems as though your troubles disappear like a feather in your way.*' It was the Frenchman, Jean-Hilaire's, favourite song of the moment, and one that he played over and over on the gramophone that lived permanently in the crew tent. He claimed it was as good a way as any to perfect his English. The entire flight had managed to squeeze themselves into the station wagon: three in the front, and seven in the back, including Dorothy and her friend Jean. Eric, as the only man in the entire squadron who refused the temptations of alcohol, sat next to Jimmy, who was driving, and warning him about any particularly sharp corners or potential hazards ahead.

'Encore!' shouted Jean-Hilaire, and they all began the song again.

'I think I'm going to be sick,' said Dorothy suddenly.

'Stop the car!' yelled Harry.

'What, now?' said Jimmy.

'Quickly!' shouted Harry as Dorothy began clutching her hand to her mouth. Jimmy slammed on the brakes and the Humber screeched, swerved and hit the side of a stone wall, the car grinding and scraping against the rock until it finally came to a halt. There was a brief moment of silence then Jimmy said, 'Right, out you pop then, Dorothy.'

Edward immediately began laughing. Soon his stomach ached with laughter, and every time he'd just about recovered he thought of Jimmy saying that, and started laughing again. Harry was laughing too, as were the others, while Jean stood with Dorothy, now doubled up by the side of the road. When everyone finally recovered, Jimmy and Eric had a look at the damage. In the dark it was hard to tell exactly how severe it was, but the fender looked to be badly mashed. Everyone stood around smoking, senses dulled and lethargic, their energy suddenly spent. After yanking the fender free from the wheel, they piled back in and set off again, but the Humber was far from well; a strange knocking sound was coming from the engine, and Jimmy announced that the steering was not as it should be. 'So I need you to be extra vigilant, Eric,' he added, his lips clamped round a cigarette.

'It would be ironic,' said Harry, 'if we were all to die now, don't you think? I mean, Eddie managed to make it back with no fuel and an unhealthy amount of fog, but I bet our odds of making it in one piece back to the Droskyn Castle are significantly less.' No-one disputed Harry's observation, not even Jimmy, but a short while later they turned into the familiar hotel driveway and crunched to a halt on the gravel. Despite the danger, half the pilots were already sound asleep, Dorothy included.

When Harry and Edward reached their room, they both stretched out on their beds still fully clothed.

'You know what? I don't think we're going to die,' said Edward. 'I think we're going to be all right.'

'Glad to hear it,' said Harry.

'This morning, I really thought I might. But you and I, Harry – someone's keeping a watch over us. You'll see.' This time there was no reply, but the deep and heavy breathing of one already asleep.

Cornwall – May, 1995

Edward was humming *When Somebody Thinks You're Wonderful* to himself as he drove towards Perranporth. A few miles ahead he saw the long strip of beach, misty from sea spray, but to the left the land rose steeply. Incredible, he thought, how perched they'd been up there. Having finally reached the town, he climbed up the hill towards St Agnes, along a road thick with vivid yellow gorse. He could not see the airfield, but sensed it was somewhere beyond the high hedgerows. A sign to 'Perranporth Aerodrome'. Edward turned right, the road narrowing further as the hedgerows grew higher until he eventually reached a bedraggled entranceway marked by a wooden sign, and lined either side by thick clumps of brambles. Mounting apprehension had accompanied him on this last part of the journey. In his mind he could remember it vividly, but he had not been back once since the squadron had moved further down the coast to Portreath – and according to his logbook, that had been on 6th December, 1941. Over fifty-three years! The world had changed so much in that time. He could hardly expect Perranporth to be any different. Turning in, he drove carefully around the potholes in the ruptured tarmac, and followed the driveway until he saw the white-washed control tower. A few cars were parked behind, so he pulled in beside them.

He sat in the car for a moment, hands still clutching the steering wheel. There were moments when he seemed to be able to disengage his mind, and think about what he was doing in a more rational and pragmatic light. And during such moments this journey of his seemed so ridiculous, so pointless. What on earth was he hoping to find?

Shaking his head, he got out of the car. *Come on,* he thought. *Cornwall's the easy part,* then he mumbled, 'Some good times.' His legs felt wooden and stiff, so he stretched, rubbed his knees, then walked over to the control tower. The place seemed curiously deserted and quiet. Three light aircraft were parked up on the grass in front of the tower, but he could not see any other planes. Outside an open door on the ground floor was a sign saying 'Reception'.

Stepping gingerly inside, Edward saw a single desk cluttered with paper and flying magazines. Local flying charts and fliers vied for wall space. From another room off to the side he heard voices, so clearing his throat, he said, 'Hello?'

A middle-aged man in a baseball cap appeared. 'Sorry,' he said. 'I'm Brian, can I help?'

'I hope so,' Edward began. 'I flew here during the war and was wondering whether I might have a look around?'

The man smiled encouragingly. 'Of course. When were you here?'

'Nineteen forty-one.'

The man nodded. 'At the beginning, then.'

'Well, not long after.'

'One of our members flew Typhoons here, but that was later in the war.' He shuffled a few pieces of paper on the desk, as though looking for something. 'It's a shame he's not here today. Anyway, yes, feel free to look around all you want. There's quite a lot left, actually. In fact, it's one of the best-preserved Fighter Command airfields in the country. You must have been flying Spits?'

Edward nodded. '324 Squadron.'

Brian nodded. 'Of course. Are you happy going round on your own, or would you like me to show you about?'

'No, no, please don't trouble yourself. Very kind of you, but I'll just wander round on my own. And try to keep out of the way of any planes.'

'Well if you're sure –'

'Quite sure, honestly.'

'Most of the blast pens are the far side. But you can walk along the edge of the old perimeter track. You'll be quite safe there.'

Edward thanked him and went back out again. It was another warm, bright day, the mid-afternoon sun still high in the sky. A light breeze wafted across the airfield. Rabbits scurried across the thick, tufty grass at the edge of the field. Edward looked around. Unmistakably the same place, but an air of desolation seemed to have fallen upon it. The tarmac along the perimeter track was veined with thick cracks and splattered with round coppery circles of lichen. He paused by the beginning of the old main runway and looked down it – at the huge dip and rise, and wondered again how they could ever have landed there. Beyond, he saw the old blast pens rising out of the ground, now covered in long, dense grass. He wondered whether they still checked for mine shafts every morning, and smiled to himself. Had they really strapped their Spitfires to the ground? They had; his memory had not been lying.

A Cessna landed as he ambled around the edge of the airfield. Several bunkers and more blast pens. He walked up to one with a double berth, stretched down and felt the grass. It was dry, so he sat down for a moment, trying to picture himself taxiing his Spitfire in at the end of a sortie. Faces from the past stirred in his mind. Hewitson, stocky with a flat nose that had been broken more than once; Parker, taller, thin as a rake and with his thick local accent. Yes, he remembered Parker had been from round these parts. He could hear their voices, quite distinctly, from over the years, could see Parker buffing the Perspex of the windscreen and saying, 'Clean and clear as day, sir,' while Hewitson, whistling tunelessly, fussed underneath the wing.

Edward stood up and walked towards the cliffs. Gulls were crying and swirling, while above him skylarks sang busily. *The sound of summer,* he thought. There had been plenty of skylarks in 1941, too. He breathed in deeply; the air was thick with the scent of prickly gorse and wild grass. Smell and sound: the most evocative of senses, and for a brief moment the passage of time seemed to have closed. Below him, some three hundred feet, the breakers crashed against the jagged cliff face. It must have been here, he thought. About halfway between the crew room and the first blast pen. The night after his first encounter with the enemy. The Humber had been beyond repair after Jimmy's brush with the wall, and although it had got them back to the hotel and even staggered to the airfield the following morning, the clanging had worsened and steam was hissing from the radiator. Jimmy had been over to the repair tents, but the senior mechanic had taken one look at it and told him what they'd all already known.

Over lunch, Jimmy had told the 'B' Flight pilots his plan. 'Now I need absolute secrecy, all right? Not a word to anyone.' They had all nodded. 'Good. Tonight we're going to push it over the cliff. We're going to say the wind got it.' He grinned at them sheepishly. 'Later tonight, when I give you the nod, we'll all walk over from the hotel.

I've already parked it up in such a way that it's pointing towards the cliff. A few heaves and it'll be just another casualty of war.'

And that was precisely what they had done: stealing out of the hotel some time after ten o'clock that night, sniggering conspiratorially and walking the mile across country to the airfield. There had been a three-quarter moon, with clouds racing dramatically across the sky, so that after just a few minutes they could see their way clearly; could see the dark noses of the Spitfires pointing imperiously skywards, could see the tents and buildings of the airfield, and the vast, wide openness of the sea.

Another strong wind was blowing. Jimmy had released the handbrake and then called out, 'Push!' Heaving and groaning, they managed to get the Humber rolling, gently at first, then as the gradient suddenly sharpened it had run away from them, bouncing over the thick clumps of grass before finally disappearing over the edge. The noise at the bottom had been terrific.

Everyone had known, of course, although the conspirators had all kept up the charade. If Sam had been at all bothered by the loss of the Humber, he never once showed it, and a few days later another had arrived. The station commander at Portreath had apparently been demanding a new one for a while; 324 Squadron had simply inherited his old one.

Edward gingerly crept towards the edge of the cliff and peered down at the swirling white spray crashing against the shiny rocks. *It must be down there somewhere,* he thought. And it was on these cliffs that he and Harry and the others would go hunting for seagulls' eggs. It had been something to do; something to eat: jackets off, sleeves rolled up, carefully clambering down the steep slopes. *My God, but it's high up,* he thought. *Three hundred feet! What a place for an airfield.*

Later he drove to Droskyn Castle. Before he left Somerset, he had already discovered it was no longer a hotel, but he was anxious to see it all the same. Turning the corner, there it was – unmistakable, with its grey walls and castellated roof. Perched high on the cliff, overlooking the long, golden beach of Perranporth, he marvelled at its setting. Had they appreciated it then? Not really. To begin with, he had been quite put out that they were been expected to share their living quarters with paying guests. They'd appreciated the beach more. It had been strewn with wire back then, but that hadn't stopped them. There were many occasions when he and Harry and the others had gone swimming. Being pummelled by the icy breakers had been invigorating.

Droskyn Castle was still lived in, it seemed. The gardens looked trim, the paint on the walls and windows fresh. Edward walked around it, trying to remember which of the windows belonged to the room he had shared with Harry. It had been at the side of the house, overlooking the beach, and in their time was always open; both had hated to sleep without a draught. They were shut now, with little sign of life. Edward felt suddenly lonely, and for the first time in a very long while, wished he had the company of one or other of his old squadron fellows. His time with the squadron had been frustrating in many ways, but the camaraderie – well, it could not have been faulted. Standing alone on the driveway, gazing up at the place that had once been so bursting with life and vitality, he wondered who was still alive. Scotty had died – he'd read his obituary recently; he'd gone on to be a well-known architect after the war. Sam had been moved up before he and Harry had left. Perhaps he was still alive. Jean-Hilaire had later taken over command of a Typhoon squadron, but had been killed over Normandy; Jimmy had survived the war, but had been decapitated in a flying accident a few years later – that had seemed particularly cruel. Eric had presumably returned to New Zealand. Harry – well, that was another matter. He had no idea what had happened to any of the others or what had become of Hewitson and Parker. Perhaps Parker was still living in the area. He almost wished he'd put his name on the squadron notice board at Hyde Park.

Returning to his car, he looked briefly at the map then set off once more, glancing up into his rear-view mirror as Droskyn Castle disappeared behind a bend in the drive.

It was early evening by the time he reached St Ives, and he was beginning to feel tired. Still, he was pleased he'd made the effort: the town was a small distance beyond Portreath, but when he'd discovered that the Tregenna Castle Hotel was still going strong, he had been determined that he should stay there.

During the war, it had been a typical English country hotel: wood panelling, open fires, faded prints and wallpaper on the walls. But it had been a big place even then; regular dances had been held every weekend with jazz bands and enough drink to keep everyone going. With the shortening days of winter, there had been even less flying and more time off duty. Saturday nights at the Tregenna Castle were looked forward to all week. There was no shortage of girls to dance with. As well as the locals, the area was awash with Land Girls and numerous WAAFs from the nearby fighter stations.

It was smarter now than he remembered: he couldn't recall there being a golf course then, nor a row of flagpoles near the main entrance; and ivy now covered the front where once it had been simply bare brick. But having taken his case to his room, he decided to have a quick explore before dinner. The place stirred his memory. Once again, things he had not thought about for decades were propelled to the forefront of his mind. Faces from the past, snippets of conversation. Fighter pilots had still been highly regarded in Britain in 1941 – it was why they were able to get away with things that others could not, such as swimming on beaches protected by barbed wire, or pushing damaged cars over cliffs. The silver wings above the breast pocket and the top button undone on their tunic singled them out, giving them a cachet unique amongst the services. It had counted less for someone like Harry, who could talk the hind legs off anyone, with or without his uniform; but for an essentially introverted person like himself, the pride he had felt when wearing his uniform in public, combined with the solidarity of his fellow pilots, had given him added confidence, even swagger. Even so, chatting up girls had not come naturally. 'Always say their name as much as possible and ask them questions about themselves,' Harry had suggested, but however sound this advice may have been, Edward knew his efforts at easy charm sounded unconvincing.

But he had not needed to display much charm with Betty. She was a Land Girl on a nearby farm and latched onto Edward, suggesting he might like to dance with her. She was small but pretty, with bright lipstick and hair curled up onto her head. From Croydon – or somewhere like that. Edward had danced with her most of the night, and had bought her drinks, and then she had suggested they go outside. 'It's very hot in here. Come on, let's get some air,' and she had taken his hand and led him through the smoke and heaving throng of people.

They'd walked out of the front of the hotel and down some steps to the terrace.

'Cigarette?' said Edward, flicking open his new case with élan.

'Thanks,' she said, one arm clutched around his. And then they talked, mostly, he realised later, about flying and the escapades he and the other pilots had got up to, until she said, 'Look, you'll probably think I'm terribly forward, but there's something I've just got to do.' Lifting a hand to his face, she'd leant up and kissed him, first on the lips, and then, to his utter astonishment, thrusting her tongue into his mouth.

Edward found the terrace and sat down on a bench. St Ives Bay was bathed in evening sunlight. Of course, back then it had been both cold and pitch dark. Had there been a bench? In his mind's eye, they had sat on a stone wall; at any rate, he'd enjoyed kissing Betty, particularly after he'd got over his initial surprise. For at least a week he had been sure he was madly in love, and then he had been posted away. He'd taken her out one afternoon and eaten fish and chips in St Ives, and they'd met up at the dance the following week, but then they'd been separated forever. *Such a brief time together!* He chuckled to himself. But it had been just as well. In his mind, she had remained as she'd been then: young, vivacious, pretty and determined to step out with a pilot. The first person he had ever properly kissed.

By that time he had been itching to be posted – and despite his youthful passion for Betty, she had not been a good enough reason to stay with 324 Squadron. After his dinner in the hotel dining room, Edward had gone back up to his room and had taken out his logbook, which had been carefully wrapped and packed in his case. No wonder he'd been bored. Day after day, it had been the same, relentlessly all through August, September and on into the winter: 'Sector recco, 1.20; convoy patrol, 2.05; formation flying, .40; convoy patrol, 1.25; local flying, .25; dogfight, .50'. During reconnaissance flights they had rarely found anything. By one entry he had written, 'Had a squirt at a Ju 88, but lost it in cloud', but that had been an exception. Dogfighting was merely practising, invariably with Harry; local flying could have been anything: testing a change on the Spitfire, navigation practice, once even a display over Truro during a presentation to the Spitfire Fund. Short flights all – except one. On 13th December, 1941, he had written 'local flying' then had marked one hour forty minutes alongside. *Ah, yes,* Edward laughed to himself, *I remember that one.*

At the beginning of December, Sam was moved away from 324 Squadron. At thirty, he was already older than most fighter pilots, and with his promotion came a staff job at group headquarters. Command of the squadron was handed over to Jimmy. The other pilots were happy with this arrangement, but despite his combat record and despite his considerable experience, Jimmy was still only twenty-one.

A week into his new command, the squadron was moved further west to Portreath. None of the pilots were happy about this. It was regarded as a demotion and a further slap in the face. 'Jesus!' Jimmy had riled. 'Who the hell do they think we are? 324's only one of the bloody top-scoring squadrons in the Battle of Britain and now we're kicked even further away from the action. Those fucking bigwigs want their heads examining.' It wasn't just the move; the bad weather and short days did little to help, and to make matters worse, the squadron had been re-equipped with long-range Spitfires, with a permanent auxiliary fuel tank slung across the port wing. Now they could fly even longer convoy patrols, but with less speed and with something of the Spitfire's natural agility shaved away. A gloom had settled over the squadron.

12th December. Another grey, cold day. Even Cornwall had looked drab: the hedgerows and dark skeletal trees sodden and dripping after a night of heavy rain. The patchwork of fields had turned a brackish green, while the sea spreading away from the coast had turned deep and menacing and grey. Edward and Harry had practised dogfighting for half an hour, but otherwise there had been no flying. For much of the day, they had hung about the dispersal drinking mugs of tea, playing cards, and reading magazines.

'Let's go out tonight,' said Harry over dinner at the mess. 'I want to get out of here for a few hours.'

Edward nodded. 'Good idea.'

Eric, who was sitting with them, said, 'We can take my car if you like.'

They drove towards St Ives, the houses, villages, and towns of Cornwall shrouded by the black winter night. Not a single light pierced the dark – not one prick of brightness – only the faint beam from Eric's headlights. They said little, the three of them, sitting hunched in their Irvins, collars raised up against the cold.

The Tregenna Castle was quiet. Midweek, and the young holidaymakers of the summer had gone. Even local people seemed to have shut up shop, preferring to stay in, conserving every penny for the long haul. In the bar, the small fire, with its green tiled surround, glowed gently.

'Well, cheers,' said Harry as he brought over the drinks. 'And here's hoping things will pick up soon.'

'I'll drink to that,' said Edward.

'Actually, I'm hoping they will sooner rather than later,' said Eric. 'I've applied for a transfer.'

Edward and Harry looked at him incredulously. 'To what?' asked Harry.

'Photo reconnaissance.'

'PR?' said Edward. 'Why? Why would you want to do that?'

'I'll most probably still be flying Spits, but I won't have to kill anyone. That appeals, actually.'

'Well,' said Harry, running his hands through his hair. 'Well, well. Good for you, Eric.'

'When d'you think you'll hear?' Edward asked.

Eric shrugged. 'Don't know. Might never happen. But fairly soon, I should think. They'll either want me or they won't.'

'Does Jimmy know about it?'

'No. You two are the first people I've told. Didn't think there was any point saying anything until I knew for sure. But I hope it does happen – I think it'll be exciting work.'

'Dangerous, Eric,' said Harry. 'No guns.'

'But a faster Spitfire. Anyway, all flying's dangerous. Landing among the mineshafts of Perranporth was dangerous.' He grinned. 'And anyway, the PR Spits operate at pretty high altitude, you know. I really hope I get accepted. It's got to be better than this.'

'That's true enough,' said Edward. 'I'm so fed up with convoy patrols. I just don't see the point of them. I mean, further up the Channel, in the Pas de Calais, fair enough. But down here – it's a waste of bloody time. When was the last time we intercepted anything?'

'We saw that Heinkel the other day,' said Harry.

'Yes, but we didn't get near it, did we? When did we actually see any Jerries attacking any ships? Never. They're not interested in attacking that far from France. I tell you, we're completely wasted here. They should send us back to 11 Group.'

'Perhaps they think our presence is preventative,' suggested Eric. 'Don't get me wrong, I agree with you, Eddie. But there must be a reason for it, and a reason for sending us to Portreath and another squadron to Perranporth.'

Harry said, 'We'll get some action eventually. They can't keep us here forever.'

'But Eric's not prepared to wait,' said Edward. They were silent for a moment, each staring into their beer.

'I don't think Jimmy's happy,' said Harry at last.

'No,' agreed Eric. 'Can't say I blame him, especially with Blackwood breathing down his neck. Sam had it pretty easy at Perranporth.'

'What he lost in facilities, he gained in independence.' Harry smiled ruefully.

'Exactly. Sam was in charge of the whole show, wasn't he? But Jimmy's not the station commander at Portreath. That's Blackwood's job, and it's pretty clear he doesn't think much of the bigwigs handing over squadrons to twenty-one-year-olds, even if they've more experience than most people twice their age.'

'I wish we had the old Jimmy back, though,' sighed Harry. 'He's become too serious.'

'It's a big deal, though,' said Eric. 'It's a big leap, isn't it, from commanding a flight to being in charge of an entire squadron.'

'He's just fed up with the new Spits and Blackwood if you ask me,' said Edward. 'Can't say I blame him.'

Harry leant back in his chair and stretched – *what can you do?* – then said, 'It's winter. Everything seems worse in winter. Short days, grey skies.'

'And the war's going badly,' added Eric. 'Do you think there'll ever be any good news?'

'Tobruk's been relieved,' said Harry. 'We haven't been invaded.'

'They won't need to, the amount of ships they're sinking in the Atlantic.'

'Stop being so bloody gloomy. We'll turn it around, you'll see. Anyway, let's talk about something else. Girls, for example. The dance on Saturday.'

Eric laughed. 'That's what I like about you, Harry: your unflinching ability to see the best in everything.'

'Well, there's no point in letting things get to you.'

Edward looked at him and smiled. He was so thankful to have had Harry by his side all this time. What good fortune it had been. Despite the disappointments of recent months, he knew he had much to thank the RAF for; for them to have stayed together this long was unusual, he knew. Other friends from Cambridge and Canada had been spread all over the country and beyond. And Eric was right about Harry: time and again his good humour and even temperament had been a source of comfort. Edward wondered how he would have survived those long weeks in Nova Scotia without Harry; he would have surely gone mad! He thought again about his friend as they drove back to Portreath later. He thought about how much he had come to depend upon him. Of course, he liked most of the others in the squadron – everyone got on well enough – but he could think of no-one in the world he would rather be with. They had spent so much time together since that providential meeting at Liverpool Street, knew so much about one another – foibles, habits, history – that he started to feeling maudlin about the inevitable day when they would be separated. At least, he thought, by staying in the squadron, they were kept together. It was no small consolation.

But even Harry was beginning to find life humdrum, as he confessed to Edward later when they were back in their room at Portreath. 'Maybe we should try and transfer too,' he said. He was lying on his bed, hands behind his head, staring up at the ceiling.

'What, to PR?'

'No. Oh, I don't know. But I'm beginning to agree with you, Eddie. We need some excitement.'

Another day with little prospect of flying. No convoys, and no enemy reconnaissance aircraft despite skies of wide open blue. At eleven, having been sitting in the crew room all morning, 'B' Flight were stood down. Rather than go back to the mess, however, Edward and Harry asked Jimmy whether they could take up the Spitfires. 'A bit of local flying,' said Harry. 'Shame to stay stuck on the ground on a day like this.'

'All right,' said Jimmy, returning to the paperwork on his desk. 'But don't be too long – I'm getting flak about using too much fuel.'

The long leg of Cornwall spread away beneath them as they climbed through the clear winter sky. The sea twinkled before them like a burnished carpet. Edward glanced over at Harry, some fifty yards off his starboard wing, and waved, then peeled off and dived. An idea had come to him; he hoped Harry was following and glancing back, grinned with satisfaction to see the other Spitfire behind him. The coast slipped beneath them and they headed out over the sea.

Harry's voice came through Edward's headset. 'Um, this isn't very local, Eddie.'

'Well, perhaps a bit further than normal,' he replied, and looked at his altimeter. Three thousand and still losing height.

'Eddie, where are we heading?'

'We both need some excitement. I thought we could go over to France and give the Germans a bit of a dust-down.'

'Are you mad?' Even through the static, Edward heard the incredulity – alarm even – in Harry's voice.

'We'll go under radar. It happened all the time during the Battle of Brit. Come on, we can show them what we can do.'

Silence, then Harry said, 'You lead. Over.'

Edward took them down to just a hundred feet above water, the glistening sea sweeping beneath them. His heart was pumping in his chest, but he felt exhilarated. He'd not planned this; not woken that morning with thoughts of a flight to France. But as they'd climbed high over south-west England, he'd remembered Sam and Jimmy talking about following 109s all the way back over the Channel. On one occasion, Jimmy had caught up with his Messerschmitt, and seen it disappear into the sea just half a mile from the enemy coast. He'd thought – to hell with it, I'm here now, might as well give them something to remember me by. And so he'd cleared the coast, spotted an airfield and shot up everything he could see, and hedge-hopped back to the Channel again. That had been in the Pas de

Calais, and the surprise of seeing a Spitfire swooping low over the French countryside had caught the Germans completely off guard. As Cornwall had shimmered emerald green that morning, it had occurred to Edward that the Germans would be even more surprised to see two Spitfires over the Brittany peninsula: they weren't supposed to have the range. And of course, normally they wouldn't, but with their new auxiliary tanks – well, that put a different complexion on things. Edward grinned to himself. It wouldn't take long. Twenty-five minutes there, ten minutes over France, back at Portreath in under two hours.

Edward took a deep breath as the French coast loomed. He'd not been to France before, but the Brittany cliffs looked just like those of Cornwall, and for the briefest of moments he had to check himself that they hadn't flown in a huge circle. But no, a glance at his compass confirmed they were in the right place. The coast now hurtled towards them and they roared over land at just fifty feet above the ground. Edward glanced over at Harry, still hugging his starboard wing, and waved. He took another deep breath. Below, brown cows began stampeding in a field; a man on a bicycle stopped and looked up as they thundered overhead. *We're over France!* he thought. Below were the enemy, and they were flying over them in broad daylight; but Edward felt empowered, invincible. He scanned the countryside, climbing for a better look, then spotted an airfield away to the east, just as he'd hoped they would. He waved again at Harry, pointing, then banked, the horizon swivelling, before straightening once more. The criss-cross of laid runways shone vividly in the sun, but dotted around the airfield were a number of aircraft, bombers, and, it seemed, fighters too. They were actually there; real enemy aircraft, with black crosses on the wings and along their fuselages. He breathed in and out rapidly, switched the gun safety catch, and with his thumb hovering over the gun button said, out loud, 'OK, here goes.'

He opened fire too early, the airframe shuddering as the eight machine guns drummed out bullets; he could see tracer initially falling short of the airfield. A moment later, he was over a line of aircraft, bullets still pouring from his wings. Men below were running. An explosion to his right – Harry had hit something. *Was that an aircraft?* Just a few seconds was all it took, and then they were over open fields once more. Edward looked behind him, thick smoke already erupting into the sky. Complete surprise! He grinned at Harry, who signalled back towards the coast. *All right,* Edward nodded, but then saw a column of army trucks winding its way along a country road. Circling, he lined up behind them and as he opened fire once more watched with delight as grey-clad men flung themselves out of the vehicles and jumped for their lives. One truck ran off the road. Pricks of dust spat into the air where his bullets hit. It was hard to keep his line of fire perfectly straight, but enough had hit their target – he could see that clearly enough. Once past the column, he banked again, away over a wood, saw that Harry was still following close behind, and headed for the coast. Edward laughed out loud, and seeing a French farm below and farm workers in the yard, waggled his wings, whooping with joy as he did so. He sighed with satisfaction. Never had he felt so alive. The sea stretched ahead of them. How easy it had been – those Germans had hardly known what had hit them!

Edward was still congratulating himself as puffs of anti-aircraft fire begun bursting around him, and arcs of tracer streamed into the sky. *Shit,* he thought, as his plane jolted and lurched. Twin lines of purple tracer were arcing slowly towards him, only to accelerate over his port wing. Another burst of flak – this time uncomfortably close, and the stick was jolted momentarily from his hand. He turned and twisted his aircraft and then he was back over the coast once more. Edward breathed a deep sigh of relief, but as he did so heard a huge crack, saw the horizon swivel, and smelled the acrid stench of cordite fill his cockpit. Clutching the stick, he managed to correct himself, but the controls felt lopsided, pulling to his left. Then he noticed the gaping hole the size of a football in his starboard wing. *Jesus Christ!* he cursed. *Where's Harry?* He frantically turned his head – nothing. *Come on Harry, where are you?* He turned his head again, felt the straps of his harness cut into his shoulders, but there was still no sign of him. Cold sweat trickled down the side of his face. His heart hammered. *Come on Harry, where the hell are you?* A roar of power, and the other Spitfire suddenly loomed up beside him from under his port wing. *Harry – thank God. Where did you come from?*

Out over the Channel, the sense of exhilaration returned, despite the strain of holding the control column to the right to correct the yaw from the hole in the wing; in all other respects, his Spitfire was flying perfectly, gauges all correct. As they drew closer to the Cornish coast they climbed steadily, passing over the glove of the Falmouth estuary at some three thousand feet. Several fishing boats were heading for port, tiny dots on a placid deep blue sea. Away to his left, the Helford river twinkled in the winter sunlight, silvery bright amidst the patchwork of green. A mass of cumulus rushed towards him, briefly enveloped his plane, then dispersed. These few clouds bathed the ground below in dark shadow. And there was Portreath, spread out below on the lip of the north Cornish coast.

Hewitson and Parker were agog. Where had they been? Why were the canvas patches over the gun ports blown? What had he done to his wing? 'Ah, sorry about that,' Edward told them. 'A bit of flak coming back over the French coast.'

'French coast, sir?'

'Yes, we shot up a German airfield.' But he found his feigned casualness impossible to keep up; grinning helplessly, he left his speechless ground crew and bounded over towards Harry.

'You madman!' laughed Harry.

'Well, we showed them, didn't we? How many planes do you think we knocked out? I must have hit at least half a dozen, and something you hit exploded all right.'

'A bowser, I think. I don't know, but they certainly weren't expecting it, were they? How's your wing?'

'All right – bit of a hole but nothing that can't be fixed.'

'I hate to think what Jimmy's going to say.'

Edward had not given any thought to that. In the excitement, it simply hadn't occurred to him. 'He'll be all right, I'm sure. Especially if it's confirmed we knocked out some enemy planes and army trucks.'

'Maybe.' Harry sounded doubtful.

They were summoned into Jimmy's office almost the moment they walked into the crew room. The other pilots crowded around them, anxious to know what they'd been doing, but Scotty tapped them on the shoulder. 'CO wants you next door, now,' he said, looking grave.

Jimmy was leaning on his desk, hands clenched together. 'Just what the hell do you think you've been doing?'

'We flew over to Brittany,' Edward told him.

'You did *what?*'

'Shot up an airfield and some trucks,' added Harry. 'Surprised them completely.'

'For fuck's sake,' said Jimmy, running his hands through his hair. 'It's time you bloody grew up a bit, both of you. We're fighting a war here, not trying to keep you personally entertained. So you're a bit fed up with convoy patrols – so fucking what? So's everybody, but it's not up to you to go spraying bullets all over France just because you want some fucking excitement. What if you'd been shot down? All this time, all the training you've been through, and you go and get killed on some hair-brain free flight over Brittany? Jesus! You could be court-martialled for this. Christ, I could sack you both here and now. As it is, you're both grounded until I say otherwise.' He was silent for a moment, then added, 'You know, I expected better from both of you. It's a hard enough job being CO here as it is, without you two making my life even more difficult. I knew you were headstrong – you especially, Eddie – but I had thought I could trust you. Now get out, keep out of my way for a few days, and you both better hope no-one else finds out about this.'

As it turned out, Jimmy later received a call of congratulations from group headquarters. Turned out a signal had been intercepted in which the Germans had reported five aircraft written off and a further four damaged. Not that either Edward or Harry knew for quite some days; as Jimmy later admitted, he wanted them to suffer for their crimes.

The bad weather returned, and the pilots found themselves spending even more of their time in the dank crew room, huddled around the fire, losing money at cards and wondering whether they would ever be posted to somewhere more interesting.

PART II

Malta

Somerset – June, 1995

The weather had turned, summer seemingly forgotten. The horse chestnuts outside Edward's close drooped, the leaves heavy with dripping rain. The first two games of cricket after his return from Cornwall had been cancelled and he found himself more house-bound than he'd have liked. And restless, too. He'd enjoyed his trip to Cornwall – more than he'd thought he would. Admitting this to himself had been hard, but once he'd accepted the fact, he felt it was quite all right to look through his metal tin once again, to reread his logbook, and even to take a book about the Battle of Britain out of the small library in the town.

The disrupted nights continued, however. He had told himself that revisiting his old Cornish haunts would put his mind at rest, but he'd known that that wouldn't be the case. How could it? Nothing had really happened there; nothing worth keeping buried for fifty years, at any rate. But the memories had flooded back – there was so much that he'd thought had been forgotten. It had been strange, though, to come face to face with his younger self, a person he knew he had once been, but whom he now barely recognised. That flight to Brittany was a case in point. What had he been thinking? So reckless; and selfish too – he could have made things very awkward for Jimmy. He chuckled. *Ah well, no real harm done.* And then he laughed again, thinking what some of his old colleagues at Myddleton would have said if they'd been told the story. They'd never have believed it. Old Icy Enderby? Never! You're pulling my leg!

Several times he dug out Andrew Fisher's address. Once he even began writing a letter but screwed it up and threw it away. *You're not ready,* he told himself. On this matter, he was being truthful. He wished he still had a picture of Harry. There had been a number, and he remembered one taken on the cliffs at Perranporth; they'd been collecting seagulls' eggs and one of the others had taken a photo-graph of them grinning triumphantly, each holding up an egg between their fingers. He'd taken a number himself, but they'd long since gone.

But if Edward thought hard, an image of Harry reappeared from the deep recesses of his mind – a little blurred perhaps, but quite definitely the friend he'd once known: Harry's had been a gentle face, deep brown eyes and eyebrows. Never any blemishes – no pimples or rash from shaving daily – as he did meticulously, even on Malta. 'I need to,' he'd once told Edward. 'A couple of days and I look like I've almost a beard.' In his mind's eye, Edward pictured him smiling: Harry had always smiled a lot; he was a happy person, always looking on the bright side, even when things had been desperate – as they frequently had during those dark months of 1942. Everyone liked Harry – he was impossible not to like. There were better pilots than him – or rather, better *fighter* pilots; Harry lacked the killer instinct.

And what about his voice? Edward closed his eyes, leant his head against the back of his armchair and thought for a moment. A soft voice, unhurried. As a boy and a young man, Edward had always gabbled – especially when he was excited, when he couldn't get the words out fast enough. 'Slow down and start again,' had been an oft-repeated phrase of his parents. Not at all like Harry, who'd always been so laid back. By God, but he'd been a good influence, and a good friend. Of course, Edward had known they wouldn't stick together forever – that could never happen, but if Harry had been an invaluable friend throughout their training and time with 324 Squadron, then he had been a rock on Malta. Edward sighed. He wondered what would have happened if Harry hadn't been there with him. Wondered whether he'd still be alive today, half a century on. He doubted it somehow. 'Where are you now, Harry?' he muttered, and felt his throat contract and his heart throb. And so that was why he couldn't write to Andrew Fisher now. He wouldn't be giving the whole picture, the complete story.

He'd known it ever since he set off for Cornwall, but only now, in the first week of June, did Edward finally accept the moment was almost upon him; it was time for him to go back to Malta. There had been ghosts in Cornwall, yes, but it was not memories from those days that were ruining his nights. No, the images that made him writhe and sweat in his bed were from later – from that tiny Mediterranean island. And from Italy. Only the night before he'd dreamed of coming into land with Messerschmitts firing at him from every direction. The undercarriage of his plane had buckled on impact, the aircraft screeching and tearing down the dusty runway. Then there had been flames, burning his legs and hands, and he'd been screaming, watching them melt before his eyes; but before his final moment came, he had suddenly become an observer, watching from the outside as a pilot squealed from within a burning cockpit. That was Malta, all right, and that was the image of the place seared into his mind: a hellhole. But of course, it wasn't a hellhole any more – not in that way at any rate – and this was why he felt certain that going there now was his only chance of banishing these fiends that plagued him. He remembered a line his mother used to say whenever he was ill as a child and the mercury in the thermometer continued to rise: 'You have to feel worse before you can get better.' He could picture her saying it, hovering in front of him with a teaspoon full of disgusting medicine. *How true that was.*

God only knew what the place was like now – not British any more, that much he knew. And it was only small. Eighteen miles by nine, or something like that. It was bound to have changed beyond recognition. Almost a completely different place. But it was no good trying to wriggle out of it with such talk. He *had* to go, that was all there was to it, no matter what he found when he got there. And after Malta, Italy. *Be methodical,* he told himself again. *One thing at a time.*

So the very next day, the first of the new month, he drove himself into Wincanton and visited the travel agent there. Flights to Malta were more costly than he'd imagined, but there were good package deals. 'How about this?' said the girl. 'You get your flights, seven nights in a four-star hotel and full board of dinner and breakfast.' She circled the hotel in a brochure with her biro, then eyed him intently. 'Actually, the Preluna's lovely,' said the girl. 'I've been there. Got its own pool and everything, and right by the sea. I can ask them for a sea view for you.'

'Where would I fly from?'

'Gatwick.'

'Hmm,' he said. *Motorways. The M25 – of course, it was unavoidable.*

The girl eyed him again, saw him wavering. 'I can hold it for you if you like,' she said. She tapped into a computer, scanned the screen, then said, 'Yes, if you book now, we can keep it open for you for forty-eight hours.'

'All right,' said Edward. 'I'll do that.' He wondered whether there was a train from Brampton Cary to Gatwick, one that did not involve hundreds of changes and conflicting timetables.

As he stepped out of the travel agent onto the high street, he bumped into Mark Withers, one of his old colleagues from the school.

'Edward!' said Mark. 'Going on holiday?'

Edward cursed to himself. *None of your bloody business – and it's hardly a holiday, anyway.* 'Um, possibly.'

'Christ! That must be a first, isn't it? Going before the end of the cricketing term?'

'It's raining so much. I won't miss a thing.'

Mark laughed. 'Fair point. Well, be seeing you.'

What did Mark know? Like everyone else at the school, they thought they knew Edward Enderby. *They don't know me at all,* he thought, and suddenly rather resented it. He had only himself to blame. 'It's your own fault,' he mumbled to himself.

Driving home again, Edward decided he *would* do as the travel agent suggested. As soon he was back, he would phone and confirm the booking. He wished Harry could be with him now. Wished Lucky or Laurie or Alex or even Michael Lindsay – any of his former comrades – could be with him, just as he'd wished he could have talked to some of those from the old days when he'd been in Cornwall. Just for one evening. He wished he'd made a note of the squadron associations listed in the Veterans' Link at Hyde Park. *If only I'd had that drink with Michael and Pete Summersby,* he thought.

Back in the calm order of his small house, he made a pot of tea, then sat down to think about how he could track down details of his old Squadron Associations. It was Pete Summersby he needed. Pete would know everything, just as he'd seemed to know everything during their time together on Malta. Had Pete said where he lived? Edward closed his eyes, rubbed his forehead. No – or if he had, he'd forgotten. Taking the notepad and biro from the table next to his chair, he glanced at Cynthia's photograph, then lifted the telephone and asked directory enquiries for three numbers: the Imperial War Museum, the RAF Museum in Hendon, and the RAF Club. Only on the third call, to the RAF Club, did he get anywhere. At first the receptionist sounded blank, as though he were speaking a different language from a different age, but then she passed him on to one of her colleagues. The man at the end of the line didn't have details of all the squadron associations, but he did know Pete Summersby. 'Stays with us regularly,' he said.

'Do you think you could give me his address or number?' Edward asked.

'Well, we're not supposed to,' said the voice. 'Um . . . let me see.' He paused for a moment. 'Yes, here it is. Lives in Norfolk.' Another pause. 'Look, I'm sure he won't mind. He's very friendly is Mr Summersby. Perhaps you could explain to him . . . ?'

'Of course – I'll make sure you don't get in trouble. Thank you,' he said. 'You've been very kind.'

Edward had begun to write a letter to Pete, but having already booked his holiday, felt impatient: he was flying out in six days' time and did not want to have to wait for correspondence. So having held off until after the six o'clock watershed, he dialled the number, his heart quickening as he did so. *What are you scared of, you fool?* The dialling tone rang, once, twice – more than a dozen times.

'Hello?' said a voice just as Edward was about to ring off, a female voice.

'Um, hello, forgive me, it's, er, Edward Enderby here. I'm after Pete Summersby. Is this the right number?'

'Yes, hold on.' Edward heard the receiver being put down, then the voice yelled, 'Dad! For you.' A television was blaring in the background. Edward heard mutterings: 'Who is it?' 'Dunno, Edward somebody,' and footsteps. A clunk as the receiver was lifted, then Pete's voice. 'Hello, yes, Pete Summersby speaking.'

'Pete, it's Edward Enderby here.'

'Ah, Squadron Leader, sir!'

'No need for all that – Edward, please.'

'Well, good to hear from you – sorry we missed you at Hyde Park. Terrific do, though, didn't you think?'

'Ah, yes, well, and I'm sorry I missed you too – I'm afraid it was really my grandson's day. We got waylaid at some stall or other. But it would be good to, ah, catch up soon. Talk about the old days and so on.'

'You must come to one of our get-togethers. Join the Association. I'll send you the details.'

'I'd like that.' Edward gave Pete his address, wondering, *do I really?*

'It'll be great to have you on board. There's a number of people you'll know.' He went through a list of former pilots and ground crew as well as various sons and daughters who had joined the Association, telling Edward at length about where they were living, what they had done with their lives, and anecdotes from recent meetings. A stream of enthusiastic chatter, to which Edward interjected occasionally with 'Really?' and, 'Gosh, how extraordinary!' and, 'Oh good,' all the while thinking, *this is his life now.* Eventually he managed to say, 'Actually, Pete, I'm going to Malta next week.'

'Malta? It's wonderful. I've been going back every April for the past six years. You know what, you should look up Lucky Santini while you're there. You remember Lucky?'

'Lucky? Of course!' For a moment, Edward scarcely dared believe he had heard correctly. Lucky was alive? His mood soared, his heart sang. Lucky was alive! It hadn't occurred to him that he could be. A real friend, someone with whom he had lived and fought throughout those months. Someone who was a link between the past and present.

'Lives on Gozo – has done for years. Didn't you know?'

'No, no I didn't. I haven't seen or spoken to anyone from the squadron in years. Since the war, really.'

'Well, you must definitely get in touch. He's got a nice place – an old farmhouse. Easy to get to, really. You just catch a ferry from Marsamxett Harbour. He's rather too fond of a drink, but . . . well, who isn't? Let me dig out his details.'

Afterwards, Edward poured himself a Scotch. He was not a great drinker – a gin and tonic occasionally, or a sherry, and sometimes a glass of wine with his supper, but he felt overwrought suddenly, and the searing taste of whisky burning down his throat calmed him. So Lucky was alive! It really was the most marvellous news he'd heard in a long time. He wondered whether he had ever kept all the photographs he'd taken – Lucky always seemed to have a camera in his hand, although God only knew where he'd got the film from. A closely guarded secret, if Edward remembered rightly. *I'd like to see some of those,* he thought.

And yet he was afraid too; afraid of what he would find there. Not for the first time, he wondered whether he had the strength to cope. Physically, he was as fit as he could possibly hope for at seventy-two; but it wasn't his body he was worried about. The circles of the whirlpool were tightening, and the closer he got to the centre, the harder it was going to be to drag himself back out again. These voices from the past, they were calling to him ever more strongly now. They filled him with both mounting excitement and dread.

Malta – February, 1942

Dawn, 21st February. Down dimly lit corridors, with their endless lines of grey pipes, through a hatchway, tramping up a metal staircase and into the dining room, with its smell of grease and bacon. HMS *Furious* suddenly rolled slightly and Edward clutched a chair to steady himself, muttering as he did so. None of them spoke as they lined up in front of the serving hatch. Plates of dry-looking scrambled eggs and fatty bacon were handed to each pilot in turn; then, still yawning, they made their way to the tables.

Furious rolled again as Edward sat down next to Harry. His stomach heaved. Shouts came from the kitchens, but the pilots were subdued. No-one spoke much.

'All right?' said Harry.

Edward nodded. 'Didn't sleep much. Did you?'

'Er, no. Don't think the hammock is much of a bed.'

'I didn't mind that so much – it was the noise. A bloody racket all night. Every single movement on the ship seemed to reverberate round the cabin.'

'Let's hope we don't fall asleep on the flight.' He smiled, then said, 'Who'd want to be in the Navy?'

Edward felt another wave of nausea and looked down at his plate of rapidly cooling food. He'd never felt less like eating, but knew he should try and swallow something before the long journey. And it might be the last cooked breakfast they had in a while. Food was scarce on Malta. He sliced into a piece of bacon. It was salty and greasy on his tongue; he hoped he wouldn't vomit in the cockpit.

Fifteen minutes later, all ten of them were up on the flight deck, making their way towards the operations room for a final briefing. A strong wind whipped over the sea and across the ship, and in his cotton tropical uniform, Edward shivered. First light streaked across the horizon, but it was going to be a grey, dull morning. He looked at the Hurricanes already brought up onto the flight deck, the wings visibly shaking in the wind. They looked menacing, spectral.

A Fleet Air Arm captain briefed them. The *Furious* would change course into the wind – reckoned to be just under thirty knots. One of his pilots would lead them in a Fulmar; he would take off first, then they would follow in turns. The Fulmar pilot would lead them as far as Bizerte on the Tunisian coast, then they would be on their own. Enemy fighters were stationed on the tiny island of Pantelleria – it was important to try and avoid them, and, they were told, to fly high over Tunisia in case there were any German or Vichy French aircraft about there. 'So keep a good look-out at all times,' he told them. *Yes, yes,* thought Edward. They would then fly over the Cap Bon peninsula, and out over the Mediterranean once more. 'Also watch out for Italian planes on Lampedusa,' he warned them. From there on, it was a simple stretch to Malta. Just over seven hundred miles; with an extra eighty-eight gallon drop tank, they should have fuel to spare. At a steady cruising speed, they were expected on the island by 9.30 – a journey of around three hours.

Squadron Leader Hammond stood up. 'R/T silence, all right? We're lined by enemy coastlines all the way, so it's essential we don't give them anything to get excited about. As we get nearer we'll tune in to the Malta frequency and let them lead us in. We'll be flying at around 20,000 feet, and let's spread ourselves out a bit – we don't want to waste energy flying close formation. Clear enough?' 'Butch' Hammond, as he was known, late twenties, a veteran of France and the Battle of Britain, and square-jawed with curly hair tightly oiled to his scalp. He *looked* like a leader, Edward thought; as though he'd been the rugger captain at school. He'd been struck by that from the moment they had all met.

Afterwards, they trooped outside again back onto the flight deck, and made for their Hurricanes. The maps and notes in Edward's hand flapped noisily in the wind, and gusts of salty spray washed over the deck. His parachute clunked against the back of his legs. He wished there had been an opportunity to practise flying off the aircraft carrier. So it had been done before – *Furious* had already made four such trips, they'd been told. *Well, terrific, but that's small comfort.* The flight deck still looked uncomfortably short, and he wished someone had taken out the old biplane ramp still sticking up two-thirds the way down. The deck was busy with seamen and naval ground crew. Men shouted and hurried between aircraft as the *Furious* and her escort of destroyers surged forward, giving an air of urgency, as though something important were about to happen.

Then Edward remembered that he was about to play a central part in that.

Edward clambered onto the wing, feeling the Hurricane shudder in the wind as he did so. Inside, the cockpit was even more cramped than he remembered from his days at OTU. Each pilot had been allowed just thirty pounds of kit, most of which he had wedged either side of the seat the previous evening: one change of clothes, a peaked cap, a couple of novels, shaving kit and toothbrush; notebook and logbook. That was all, really. Nor were the planes armed: the eight machine guns were considered too heavy. In their place had been jammed as many packets of cigarettes as the gun ports would allow. 'They're short of cigarettes on Malta,' Hammond had explained. 'But what if we're attacked?' Edward had asked him. Butch had shrugged. 'Let's hope we're not.'

Edward struggled to get comfortable. He felt hemmed in, while underneath his backside was a packed inflatable dinghy; he was already sitting on his parachute and his head almost touched the top of the canopy. *Three hours of this.* He prayed the switch on his overload tank would work – he'd checked it twice the day before and it had seemed to be working fine, but if anything went wrong . . . He closed his eyes, took a deep breath.

The ship suddenly turned, tilting as it did so. Edward looked up in alarm. And the *Furious* was building up speed too, scything into the wind, with great sheets of spray showering the deck. The five aircraft in front of Edward began starting up, one by one, licks of flame and smoke briefly flickering from the exhaust stubs. Having primed the engine, Edward set the throttle, flicked on the magneto switches, then pressed the starter button. *Please start.* The propeller jerked, stopped, jerked again, then the engine erupted into life, the airscrew now just a whirr in front of him. *Thank you.* Throttling back to warm the engine, he waited. The deck officer, his flag aloft, was now standing in front of Butch Hammond, the first in line. Edward could see the leading Hurricane shaking with the force of the revs. The flag dropped and the aircraft hurtled down the deck, lifted off the ramp, dropped again, then slowly rose into the air once more.

Harry was third off. Edward watched breathlessly as his friend disappeared over the end of the aircraft carrier, only to reappear moments later. Another sigh of relief. The fourth and fifth followed, and then Edward was being motioned to taxi to the end of the deck and to line himself up on the white central line. With both arms raised, the flight-deck officer looked at him. Edward opened the throttle, felt the airframe rattle and shake and gave a wave. His mouth felt dry, his stomach dull. His heart drummed in his chest. *Here goes.* The flight-deck officer dropped his flag, Edward released the brakes, and the Hurricane sped down the flight deck, Edward jolting and shaking in his seat. *Come on, come on,* he thought. The Hurricane hit the ramp, flew into the air, Edward pulled back on the stick, and then, as he willed the plane to take to the sky, it lifted off past the end of the flight deck. Glancing behind him, he saw the *Furious* shrink. Breathing out heavily, he grinned to himself – *thank God that's over* – and then climbed up to join the others, now circling over the convoy below.

All ten of them took off successfully, and having formed up on the Fulmar, began the climb high into an unfamiliar sky. For a while Edward continued to twist and turn his head, constantly checking the sky, but as the minutes passed, so he began to feel calmer. He'd been so anxious about simply getting into the air that the danger from enemy aircraft seemed far less in comparison. And the sky was so vast, so utterly empty, and with fellow Hurricanes either side of him, his thoughts began to wander.

It was, he thought, incredible to think that so little had happened for months on end, and then within two weeks he was flying over the Mediterranean on his way to Malta. It was Scotty who'd started the ball rolling. Another morning sat in the crew room at Portreath; another morning when there had been little flying. And then Scotty had wandered in and asked if anyone fancied a posting to Burma. They were aware of what was going on in the Far East – the Japanese had rampaged down through Malaya and were threatening Singapore. In the Philippines, the Americans had not fared much better. The prospect of joining Air Command, India, seemed fraught with risk. No-one had put their hand up. Scotty had shrugged – *I don't blame you* – and wandered back to his office.

But by the end of the day, Edward and Harry had talked each other into offering their services. At least it would be a change; at least they would see some action. At least it would be better than staying put in Portreath, a place from which it seemed they would never be posted. 'And they need *two* volunteers,' pointed out Harry. 'When's that chance going to come along again? If we both go, then we can stick together.'

Jimmy took their decision well. He'd long since forgiven Edward for his free flight over Brittany; in recent weeks, he'd even returned to something like his old self. He had been surprised, however. 'You must know you should never volunteer for anything – it's a golden rule,' he told them.

'Our minds are made up,' said Harry.

Jimmy nodded. 'Yes, I can see that. Well, you'll be missed.'

They left the squadron the following day, after a drunken send-off at the Tregenna Castle, heading their separate ways for ten days' embarkation leave. Edward had been at home only a few days when he received a telegram telling him his posting had been changed. With mounting anxiety, he had rung Harry, but to his great relief, discovered his friend had received the same notice. Instead, they would be going to the Middle East.

For the last couple of days of his leave, Edward had felt impatient and anxious to get going, but as he packed and looked round his bedroom for the last time in God only knew how many months – even years – he wondered whether he might be reprieved, that another telegram would arrive informing him he would be staying in England after all. On the walls hung framed team photographs from his schooldays. Above his bed there was still the woodland picture of fairies and elves that had been in his room all his life – it had been there since his earliest memories. Only now did he realise how childish it was, how unsuitable it was for a fighter pilot in the Royal Air Force. Other nick-nacks littered the room: a cricket bat, boxing gloves and a deflated rugger ball. The Meccano aeroplane he had made many years before. A boy's room.

'I know you're grown up now,' his mother had said at the station, 'but you're still my little boy.'

'Come on, Angela, you're embarrassing the lad,' said his father. His mother had tried hard not to cry, but had been unable to stop herself, dabbing her eyes with her handkerchief. Edward had felt like crying himself. Why was it worse this time? *Because I'm going to the*

Middle East, he thought. There would be no more empty days flying tedious convoy patrols. The Middle East, as everyone knew – as his mother and father knew – was the one place where British forces were still actively fighting Germany; and he would be in the thick of it. His mother was crying because she knew there was every chance she would never see him again.

Friday, 13th February, 1942. An inauspicious day on which to begin their journey. Edward had met Harry in London the night before, and then they had joined three others at Paddington – a wiry Australian, Laurie Bowles; a tall, athletic-looking American, Lucky Santini; and a Scottish sergeant pilot called Alex McLeish. Only Edward and Harry knew one another. They all shook hands, eyeing each other. Edward noticed both Laurie and Alex wore the purple and white ribbon of a DFC above their breast pocket. It was raining as they pulled out of the station. London looked tired, Edward thought. Blackened buildings, and occasionally a gaping hole where once a building – or several buildings – had stood. It was still raining by the time they reached Reading.

'Bastard English weather,' muttered Laurie.

'You clearly haven't been to Scotland,' said Alex.

'No, and I don't think I want to.'

'Believe me, you do,' said Lucky. 'Scotland is an amazing place.'

'Anyway, might be the last rain we see in a long time,' added Harry. 'Doesn't rain much in North Africa.'

'North Africa?' said Laurie. 'We're not going to North Africa. No, mate. Reckon we're heading for Malta.'

'Malta?' Edward sat up.

'Yup. That's what I heard.' Laurie had come from Biggin Hill, part of 11 Group. It was a large fighter station, and, as he put it, a lot of 'top brass' were always passing through. If you wanted to know what was going on, then Biggin was the place to find out. 'My old CO got it from the Winco, and the Winco heard it from someone at Air Ministry. They've only got Hurricanes out there, but they're going to send some Spits. And Spitfire pilots. You all flown Spits?' They nodded. 'Well, then. In my limited experience, these rumours usually tend to be right.'

'Malta,' said Harry, 'Jesus.'

'Malta? Where the hell's that?' said Lucky.

'It's an island in the Mediterranean. About halfway along,' said Harry.

Lucky looked doubtful. 'Never heard of it.'

Laurie grinned. 'You have now. Fiery little place just at the minute – it'll be a bit different from rhubarbs over France at any rate.' Edward looked at him, noticing the way Laurie constantly jigged his leg and drummed his fingers.

The train trundled west, through damp, grey towns: Hungerford, Swindon, Taunton, Exeter; a long, faltering journey, but which gave them a chance to talk. Edward was glad not to sit in silence; it wasn't good to think too hard about things. Why 'Lucky'? Harry asked.

'Like Lucky Luciano,' he replied. 'You know, the gangster? My name's Luciano. I never use it, though. Never have. Always been Lucky.'

'Have you?' asked Harry.

'I guess so. Survived so far, haven't I?' He was from California. Burbank. 'It's near Hollywood,' he told them. His father had died when he was young, so his mother had been forced to go out and work. There wasn't much time for him, and even less when she married again and had two more children. Lucky waved his hand at them. 'Look, I didn't care too much. Meant no-one was checking up on me. Leastways, that's the way I looked at it.' He'd always loved planes, right from when he was a boy, when he used to bunk off school and sneak down to the Metropolitan airdrome to watch the airplanes. They got to know him and started giving him odd jobs, cleaning the planes, sweeping out hangars.

'Did you ever see any film stars?' asked Edward.

'Oh, sure. Movie stars have been flying ever since airplanes were invented. Yeah, I saw loads of them. Gable, Garbo; Errol Flynn. We had them all coming through. You should see my autograph book.'

Edward was impressed. He'd seen *Dawn Patrol* the summer he left school. At the time he'd thought it the best film he'd ever seen, and it had been a greater influence on his desire to fly than he was ever willing to confess.

Lucky was not to be drawn into anecdotes about film stars, however. 'I couldn't give a damn about Hollywood,' he told them. 'Airplanes was what got me going.' Later on, when he was fifteen and had finished with school, he got a job working for Lockheed, the aircraft manufacturers. He saved and hoarded, continued hanging out with the fliers, and eventually had enough stashed away to learn to fly himself. 'Boy, that was a great moment,' he told them, closing his eyes and sighing as he remembered that first flight. 'But I guess you guys would know all about that. Pure heaven.' By the time he was eighteen he had a part share in a plane of his own. 'A Laird Speedwing – a hundred horsepower, but a great little bird all the same.' And then the war came along and America wasn't in it. Lucky figured they would be before too long and so applied to join the air force. He didn't like what he'd seen of Hitler or the Nazis, but really, he just wanted to fly. He'd become bored of flying hundred-horsepower aircraft. 'I saw these thousand-horsepower birds, and wanted a piece of it myself. Christ, who wouldn't?'

'So what happened?' asked Edward.

'Failed my goddam medical. Apparently, I have some kind of stigma in my eye. So I tried to join the navy fliers, but the same thing happened. "Sorry son, you're eyes aren't up to it." Don't give me that crap, I told them, but they weren't interested. Of course, the sons of bitches would welcome me with open arms now, but back in 1939 they were a bit more picky.' But the RAF was desperate for experienced pilots, and wasn't too bothered about stigmas. He found out about the Clayton Knight Committee, who were in Los Angeles and screening young pilots like himself, and helping them to join the RAF in Canada. An interview at the Hollywood Roosevelt Hotel and he was in. 'No damned questions about my eyes.' Before he knew it, he was on a ship to Britain. He arrived at Greenock, on the Clyde, just over a year before. Coming off the boat, he was met by a Scottish lady handing out mugs of tea. 'I couldn't believe it. I'd come all this way and the first thing I do is drink tea.' In the distance he'd seen the mountains and decided that one day he'd come back and visit. A few months later he was given a week's leave, so suffering a long and arduous train journey, he and a friend went back to Scotland and spent a week walking around Oban. 'There's nothing like the Highlands in California, I can tell you.' After completing his training, he had joined the Eagle Squadron, along with all the other American volunteers, and had slowly but surely got used to the English way of doing things. He liked the RAF. Liked their attitude and liked their easy-going approach. When rumours began that the American squadrons were going to be absorbed into the US Air Force, he made up his mind to volunteer for the first overseas posting he could. That way, he figured, he could stay with the RAF. 'So here I am,' he said, 'for better or worse.' He smoothed his dark, finely combed hair and movie-star moustache. Despite a long, cold winter in Britain, he still glowed with good health. 'I mean,' he added, 'if Uncle Sam didn't want me back in '39, I don't see why they should have me now I've earned my pips.' Pulling a packet of cigarettes from his pocket, he flicked one into his mouth, winked, then flipped open his lighter and lit it with one hand. A perfect trio of smoke rings drifted out into the compartment. 'Anyway,' he said, 'I want to hear about you guys.'

Edward and Harry spoke in tandem. Their sorry tale of squadron life in Cornwall was met with sympathy. 'And I thought fighter sweeps were bad enough,' said Laurie. Like Lucky, Laurie had also had a lifelong passion for aeroplanes. Brought up on a farm in northern New South Wales, his father and uncles had bought one together when he was still a boy. 'They made a heck of a difference. Jesus, our farm was probably the same size as England. Well, maybe not *that* big, but bloody big all the same.' He could fly by the time he was fifteen – so could all his brothers. 'All five of us, so then we got another one – a Tiger Moth. She was an absolute beaut.' But one of his brothers had crashed it. 'Yeah, he was getting a bit carried away with himself, doing acrobatics and all that shit, and crashed straight into the ground.'

'What happened to him?' asked Edward.

'Well, he killed himself, didn't he? Bloody idiot.' He sighed, looked out of the window, then said, 'Mum wasn't so happy about us all flying after that, but it didn't stop me.' There wasn't enough work – or money – for all of them to stay on the farm, not with all his cousins as well. So he said his farewells, headed to Sydney and got the boat to England. He'd never been on a ship before. Had never even seen the sea. He was sick as a dog all the way to England, but after what seemed like forever, the ship eventually reached Liverpool. 'I got here the same day Chamberlain came back from meeting Hitler and flapping his piece of paper. Joined the Air Force as soon as I could.'

'And you haven't been home since?' said Edward.

'Well, no. Of course not. There's the small matter of a war on. But it's OK. I get letters.' Two of his brothers had since joined the army. They were now in the Middle East, and that was one of the reasons he'd been so keen to volunteer for the overseas posting. He'd hoped he might bump into them, and was disappointed when he discovered they were almost certainly headed for Malta. 'But it was too late then. My CO said you should never volunteer for anything, and he was right.'

'Our CO said the same,' said Harry.

Edward warmed to these men. It was funny, he reflected, how some people you took to immediately and others you didn't, often for no reason that could be defined. But already he felt a growing sense of solidarity, that they were headed on this venture together, creating a bond before they'd barely started. He looked across at Alex. Pale skin, fair hair and eyebrows so blond they were hardly visible. Of them all, Alex had said the least, had been the quietest. Leaning his hand against the window, he was gazing out at the bleak countryside, an expression of wistfulness etched across his face.

'What about you, Alex?' asked Lucky. 'Did you volunteer for this caper?'

Alex shook his head. 'No,' he said, his voice soft, but with a distinct brogue. 'I've heard that rule as well, you know, only I've always stuck to it.' He smiled ruefully. 'No, I've been instructing for the past nine months.' He had joined the RAF before the war. His father had been a shepherd in Perthshire, and Alex had been expected to follow suit – a life of trudging up and down mountains, tending to the sheep. But then he'd seen a recruitment poster in Pitlochry – this was in 1938, after the Munich Crisis – and without telling his parents, he'd taken a train to Glasgow and joined up. Just like that. He'd never expected to be a pilot – he'd assumed he'd be crew – but had found himself picked out. Not that he was complaining. 'Who would turn down a chance to fly?' he said. Two weeks before the war broke out, he was posted. His squadron, took part in the battle over Dunkirk, then fought through much of the Battle of Britain. He said little about it; you didn't brag. At the end of August that summer, the squadron was moved north, out of the front line of battle. They were at Drem in Scotland when Alex was posted to Wales as an instructor. It was there that he'd met Joan –

she was a WAAF, working with the ground controller. 'Then suddenly I was told my instructing days were over and that I'd been posted overseas,' he said.

'You didn't want that?' asked Harry.

'No. You see, I've only been married three weeks. I'd never have done it if I'd known I was about to be posted. It's not really fair on Joan. We'd only just found ourselves somewhere to live.' He smiled again sadly.

'You must have known it was on the cards,' said Laurie.

'No, not at all. I thought I'd be staying in Britain for some time to come. You see, I'd been told that I was likely to be posted to Hawkers as a test pilot. Now I don't know when I'll see her again. I'm worried my letters won't get through from Malta.'

'Of course they will,' said Harry. They were all silent for a while after that. Alex didn't look very old, but by being married, he had already placed himself on a different level from the others. Edward thought about Betty at the Tregenna Castle. He couldn't ever imagine being married. Couldn't imagine falling in love. His mother was the only member of the female sex he'd ever really known, and he was glad about that, grateful that he wasn't in Alex's shoes.

Plymouth – at last. An RAF truck was waiting for them and took them to the Grand Hotel, requisitioned entirely by the RAF, where they met the other six pilots – all of whom had been flown down earlier in the day. Squadron Leader Butch Hammond was in command: a pre-war regular, an ace twice over and with two DFCs to his name. And grey eyes underneath his dark hair, eyes that bored into the newcomers suspiciously. 'Seen much action?' he asked Edward and Harry.

'Not very much, sir,' Harry replied. 'We've been in a quiet sector. But we've done plenty of flying. Built up our hours.'

Hammond raised an eyebrow. 'Flying's one thing,' he said. 'Being a fighter pilot's quite another.' He looked at Edward. 'And you volunteered for this, did you?'

'Yes, sir.'

Hammond nodded. 'I see,' he said, then after clearing his throat, turned to them all. 'Well, we'll be flying out to Gibraltar tomorrow morning. Can't say much more now – but all will be revealed soon enough.'

Dinner in the plush hotel dining room – thin soup and a potato-rich pie – followed by drinks at the bar afterwards: watery beer and whisky. There was a Canadian amongst them, too – Ken Bartlett – and an Irishman – Paddy Milligan. Men from across the free world, brought together in this once grand Devon hotel on a grey winter's day, only to be sent to some tiny outpost in the middle of the Mediterranean. Since leaving India as a boy, Edward had rarely spoken with anyone who was not English. How that had changed since he'd joined the RAF. And what struck him was how similar they all were: whether French, Canadian, American or Irish, one young man was much the same as another.

The following morning the weather had worsened. At Mountbatten seaplane base, the Catalinas bobbed and rocked on a restless deep green sea. There was talk of postponing the flight – the sea looked too rough – but in the end they went, knocked and jolted as the flying boat crashed over the waves and eventually heaved itself into the air. None of them looked comfortable – they were bad passengers to a man, but that was hardly surprising: it wasn't the fighter pilot way to be flown by someone else. Thunderstorms harangued them all the way across the Bay of Biscay, the Catalina pitching and falling as though it were still on the sea; they had to stay low to avoid the enemy radar, but at least the bad weather kept any stray marauders out of their way.

Over nine hours later, having skirted around the Iberian Peninsula, they turned in on Cape St Vincent on the final stretch to Gibraltar. Although the sun had long-since set, Gibraltar itself shone brightly from the twinkle of thousands of lights, as did Algeciras, across the straits in Spanish Morocco. After more than two years of blackouts back home in Britain, this dazzling illumination seemed almost fantastical. It was not just the lights: at the Bristol Hotel they dined on fat steaks and claret and ate sweet pastries, the kind of meal they had all but forgotten about.

Later, they received a briefing in the bar, the sun-scorched Air Commodore constantly looking around him, and speaking in hushed tones. 'Spies are everywhere,' he explained. 'One can never be too careful.' They were to stay in Gibraltar another day and night, he told them. HMS *Furious* was due in the following morning, their Spitfires already aboard. At dawn the next day – 20th February – they would set sail, steaming back out into the Atlantic to fool the spies, then, in the dead of a moonless night, would creep back through the straits and into the Mediterranean. That way, he assured them, the fascist observers at Algeciras would be none the wiser.

Two nights of crisp, clean sheets, and a day of ambling through the spice-scented bazaars. 'I feel like I'm on holiday,' said Harry as they sat at an outside café.

'We are, in a way,' said Edward. 'For a day at any rate.'

Harry looked up and closed his eyes, letting the sun beat down upon his face. 'I can hardly believe this is winter. This posting's looking even better.'

Edward laughed. 'Just think of them all still stuck in Portreath. They don't know what they're missing.' They were silent for a moment, then Edward said, 'It's going to be quite rough in Malta, isn't it? I mean, things are pretty desperate there.'

Harry nodded.

'But we'll be all right, won't we?' Edward continued. Harry lit a cigarette, and exhaled a cloud of swirling blue-grey smoke into the sky.

'Of course we will. I don't think you and I will die. I don't know why, but I do feel it very strongly.' He looked at Edward intently. 'I am scared, though.'

'So am I.'

Harry's face brightened. 'Are you? So it's not just me, then.'

Later, they strolled past well-stocked shops and bought presents for their parents, which they later posted from the hotel. They looked at *Furious* lying in port. She looked huge, but Edward had hoped she'd be bigger. Taking off from her flight deck was beginning to worry him. He just prayed that Harry's hunch about them was right.

They left at dawn the following day, as planned, the wind cutting up once more the moment they headed back out into the desolate Atlantic. Everything was exactly as the Air Commodore had outlined, except in one important aspect. The promised Spitfires were not on board. 'Seems they never made it to Greenock in the first place,' Hammond told them. 'Apparently, we'll get them in a couple of weeks, although I'll believe it when I see it. In the meantime, we're going to have fly in yet more Hurricanes.' There was a collective groan at this news. 'Hurricanes?' said Laurie Bowles. 'What use are they going to be?'

'I'm not sure I can remember how to fly one, sir,' said Lucky. He was joking, but Edward was worried. It had been over seven months since he'd been in a Hurricane, and now he was expected to fly off in one from a horribly short-looking runway in the middle of the sea. All that day at sea, he spent his time familiarising himself with his allocated aircraft, sitting in the cockpit, going through the normal pre-flight checks, adjusting the settings and repeatedly making sure the changeover on his fuel tanks was working. As the day had worn on, so his fears had increased. He began to think he was trapped and that he would never stand on dry land again. By the time they had finished dinner, he was so wound up, Harry had to take him to the wardroom for several large drinks. He'd hoped whisky would help him sleep, but the clangings and tapping resonating around the iron hull and the discomfort of the netted hammocks kept him awake for much of the night. He prayed he would never have to go through the experience again.

But he'd made it. He'd successfully taken off, and was now flying high over the Mediterranean, the sun high above him, shining down through the Perspex canopy. Even a fighter plane appeared large on the ground, yet here they were, ten specks coasting at twenty thousand feet. So precarious, and yet Edward felt quite secure, the harness tight around him, the cockpit snug and crammed with things that were so familiar to him. He glanced down at the sea, shimmering in the sunlight, drifting and dancing as the winds from North Africa blew across it, rippling it into strange patterns.

At long last, Edward spied Malta. The cloud had cleared east of Cap Bon, so that now the sky and sea merged along a hazy grey line some way in the distance. But there, ahead of him, like a dusty autumn leaf, lay Malta. It was an image of utter calm and peacefulness. He glanced at his watch. Just after half-past nine. *Almost on time.*

Soon after he heard Hammond trying to make contact with Malta. A German voice crackled in his ear, Butch cursed then called again and this time reached the RAF ground controller on the island. 'Pancake as soon as you can,' the controller told them. 'You're a few minutes late and we usually get a raid at around ten.' They were told to split into two formations. Half were to land at Luqa, half at Takali. Edward was directed to the latter. The Island was fast looming towards them now, the deep azure of the Mediterranean turning vivid turquoise as it lapped the edges of the Island. So inviting. Edward wanted to leap in and swim. They had already dropped to ten thousand, but now Hammond brought them even lower. Their marker was the tiny island of Filfla, an outcrop to the south. Edward spotted it. Two thousand feet, and cutting the throttle. He felt his heart quicken again. *So this is Malta.* He could see the distinct inlet of Grand Harbour, and the finger of Valletta – a plume of smoke wafted high into the sky above; he could see the whole island laid out before him. *So small,* he thought. Fifteen hundred feet. Villages and towns dotted a patchwork landscape of differing hues of dust-gold and brown. Spires and pinnacles of the Island's many churches stood proudly against the skyline. The first five were coming into land over Luqa – Edward watched them turn in, flashing blue undersides, their wheels lowering into position. Moments later, he spotted Takali, with its blast shelters dotted around the perimeter. Away to the east was another town and a church with a huge dome, dominating the whole settlement; to the north a further town perched high on a hill, and yet another church towering high over the airfield below.

'Blue section – break!' said Lucky, the section leader. Throttle back – but not as much as a Spitfire; you couldn't glide in with a Hurricane. Undercarriage down. Edward heard the gentle whirr as the wheels lowered and clicked into place. Ahead of him was Lucky; one had already touched down, another was about to. *Five minutes to ten.* The cockpit felt suddenly close and claustrophobic, so he pulled off his mask and yanked back the hood on its runners, a blast of air and dust greeting him.

Lucky touched down ahead of him, dust whipping up around him, then Edward watched the runway accelerate towards him until it was lost behind the great nose of the plane. A jolt and he had made it, back on land once more.

He taxied off the main strip – there was no runway as such. Through the clouds of dust, two ground crew appeared and after motioning him to stop, jumped onto the wing. 'Head round to the left,' one of them yelled. 'We're expecting a raid any minute.'

Edward did as he was bidden, bumping over the rough ground. 'Here,' said one of the men eventually, pointing towards a U-shaped wall of old four-gallon fuel cans. Edward turned in, braked and cut the engine, and took off his helmet.

'Quickly!' said one of the ground crew. Edward was suddenly conscious that an air-raid siren was wailing hauntingly over the island. 'Leave your stuff for the moment,' said the man. Fumbling with his harness buckle, Edward frantically tried to free himself. The first explosions were dully detonating from the south. *Free at last – thank God*. He pushed himself up, his legs stiff, and lowered himself onto the wing, then jumped awkwardly onto the ground, turning his ankle as his did so.

'Come on, sir!' said the man, holding out a hand. Edward took it, and pulled himself up, and hobbled after him. Fifty yards away, there was a long narrow slit trench. There were several ground crew already there as Edward dropped in.

'Eddie – you made it!' said Lucky. 'Jesus, what kind of welcome is this?'

Seconds later, Harry also joined them. The explosions were getting closer.

'That's Luqa, sir,' said the man who had jumped on Edward's wing. 'I'm Summersby by the way,' he added. 'Very glad to see you all.'

'Bloody hell, I hope the first lot got down in time,' said Harry. Another explosion, louder this time, followed by the screaming and whistling of more bombs and the roar of aero engines. The ground shuddered and shook, the noise deafening. The pilots, without helmets, covered their heads instinctively with their hands and crouched as low as they could into the ground. More screaming from the sky, and more explosions, and this time it seemed as though the eruptions were just yards from where they were crouching. Edward grimaced, as showers of mud, grit and fragments of stone clattered down around and over them. They heard the bombers drifting away, but now they could hear the whirr of more engines, lighter, more refined this time. Edward had just guessed they must be enemy fighters when they opened fire, machine-gun bullets spitting over the airfield. Another smaller explosion as an aircraft was hit and burst into flames.

And then they were gone. Slowly, gingerly, they lifted their heads. The airfield, the whole Island it seemed, was covered in dust and smoke. They all coughed, choking on the acrid fumes. Two separate columns of thick black smoke were already billowing high into the sky.

'Bollocks,' said Summersby. 'Another plane and a bowser. That's the last one gone.'

As the dust and smoke began to settle, the men emerged from their slit trenches. With his handkerchief over his mouth, Edward walked unsteadily towards his Hurricane. His legs felt weak, his head whirred, and his ears were ringing shrilly. His aircraft was covered with dirt and grit, but otherwise it appeared to be in one piece. He looked around, and gasped. New bomb craters littered the airfield where, just a few minutes before, they had landed. Scattered elsewhere were the remains of numerous burnt-out aircraft – skeletal and charred Hurricanes, but bombers too, Wellingtons and Blenheims. Dotted in between were countless little red flags, sticking up through the wispy dried grass.

Edward turned and saw that Summersby was standing next to him. 'What are those flags?' he asked.

'Unexploded bombs. You wouldn't believe the number of duds and delayed-action stuff they lob down on us.' The other Hurricanes parked around the perimeter looked battered and tired. One had a completely different airscrew, most were roughly patched; all were chipped and streaked with oil.

Harry and Lucky walked over. They looked ashen. Lucky turned to Summersby. 'How many aircraft have we got here?'

'Hard to say, sir. In total, around fifty-odd, but some of those are in pieces, and most aren't actually serviceable as such. Numbers have been going down pretty fast in the last few days. Two days ago we had just eleven.'

'Eleven?' All three stared incredulously at the airman.

'There were only nine fit to fly this morning, so assuming your ten are all right, that puts us up to nineteen.'

'Jesus,' mumbled Lucky. 'And the Krauts? Just a little more than that, right?'

Summersby nodded slowly. 'Hundreds.'

They looked at each other. Words were pointless.

Malta – February, 1942

10.30 a.m., 21st February, 1942. A Saturday, not that it made any difference. Edward had been on the island little more than an hour when six Hurricanes came into land, one with its engine spluttering. Edward watched. They all made it safely down, but the last, the one smoking slightly, cut its engine almost immediately and rolled to a standstill. While the others taxied off towards their blast shelters, this lone aircraft remained in the middle of the dusty field, the pilot making no effort to get out. A number of airmen rushed over. Some shouting followed, then the pilot was pulled from the cockpit and lowered carefully onto the ground. Slowly he was helped back onto his feet, and, with an airman taking each arm, led towards dispersal. Edward rubbed his eyes and ran his hands through his hair. It was a bright day, the sun bearing down from a deep, cloudless sky, and warm – but not stifling – with a cooling breeze.

Edward stumbled back to his Hurricane, swept the worst of the debris from the port wing with his hand, then clambered up to gather his belongings, placing them together in a canvas knapsack he had brought especially for the purpose. Several ground crew were already swarming over his plane, gleefully pulling up the gun ports with bayonets, and ripping out cartons of Camel cigarettes, medical supplies and other goodies stashed there. Armourers hurried up to the Hurricane with machine guns and ammunition boxes, while other men – soldiers, not RAF – strained under the weight of carrying stacks of four-gallon tin cans of petrol. Cans, boxes, oil-stained men with toolboxes. Edward looked at them, bewildered. Already, the craters were being filled in – more soldiers, their legs and arms fried a deep brown under threadbare KD shorts and shirts.

Lucky and Harry called to him. The two of them were standing with another of the ground crew; Summersby had vanished. As Edward joined them, a soldier walked past with wide, staring eyes and mouth spread in a grin. He turned his head and laughed at them, then ran towards another of the planes. 'Don't mind him,' said the erk. 'He's gone a bit loopy. We all get a bit bomb-happy from time to time.' The pilots nodded, *oh, I see.*

'Where are we supposed to go?' Edward asked, his parachute, knapsack and helmet bundled in his arms.

'To dispersal, apparently,' said Harry, pointing to one end of the airfield. Hundreds of men were scurrying busily, RAF and Army mixed together.

'Jesus,' said Lucky again. 'What the hell is this place we've come to?'

Dispersal was a battered-looking concrete shed, pockmarked with shrapnel blasts. Alex and the fifth pilot among them, another Englishman named Don Routledge, were already standing outside, talking to an exhausted-looking squadron leader. Several pilots lolled on a number of canvas stretchers placed in front of the building, while others squatted on lumps of rock. They, too, wore a variety of battered clothes, in various hues of cream and khaki.

'Ah, welcome,' said the Squadron Leader as the three of them reached dispersal. 'Tony Pallister. I'm in charge of 636 Squadron here. Sorry about the welcome, but if there's one thing I'll say for Jerry, it's that he's regular as clockwork. There's usually another visit early afternoon. Never many bombers during the day, although they always come protected by swarms of 109s. Then things start hotting up again once it gets dark. Hundreds of the bastards. They like to keep us awake.' He grinned, showing black gaps between his teeth. He looked around, making a sweep with his hands before clapping them together again. 'Well,' he said. 'I imagine this must all be a bit of a surprise. A bit different from what you've been used to in England. I'm afraid it is all rather frugal. Everything's a bit limited. We never seem to have enough of anything. The erks have to work like demons, and really it's amazing what they manage. We've even had to strip down two aircraft with not much wrong with them for spares. Ridiculous really, but what can you do? Anyway, gorgeous day.'

'Is it always like this?' asked Harry.

'God, no. We've had terrible weather this year. January was atrocious, although we weren't complaining. Didn't see Jerry for days at a time – it was bliss. No, it's only in the past week or two that things seem to have picked up. This place dries pretty quickly. You'd never guess it was completely waterlogged a few weeks back. Like a bloody lake. We had a bit of riot as quite a lot of snipe suddenly came in. It was like something out of the Fens. Anyway, we all took potshots. Boosted the daily ration no end.' Edward looked across at the dusty bowl in front of him. He could not imagine it ever looking like any part of England. 'Fiendishly hot in the summer of course,' added Pallister. 'So hot you have to watch yourself getting into your aircraft. I got some quite nasty burns last summer.' He scratched his chin thoughtfully, then said, 'I have to say, we're all feeling a bit blue that you've not come with Spitfires.'

'So are we,' said Lucky.

'Any idea when they might be coming?' Tony asked. 'We're usually the last to know.'

Lucky shrugged. 'Well, sir, soon I'd guess – in the next week, or so we were told at Gib.'

'Less of the sir, all right? Tony's fine.' He rubbed the back of his head, and tutted. 'It's always a couple of weeks.' Another weather-beaten young man with thick, matted brown hair ambled over. 'Ah,' said Tony, 'meet Chuck Cartwright. He's 'A' Flight commander.'

Chuck held out a hand to them all. 'Hi,' he said. They introduced themselves, then looking at Lucky, Chuck said, 'American, right?'

'Right. Burbank, California. You? You're Canadian.'

Chuck grinned. 'You bet. Vancouver.'

'We've got all sorts here,' said Tony. 'Aussies, Kiwis, Canadians, Rhodesians, a couple of Yanks in 126 Squadron. Even a few Englishmen.' He introduced a few more of the pilots, and pointed out those who were asleep. Edward noticed that many of the pilots absent-mindedly scratched themselves – on their arms, or legs or head; even those asleep, rather like a dozing dog in a patch of sun. He peered into the dispersal hut. A few chairs, a couple of large rocks and the remains of another wooden chair scattered and splintered on the ground. Pictures of naked women glued roughly to the wall flapped gently in the breeze. Edward looked down and saw a lizard scamper across his foot, then stepped outside again to stand with the others. Creaking towards them was an old wooden cart full of fuel cans, pulled by a skinny mule nodding its head slowly and mournfully. A Maltese man, a wide hat on his head and a thick moustache covering his top lip, clutched a whip, his shoulders hunched. 'Bit of a bore actually, but we've just lost our last bowser,' said Tony. 'Can't see how we're ever going to get another one, so that means doing it all by hand from now on – with, of course, a bit of help from the locals.' They all followed his gaze towards the cart as it plodded slowly towards them.

'Anyway,' said Tony. 'This is Takali, for better or worse. We spend a lot of time here at dispersal, although as you can see, we keep the aircraft pretty spread out around the airfield.' He looked behind him. 'No buildings as such. Most maintenance is done in the pit over there and in the caves.' He gestured towards a rough cliff that bordered the edge of the field. Caves had been dug into the cliff, but in front was a large seventy yard-long trench. 'It protects us from the worst of the blast, and so far, we've had no direct hits. As I say, the erks do amazing things here. Extraordinary in the circumstances.'

'Was the pilot all right?' Edward asked. 'The one that just came in?'

'Bobby? Yes, he should be. A bullet grazed his head. I think he's suffering concussion more than anything.'

'And what's that?' asked Harry, pointing to a lone building standing shakily on the far side of the airfield.

'The Mad House,' Chuck told them. He grinned. 'We were still using that as a mess when we first got here. Amazing place, all marble and grand staircases. Of course, it was a lot bigger then.'

'I think Jerry uses it as a marker,' added Tony. 'They've been chipping away at it bit by bit, but it refuses to collapse completely. Can't imagine it'll be with us for much longer, though.'

'Nah. Give it another six weeks, max,' said Chuck.

The grinding of gears made them turn. Coming towards them was a bus, wheezing gently and clattering whenever it hit a rut or went over a rough bit of ground. 'This should be the others,' said Tony. They watched as the bus drew towards them. 'That's seen better days,' Harry muttered to Edward. All the glass from the windscreen and windows had gone, as had one of the wings. Bullet holes peppered its sides, while one half of the bonnet flapped loosely, shaking from the uneasy rhythms of the engine.

'Well, on you get,' said Tony. 'This is going to take you to your quarters. See you later.'

They joined the other five pilots, all of whom had made it safely, but who were equally dazed by their first hour on the Island. Back around the airfield they jolted, before joining a road that led towards the citadel on the hill that overlooked Takali. Rubble littered their way. For the most part, the driver was able to easily wind his way through, but occasionally rock scraped against the side of the bus, grinding noisily and causing the bus to judder and the pilots to clutch their seats. No-one said much. What was there to say? Most had volunteered for this. Edward looked at Harry, and smiled weakly. *What have we done?*

The bus began to climb up a long hill towards the town. Edward looked out through the glassless window, squinting from the dust worked up by the bus, towards the towering walls and buildings of the citadel, and the great dome and pinnacles of the church. The ground then dropped and rose again, climbing towards another cluster of buildings and what appeared to be a clock tower, standing proudly against the blue sky. 'I don't know anything about this place,' he said to Harry. 'I didn't even really know where it was until we reached Gib.'

'All I know is that St Paul was washed up here during a storm,' Harry told him. 'And there was a siege in fifteen-sixty-something. The Knights Templars held out against the Turks.'

'How on earth do you know that?'

Harry shrugged. 'Nelson came here too, after the Battle of the Nile, and helped the Maltese kick out the French. That's when it became British – or around then, anyway. Didn't you do any history at school?'

'Yes, but not that.'

The driver crunched the gears again, the engine coughed, and the bus came almost to a standstill before lurching forward again just as the first buildings rose directly beside them. Then the driver turned, climbed a further stretch of even steeper hill and stuttered into a market square that overlooked almost the entire Island. The town was bare of almost any vehicles, save an equally dilapidated but less bullet-riddled bus. Mules stood forlornly at the head of carts, their ribs bulging through mangy coats. Maltese men and women ambled past; children, many without shoes, ran and shouted.

They trundled on, past the market square and onto a stone bridge across what appeared to be a dried moat, and under a large ornate gateway. It reminded Edward of the castles of North Wales he had visited as a boy. He thought: we're the knights of this new siege, and wondered whether the men of four centuries before had walked beneath these same gates with similar waves of nausea and dread churning in their stomachs.

The citadel was quiet and still. High walls loomed above them, casting dark shadows across their way. The din of the engine, its rough spluttering, was accentuated in these closed surroundings. They turned a corner, down a narrow street, then emerged into a courtyard before an ornate palazzo. The driver braked squeakily and brought them to a halt. 'Here we are,' he said in a thick accent.

The Xara Palace – pronounced *Shara*. Owned by the Baron Chapelle, a Maltese Knight of St John, but requisitioned by the RAF, and one of the largest houses in the ancient citadel of Mdina. The pilots stepped out, clutching their bags. Flight Lieutenant Bagshawe, the intelligence officer at Takali, ushered them into a long cool hallway of thick stone. It seemed dark after the brightness outside, the air filled with a damp mustiness. 'Most of us are here now,' he said. 'The officers at any rate. The night-fighter boys were the first in, but most of the other places have all been bombed out. So far, this has proved impregnable.' He looked around, then touched a chair. 'Touch wood.' Bagshawe was short, with a clipped and greying moustache. Edward guessed he was about forty. He spoke with a faint Scottish lilt. 'I'll show you your rooms, and the mess. We'll have lunch then get you back to the airfield. Sound all right?'

The rooms were large, with high ceilings, wooden floorboards and thick walls. Butch Hammond was given a room of his own, while the others were split into threes. Edward and Harry were put in a room with Lucky. The paint was peeling in the corners and spots of mould flecked one wall, but although the same pervading smell of damp filled the air, it was front-facing, built into the bastion walls. Harry pushed back the wooden shutters and looked out of the window. 'My God,' he said, 'what a view.' Edward and Lucky came over. Below, a mile or two away, was Takali, but beyond they could see a number of small towns and villages, church towers and domes rising above the houses. In the far distance were the harbours, and the capital, Valletta. Smoke was still drifting into the sky. Further south, Luqa airfield was also clearly visible. 'Must be the best view on the Island,' said Edward.

It wasn't. Two floors above them was the mess, with its open balcony. From here, even more of the Island lay spread before them. 'Just there – almost next door – with the clock tower, that's Imtarfa,' Bagshawe told the assembled pilots. 'The military hospital. I'm afraid the enemy use the tower as another bomb marker for Takali. Rather unfortunate, really. And that's Mostar,' he continued, pointing to a huge domed church that dominated the town just beyond the northern edge of Takali. 'Bloody good mess, don't you think? Now I'm afraid I can't tell yet which of the three fighter squadrons you'll be joining, but you will be staying put here and operating from Takali. The AOC is going to visit this evening along with Woody, the Ground Controller, so I'm sure they'll put you in the picture then.'

Lunch in the Mess. Two thin slices of corned beef and a slab of stale bread. Edward was starving – breakfast felt like a lifetime ago and he was still hungry after he'd eaten what he'd been given. He was not alone. Most of the pilots looked dejected. 'It hadn't occurred to me that there wouldn't be much food,' Harry said to him. 'I mean, it's obvious when you think about it – the Island's under siege – but this is going to take some getting used to.'

'You're telling me. I wonder what the drink situation is like.'

'Probably not very good. Eddie, what are we going to do?'

They were told the bus would collect them again at three. Edward was getting some sleep when, just after two o'clock, air-raid sirens began wailing over the Island. He woke feeling disorientated, then Lucky came in and said, 'Come on, we're going up to the balcony to watch.'

'Shouldn't we be taking cover in some kind of shelter?'

'Do you know where it is?'

'No,' Edward confessed.

'Well, then. Anyway, look at the width of these walls.'

A number of pilots were already there, including some of those who had been at Takali earlier, leaning on the wooden balcony to watch the show. Eight Hurricanes had taken off already, but were now out of sight. The bombers were still invisible when the first puffs of anti-aircraft fire began peppering the sky, their reports following hollowly some seconds later. Once again, the enemy had made for the docks first. Explosions and the muffled crump of bombs exploding began filling the air. More smoke shrouded the harbours.

'Here they come,' said someone. Edward strained his eyes, then saw a formation of around ten bombers wheeling over Hal Far and Luqa airfields. Tiny dots began swirling high above. 'The Hurricanes,' said Hammond. One bomber was seen diving towards the sea, smoke trailing. They all cheered. The guns based around the airfields began opening up, deep, sharp cracks from the heavy guns and a lighter, more rapid rate of fire from the Bofors. Black puffs dotted the skyline. Suddenly enemy bombers were diving over Takali once more, the anti-aircraft guns and sound of exploding bombs now quite deafening, even from where the pilots were watching. The airfield disappeared under a cloud of dust, smoke and debris, then five 109s appeared through the haze, just fifty feet from the ground, climbed and screamed over them.

'Bloody nerve!' shouted Hammond, who shook his clenched fist at them as they disappeared from sight. 'Just wait 'til I have a go at those bastards.' He glowered at the other pilots, then turned and went inside.

An afternoon spent hanging around dispersal, talking to the old hands and trying to make a rapid adjustment to their new surroundings. Most of 636 Squadron had disappeared. They appeared to work in shifts; 126 Squadron was now on duty. 'There's no point in us all being here,' said one. 'After all, there's nothing like enough aircraft for us all.' The steamroller had been damaged on the last raid, so a number of the ground crew were frantically trying to repair it. 'Without it we're buggered,' said another of the pilots. 'It's hard enough filling in the craters as it is.'

Edward listened attentively. It seemed Takali had only recently started to come under regular and heavy attack. During the first week of February, the pre-war station offices had been destroyed. A week later, the old barracks blocks, where the ground crew had lived, had also been destroyed. Rubble and contorted steel lay heaped in piles; shards of glass twinkled in the sunlight. Their ten Hurricanes were the first fighters to arrive on the island since the previous November. 'These crates we've been flying are pieces of crap,' said one. He was an American – there were a number in the squadron, all volunteers. 'Couple of weeks back, my engine cut out on me *five* times.' He held up his hand to emphasise the point.

'What did you do?' asked Harry.

'Well, fortunately it was while we were providing air cover for a ship, so I kept diving and the engine started again. If there'd been any yellow-nosed fuckers humming around I'd have been toast. Another of the guys was coming in to land and a hundred feet off the deck his engine seized completely. Of course, he had to crash land. What else could he do? Let me tell you, this is no place to crash land in a hurry. You may or may not have noticed, but the whole goddam place is covered with stone walls – there's not a field on the island long enough to land a plane. So he crashes straight into one of these walls, smashes his head open on the gunsight, and breaks his shoulder. And he was lucky. The Hurricane was nothing but a piece of scrap. And he was a good guy.' He cleared his throat, spat, then said, 'Ah, hell. I tell you, it's bad enough trying to fight when you're completely outnumbered without that kind of shit happening.' Even a brand-new Hurricane straight out of the factory would struggle against the latest 109s and Italian Macchi 202s, he told them, but the ones they had on Malta had been repaired and botched and patched up so many times, and often with ill-matching parts, that their performance levels had shrunk further. It took them at least fifteen minutes to climb to fifteen thousand feet, by which time the enemy were already over the Island. 'The moment you try to attack a bomber, you've got half a dozen 109s and 202s bearing down upon you.'

'So what are the tactics?' asked Edward.

'Tactics?' The pilot snorted. 'There aren't any. Have a quick squirt at the bombers and pray to God you haven't already been hit yourself so you can dive out of the way. Hit the deck, then home.' Landing was also hazardous in the extreme, he warned them, because by that time, the airfield would be covered in bomb craters. 'Look, sorry,' he said. 'I'm not trying to put the fear of God into you or anything, but there's no point beating about the bush. We haven't a hope in hell here. Not until they give us some better machines in which to take on these fucking Krauts and Eyeties. Better machines and plenty of 'em.'

*

7.10 p.m. Air Vice-Marshal Hugh Pughe Lloyd strode into the mess at the Xara Palace, followed by Group Captain 'Woody' Woodhall. 'Good evening, gentlemen,' said the Island's commanding officer, then turned to face them, hands on his hips, legs spaced apart, and with his cigarette holder still clamped into one side of his mouth. He stared at the pilots assembled in front of him, his pale eyes sweeping briefly from man to man. Two creases ran from either side of his nose to the corners of his mouth. Almost a sneer, Edward thought. 'Hugh Pughe' the others had called him; everyone seemed to have a nickname, even the chief.

'Welcome to Malta,' he began. 'I know most of you have volunteered to come here and for that I'm most grateful. We are in the middle of a deadly battle, and each and every one of you will play a critical role. History is being made, and you are a part of it. Remember that.' He paused dramatically. The room was utterly silent. Edward had a sudden urge to cough, but managed to control himself until Lloyd began speaking again. 'We are in the middle of a siege, gentlemen, a siege that began twenty months ago when the Italians declared war on Britain and began sending their bombers over. Well, let me tell you that things have hotted up considerably in recent months. As you will no doubt have already discovered, the Germans have joined in too, and I'm afraid right now we have our backs to the wall. Hitler and the *Duce* have assembled a mighty air fleet against us. On Sicily there are over five hundred German and Italian aircraft – you've seen some of them already, I think. We have nothing like that number. We ask a lot of our fighter pilots, but so far no man has let us down. You are the Island's defenders – you and the artillery. The gunners are splendid fellows and you will find them worthy comrades, but I'm not going to deny that a hard and arduous task faces you. Now I know you have flown in new Hurricanes, but you have all been brought here because you are Spitfire pilots, and when the Spitfires arrive – and they will arrive, very soon – you will be flying them. More will follow, and more complete squadrons, and then we will show the enemy that they've picked a fight with the wrong people. I know the German, gentleman. I fought him in the last war and believe me, he hasn't changed a bit. He's still nothing but a cowardly bully. And like all bullies, when hit back, he doesn't like it.' From outside a faint whirr could be heard, becoming rapidly louder. Harry nudged Edward. The others began looking around and even Hugh Pughe stopped and listened. 'A slight interruption I believe, gentlemen,' said Lloyd, just as the sirens rang out once more. Moments later there was a whistling in the air. Edward's heart seemed to freeze in his chest. An explosion shook the building, bursting the wooden window shutters inwards. Scraping chairs as the pilots quickly lay down on the floor, hands over their heads. Only Lloyd remained standing, defiantly leaning against one of the walls. More bombs followed in quick succession. Edward glanced at Harry, saw him grimacing, his eyes shut tight. The noise was deafening, the whistling a terrible sound that seemed to signal an inevitable death. The building shook repeatedly, dust fell from the ceiling, followed by a chunk of plaster, which crashed to the floor and split into a million pieces.

It was over quickly. Silence returned, suddenly, save the increasingly faint whirr of aero-engines. *I'm still alive*, thought Edward, lifting his head. Hugh Pughe was back in the centre of the room. 'All right, gentlemen, as I was saying.' Bashfully, the pilots clambered to their feet, dusting themselves down as they did so. Edward was glad for his chair; his legs felt weak. So this was life in the front line, he thought: bombed day and night, never knowing when a hundred-pound lump of iron and high explosive might land on your head. Harry looked pale. *He's thinking the same*, thought Edward. Even Lucky was chewing his nails.

'As I was saying,' said the AOC once more. '636 Squadron has suffered badly over the past ten days. They're low on pilots and are barely operational. But I'm re-forming it as of now. You men are going to provide the nucleus of the new Spitfire strike force, and all of you will be joining 636 immediately – all except Squadron Leader Hammond, who is promoted to Wing Commander and will become station commander at Takali. Squadron Leader Pallister will be your immediate CO, but Hammond will be responsible for turning you and later squadrons into the fist that strikes back at the Hun. Don't forget that Malta's primary role is an offensive one. We might not be taking the fight to the enemy much at the moment, but we will again, and soon. We *will* have our day, and it will be you who will be able to savour that victory. Years from now, you'll all be proud to have been here. This is a great air battle and we are going to win. All clear?' The pilots nodded. 'And one final thing.' He swept his eyes over them once more. 'Good luck, gentlemen.'

Later, in their room. The canvas camp bed was rather like a stretcher and not quite wide enough to ever get really comfortable. Edward lay on his back, hands behind his head, staring up at the dark nothingness above him. A monumentally long day – were they really still on the *Furious* this morning? – but despite his exhaustion, he could not sleep.

He heard Harry try and turn, and so sighed quite audibly to let the other two know he was still awake. No response. *Lucky them,* he thought. He wondered how he was going to get through the next few months – through even the next few days. He knew he would be flying some time very soon, but that American had put the wind up him, and he prayed that when he did fly, it would be in one of the new Hurricanes and not some wreck in which his engine was likely to seize. And although he now had plenty of flying experience and knew how to handle a plane, he and Harry were horribly untested in action. Adventure, action, excitement: it was what they had craved – he especially – and yet already he realised what a fool he'd been. A wave of despair swept over him. He no longer trusted his ability; he'd had no idea the front line could be like this. What a difference from England, where new Spitfires and new parts arrived regularly, where there was plenty to eat, and pubs to visit and girls to dance with at weekends. Where he could visit his parents every few weeks. He thought of his parents now, of his mother trying hard not to cry, and the swagger with which he'd told her not to worry about him, that he would be fine. Now he wasn't so sure. And yet the AOC's speech had stirred him, appealing to some of the romantic notions he had felt on leaving England; that they were on a crusade like the knights of old. They were even living within the bastion walls of a medieval fortress. All he had to do, he now told himself, was survive until the promised Spitfires arrived. Everything would be better then. In the meantime – well, they were here, and there was nothing they could do about it.

The air-raid siren suddenly burst into life. *Again?* And once more, the gap between beginning its wailing and the whistle of bombs was desperately small. The already familiar hum of aero-engines could be heard, then explosions from over the airfield, the thunder of the 3.7 inch guns and the pom-pom-pom of the Bofors. Lucky and Harry were awake now, cursing, Lucky ranting and swearing that he was going to make them pay. The explosions drew nearer, until they heard the whistle of the bombs falling from the sky, and felt the ancient palace tremble. 'Best to stay where you are during a night raid,' they had been told that afternoon. 'Otherwise you'll never get any sleep. In any case, the walls are as good as any shelter.' What about the roof? Edward had wanted to ask, but had not dared. And so they stayed in their beds, Edward wearing his tin hat, clutching his sheets, and praying they might be spared.

Dust and bits of plaster clattered onto his helmet. 'Who's wearing their tin hat?' asked Lucky.

'Me,' said Edward and Harry together.

'I've got mine a bit lower down,' he told them, 'where it really matters.' And then they all began to laugh.

'It's not funny,' yelled Harry, as their laughter grew increasingly hysterical. A final crash nearby, followed by more plaster pattering down onto their steel helmets, and prompting a renewal of uncontrollable laughter. Overhead, the bombers whirred back into the night. A stillness returned once more to the besieged island.

Everything about Malta had shocked Edward – the toughness, the shortages of absolutely everything, the appalling conditions in which they were expected to operate. His first flight from the island had been two days after his arrival. Not in one of the new planes, but an old model, a relic of the last large batch the previous November. No form 700 to sign off – when he'd mentioned it, the fitter had looked at him blankly.

'Form 700, sir?'

'Yes, the form 700,' he had said. 'The form that you should tick when you're going through the daily servicing.'

The erk had still looked blank.

'You do service them daily, don't you?'

'Yes, sir, as best we can.'

The machine hardly inspired confidence. Paint flecked, squadron symbols roughly hand-painted over old ones, streaks of oil running down the cowling. The tyres on the wheels looked horribly flat. Edward took off, feeling every bump and jolt as he rumbled down the runway. Some bombers had been spotted taking off from northern Sicily. 'Big jobs,' Woody, the Ground Controller had told them. 'Looks like just a handful. Four, I would say.' The three of them climbed slowly. Edward kept the throttle as wide open as he could, but its sluggishness still took him aback, the engine screaming, and the airframe shaking violently as they struggled to gain height. Out over the sea, twinkling in the sunlight. Higher they climbed, into the sun, until they had reached twenty-four thousand feet, then they turned, sun behind them with Malta away below, tiny and insignificant.

Chuck Cartwright was leading. 'This is Tiger Leader. Can't see a thing.'

'Chuck, they're at angels seventeen.' Woody's voice, rising up from Fighter Control, deep underground beneath Valletta, was calm, steady. 'They've some little jobs with them, travelling fast at angels twenty so keep a good lookout.'

Edward looked around, but could see nothing. According to

Woody, the bombers should be some seven thousand feet beneath them. Then way below, and almost over Malta, he spotted the distinct shape of four Junkers 88s.

Chuck had spotted them too. 'OK, I see them,' he said leading them into a dive. Go for the bombers, Hugh Pughe had told them that first night, always the bombers, but just watch your arses for the little jobs. So now they dived, engines screaming once more. Edward glanced at his dials, the arrows all flickering wildly. Once more the airframe shook violently. His heart was drumming, but even then he felt more concerned about whether his Hurricane would remain in one piece than he did about having to fire or be fired on.

They dived behind, apparently unseen, but by then it was too late. Both bombers and Messerschmitts were away from them before they even got close. Even with his throttle through the gate, Edward's Hurricane was struggling to gain three hundred miles an hour. The enemy simply pulled away.

Soon after they were coming into land again, circling in from the south. An aircraft was on fire, thick black smoke billowing up into the sky and partly covering the airfield. Chuck came in first followed by the Rhodesian, Zulu Purnell. Edward lowered the undercarriage, but nothing happened. His manifold pressure was now rising violently, as was his temperature gauge. Ripping off his oxygen mask, his breathing quickened dramatically. Someone fired a flare – *your wheels are still up* – so he opened the throttle as much as he dared, and banking, turned again, pressing the undercarriage lever again and again, until at last – *thank God* – he heard the familiar whirr as the wheels dropped into place. Touching down, he closed his eyes, relief surging through him, then opened them again only to see, too late, a large pothole, the remains of a poorly repaired bomb crater, looming towards him. Braking hard he veered violently to one side but not before his port-side wheel had clipped the edge of the hole, causing the leg to collapse. As the aircraft toppled over and lurched to one side, a wing scraping angrily along the ground and the wooden propeller shattering and splintering before his eyes, Edward wondered whether he would survive. Utterly powerless to do anything about it, he felt surprisingly detached, as though it was happening to someone else rather than himself. As he continued to race along the ground, jolted and thrown about the cockpit despite his harness, he saw that the Hurricane was circling in a wide arc towards a parked Beaufort on the far side of the field. 'Oh please, no,' he said aloud, and shielded his arms to his face. Seconds passed, but finally the machine ground to a halt. Edward lowered his arms. The Beaufort stood directly in front of him, just fifteen yards away.

Harry had been one of the first to the scene, having run across the airfield along with a number of ground crew the moment Edward had lost a wheel.

'My God, Eddie, are you all right?' he said as Edward slid off the wing.

'I think so.' He felt something running down his face, and lifting a hand touched it and saw that his fingers were red with blood.

'Let me look. Take your helmet off.'

Edward did so, and watched Harry as his friend peered at his head.

'You've just nicked it, I think. Hurt anywhere else?'

'No – knee's a bit sore, but no, otherwise, I think I'm fine.'

'Jesus, you had me worried.'

Edward had not flown since. Butch had been as good as his word, although most days they'd been on standby – 'A' Flight in the morning, 'B' Flight in the afternoon, and then vice versa. Anyway, there were hardly ever enough planes to fly; more often than not only one section would ever get airborne. The rest of the time, they sat around the stone hut at dispersal, playing cards, writing letters, watching the lizards dart between the rocks. And when they were not flying, they were frequently ordered to help build aircraft blast pens, filling disused four-gallon fuel cans with sand and grit, then piling them high into a U-shaped wall. Laborious manual labour interspersed by moments of sheer terror as half a dozen Junkers screamed overhead, dropping their bombs. Almost worse were the fighters – mostly 109s, who suddenly appeared, fifty feet off the ground, tearing over the airfield and peppering the ground with machine-gun bullets and cannon fire, lines of dust and razor-sharp rock splinters bursting lethally into the air. The ack-ack teams pounded away furiously, but what chance did they have when the Messerschmitts sneaked upon them and flew over in a blur at over three-hundred-and-fifty miles per hour?

At least they had Butch Hammond. The new Wing Commander had not waited long to exert his influence. Just a few days after his arrival, he called all three squadrons for a talk in the mess at the Xara Palace. He stood before them as Hugh Pughe had the night they arrived, but, Edward thought, Butch cut a more imposing figure. Taller than the AOC, his oiled hair combed back against his scalp, he picked nonchalantly at a fingernail until everyone quietened down.

'All right, everyone,' he said eventually to the more than sixty pilots assembled. His voice was deep and clear, almost a growl. 'I know what you're all feeling. The Hurricanes are a disgrace and you're not very happy about it. Well, neither am I, but until the Spits get here we're just going to have to make the best of what we've got, and that means flying these old crates as effectively as we possibly can.' He paused, eyeing his congregation. Someone coughed. Hammond placed his hands on his waist, legs apart. 'We've got to change how we fly. There's no place now for tight-formation vics of three aircraft. At the speed these Hurricanes can go, all we're doing is offering a bigger target for Mr Messerschmitt's fighters. From now on, we will only fly in pairs and fours, and so on. Leader and wingman, and at a healthy distance apart. The leader will go after the bomber and the wingman will follow, watching the leader's arse for any attack by the 109s. Each section will now consist of not three, but four pilots. It's the same system the Germans use and, as I think you'll agree, they've more than ably proved its effectiveness. I've also had a word with the ack-ack boys. They do a bloody good job, but they've promised to step up efforts to protect the airfields, and will do their best to send up as thick a wall of steel as they possibly can when you're all coming in to land. They understand the need to keep the 109s out of harm's way when you're landing.' He paused again, then said, 'Now, I'm afraid there's been a fuck-up at Gib. The Spitfires are going to be delayed.' The whole room let out a collective groan. 'I know,' he said, 'it's bloody typical. Apparently, some modifications need to be made before they can go on the aircraft carrier, but we've been assured we're talking about only a couple of days. That means they should be here around 6th or 7th March. Until then, we're going to keep flying to an absolute minimum. All right? Everyone clear about what I've said? Squadron

Leaders and Flight Commanders have already been briefed, so if anyone's unsure about the new finger-four system, ask them, or see me personally.' He cleared his throat. 'We've got to keep our heads and make sure we keep as sound in body and spirit as we possibly can.'

Moments after he finished, the bombers returned again. Once more the pilots collapsed onto the ground, clutching their heads as the whistle and explosions of bombs and the crack of anti-aircraft fire shattered the air and shook even the great bastions of Mdina.

7th March, 1942. Fifteen Spitfires finally appeared over the island, touching down on Takali as surviving Hurricanes circled above them. Somehow, news that the Spitfires were coming had spread throughout the Island, because there to witness this historic scene were hundreds of Maltese – workers and civilians, men and women, old and young – who clapped and cheered as the first one safely touched down. Not a single enemy bomber had appeared, not even while the ground crew frantically took off the extra petrol tanks and began servicing the aircraft ready for action. It was not until well into the afternoon that any enemy bombers made a raid, and even then their appearance was, for once, a fairly lacklustre affair, and concentrated on Luqa rather than Takali. A miracle had occurred, the Maltese exclaimed. As the pilots returned to Mdina at the end of the day, an old woman approached them. 'First these magnificent aircraft arrive,' she said, waving her finger at them, 'then of the Germans, there is barely a sign. God is with us. God will save Malta.'

Edward wondered whether she was right. Despite the vast number of churches he had seen when he had first flown over the island, and despite the fact that the huge dome of Mostar's church could be so clearly seen from the airfield, he had given little thought to the religiousness of the Maltese people. Really, he'd barely given them much thought at all: they were just there, dirty-looking and threadbare, olive-skinned men with dark hair and whiskers, servants at the Xara Palace or bringing fuel carts up to the airfield. In Rabat and Mdina, the children were filthy, faces smudged, their hair matted and dusty, feet often shoeless.

For the first time in his life, he envied those for whom a belief in

God meant so much. That faith, that comfort – he wished he could draw strength from it at such a time.

The subject of religion came up again later that evening in the mess, as Edward played poker with Laurie, Harry and Alex McLeish.

'Amazing, don't you think, how the Maltese thank God rather than the British government?' said Laurie.

'Oh, I don't know,' said Harry. 'They're a devout people. The church is at the very heart of their lives.'

'Yeah, I'd noticed that,' said Laurie

'It's easy to forget that this is their island,' Harry continued. 'I mean, we think we're fighting out here to help save Britain and beat Germany, but the Maltese see it differently. We're here to help God save them and the Island. For them this is like two summers ago in England, when we all expected German paratroopers any moment.'

Yes, thought Edward, *you're right.* 'It must be good to be able to place such faith in God,' he said. 'I can't say it's ever really done much for me – religion, I mean. I always associate God with my village church as a boy and chapel at school. Repeating the same old guff over and over.'

'I think He's a great comfort,' said Alex. 'Gives life meaning.'

'I'm glad for you, Alex,' said Lucky. 'Red's the same – prays regular as clockwork, but then he's from God-fearing Tennessee where they're all a bit that way inclined. But let me tell you something: they're going to need all the faith they can get their hands on. Fifteen Spits ain't going to go very far.'

'More will come now,' said Harry. 'That's what Baggy said.'

'Good,' said Laurie, 'because I'm sick of those fucking Hurricanes. If I die because of engine failure, I'm not going to be happy.'

Bagshawe walked in a moment later behind Butch Hammond. They were both holding tumblers of something pale. 'All right, chaps?' said Butch, glancing at their group.

'Just talking about the Spits, sir,' said Laurie. 'The Malts think they were sent from God not the Air Ministry.'

'I think they might be right,' said Butch, and wandered off. Bagshawe, meanwhile, paused, glanced at Laurie's hand, then winked at the others.

'What did he mean by that, Baggy?' asked Laurie.

'Let's just say Butch doesn't think too much about the Air Ministry's willingness to give us Spits. Or, to put it another way, if they'd sent a few more Spits last year it might have made life here a bit easier.'

'So what the hell's been taking them so long?' asked Lucky.

Bagshawe shrugged, and took a sip of his drink. 'Put it down to some pen-pusher back at Air Ministry. There's plenty of Spits back in Britain. Thousands, even. They've given technical reasons as their excuse – that the Spitfire's undercarriage is too narrow for dirt airfields, that the air filters weren't ready, that it would be too difficult to get them here, and so on and so on.'

'But that's rubbish,' said Edward.

'Of course it is. But you have to remember that there are lots of people running this war who are stupid and ignorant, and who can't see beyond their own back yard. Butch has been raising merry hell about it since he's been here. Threatened to resign last week.'

Lucky whistled.

'Good old Butch,' said Harry.

'Yes, we're lucky to have him.'

Edward had never been good at cards, which was unfortunate because there was often little else to do. Having lost the best part of a pound, he left the others to it and, putting on a sweater and his battle-blouse, went outside to the balcony for a cigarette. The cigarettes they'd brought out with them had already gone and it was hard to stretch out the weekly ration of one packet of low-grade Egyptian cigarettes a week. But a smoke last thing at night had already become a treasured ritual. Cupping his hands to hide the match, he lit one and watched the blue smoke roll into the windless air. He breathed in deeply, the sharp, clean air mingling with the smoke. Not a single light twinkled, but a half moon bathed the island in a soft, milky light. So peaceful, so quiet, the dark sea stretching away to infinity beyond the craggy coastline. *This place*, he thought. Just under three weeks ago, he'd barely heard of it; now he wondered whether he would ever leave.

He thought of the death and violence he'd already witnessed. On his fourth day, one man from the Buffs had been killed and three others were seriously wounded. He'd not seen it, but the news had chilled him; there'd been just a single death during his training when a pupil pilot had stalled and crashed in Canada, and not one during his time with 324 Squadron. Then, just three days before, he and Zulu Purnell had been helping build another blast shelter at the far end of the airfield when three Junkers 88s had dived on Takali. They and the other men all ran for the nearest slit trench – all except one, a ginger-haired lad, who shouted, 'I'm going to get you, you fucking Jerry bastards!' and had run over to the mounted Lewis gun fifty yards away and had begun firing furiously. A single bomb fell near them. In the slit trench, Edward heard the whistle, then Zulu said, 'Jesus Christ!' and clutched his hands over his head, as the ground shuddered and debris rained down on them. One of the erks said, 'Oh my God, Rusty!' The Lewis gun was no longer firing; the bombers had gone and so they all clambered out of the slit trench, dazed and covered in grit, flapping hands in front of their faces to clear away the clouds of smoke and dust. 'Rusty?' one of the men shouted, then another said, 'Oh my God! Oh, Christ, no!' Edward and Zulu rushed over. The man was standing by a single leg, still socked and booted. Edward gasped, and as the dust cleared a stray dog trotted past, Rusty's ginger scalp between its teeth.

He'd vomited. Death had always been something abstract – something that happened, but was never witnessed. But the end for this man, so very alive one minute, and so violently and with so little dignity killed a moment later, shocked him deeply.

Worse was to follow. There had still been some flying, and just yesterday Chuck and Harry had been sent up after some Stukas that were reported to be heading for the harbours. Normally, Zulu would have been flying as Chuck's wingman, but he had a touch of Malta Dog – dysentery – and was sick in bed. They'd actually caught up with the dive-bombers and Chuck had even shot one down. But just as they were about to land again, the 109s had shown up. Harry had made it safely – somehow dodging the bullets – but Buck's plane was riddled and before his wheels even touched the ground, the ruptured petrol tanks, still half full, had burst into flames. They'd all seen it. Buck's Hurricane seemed to buckle, and plummeted onto the rough field, scraping uncontrollably until it came to rest just a short distance from Harry. From the dispersal hut, the other pilots watched as Buck, slowly enveloped by flames, struggled to get out before disappearing amidst the dense, dark smoke that shrouded him. The death of Rusty had been grotesque, but Edward had not known him; Chuck had been his Section Leader, a stalwart of the squadron. A friend to many.

Standing out there on the balcony, the Island so deceptively peaceful, Edward lit another cigarette – a rare extravagance – and noticed that as he cupped his hands, they were shaking again.

'Here you are.'

Edward turned. 'Harry. I just needed some air. I think I'm going to have to stop playing cards. I'm going to be skint in no time.'

Harry smiled. 'It would be a little foolish to come back broke from an island where there is nothing to spend your money on.' He lit a cigarette himself, then sighed. 'What have we done, Eddie?'

'What, coming here?' Harry nodded. 'I don't know.'

'I can't stop thinking about Chuck,' said Harry. 'I could see him. Could see him and hear him struggling for his life. I don't think I'll ever forget it. And the worse thing is, I did nothing to help him. I was only thirty yards away. I should have run over to him straight away, tried to get him out.'

'Harry, there was nothing you could have done.'

'There was. I should have run to him, but I was paralysed where I was – I was scared, terrified that I would get burnt too.' He turned away and wiped one eye with the back of his hand. 'Christ,' he said. 'What is this place we've come to?'

Edward put a hand on his shoulder. *It'll be OK.* They stood for a moment, smoking, neither saying anything. Then Edward said, 'Would you have volunteered if I hadn't wanted to?'

'Would you if I hadn't?'

They were silent again for a moment until Edward said, 'I wonder whether God *is* on our side.'

'I don't know. But I do know I've done more praying since I've been here than I've ever done in my life. I hope someone's watching out for us. Perhaps it's not the God we know from church, but it's good to think that there's more to it than this, don't you think? That Buck's up there somewhere, in a better place?'

Edward shivered. 'It's cold.'

'Yes – let's go in, Eddie.'

*

Tuesday, 10th March. It had taken three whole days to get the Spitfires ready. They had arrived with the wrong paint scheme, without their guns and cannons properly synchronised. New paint had to be found and mixed up – and this took time – and although most of the 634 Squadron pilots were given a brief test flight on the ninth, it wasn't until shortly after ten the following morning that seven of the new Spitfires were scrambled along with a dozen Hurricanes from Takali and Hal Far.

Butch Hammond had briefed the pilots the night before. As in the Battle of Britain, attacking enemy bombers would be the task of the Hurricanes, he told them. The Spitfires would climb as high as they could, and then, with the sun behind them, would dive and shoot down any escorting enemy fighters. He made it all sound so simple. 'Tomorrow,' he reminded them, 'will be the first time the Spitfire has been in action against the enemy operating from outside the British Isles.' Holding up his hands he said, 'I know – unbelievable isn't it? Two-and-a-half years we've been fighting this war. It's been a long time coming, but those of you lucky enough to be flying them tomorrow can feel rightly proud.'

Since tramping the two-and-a-half miles from Mdina to Takali at first light that morning, it had felt like a long wait. The day had begun grey, and as the morning grew, the thin layer of cloud that covered the Island seemed unwilling to disperse. Laurie Bowles had even begun taking bets that no enemy aircraft would turn up until after the changeover with 'B' Flight at one o'clock.

'You're a fool, Laurie,' Bagshawe had told him.

'It's sod's law, Baggy.'

'But the Germans like to attack just before elevenses. You can set your watch by it. However good their planes might be, and however skilled their pilots, they simply cannot bring themselves to disrupt a well-worn routine.'

Butch Hammond had also been pacing impatiently. He had arrived at dispersal soon after the rest of the pilots, already wearing his mae west and clutching his flying helmet and goggles. 'Well, I'm not going to miss this,' he had told them. Tony had been told to lead Blue section, he would take Green. Four and three – only seven Spitfires were ready and serviceable.

But Bagshawe had been right. Just after ten in the morning, the field telephone rang: a small number of 'big jobs' were on their way. Off the pilots ran, as the engines were primed and started by the waiting ground crew, erupting with a guttural roar. As he neared his blast pen, Edward saw his rigger jump out. 'Good luck, sir,' the airman called out as Edward grabbed his parachute and dinghy pack, clambered onto the wing and lowered himself into the comfortingly familiar pale green cockpit. Moments later, he was taxiing out, watching Butch and his two wingmen thunder down the runway and lift into the sky, a cloud of dust in their wake. And then it was his turn, Tony and Zulu on his left, Harry on his right. Further away, four Hurricanes were also taking off in a line, as Edward gunned his throttle and hurtled down the brown dusty field. Sixty, seventy, eighty, and then ninety miles an hour, a monstrous surge of power that pinned him into his seat. Easing back on the stick, he felt himself rise into the sky, the fields, walls and villages of Malta disappearing beneath him.

Butch had said they could feel proud – well, Edward did. As they climbed to 19,000 feet, through the cloud layer and into the bright burning blue, he glanced around him at the rest of Blue Section, Tony and Zulu ahead and slightly above him, Harry behind, some fifty yards off his starboard wing. Higher still was the section of three Spitfires, Butch out in front, the new deep blue of the underside of their aircraft blending with the richness of the sky. His heart pounded in his chest, that now familiar nausea sat hollowly in his stomach, yet he felt exhilarated too. He twisted and turned his head, squinting as the sun behind him bore down upon them. *Yes,* he thought, *this is much better.* They'd flown Mark IIs in Cornwall, but these new Mark Vs were wonderful; the difference in power over the Hurricanes was extraordinary. In this machine they would show the 109s what they could do. At that moment, he felt invincible once more.

Moments later, enemy fighters were spotted below them and Tony was leading them into attack. A deep breath – a glance at Harry – and then Edward pulled the stick over, watch the horizon swivel, and heard the engine begin to scream. They were upon the 109s in moments. Several thousand feet above and behind the bombers, the enemy never saw the Spitfires coming until Tony opened fire, sending the first spiralling out to sea. Edward heard the anguished radio chatter of the German pilots, watched them frantically break, but managed to latch onto the tail of one, so close he could see its mottled sand and grey fuselage clearly, with its squadron markings and black crosses on the wings vivid and sharp. He even saw the pilot turn his head towards him. Edward fired, watched the tracer from a brief few-second burst of cannon and machine-gun fire streak across the sky and knock off pieces of the 109's tail, which then floated like leaves into the sky.

Another glance behind – *where is everyone?* – then he turned back to the Messerschmitt in front of him, twisting and turning out to sea. Edward fired again, but this time his shots were wide. *Keep still, you bastard.* Back and forth, turning so tight that at times Edward felt his vision blurring, the force of gravity pressing him into his seat. Down they flew, through the cloud, Malta now far behind, until they were just above the wave tops. *Damn!* thought Edward. Ahead, Sicily loomed, the eerie peak of Mount Etna pointing through the haze, dominating the entire island.

He thought for a moment; he was getting too close to enemy shores. *Shit,* he cursed to himself. Just a few inches to the left on that first burst, and he'd have had him. 'Come on,' he told himself out loud, 'time to go home.' Banking, he made one last glance at the Messerschmitt, and saw the German pilot waggle his wings. A sign of respect? Or, *you can't catch me – up yours, Tommy?* Edward couldn't say.

As he landed back down again just under ten minutes later, a number of other Spitfires were taxiing back to their blast pens. Ahead, at the far end of the airfield, lay the remains of another smashed-up Hurricane. He felt suddenly exhausted. Sweat ran from under his helmet and down his face. His shirt clung to his back.

The noise of battle, of aero-engines, of the drum of machine guns and cannon, still rang in his ears, even after he had reached his blast pen, cut the engine and seen the propeller click to a halt. The rapidly cooling engine ticked furiously as Edward undid his wires and harness and heaved himself out of the cockpit.

'You fired your guns then, sir,' said the rigger.

'Yes.'

'Any joy?'

'Took off pieces of his tail but he didn't go down. But we bounced them, you know. They never saw us coming. Tony definitely got one – I saw it. I don't know about the others.'

'Well, they're all back. The Spits that is.'

Edward saw a column of smoke rising from the centre of the Island, a few miles to the west. 'Is that another one?'

'A Hurricane, I'm afraid. Not sure who yet. He came down about twenty minutes ago.'

'Parachute?'

The erk shook his head.

Edward nodded – it was pointless to say anything – then began to walk back to dispersal.

Two more raids appeared over the Island before 'A' Flight were stood down, but on both occasions they were alerted too late. On the second, Edward took off again with the rest of Blue section, but they found nothing; the bombers had reached Hal Far by coming in low under the radar, hitting the officers' mess and quarters, and disappearing again before the Spitfires had barely managed to take off. Then later that afternoon, Edward, Harry and a number of the other 'A' Flight pilots watched a raid of over forty enemy bombers from the balcony of the Xara Palace. Bombs exploded, the chatter of machine guns rang out, engines raced and choked, black puffs dotted the sky; and when the display was over, the airfields of Luqa and Hal Far, away to the south, lay shrouded in dust and smoke, and John McAfferty, a Scottish pilot from 'B' Flight, was being taken to the hospital at Imtarfa, his parachute having failed to properly open. They had watched his Spitfire hurtle into the ground near the Dingli cliffs, a long streak of dark smoke trailing behind. And they'd all flinched a bit as they saw the tiny fireball over five miles away, then, a few seconds later, heard the explosion. John had been due to be posted home a few days later. Instead, they buried him, beneath the orange soil of a rapidly growing cemetery on the hills south of Valletta.

Malta – June, 1995

Edward had asked for a window seat and had been given one, near the front of the plane. He'd brought a book with him, but read little; once they began flying over central France, the cloud cleared, leaving Europe spread out clearly below: the patchwork of clays and greens of France, then the magnificence of the Alps, the peaks – some still capped white with snow – rising up almost to meet them as they flew south. Edward found it fascinating, mesmerising even. Then down below was Italy and he looked away, back to his paperback for a few minutes. *Later,* he thought. *Malta first.* Next time he looked they were travelling over the sea until they reached Sicily, and *yes,* there was Etna, still dominating the entire island. And then it really was just a hop away. Fifteen minutes it had taken the German and Italian fighters to reach Malta; fifteen minutes it had taken the Allies to fly over Sicily during the invasion in '43. As the plane flew back out to sea, leaving the Sicilian coast behind, Edward glanced at his watch. Sure enough, just under a quarter of an hour later they had reached Malta, and there it was, just as he remembered, the summer heat almost shimmering off the dusty villages and fields as they circled overhead and prepared to land.

The Boeing banked, and Edward felt himself almost looking down directly over Grand Harbour – the finger of Valletta and the Three Cities – their distinct outline so very familiar, so that the years, the long passage of time, seemed to slip away.

Luqa, of course, was very different – utterly unrecognisable from the wrecked, blasted airfield he remembered landing on occasionally, with its innumerable unexploded bombs and burntout remains of aircraft littered from one side to the other. He was also surprised by the vast numbers of cars, trucks and buses, and by the endless building work that seemed to be going on. 'It's all started in the last few years,' his taxi driver told him. 'Building, building, building. A lot of money coming in from outside, and of course, Malta's a great holiday destination now. It's big business.'

He was driven straight to the hotel in Sliema, bypassing the finger of Floriana and Valletta. Pleasure boats and yachts, their white hulls and masts dazzlingly bright in the afternoon sunlight, crammed into the creeks and inlets of Marsamxett Harbour. Then they briefly left the sea behind, hurtling down a long street that Edward was sure had been open country when he had last been there, the driver weaving in between and past exhaust-billowing lorries and knocked-about yellow buses. The sea suddenly reappeared and they were driving along an esplanade, the blue sea one side, and a line of hotels on the other. Moments later, the driver pulled the car over and Edward was clambering out, and a porter was hurrying down the steps and offering to take his case.

'Welcome to Malta, sir,' said the porter. 'Is this your first time here?'

Several times during the last week he'd picked up the phone to ring Lucky, but it had been such a long time since he'd spoken to him that he could never quite bring himself to dial the number; telephones could be so impersonal. One couldn't see how the other person was reacting, and he didn't want to throw Lucky off guard by springing himself on him like that, a bolt from the blue. Instead he wrote him a letter, explaining that he was coming out to Malta, would love to see him if at all possible, and not to reply because he would be leaving in a few days. He gave Lucky the name of his hotel and said he would call him on his arrival. *But please don't put yourself out,* he had written. *If you are busy or away, no matter, but it would be lovely to hear from you – it's been too long.*

He had heard nothing since – he'd not really expected to – although he had half hoped Lucky might have rung *him*. Now that he was here in Malta, he felt uneasy again about making the call to a man he had not seen in half a century. *I'll ring him in the morning,* he thought as he walked into the main foyer of the hotel. *Give myself a chance to settle in.*

At the main desk, he handed over his passport and filled in the registration form. 'There's a message for you, sir,' said the receptionist, and handed him an unsealed envelope.

'Ah, thank you,' said Edward, pulling out the note immediately. *Eddie – will see you in foyer Preluna 7 p.m. tonight. Lucky.* Edward put a hand on the counter, then shakily folded the paper and put it in his pocket. Tonight! That only gave him a few hours.

In his room he unpacked, hanging his shirts, trousers, and jackets – a light summer one and a dark blue blazer – in the cupboard. He wasn't sure what he should wear. Normally he wore a tie, but it was hot, far hotter than in England, and he didn't want to seem either too formal or feel uncomfortable. And yet, just to wear an open-necked shirt seemed too far the other way. What if Lucky wanted them to go out to dinner? He would need a jacket, then. 'You're being ridiculous,' he told himself out loud, and went out onto his small balcony. The Mediterranean twinkled in the late afternoon sunlight, cool and inviting. Children shouted and screamed from the pool on the rocks the far side of the road. He looked at his watch – *ten past five. Just under two hours.* He went inside, sat on the bed, stood up again, then decided he would go for a brief walk. A stroll along the seafront, then perhaps tea and a shower. Not for the first time, he wondered whether he was making a terrible mistake.

Wearing a light blue shirt, linen summer jacket, *and* a tie, Edward exited the lift in the foyer at just a few minutes before seven. He spotted Lucky immediately – thick hair still swept back, and like his own, with plenty of dark remaining. But then suddenly he wasn't so sure. Last time he'd seen Lucky, he'd been in RAF blue, peaked cap on his head, and he'd been only about twenty-five; this man's face was lined, with bags under the eyes and liver spots on his forehead. And he was wearing a garish Hawaiian shirt, baggy linen trousers and sandals. Could it really be him? He stopped by the lift a moment, then caught Lucky's eye and at that moment knew for sure.

'Eddie Enderby!' cried Lucky, standing up immediately. 'God-damn! Christ, how long has it been? Fifty years at least! How the hell are you?'

They shook hands, Lucky clasping him by the shoulder as he did so.

'Very well, Lucky. Very well. And you?'

'Ah, can't complain. Well, not too much anyways.' They both eyed each other – *is it really you?* Edward smelt a waft of alcohol on Lucky's breath. 'I don't believe it,' said Lucky, shaking his head. Suddenly Edward could think of nothing to say.

'Look, I thought we could go and get a drink or two, then have some dinner. I've booked us into the Phoenicia. Have you been back up to Valletta yet?'

'No,' said Edward. 'The Phoenicia? Is that the same –?'

'Yeah, it most certainly is. Remember it? Thought you'd like that. And the food's a little better than you might remember.'

'Sounds wonderful, Lucky.'

'And you remember the Xara Palace? Course you do. Well, someone's just gone and bought it and they're going to turn it into a hotel. Next year, you'll be able to come over and stay in our old room. Amazing, ain't it?'

'The Xara Palace. My God.'

Parked directly outside was Lucky's car, an ageing 2CV with a dented front wing. 'Jump in,' Lucky told him, and for a moment Edward wondered whether he should suggest a taxi instead. But Lucky had already got in and was opening the passenger door. 'I apologise,' he said, 'she's not pretty, but when I moved over here, I realised there was no point in getting anything very smart. The Malts drive like lunatics and it's not like I ever go very far. Well, you can't – there's nowhere to go.'

'Must be a bit different from America.'

Lucky laughed. 'You're telling me. I certainly had some big cars out there. But I kind of prefer this one, to be honest. It's easy to repair and I don't get too upset if someone dents a fender or something.'

If Lucky's drinking affected his driving, Edward could not spot it. He seemed in control. Had it not been for the smell of his breath, Edward would have sworn Lucky was completely sober.

A yellow bus, even more aged than Lucky's Citroën, spluttered up the hill from the harbour, thick exhaust smoke belching from its behind.

'What a lot of old buses they have here,' said Edward.

'Incredible, aren't they? You can buy little models of them in every tourist shop in town, although the toy versions never have that dented, fully polluting style of the real ones. Still, they're a damn sight better than that one that picked us up when we first got here. Remember that?'

'How could I forget it?'

'Jesus,' muttered Lucky. 'I don't know how we did it.'

'No.'

The briefest of pauses, then Lucky said, 'Look at Valletta now. That dome wasn't there in our day, and there's a lot less rubble about, but otherwise it looks much the same.'

Edward looked, muttered, 'Stunning,' then said, 'But you live on Gozo, don't you, Lucky?'

'Yeah. Got an old farmhouse. I bought it nearly ten years ago now.'

'Well, it's very good of you to come over to see me.'

Lucky turned and grinned. 'Anything for an old pal. But seriously, it's no sweat coming over. I get in my car, jump on the ferry, and just over twenty minutes later I'm driving onto Malta. And as I said, it takes no time to drive down here. Nothing does.'

'And you'll go back tonight?'

'Sure. Last ferry doesn't go 'til after eleven.'

And so it continued on the short journey to the Phoenicia: observations about Malta and the Maltese, and the weather forecast for the next week (hot and cloudless), until they reached Floriana and Edward began seeing once-familiar landmarks and felt the passage of time slipping away. 'St Publius,' he mumbled.

'What? Oh, yes,' said Lucky. 'And look at the clock on the left.'

Edward looked. 'It's stopped.'

'Exactly. 7.40 – the time the place was bombed. It's been that way since 1942.'

Edward shook his head, then saw they had reached the hotel. It looked almost exactly as he remembered. And opposite was the bus station, where it had always been. Busier, of course, but otherwise much the same.

'And that's the RAF memorial,' said Lucky pointing to a tall eagle-crested column as they got out of the car. 'We can have a look at it. There's a number of names on there that you'll recognise.'

'Yes – I'd like that.' *But not now,* he thought and was glad when Lucky said, 'But first things first: a drink.'

It was still hot outside and already Edward felt in need of cool air and, if he was honest, a drink. The bar provided both. 'What'll you have?' Lucky asked him.

'Gin and tonic, please. With ice.'

'Goes without saying.' He turned to the barman. 'Gin and tonic and a negroni. It's one thing I'll say about you British – you never have cottoned on to ice.'

Edward shrugged. 'I suppose it's rarely warm enough to warrant it.'

'Maybe that's it.' Lucky chuckled and led Edward to a table next to a large indoor fern. 'Cheers,' he said, chinking Edward's glass. 'Damn good to see you, Eddie. I'm trying to think when I last saw you. In England, just after the end of the war.'

'Yes, it must have been. A long time ago.'

Lucky opened his mouth as though he were about to say something, then stopped. 'Well, now,' he said after a moment, 'I want to hear all about what you've been up to for the last fifty years.'

Edward smiled. 'Surprisingly little. At any rate, very little when one considers how much happened during the war.' He told Lucky briefly: about leaving the RAF, marrying Cynthia and his son, Simon, about the school and a lifetime in teaching.

'Christ, I envy you,' said Lucky, finishing his negroni. He looked around, caught a waiter's eye and raised his glass – *another, please* – then turned to Edward. 'How you doin', Eddie? Need a refill?'

'No, I'm fine for the moment, thanks.'

Lucky whistled. 'Boy, do I envy you,' he said again.

'I can't think why. It's been a pretty ordinary life. Dull even.'

'But you settled down afterwards, didn't you? Found stability.'

'I suppose so. In a way.'

Lucky rubbed his neck. 'Well, that's why I envy you.'

Edward eyed him – *go on. I'm listening.*

Lucky sighed, his eyes suddenly distant and wistful. 'I've never really managed to settle,' he said at last. 'I stayed in the RAF as long as I could after the war, but it got kind of boring, so I thought I should head back to the States – after all, I hadn't been back home for the best part of six years. Hadn't seen my family at all in that time. It wasn't the same, though.' His mother had remarried just after he'd joined up, had had more kids, and on Lucky's return, his stepfather made it pretty clear that he didn't want his stepson hanging around about the place. So he left Burbank and headed down to San Diego and began teaching flying at a civilian airfield there. He soon got bored of that too, had a fight with his boss, and was given the boot. For several years he bummed about California, teaching flying and occasionally taking charter flights up and down the coast. Then he met his future wife, Celeste. 'She was a good girl,' he said, 'and her old man sat me down one day and told me he wanted me to join the family construction business. So I married Celeste and quit flying and settled down.' For several years all went well. They were living 'the American dream' in a quiet town north of San Francisco, had a couple of kids, and Lucky was becoming respectable. 'I know, hard to imagine, but it's true.'

But it didn't last. After a while he started to get itchy feet again. 'I wasn't sleeping well, either,' he told Edward. 'You know: bad dreams.'

Edward nodded. *Yes, I know about those.*

'So anyway, I started to drink a bit. I found that if I went to bed with a bit of alcohol inside me, then I slept better. I guess it helped me to forget. And I missed the flying, too. You know, flying was my life when I was younger. The thrill, the excitement of being around those wonderful machines, of taking them high into the sky where no-one could get you. I used to think the sky was my own private kingdom. I liked my father-in-law, don't get me wrong, but he was always there, breathing down my neck. And he didn't like a man who drank.'

Edward sensed what was coming.

'So I started drinking a bit more. Sometimes quite a lot. Sometimes things got a bit out of hand with Celeste . . . you know?' He eyed Edward carefully, but Edward simply nodded. 'I'm not proud of myself,' he said, looking away. Later, he started arguing with his father-in-law. This went on for a few years: occasionally going too far and smacking Celeste, fighting with his father-in-law, winding up drunk more often than was good for anyone. Then one day he got back from work and found that Celeste and the kids had gone. When he went round to his in-laws' house, his father-in-law told him he was fired and that he was no longer welcome in their house. 'He said to me, "D'you think you're the only man in America who lived through the war?" He was right, of course,' said Lucky.

'What did you do?'

'I cleaned up. Went sober for a while. Didn't touch a drop for a dozen years. And I went back to flying. Moved up to Seattle, began instructing again, and with a friend bought into a business that ran tours to Alaska. The most goddam beautiful flying I ever did.' For a while Lucky found peace. But then the nightmares began again and this time he had a full-blown breakdown. 'I was a mess. I suddenly realised how lonesome I was. I hardly ever saw my kids, had lost my wife, and most of my greatest pals in life were dead.' Somehow, he pulled himself together. 'God knows how,' he said, rubbing his forehead. He was still a half-owner of the flying school, a business that was expanding without him. In 1982 he sold up, and decided to go travelling. He went to Britain, back to some of the places he'd known during the war, then travelled on through France and eventually wound up on Malta. 'I never left,' he said and for a moment Edward wondered whether he meant in 1942 or forty years later. Lucky finished his drink with a flourish. 'Well, it's a damn sight nicer here than it used to be in the old days. And I had a bit of money, property was cheap, and I suddenly thought – what the heck, I might as well stay here.'

He suddenly grinned, as though momentarily embarrassed. 'I've been talking too long. I apologise. You can probably tell I don't get to speak about this stuff too much – but, well, you understand Eddie, you know what it's like . . .'

'Don't apologise. I'm sorry you've had a tough time.' Edward smiled at him; Lucky had always worn his heart on his sleeve, even all those years ago.

'Yeah, well, anyway. Time to eat. You must be hungry.'

Once sat at their table, however, and having ordered a bottle of wine, Lucky needed little encouragement to talk some more: one story after another – about his former father-in-law, about misadventures flying over Alaska, and his contact with some of his fellow Eagle Squadron pilots. Lucky was a member of the Eagle Squadron Association, and received regular newsletters. The last time he'd been back to the States had been for a reunion in Charleston.

'Do you miss America?' Edward asked him.

'Do I miss America,' Lucky repeated, turning his wine glass in his hand. 'No. I can't say that I do. I wish I did. I dunno. I suppose in some ways I left America behind when I joined the RAF. I'd been rejected by the US military, and by the time I came back I reckon I was pretty anglicised. Jesus, six years is a long time to be away. And when I got back everything was different. I missed the excitement of flying, but you know what else? I missed the camaraderie. God knows, I really missed that. Nothing has come close to that. What you feel for a bunch of guys that you're living and dying with . . . like we were on Malta back then. I guess everyone else has been a bit of a disappointment. And sure, I know after the war everyone was in the same boat, but in California there wasn't anyone who knew a goddam thing about Malta and what had gone on there. Hell, most people in California didn't even know Malta existed. In California it was all about the Pacific war. That's what counted. If I'd flown over the goddam Solomons or something I'd have probably settled back into life just fine.' He took a deep drink from his glass. 'So now I have a wife I haven't spoken to in years, and a grown-up son and daughter who I see once in a blue moon. I've even got grandkids – five of 'em. I guess I'll probably go back and see them some time in the next year or so. Or maybe they can come and visit me . . .' He let the sentence trail. 'I used to think I *was* Lucky. Now I'm not so sure. What's that line? "They shall not grow old as we grow old". Do you ever think about that, Eddie? Do you ever think sometimes that those guys were the lucky ones?'

'Sometimes.'

'I mean, Christ. Sometimes I think that the only useful thing I've ever done in my life is the five years I spent fighting in the war. That was a time when I was doing something with my life, something worthwhile, you know?' He rubbed his forehead, then ran his hands through his hair.

Edward looked at him. 'I think we've all suffered our fair share,' he mumbled.

'Ah, I dunno,' Lucky continued. 'To think I was so happy when the war was over. I've made it, I thought, I've survived. But now I'm really not so sure. We left a large part of ourselves behind, didn't we, Eddie?'

Lucky had insisted on paying, and Edward had insisted on taking a taxi back to his hotel in Sliema. On this, Lucky had acquiesced; he had been too drunk to do otherwise. He had wondered how on earth Lucky would be able to drive back to the ferry, and had even thought about suggesting he stay the night in the Phoenicia, so he was relieved when, the following morning, Lucky rang him in his hotel room.

'Morning, Eddie, how are ya?'

'Very well. And thank you again for a delicious dinner.'

'Ah, don't mention it. The least I could do after making you listen to the ramblings of an old drunk all night. Anyway, I apologise profusely.'

'You've nothing to apologise for.'

'Well, you're too kind. Anyway, listen, do you want to meet up today? We can visit some of our old haunts.'

'Yes, of course. So long as you don't mind trekking over from Gozo again.'

'Are you kidding? What else would I do all day?'

And so it was arranged. After all, Edward told himself, revisiting old haunts was why he had come back to Malta.

'I thought we could have a look around Valletta,' said Lucky when they met up again in the foyer of the Preluna. It was shortly after eleven in the morning. He was wearing another Hawaiian shirt and Edward was glad he had decided to forego his tie. 'If it's okay with you, we'll leave the car here, and walk down to the harbour,' added Lucky. 'Then we can get the foot-ferry across. And there's always a welcome breeze across the harbour. But I warn you: it's a steep climb the other side.'

Outside, it was another baking hot, cloudless day, the sky a deep, rich blue.

'I'd forgotten how hot it can be,' said Edward as they stepped out into the bright sunshine.

'Gets worse in August, but you're right. I remember that June we were here. Almost no food and relentlessly hot.'

'I burnt my hand once getting into my plane. For some reason I hadn't put on my glove. I got really bad blisters along the tops of my fingers.'

'And nowhere really to get much shade.'

'Well, dispersal certainly didn't have a roof by then.'

They walked down the narrow hill to the corniche, busy with traffic and people alike. Sightseeing boats lined the harbour front, their vividly coloured stands vying for space alongside the ice-cream kiosks.

'Over here,' said Lucky, pointing to a small boat and the line of people queuing to board.

'I can't get over how thriving the place seems to be,' said Edward. 'When we left in July '42, this place was a ghost town. I distinctly remember coming down to Sliema – some of the 601 Squadron boys had a house here – and there was barely a soul about. The harbour was full of wrecks, the submariners had packed up and gone to Alex, and the streets were strewn with piles of rubble. I don't know what I expected, but the difference is so marked.'

'Fifty years is a long time, Eddie. Still, I think if you'd come back twenty years ago it would have looked pretty run down. Malta's only just recently begun to take off, you know.'

Fifteen minutes later, they were stepping off the ferry and beginning the climb up to the centre of Valletta. The place was a city of light and shadows that day. Burnished white limestone, dazzling in the heat, then cool and dark where the tall stonework masked the sun. They took their time to climb the steep streets, pausing frequently to catch their breath.

'Hard work, eh?' said Lucky as the steps briefly levelled off.

'But worth it. The views are marvellous. Anyway, there's no rush, is there?'

'That's true. And as old men we should take things slow,' Lucky chuckled. 'Although you're still pretty sprightly, Eddie. Do you work out or anything?'

Edward laughed. 'What – you mean go to a gym?'

'Sure – or swimming or something.'

'No,' he said, still laughing. 'Nothing like that. I don't eat too much, and I do a lot of walking. Seems to do the trick.'

They continued on up towards the heart of the city, Edward glancing at the old dust-laden doorways and the names above them: Galea, Grech, Borg, Vella, the Maltese Smith and Jones. Old British postboxes and telephone boxes still stood on street corners, still bright red, even though the hundred-and-seventy-year union had been over for more than twenty years.

They passed over a long, dark, narrow street.

'Remember this?'

'My God, yes – it's the Gut!' Edward exclaimed. 'But where have all the bars gone? This place used to be heaving.'

'Not any more. Only time I've ever slept with a hooker was down here.' Lucky grinned.

'Really?' Edward was surprised. 'I don't remember you saying anything at the time.'

'I swear it. It was near the end of our time here. I managed to borrow a bicycle. It was in the middle of the afternoon. To be honest, I just wanted some female company, but actually I got a bit more than that.' He winked.

Edward laughed. 'Lucky – you are extraordinary. I hardly remember talking to any women at all for the whole time I was here. I *thought* about them, and certainly when we were first here, Harry and I used to come into Valletta to go to the cinema quite a lot, just so we could remember what beautiful women looked like. It didn't really matter that the films were always hugely out of date, or that we'd seen them before in England. I didn't mind how many times I watched Dorothy Lamour.'

'There were still a few English girls here. I remember that time with you and Harry singing in the Snakepit.'

Yes, thought Edward, *I remember that. How could I forget?*

They had now reached a large square, filled with tables and brightly coloured sunshades. White-jacketed waiters from the cafés and restaurants around the edge of the square scurried between tables. Lucky suggested they have a drink. 'Don't look so worried, Eddie – only a coffee, all right?' They found a table, sat down and Lucky stretched. 'Must have been March '42. Right after Takali was hit so bad.'

'You're right,' said Edward, 'because those girls left only a few weeks later.'

He closed his eyes for a moment, the dry heat burning his face. It was a pleasant sensation now that he was sitting still. *Close your eyes,* he thought, *and you can be any age and in any time.* And so Edward began remembering once more, back to an afternoon in Valletta, not so very far from where he was sitting now.

Malta – March, 1942

Valletta, 20th March, 1942. It had been Lucky's idea to make a visit to the island's capital. 'I've got to get away from this dump,' he'd said the moment 'A' Flight had been stood down. 'Anywhere but here.' Butch Hammond had overheard him and had offered him a lift to the Hole.

'Any other takers?' Butch had asked. Well, there weren't many who would miss the opportunity of a ride into Valletta. Most of the flight took up his offer, Edward and Harry included. 'You'll have to make your own way back, though,' Butch had warned them. *Whatever* – they would cross that path as and when.

Butch dropped them in Castile Square, near the entrance to the Hole, the deep underground nerve centre of Malta's war effort. They clambered out of the back of the truck opposite a long queue of women, children and the elderly, snaking down Windmill Street from the square, between piles of rubble. They were waiting patiently for their turn at the Victory Kitchen, one of a number of canteens where islanders could still get a cooked meal of sorts; with almost no kerosene and even less wood, there was little cooking to be done at home or in the numerous shelters dug into the rock.

For a moment the pilots all stood looking at each other – *what now?* Edward stared at the long line of people, most of whom were silently watching this sudden arrival. They looked miserable, Edward thought. A group of children suddenly ran out towards them, shouting 'Spitfire, Spitfire!' their arms outstretched.

'Nice to be appreciated,' muttered Laurie Bowles, and reached into his pocket for some coins to give to them. The others did the same.

Harry said, 'What about the Snakepit?' He looked at his watch. 'It's only just one-thirty. Some of the girls might still be there.'

The others nodded, and so they walked noisily down past the Opera House, turned right into Kingsway and on to the Union Club. There was laughter coming from the Snakepit, the Club's bar.

'A party!' said Harry, rubbing his hands together.

The long, narrow bar was busier than usual: along with the usual army officers on their weekly leave, and desk men from the Hole, there was also a group of submariners standing by the bar.

'Ah, the gallant flyboys!' shouted one of the submariners. 'Where were you this morning?'

'Shooting down Germans,' said Zulu Purnell.

'Not the ones that bombed the Lazzaretto you weren't,' said another of the submariners.

'Well, we can only apologise,' said Zulu, 'and promise to try harder next time. But there are rather a lot of them, I'm afraid, and not so very many of us.'

'Apology accepted – don't listen to him,' said the first submariner. 'Anyway, have a drink. What'll it be?'

'What are you guys on?' asked Lucky.

'We're working our way through the Pimms, although we've only just got here, so we're still on Number Ones.'

'Great,' said Lucky, and introduced himself.

'David Timpson,' said the first submariner. 'We're from the *Usher*. Just back in this morning. You're a Yank, aren't you? We've just had a Yank on our boat. Odd sort of fellow – a journalist.'

'Most of us are a bit strange, aren't we Red?' said Lucky, turning to Red O'Neill.

'Hell, yeah,' said Red. 'Must be to have believed that guy who told us we were coming here on vacation.' Everyone laughed; Edward noticed a palpable release of tension in the air.

'You just back from patrol?' Edward asked one of the submariners, a young flaxen-haired man whose jawline was covered with tiny shaving cuts.

'Yes – got in a couple of hours back.' He raised his glass. 'And pretty hairy it was, too. It's bad enough being hounded by destroyers without being shot at the moment you get back to harbour. We had to drop to the bottom and wait for them to bugger off again. Still, we're here now. I've been looking forward to this ever since we left port twelve days ago.'

Edward felt a nudge in his side. 'Don't look now,' said Harry, 'but there are some very lovely-looking girls sitting over there.'

Edward turned immediately, caught one of the girls' eye, and feeling himself redden, hastily looked away again. 'But they're talking to some army fellows.'

'And?'

'Well, they're clearly spoken for.'

'Nonsense. Didn't you see how quickly that girl caught your eye? She's desperate for us to come over and rescue her. Those officers are probably boring them to death with stories of building defence posts on Dingli Cliffs or something. Come on.' He moved away from the crowd of pilots and submariners, Edward following.

'Afternoon, ladies – and gentlemen,' said, Harry. 'Mind if we join you?'

'Please do,' said one of the girls.

The Army officers, a captain and a lieutenant from the Devons, looked at each other, then the Captain said, 'No, of course not.'

Harry pulled up two seats and they introduced themselves. 'Elizabeth and Kitty,' said Harry, repeating their names, 'and what do you do?'

The girls smiled at each other, Harry laughed, then Kitty said, 'We're cipher clerks.'

'In the Hole?'

'Yes. We work in intelligence, transcribing codes, but of course it's very hush-hush,' Kitty continued. 'We couldn't possibly divulge a thing more.'

'God forbid,' said Harry.

Edward smiled too, but could think of little to say. The girls were certainly pretty: Elizabeth, fair-haired and with intelligent, sharp features, while Kitty was more petite, with straight dark hair, bright red lips and dark eyes that seemed to be watching Harry intently. 'Can I get anyone a drink?' he asked.

'Of course, how rude of us,' exclaimed Harry. 'A drink, ladies? Chaps?'

'Yes, please,' said Kitty. 'Pink gin for me.'

'Same for me,' smiled Elizabeth, then turning to Edward, said, 'Thank you, Eddie.'

Edward nodded, then looked at the two officers. 'All right,' said the captain. 'Don't mind if I do. We'll have the same.'

Edward left Harry and made his way back to the bar.

'Eddie,' said Zulu Purnell, 'there you are. Guess what? The sailor boys are challenging us.'

'To what?'

'To a gharrie race,' said another of the submariners. 'An absolute tradition. Up round Castile Square and back down again. The winner gets . . .' He looked around, then said, 'I don't what the winner gets yet. We'll think of something. But this time it's going to be Royal Navy versus RAF.'

'All right,' said Edward. 'But can I finish my drink first?'

'Take your time, take your time,' said the submariner. 'We'll have a few more drinks yet. We find a bit of alcohol improves our speed.'

'Fuel is crucial,' said another.

When Edward returned with the drinks, Harry was deep in conversation with Kitty and Elizabeth, his head leaned in towards them. The army officers sat morosely to one side. 'Ah, there you are, Eddie,' said Harry. 'Kitty and Elizabeth have just been telling me about getting stuck on the Island. They've been here since 1939. Imagine that.'

'A long time,' said Edward.

'Very,' agreed Harry. 'And the Captain and Lieutenant here have been here since the beginning of 1940. The difference, of course, is that the Devons were ordered here; the girls chose to stay and do their bit.'

'But I volunteered to join the Army in the first place,' said the Lieutenant. 'I didn't wait for conscription.'

Harry turned to him. 'Good for you, but you have to admit the girls were pretty gutsy to stay here.'

'Oh, hardly,' said Elizabeth. 'Our fathers were posted here before the war – with the Navy – and although they were both recalled to England, our parents thought we would be safer here. And we were until Mussolini decided to join in.'

'And after that, I suppose it was a bit difficult to get back again,' said Edward.

'We could have gone to Egypt,' said Kitty, 'and then either stayed there or taken a boat back round the Cape, but – well, we thought we could be more use here.'

'I call that very brave,' said Harry. 'Don't you agree, chaps?' The Army men nodded.

'And anyway, my husband is in the Dorsets,' said Elizabeth, 'and I wanted to be near him.'

'You're married?' exclaimed Edward, then felt himself blush once more.

Elizabeth laughed, and raised her hand to show the narrow gold band and engagement ring on her finger. 'Yes, I'm married.'

'But I'm not,' added Kitty, eyeing Harry, who winked back. 'I'm deliciously free and single.'

'Where is he?' asked Edward. 'Your husband, that is?'

'He's camped out on Dingli Cliffs at the moment, waiting for enemy parachutists.'

Harry nudged Edward. 'On Dingli Cliffs, is he? Good for him. Well, we're complete novices here in comparison. We've only been here a month.'

'And what do you fly?' asked Elizabeth.

'Um, Spitfires,' said Harry.

'Spitfires? How marvellous,' said Kitty. Edward tried hard not to smile; he felt a renewed sense of pride. The army men exchanged glances.

'Saw one of your boys come down this morning,' said the captain.

'Yes, that was Mikey Lindsay,' said Harry. 'Poor sod got clobbered by half a dozen 109s. Still, he baled out no problem, and was picked up by the air-sea rescue lads. Nothing more than a graze on his arm.'

'How incredible,' said Kitty.

'Yes, it is rather, isn't it? He's being given a check-over up at Imtarfa this afternoon, but he's expected to be able to fly again tomorrow.'

'And were you two flying this morning?' asked Kitty.

'Us? Yes,' said Harry, pulling out a crumpled packet of cigarettes. 'Smoke, anyone?' The girls took one each, so too did the captain.

'Did you shoot anything down?' asked Kitty.

'Not personally. I was flying with Zulu – that stocky little Rhodesian over there.' He pointed at Zulu, who was laughing and slapping the back of one of the submariners. 'We just spent our time dodging the 109s. To be honest, we're often so out-numbered there's little opportunity to take them on. But Red over there got one. He's the tall American. And you had a go, didn't you, Eddie?'

Edward nodded. 'He was a bit far away, though.' He hoped he sounded nonchalant.

'Actually, usually the hardest thing is trying to land. The 109s tend to hang around and try and have a pop when we're coming back in. Very inconsiderate of them. Fortunately, the airfield wasn't bombed this morning, but very often you can come back in with the whole place in a right old mess, covered in smoke and dust, bomb craters everywhere.'

'So what do you do?' Elizabeth asked.

'Good question. Pray long and hard and hope for the best.' He grinned, and blew several smoke rings into the air.

'We must be getting along,' said the Captain suddenly, standing up. Turning to Edward, he said, 'Thanks for the drink,' he added, then tipping his cap, said, 'Ladies.'

The girls watched them leave, then once out of earshot, began laughing. Kitty said, 'Thank God you two showed up. Bless them, but they were very dull.'

'Really?' said Harry. 'I thought they seemed charming. A bit dour, perhaps.'

Edward looked down at his glass on the table. It had been another terrifying morning: the sky full of aircraft, mostly German and Italian, as bombers dived down over Grand Harbour and the submarine base in Marsamxett Harbour. He'd tried to stick with Zulu but it had been hard, especially with five 109s bearing down on him. For a brief moment he'd had a clear shot at another Messerschmitt, but it had been fleeting, and in his sudden excitement he'd shot wide, his tracer disappearing harmlessly out to sea. Harry had landed just after him; they'd both had the shakes as they'd lit cigarettes on their way back to dispersal.

'Eddie, are you all right?' said Harry.

Edward looked up. 'What? Oh, yes. Sorry.'

He noticed Elizabeth looking at him – *It's all right* – then he smiled bashfully.

'What you need is another drink,' said Harry. 'Let me get another round.'

'Harry's a darling,' said Kitty. 'Have you been friends long?'

'Ever since we joined up. We trained together, went operational together and even joined our first squadron together.'

'And you came out here together too?' said Elizabeth.

'Yes. We've been lucky. *I've* been lucky. Couldn't ask for a better friend.'

When Harry returned, he did so with Zulu, Lucky, Red O'Neill and half the submariners. The laughter had become even more frequent – now, someone only had to say something slightly amusing and everyone would double up with near-hysterical giggles. Most of the Pimms cups had been drunk – although on this occasion they had had to do without Numbers 5 and 6: the bar – indeed, the whole Island – was out of rye and vodka.

'It seems it's gharrie-racing time,' said Harry.

'And you two are definitely needed,' said Zulu.

Harry gave the girls their drinks, then raised his glass. 'Chin, chin,' he said.

'The ladies can be the adjudicators,' said David Timpson. 'And the winner's prize is –'

'A kiss from these very cute girls,' said Lucky.

Elizabeth and Kitty looked at one another and laughed. 'I don't know about that,' said Elizabeth. 'I mean, what *would* my husband think?'

'Oh, he'd understand,' said Lucky. 'Essential war work. A morale-booster for the troops.'

'Well, when you put it like that.' Elizabeth glanced at Kitty again and giggled. 'It's a good job we've the rest of the day off, isn't it, Kitty?'

'We'll gladly give the winning team a kiss,' said Kitty, 'but only on the cheek.'

The men groaned, but Lucky put up his hands. 'No, fair enough. It's something just to be blessed with female company.'

'And what exactly is a gharrie race?' asked Elizabeth, 'although I can guess.'

'Well,' said a tall, bearded submariner. 'We go out onto Kingsway, persuade a couple of Maltese gharrie drivers to lend us their mule and trap, and then we race each other. It's usually pretty riotous.'

They all spewed out onto Kingsway, spirits high, amidst laughing and jostling. Two of the submariners began piggyback racing.

Edward felt light-headed already. The drinks at the mess were watered down; in just a month, he had become unused to drinking so much in such a short time.

'So where the hell are these goddam carts?' asked Lucky, getting out his camera. Kingsway was largely deserted.

The bearded submariner scratched his chin. 'Um, we always used to be able to pick them up here. Maybe we should try the bus station.'

'What do you think they're eating at the Victory Kitchens?' said someone else. More laughter. They made their way up past the Opera House and through the main city gates, and there found two gharries. The Maltese drivers were only too happy to hand over the reins as coins and notes were stuffed into their pockets. 'Won't be long,' said the bearded submariner. 'Be right back. All right, two teams,' he said, turning to the assembled party.

'How many in each?' asked Zulu.

'Six? Any more and these mules will collapse.'

Zulu jumped up onto the first gharrie. 'Who's with me?' he shouted, standing up and clutching the reins. 'Yee-ha!'

'Come on,' said Harry to Edward. They clambered up beside Zulu. Lucky, Red and Laurie joined them.

'Just like being in the Wild West, eh Red?' said Zulu.

'Oh sure. All we need now is Injuns.'

'Okay, listen everyone,' shouted the bearded submariner. 'The course is this: back through City Gate, up past the Opera House to Castile Square, once round and back. That's fairly free of rubble, isn't it?'

'Come on, let's get going,' shouted another of the submariners.

'All right. Ladies? Ready?'

The girls nodded. 'Ready,' they shouted, 'Steady! Go!' With a lurch the gharries rumbled forward.

As they quickly discovered, this was no modern-day chariot race. The mules barely broke into a trot despite frantic yee-ha-ing, so by the time they reached the front of the Opera House, all the pilots except Zulu had jumped down and were pushing and pulling the cart along with the underfed mule. The submariners immediately followed their example and the pace of the race quickened, those not participating following behind and yelling shouts of encouragement. Around the square the pilots had the edge, but as they turned back down beside the Opera House once more, the submariners began to catch them, so that as they turned into the final straight leading up to the City Gate, the two gharries were neck and neck. Edward felt exhausted: his legs ached, his chest was tight and a stitch had developed across his stomach.

'Come on, lads!' screamed Zulu. 'We've got 'em now!'

But they hadn't. Both teams tried to proclaim themselves the winner, but the girls were adamant the race was a dead heat. 'So no kisses, I'm afraid.'

'Surely that's not fair,' said the bearded submariner. 'Surely you should give us all a kiss.'

'No,' said Kitty firmly. 'No winner, no kiss.'

They staggered back to the Union Club. More drinks – pink gins all round; there was no Pimms left. Edward felt his head begin to swim. Someone suggested a singing competition, and then the bearded submariner was standing on a table belting out a sea shanty about a sailor who had got up to no good during a stay in port. Edward looked up at the man: tie undone, face red, the veins on his neck bulging, spittle darting into the air. Everyone cheered. One by one the others followed: some barely made it onto the table. Laurie was so flat and tuneless, he was pulled down before he'd hardly started.

'Who hasn't sung yet?' shouted Zulu. 'Eddie and Harry! You haven't been up. Go on, your turn.'

'All right, all right,' said Edward, 'but this is going to be a duet.' Clambering onto the table amidst whistles and cheers, they stood arm in arm, precariously balanced, and began singing *Lili Marlene*. It was such an obvious song – whistled and sung endlessly by both sides all the way from Germany to North Africa and back across the Mediterranean – and yet no-one else had thought of it. Within moments everyone in the Snakepit had joined in, even, Edward noticed, Kitty and Elizabeth, and even some other officers who had only just stepped into the bar.

They sang two encores, and as they did so, Edward looked out over the room, at the haze of cigarette smoke, at the red, open-mouthed faces, and at the two girls sitting to one side, singing and laughing along with the boys. He looked down at Lucky, and at Laurie, Zulu and Red; Zulu with sweat pouring down his round face, Lucky and Red arm in arm as well. And he felt Harry's hand gripping his shoulder, swaying him from side to side as they led the now-crowded bar on the final verse:

> *'Resting in our billets, just behind the lines,*
> *Even though we're parted, your lips are close to mine.*
> *You wait where that lantern softly gleams,*
> *Your sweet face seems to haunt my dreams*
> *My Lili of the Lamplight,*
> *My own Lili Marlene.'*

When they finished, they jumped down to more cheers and whistles. Shrill, ear-piercing wolf-whistling was a talent shared by both Zulu and Lucky and they repeatedly blew them now. Kitty and Elizabeth declared that Edward and Harry were the unquestionable winners, and they kissed them both.

Soon after, the party dissolved. Everyone was drunk; the party had run its course. Outside, daylight was just beginning to fade. The pilots stumbled back up through the City Gate and soon after managed to catch one of the very few buses that still ran across the island. As the bus began trundling its way through the narrow lanes of cleared bomb damage, they sang *Lili Marlene* once more for good measure, and Zulu commented on the consideration of the Germans not to have bombed them once all afternoon.

The enemy bombers were back in force later that evening, however. It was dusk by the time the bus pulled into the main square at Rabat. As the pilots stumbled off and headed back through the gates of Mdina to the Xara Palace, the sirens began wailing once more and they paused a moment, listening to the distant thrum of aero-engines. The bombs had started falling before they reached the front door. Hurrying up the stone staircase to the balcony, they emerged to a deafening roar of engines and explosions.

'My God,' said Harry. 'Look at that.'

Row upon row of black shapes filled the sky as far as the eye could see. And they all seemed to be heading for Takali. Bombs were whistling and screaming, guns blasting. Soon the airfield was shrouded in smoke, so thick Edward could smell the cordite and dust from his vantage point two miles away. Overhead, the bombers thundered by, job done, on their way back to Sicily.

But they were back again the following morning – more than two hundred aircraft, and once again, Takali was the target. What buildings had remained were now utterly destroyed, planes were obliterated on the ground, and the airfield looked more pockmarked and cratered than the surface of the moon. In less than a day, Takali had become the most bombed airfield in the world.

In the weeks – and years even – that followed, Edward would look back upon that afternoon at the Snakepit and draw solace. An afternoon to cherish, and to remember. On Malta, there would be no more like it.

Malta – June, 1995

'What was the name of that girl Harry was so sweet on?' asked Lucky as a waiter brought over their coffee.

'Kitty,' said Edward, whisking a fly away from his face.

'Kitty,' repeated Lucky. 'Ye-es, that's right. He was pretty hooked on her for a while, wasn't he?'

Edward smiled. 'Quite bowled over, I'd say. Harry had such charm and the girls always adored him, but I think it was quite different with Kitty. I think she had the same effect on men that he did on women. After all, she was rather beautiful, wasn't she?'

'Oh, sure. She was a blinder. We were all jealous as hell.' He grinned. 'Leastways, I know I was.'

'And she'd been on the Island since before the siege began. One can only imagine what it must have been like for her: one of the best-looking girls on Malta, surrounded by thousands of sex-starved men all hanging on every word she said. Then Harry comes along. They were a match for each other – at least, I thought they were.'

'Maybe, Eddie.'

'Do you remember, he borrowed a bicycle from one of the erks? Whenever we weren't needed, he'd scurry off to Floriana – she had a flat there, and I think she was on her own by that stage because the girl she used to live with had already left the Island.'

Lucky laughed. 'Actually, now you mention it, I do recall you and I spending quite a few nights on our own. Can hardly blame him. And it wasn't as if there was so much flying at that time, anyway.'

'No.' He thought for a moment, then said, 'Yes, he really fell for Kitty.'

'I wonder whatever became of her.'

'Hm,' said Edward. He thought about telling Lucky about the time he met her later, back in England, but instead said, 'Probably married a succession of rich husbands.'

'A bit cynical for you, isn't it, Eddie?'

Edward shrugged. 'She was that sort of girl.'

They drank their coffee. Edward looked around the tables and brightly coloured sunshades, at the throng of people, laughing, talking, writing postcards. At the centre of the square, gazing down on the café scene below, stood the stone statue of Queen Victoria. *Such a sour expression,* he thought. The ageing empress, mistress of all she surveyed; she had no need of beauty.

Not for the first time Lucky said, 'How did we do it, Eddie?'

'What do you mean?'

'How did we live through those days? Jeez, but this was a tough place back then.' He wiped his mouth and shook his head. 'Hell, you know what? I think I *am* going to have a drink. Just a beer. You'll join me, Eddie?'

Why not? thought Edward. A cool glass of beer might be refreshing. 'Yes, all right.' He couldn't remember the last time he'd had a drink before six o'clock in the evening.

'You know, I just remember feeling so goddam frustrated all the time. I wanted to get up there and get at 'em, but there was never enough planes, never enough fuel, never enough anything.'

'I've still got my logbook,' said Edward. 'I've been looking through it, and you know, I flew just four times during the last two weeks of March. And every time I seemed to have written, "Jumped by successive lots of 109s", or "rather hasty landing". In April, I think I only flew five times all month.'

'Yeah, I've still got mine. I'll show you. How more of us didn't get the chop, I'll never know.' Lucky grimaced, then pushed back his chair, the noise against the stone paving loud and grating. 'Just nipping to the bathroom a moment,' he said.

Edward nodded. So much had come back to him in the past few weeks. So much that he thought had been discarded from his mind long ago. A tough place, Lucky had called it. *It wasn't just tough,* he thought, *it was brutal.* Edward suddenly shuddered, remembering the terror he'd felt as his Spitfire had been pounced on by the 109s; the near panic as he'd twisted and turned, heard bullets tearing into his fuselage. Somehow, the bullets had missed him, and somehow, he'd always managed to make it back down safely. *Why was that?* He shook his head, and found he was once again on the verge of tears – a sensation that had become all too familiar during recent weeks. *That attack on Takali,* he thought to himself . . . The ground had shuddered, pounded with the exploding bombs – it had been like an earthquake. He remembered the terror he'd felt – they had all felt.

There had been a pilot next to him who had actually soiled his pants.

A picture came into his mind: Takali, bare and rough, dotted with red flags marking the *hundreds* of unexploded and delayed-action bombs. Some people had believed that the large number of dud bombs was due to the Polish workforce in Germany doing their bit for the Allied cause. But Laurie Bowles, he remembered, had blamed the Italians. 'They've probably got too many Eyeties working on those airfields over there,' he had said. 'Lazy bastards probably don't load them up properly or something.' Every so often a delayed-action bomb had exploded – and then everyone would jump.

Lucky had wondered how they had stood it; Edward wondered too. Even the pilots had been expected to help repair the bomb damage; Butch had demanded an all-out effort. No-one had been excused. It had been exhausting work: Edward remembered the back-breaking amount of shovelling, the sense of permanent exhaustion made worse by their hunger. And the relentlessness of it all: not just the bombers, but the 109s and Italian Macchi 202s repeatedly buzzing over the airfield at zero feet and peppering the place with machine-gun and cannon-fire. These endless attacks had jarred the nerves. Jarred the nerves and made them tense and irritable. As in Cornwall, there had been too much time twiddling fingers and not enough flying – but for very different reasons: on Malta there had always been plenty for them to do, it was just that there never seemed to be enough fuel or aircraft with which to do it.

What a wreck of a place Takali had become. Even the Mad House, that strange building the far side of the airfield, had finally become a pile of rubble. There had been a week, he remembered now, where the last stubborn section had become smaller and smaller until one day it had disappeared altogether. Dispersal had been the exception, but it had become roofless, while the inside had become full of stones, rocks and shattered furniture. It had become a focal point only. He remembered how they had lain on stretchers outside, using them as sunbeds, or squatted down on rocks. Part of a wing had been adapted as a card table.

And yet they had known so little about what was going on. It amazed him now to think how little he had really thought about the siege at the time. The situation had been so dire. A convoy had reached Grand Harbour around the same time as the Takali blitz –

towards the end of March, it must have been. Except that it hadn't been a whole convoy – just two or three ships and then they'd been hit in the harbour before they'd been properly unloaded. He could picture it now: smoke as black as night rising thousands and thousands of feet into the sky for all on the Island to see.

'Eddie?'

He looked up at Lucky, who was now back and sitting opposite him once more.

'I said, there's a coupla' things I'd like to show you.'

'Oh, yes, of course.'

Lucky grinned. 'Daydreaming?'

'Just thinking about Butch.' Edward smiled.

'Butch Hammond,' mused Lucky. 'A great guy.'

'Yes, he was. And I think I appreciated his candour, even then. He wasn't afraid of telling us straight.'

Having finished their drinks, Lucky took Edward up Kingsway. 'Although it's Republic Street now,' he told Edward. 'All the old names have gone: Old Bakery Street, Windmill Street.'

'Is the Union Club still here?'

'No. Long since closed, although the branch in Sliema is still there. Close to the Preluna, actually, but I don't go in very often. I mean, I'm a member – course I am – but you still have to wear a tie and jacket and there's too many people still sipping pink gins. For them the sun is yet to set on the glorious British Empire.'

Edward was about to respond when he suddenly stopped and stared. 'The Opera House, my God.'

'Yeah,' said Lucky. 'Unbelievable, isn't it?'

7*th April.* He looked at the remains, the steps sprouting tufts of grass and weeds, the truncated pillars. The rubble had been cleared away, of course, but otherwise the once magnificent building had been left as it had become on that day in April, 1942.

'I had no idea,' said Edward. 'I just assumed it had been rebuilt, or cleared.'

'Sad, isn't it?'

'And to think we had that ridiculous gharrie race just a few days before.'

'Yeah – that was fun. And the submariners left soon after, too.'

'Yes, of course.' Edward put his hand up to shield his eyes; the sun, now high in the sky, continued to bear down relentlessly.

'Yup, the whole lot of 'em. Off to Alex. I remember when that happened – and thinking we were really up the creek.' He looked at his watch. 'Hell, we need to get a move on. C'mon, Eddie.'

'Where are we going?'

'I'll show you. Follow me.'

Away from Republic Street, Valletta was quiet, the high buildings with their distinctive window boxes and shutters casting thick shadow over much of the streets. Then, as they crossed a road, they would be dazzled by a narrow strip of blinding brightness from the sun. *These were nothing but rubble back then,* Edward thought. *Rubble and dust.* Well, there was still thick dust on many of the doors and windows, but not the thin, cloying kind that had covered everything like talcum powder. It had got everywhere – in your hair, down your trousers, in your shoes – chafing and itching; another discomfort.

They started heading downhill, the road long and straight and leading to a vivid strip of azure sea. Then they crossed over and turned towards Grand Harbour, down a flight of steps that led them by the Lower Barracca Gardens. Edward stopped, gazing across towards the Three Cities gleaming on the far side of the harbour, but Lucky said, 'Come on, Eddie, no time for that now.'

'Where are you taking me?' asked Edward again.

'We're right there – you'll see.' And as they turned the corner, Edward did see: an almost white stone rotunda perched high on the sea wall under which hung a large bell. They walked up the road and stood before the wide steps leading up towards the monument.

'Dead on time,' said Lucky, as some mechanism from within the rotunda began to click. Then the bell chimed. A low, mournful peel, but one that was loud enough to make Edward start. Back and forth swung the bell, slow, steady and haunting.

When its toll eventually came to an end, Lucky turned to Edward and said, 'The Siege Bell. It rings at noon every single day. You can hear it thirty miles out to sea.'

Lucky began climbing the steps. 'And here, let me show you something else.' Edward followed once more, and they passed through the rotunda and gazed down at a stone plinth on which lay a bronze supine figure of a man.

'How beautiful,' muttered Edward.

'Yeah, ain't it?' Lucky leant on the wall by the catafalque. 'To commemorate all those who died on Malta.' He eyed Edward a moment, then said, 'Do you ever wonder why we survived and so many of our friends didn't?'

Edward nodded.

'I do quite a bit,' continued Lucky. 'And I don't mind telling you I feel guilty about it. I think of my life and I start realising I haven't really made the most of the chance I've been given. Do you remember Zulu Purnell?'

'Of course.'

'He came down just over there.' Lucky pointed out towards the mouth of the harbour. 'I wonder if Zulu had lived and I'd died, would he have had a fuller, better life than me?'

'That's nonsense, Lucky. You can't start thinking like that.'

'But I do Eddie. I do.'

After lunch, Lucky said he had 'a few things to attend to' that afternoon, but promised to meet Edward at the hotel the following morning.

'We'll go to Ta' Qali, all right? And up to Mdina. Boy, just wait 'til you see the Xara Palace again.'

'I'd like that very much.'

'And then, Eddie,' added Lucky, clutching him by the shoulder, 'and I hope you won't take this the wrong way, but I'd really like you to come back with me to my place. Spend a coupla' days there. It's a nice house – you'll have your own room and bathroom. Will you do that? Ditch the Preluna for a bit. I mean, I know you've paid for it and everything, but my house is free, so you won't be losing out. And I've got a few things tucked away up there I'd like you to see. What do you say?'

For a moment Edward wavered. Lucky looked at him, glassy eyes searching his face.

'All right, Lucky,' he said at length. 'Why not? That would be lovely.' *This is why I'm here,* he told himself. Then he said, 'Tell me, Lucky. Whatever happened to all those pictures you used to take? I remember that camera you had. You always seemed to get film somehow.'

Lucky grinned. 'Still got 'em. One of the reasons I want you to come over to my place. There's pictures of all us: you, Zulu, Harry. The whole gang.'

Edward felt his spirits rise. 'You know, I'd love to see those, Lucky.'

'Well, come on over to Gozo and you can.'

They went their separate ways. Edward took the opportunity to do some sightseeing, something there had been little chance to do the last time he'd been there. As he ambled through the cathedral and the Grand Master's Palace, reading about the previous Great Siege, he remembered Harry's history lesson that first day they had been on the Island. *And I was the one who become a history teacher,* he thought.

Later, back at the hotel, he sat out on his narrow balcony, glad for the chance to sit quietly and collect his thoughts for a moment. He was exhausted: all that walking about. Yes, he might be fit for his age, but he'd noticed in recent years that he tended to tire more quickly. *I'm getting old,* he thought.

He was not sure how he felt. It was good seeing Lucky – he'd enjoyed talking with him over dinner the previous evening, even though Lucky had been half cut and had done most of the talking. It had made him realise he wasn't alone; Lucky, too, had suffered in the long years since the war. Of course, he and Lucky were very different, but they'd been different back in 1942 as well. They'd become good friends then, and Edward was enjoying Lucky's company every bit as much now – more than he had first expected. And today his old friend had been sober and, in truth, not so very different from the drunk version; slightly less maudlin perhaps. And the wit and irreverence that Edward had liked so much when he'd first known him was still there. He was looking forward to staying in his house; was glad that Lucky had asked him and that he had wanted him to stay.

His thoughts turned to his son, Simon. *You'd approve of me meeting up with Lucky again,* he thought, and then wondered whether one day he might bring Simon to Malta too – perhaps even with Nick. Perhaps with Katie and Lucy too. *When this is all over,*

Simon, he thought, *I'll tell you everything. I promise.* He clenched his fists and lightly tapped his leg. *Everything. But not yet.*

And what about Valletta? There was much about the city that struck him as familiar; sometimes, fifty years seemed not so very long ago. Certainly, those once dormant memories were now erupting furiously into his mind. And yet he had just spent an afternoon playing the tourist, admiring the Caravaggios and the Maltese architecture; the Island had become a *holiday* destination. Half a century before, it had been the world's worst posting. One of the most violent spots on earth.

Absent-mindedly, he rubbed the rough, melted plastic of his chair, where some earlier guest had stubbed out a cigarette. Harry had been in Valletta that day, when the Opera House had been destroyed. It had not been the only building to have been hit: the Castile, several of the old Knights of Malta *auberges,* God knows how many others. He remembered Harry telling him about it. As the bombs had started falling, he and Kitty had rushed into the nearest public shelter. 'I'd never realised what horrible, fetid places they are,' he had said to Edward the following morning. 'The smell was appalling – of sweat and piss. And it was damp and heaving with people. There was nowhere to sit. Barely anywhere to stand.' Children had been crying, others praying out loud, the wailing increasing every time another bomb dropped, shaking the ground as it exploded above. When the all clear had sounded, they had emerged, the dust still thick in the air. The scene of devastation that greeted them had shocked even Harry. 'People were just staring at the remains of the Opera House,' he'd said. 'They couldn't believe it. Nor could I, for that matter.'

April had been the worst month. Day after day, night after night, the bombers pounded Malta into dust. The Island's cities became piles of rubble. Back then, Edward had understood little about what the civilians had gone through; unlike Harry, he'd never been in one of the shelters dug out underneath Valletta, and nor had there ever been much cause to speak to many of the Maltese. How callow he had been! As pilots they'd been so wrapped up in their own desperate existence, but they had not lost their homes and possessions; they hadn't been expected to live day in, day out in a tiny stinking subterranean cubbyhole. That April the Island had been awarded the

George Cross – an unprecedented honour – but a medal could not feed, house or clothe the Islanders. And while most Maltese had been forced to stay on that accursed Island, those that could leave were doing so. Even the submariners. One of the Royal Navy's finest bases in the whole world now had no navy left at all.

And Kitty had left too. Her father had insisted; she'd wanted to stay. Wanted to stay with Harry.

'What do I do?' Harry had asked Edward one afternoon as they sat out on the balcony of the Xara Palace. Even then, Hal Far and Luqa were under attack, huge plumes of dust and smoke billowing into the sky. 'She's in danger every night. We're all right up here, but her flat's in the front line.'

'Could she move to one of the villages?'

'Then how would she get to work? She'd still have to get into Valletta every day, and even if she did manage it, she'd still run the risk of being strafed by those bastards.' He sighed, ran his hands through his hair. 'She should go. She should do as her father says. This place is too dangerous. But Eddie, I'm just so worried that I'll never see her again.'

It was a night flight. A Wellington was flying from Luqa to Gibraltar. There were a handful of spare places, and Kitty took one of them. The timing of the plane's departure was everything: after the early evening raid, but before the next. Harry had gone down to see her off, Edward remembered, then his friend had cycled back, through the dark, railing against the unfairness of it all. Somehow he'd got hold of a bottle of whisky – from the pilot of the Wellington? White Horse whisky – *yes*, Edward could even remember that. 'Eddie, I need you to get drunk with me,' Harry had said when he arrived back at the Xara Palace, and so they'd gone out, walking through the narrow streets of Mdina – the Silent City – until they reached the bastion walls that overlooked the hilltop hospital of Imtarfa. For a few hours the bombers had left the Island alone, and so the two of them had sat there, perched on the walls, legs dangling over the side, the Island around them still and eerily peaceful. And as they drank they cursed Malta and the Germans and the Italians, and they cursed themselves for being such stupid bloody fools.

And now I'm back, he thought.

Malta – April, 1942

20th April, 1942. At last, more Spitfires were about to arrive – forty-eight of them, two whole squadrons. As Hugh Pughe Lloyd had assured them at his briefing the night before, these new arrivals would, at last, make all the difference. 'With plenty of Spits we can give the Hun a bit of his own medicine,' he'd told them. 'You'll all get a good chance to send him burning into the sea. This time we're going to hurt him, and hurt him hard.'

The new Spitfires were expected to arrive just before ten that morning, but the pilots of 'A' Flight had been at dispersal since dawn. There were just six of them: Red O'Neill had been shot up and was in hospital at Imtarfa; Doug Routledge had been posted back to Britain and had not been replaced; Tony and Alex McLeish were laid low with a touch of Malta Dog; while another of the 'A' Flight pilots, Johnny Dillinger, had been moved over into 'B' Flight. Edward sat on a rock outside the shattered remnants of the hut, and watched a lizard scurry in sudden darting movements through tufts of dried grass and then disappear between some stones. He rubbed his eyes, yawned, and looked at Zulu, prostrate on a stretcher a few yards away and snoring. A tiny line of saliva ran down from the Rhodesian's mouth and chin, staining the dusty canvas.

Edward smiled to himself. Zulu had not been among the pilots to walk down from the Xara Palace a few hours before. Instead he'd met them there, still drunk, with glazed eyes after a night in Valletta with a friend of his from Luqa – a photo reconnaissance pilot newly back from Egypt and armed with bottles of brandy.

Lucky, now Flight Commander, had told him to take himself back to the mess. 'Come back when you've slept it off,' he'd said.

But Zulu had had none of it. 'A bit of kip and I'll be fine,' he had assured Lucky as he lay down on the stretcher. That had been nearly three hours ago.

It may have been quiet at dispersal, but around the airfield there was much activity. Soldiers were carrying supplies to the numerous blast pens that now dotted the perimeter in expectation of the Spitfires. In the meantime, the mechanics continued their desperate efforts to inject life into another of the sickly Spitfires that still existed, their muffled clangs and hammering resounding across the dusty field. 'Maximum effort' had been demanded from the ground crews – it was essential that as many fighters as possible were ready to provide cover for the new arrivals. The chief mechanic had told Lucky there would be six of the old Spitfires available that morning – a rarity; so far, there had been even less flying in April than there had been the previous month. On two days that month there'd been no flyable Spitfires at all. Edward had been in the air only twice, once at the beginning of the month when he'd hit a Junkers 88 before being pounced on by a flight of 109s, and again four days before, when nothing much had happened; he had been almost thankful for that. In three weeks he'd had just over an hour's flying.

Now, though, it looked as though they would all soon be airborne, so long as a raid developed before lunchtime, and no-one would bet against that. It was the reason Lucky had agreed to let Zulu stay; it would have been unforgivable to have left one of the planes on the ground. Edward stood up, threw a few pebbles at Harry, who was reading a paperback, then wandered a few yards away from dispersal, before pacing back again. A nauseous feeling sat in the pit of his stomach, and he looked up into the deep blue unending sky. So empty now, but soon it would be alive with swirling aircraft, the rattle of gunfire, and streaked with vivid white contrails and lines of black smoke. And he would be in the thick of it. He shivered involuntarily.

Perhaps Hugh Pughe was right, he thought. Perhaps these new planes would make all the difference; he wanted to believe so, and yet the enemy had so many aircraft – hundreds, not just fifty. He thought about the last new squadron to have been posted to Malta – 229, who had flown across the Mediterranean from Libya shortly after the blitz on Takali a month before. They had come with twenty-four Hurricanes, and just over three weeks later, they had lost half their pilots and the majority of their planes. Despite having had plenty of experience fighting against the Germans and Italians in North Africa, they had not managed to shoot down a single enemy plane. It wasn't their fault: it was the planes they flew and the overwhelming superiority of the enemy.

Edward's thoughts were interrupted as sirens began wailing out over the Island once again. Glancing at dispersal, he then looked at his watch: nearly nine o'clock.

'Jesus, what the hell's going on?' said Lucky. He bawled at the duty telephonist sitting outside dispersal at a rickety table. 'Get Woody on the phone pronto.'

Moments later the gunners were opening fire, the sky over the harbours and south of the Island soon became peppered with black smudges of flak. Aircraft were wheeling in between, engines screaming as they dived. Edward noticed Harry had not even looked up from his book. Lucky was on the phone, nodding, one eye still on the developing raid.

'OK, relax, fellers,' he said, having handed back the receiver. 'We're to sit this one out. Woody wants us to wait until the Spits are closer. By his reckoning, they're an hour away.'

The raid passed, the attackers never troubling either of the two main airfields. Takali's Bofors crews pounded away as a lone Junkers, trailing thick smoke, skirted nearby. Almost as quickly as it had begun, however, the attack was over and the skies were clear once more. Only the slow-drifting pall of dust and smoke that hung over the harbours remained.

A little before 10 a.m. The familiar whirr of Merlin engines could be heard. Soldiers and ground crew stopped what they were doing, looked up, pointing. There, look! The pilots watched, too, as the first specks appeared, then gradually grew until one after another, the first flight of new Spitfires began touching down amid flurries of dust. One squadron had flown into Luqa, the other, 603, into Takali. Erks leapt onto their wings, directing them to the blast pens.

'They're all down,' said Butch, who had now appeared at dispersal. All but one, an American, who had taken off with them but had then disappeared. The CO looked happier than Edward had seen him in weeks.

Soon enough, the new pilots began wandering over to dispersal. They looked dazed, bleary-eyed, and clearly dismayed at the state of their new fighter base. And white-skinned too, their new tropical kit clean and fresh. *We must have been the same*, thought Edward, and smiled to himself. He picked at the frayed edge of his cotton shorts. They had become as bleached and stained as his face and arms had been browned. The new pilots were talking, several all at once. A few 109s had been seen as they had approached the Island, but they'd not attacked; otherwise their trip had been thankfully uneventful. They'd been nervous about switching over to the overload tanks; another had lost his maps when they'd blown out of the cockpit; what was the smoke over the south of the Island? When would they be flying again?

'We've got to get your planes battle-worthy first,' Butch told them. 'But brace yourselves. We're expecting a visit any moment. Malta's a bit different to what most of you will have been used to in England. There are no massed fighter sweeps here.'

'A' Flight was finally scrambled half an hour before they were due to be stood down. Woody phoned, got Butch on the line and told him that fifty plus 'big jobs' were heading towards the Island. The inactivity of the morning was dispelled in an instant. All six pilots ran to their planes, which were close at hand. Edward ran over the rough ground, heart pounding like a hammer. Grabbing his parachute, he jumped onto the wing and hoisted himself into the cockpit. How battered his aircraft looked: paint flecked, streaked with oil stains; no squadron markings: there were not enough planes for them to belong to any one squadron in particular, and so the letters had been roughly painted over with ill-matching desert brown. Three Hurricanes roared down the runway, and then it was 'A' Flight's turn. Helmet strapped on, oxygen and radio leads plugged in, quick glance at the dials – oil pressure OK, fuel OK, signal to his fitter and rigger and ease open the throttle. *Here we go,* thought Edward, *and the next time I'm back down again* – well, he hoped for the best.

Edward was flying number two to Lucky, Harry wingman to Zulu, and Laurie leading Mike Lindsay. It was now nearly one o'clock and they flew as fast as they could to 17,000 feet. South of the Island, the six of them turned, the sun streaking across them and glinting over their canopies as it swivelled behind them. Down below, the deep blue Mediterranean twinkled, while ahead, leaf-like, Malta seemed to float upon the sea.

They saw the Stukas clearly, slowly heading towards Hal Far. Gunning the throttle, Edward followed Lucky as they dived towards them, his Spitfire bucking and jerking with the strain. The aircraft loomed towards them in no time at all. His ears raged with the change in pressure, while his whole body felt pressed into the bucket seat. His helmet was slipping, so swiftly he nudged it back off his forehead, flicked the gun safety catch to 'off' and quickly strained his head.

'109s three o'clock,' he called out.

'All right, Eddie,' replied Lucky, 'I see 'em.' Lucky pressed ahead towards the lumbering Stukas, so Edward and the others followed. He swivelled his head again. *Christ, this will be close.* The 109s were closing like angry wasps. He picked out a Stuka, drew as close as he dared, then fired a short burst from his cannon and machine guns. The aircraft juddered, he saw parts of metal fly off the Stuka, but orange tracer was now zipping over his head. No time to press the attack. Ahead of him, Lucky had turned in towards the fire and Edward followed. To his relief he saw the enemy tracer fire whistle past wide. Now there was no chance of attacking the dive bombers again – the sky was full of 109s.

'Break, Zulu!' he heard Harry call. 'For Christ's sake, break.'

'I'm hit, I'm hit!' said Zulu.

'Get out of there, get out, Zulu!' yelled Harry, as a 109 streaked past Edward, the mottled sand paintwork and squadron markings vividly clear. More tracer fizzed overhead and then the aircraft jolted as bullets tore into his fuselage. 'Shit!' he said out loud, and automatically turned once more into the fire. Four more 109s were heading straight for him, dazzling as the sun, now ahead of him, sparkled across them. Tracer curled towards him, Edward flung his Spitfire one way then another, radio static and chatter from the other pilots crackling in his ears, the horizon sliding back and forth. He flipped the plane and a Junkers 88 suddenly slid across in front of him, huge and seemingly passing just inches away, the wash from the propellers jolting his Spitfire with sudden turbulence. *Jesus, where the hell did that come from?* Edward felt his stomach lurch, then he dived and saw below and ahead of him another Messerschmitt slowing climbing towards the fray. A moment later he was right upon him, thumb pressed down on the gun button and pumping machine-gun bullets and cannon shells into it. He could see his tracer scoring hits, then a puff of smoke from the engine, the 109 wobbled, and suddenly toppled on its back and dropped out of the sky, smoke pouring in a trail behind it. But no time to think. Two more 109s were attacking him almost head on. The closing speed was nearly seven hundred miles an hour – a split second – and Edward broke left as the 109 did the same. The joystick was knocked from his hand, he was flung against his harness so that the straps tore into his barely covered shoulders, and suddenly the sky had change places with the sea. The Spitfire groaned, began shuddering, then tumbled into a diving spin. Round and round, the sea, the tan cliffs and fields of Malta rotating in a whirr. *Shit, shit!* He clutched the stick with both hands, but the controls were slack. *Come on, come on!* The sea and land were rushing towards him. *Stop this spinning.* The controls still slack in his hand. *Christ – what to do? I'm going to die.*

Then a strange calm descended upon him. He no longer heard the scream of the engine; his panic had gone. His end had come and that was that. He worried for his parents, hoped that Harry and the others might miss him a bit, but the terror had left him. *Come on,* he then told himself, *one last try.* He kicked the rudder, pushed the stick forward as far as it would go, and felt it catch – a glimmer of hope – and then the sea stopped spinning before him. *Thank God.* He eased open the throttle, pulled back the stick and suddenly, for a brief moment, the Spitfire was flying the right way up, but then a wing dropped and he felt himself being pulled over. Grabbing the stick, he pushed it to one side and the Spitfire corrected itself. Only then did he glance at his port-side wing and see a large three-foot chunk had been ripped off the end. *Jesus,* he thought. He breathed heavily, felt sweat run from underneath his helmet and down his face.

He was now only a thousand feet or so above sea level. Of the mass of swirling aircraft there was no sign, although Malta now lay just a few miles ahead of him and he could see smoke and the tiny dots of dive bombers still swarming over the airfields. His plane was shaking, the whole aircraft vibrating and creaking. Edward grimaced and he wondered how he was ever going to land again. Glancing around, the sky seemed clear behind him, so he dived gently until he was skimming the sea. The white crests of the breakers seemed so close he could almost touch them. The cockpit felt close, the heat overwhelming, and the smell of rubber, oil, and hot metal suddenly claustrophobic and cloying. Tugging off his oxygen mask, he pulled back his canopy and a blast of cool air buffeted his face.

The giant screen of Dingli Cliffs drew towards him and he climbed, clearing them with the Island suddenly spread before him. Both Takali and Luqa had been attacked – clouds of dust and smoke covered both. Above him, 109s still circled, waiting, he knew, to pounce as the defenders returned to land. Just fifty feet from the ground, he roared over the dense network of small stone-walled fields, then began circling around Takali. Smoke and dust still hid much of it, and he hoped that if he ever managed to land he would be able to avoid the bomb craters. Above, the 109s were still there, circling like vultures, ready to swoop down and tear him to pieces. He glanced at his fuel gauge – empty. He was out of ammunition too – fifteen seconds of firepower was always used up too easily. His back felt clammy, and sweat now poured down his face despite the draught from the open canopy. What to do? Risk running out of fuel and crashing into those vicious stone walls, or come in and land at Takali and hope to avoid being shot to pieces as he did so? His arms – especially his left arm – had begun to ache terribly from the strain of trying to keep the Spitfire on an even keel. For a few moments he felt paralysed with indecision. There was Imtarfa, with its clock tower, and there, as he banked gently again, was Mdina, and the Xara Palace, looming above him. He wished he could be standing on the balcony there, watching instead. Then the engine spluttered. He looked up again – *why can't you bastards piss off?* – then took a deep breath and turned in towards Takali. He lowered the undercarriage and heard the gentle hum of the hydraulics as the wheels clicked into place. Flaps down – *hold her steady* – throttle cut.

Two loud cracks and the aircraft slewed as though it had been punched by a giant sledgehammer. He looked up in his mirror and saw a yellow-nosed 109 bearing down upon him, fizzing arcs of tracer hurtling towards him. Another deafening bang, smoke billowed up from the engine, and the aircraft dropped. He was now going to hit the ground too fast – the Spitfire would tip over – so he quickly retracted the undercarriage once more and braced himself. It all happened so quickly: shells flicking past his head, the ground looming towards him, the aircraft enveloped by smoke – and that acrid stench – then he closed his eyes tightly, breathed rapidly and then felt the wind knocked out of him as the Spitfire hit the ground and continued to slide and grind and scrape along the surface. *Stop, please stop*, he prayed – and eventually it did so, amidst another cloud of choking dust and fine grit. Fumbling fingers tugged at the rest of the leads, and then he pushed himself up out of the cockpit, leapt onto the wing and to the ground, and ran as fast as could as two more Messerschmitts roared overhead, their guns firing and tearing into the wrecked Spitfire behind him.

He glanced back, tripped, and fell into a bomb crater, cutting his hands and knees as he did so. Another 109 hurtled over his head – a brief blur of silvery grey, streaked with oil – and he ducked involuntarily, then scrambled out of the hole and ran on towards a slit trench at the edge of the airfield, where several erks were still taking cover.

'You all right, sir?' It was Pete Summersby.

Edward gasped and nodded.

'Reckon they must have known the new Spits were coming. Bastards.'

Edward nodded again, then, when he finally felt his breath coming back to him, croaked, 'I'm sorry about my plane. I know how hard you worked on it.'

Pete shrugged. 'Did you get anything, sir?'

'Yes,' said Edward, then he shuddered and added, 'a 109. It went into the sea.'

'Congratulations, sir. One less Jerry to worry about.'

'I suppose so,' said Edward.

When the raiders eventually left and the dust began to settle, Edward clambered out of the slit trench and made his way back to dispersal. Harry was there, so too was Lucky. Alex and Laurie had got back safely as well, as had Mike Lindsay, although he had already been taken off to Imtarfa – a cannon shell had smashed his canopy and his face had been cut by the splinters.

'Zulu?' asked Edward.

The others shook their heads. 'A Jerry flew over his parachute and it collapsed,' said Lucky.

'Bastard did it deliberately,' said Harry. 'Must have done. He was hit, but he'd got out. I saw him. Then whoosh – just a few feet above him.'

Edward had never seen Harry so angry. Lucky shifted his feet, bit his lip and glanced at the others anxiously. Edward looked away – *we're all to blame,* he thought. *We should never have let him fly.* The intelligence officer hovered, wanting their statements. Lucky had also got a 109, Harry had seen hits on a Stuka and a Messerschmitt, and Laurie also claimed strikes on a Junkers 88. Two confirmed kills in return for one pilot dead, one wounded, two Spitfires wrecked and another badly damaged.

Soon after, they trudged back towards Mdina. Edward felt exhausted. The hill seemed longer and steeper than normal. *So Zulu's gone,* he thought. He would miss him – they all would.

'It was murder,' Harry said to him as they went back to their room to clean up. 'Nothing less. It sickens me, Eddie. How could anyone do that? How could you deliberately fly over someone so his parachute failed? So he would die a horrible death?'

Edward said nothing.

'Poor Zulu,' Harry continued. 'He would have known. For all that time that he fell, he would have known he was going to die.'

'Don't, Harry.'

'This – this *fucking* war.' He scrunched up his towel and hurled it at the wall, then walked out. Edward paused a moment, then took out his logbook. 'Squirted at Ju 87 and 109s. One 109 confirmed,' he wrote, drawing a small swastika beside it. Then he added, 'Collided with 109 head-on and crashed on landing. Zulu Purnell killed.'

The raiders returned later that afternoon. Not only were most of 'A' Flight out on the balcony of the Xara Palace to witness the attack, so too were a number of the new arrivals. Edward counted sixty bombers then gave up. For the second time that day, black bomb-burst began gushing up from the ground in huge mushrooms of smoke. Layers of the billowing cloud soon merged with one another until the entire airfield and much of the Island disappeared beneath the fog. A few minutes later they were gone. One moment the air was being ripped apart by the noise of guns, engines and explosions, while the next these had faded into nothing and then to an eerie silence. Edward glanced at some of the new pilots. They looked stunned as they gazed out at the slowly dispersing cloud. No-one said a word. The dome at Mostar gradually reappeared, then the outline of the stone-walled fields. Then so did Takali, but a number of narrow columns of smoke remained, rising like black needles into the sky.

'What are those?' asked one of the new boys standing nearby.

'Our wonderful Spitfires,' said Harry. 'Burning.'

Two days later, only seven of the new planes were still fit to fly.

Malta – May, 1942

By the last day of April, 1942, there were just seven airworthy Spitfires left. Edward had flown four times all month. The last occasion, the day after he'd crash-landed, had been another desperate melee, in which they'd once again been hopelessly outnumbered. Two more pilots had been killed and a further eight shot down. Even back on the ground, there was the relentless bombing, the ever-present danger; the aircraft graveyard at Takali was a constant reminder of the mayhem in which they found themselves. And they were hungry, too. The food on the Island had hardly been plentiful even when they'd first arrived, but by the onset of summer the shortages were beginning to be felt more keenly: a small, single rasher of bacon for breakfast, watery soup and hard bread for lunch, a ladle of goat stew or a sardine for dinner. Edward had to tighten the straps on the sides of his shorts. The relentlessness of the action, even when they were not flying, the constantly disturbed nights, the dawn starts, and the lack of basic sustenance meant that the pilots were always exhausted. Edward had never felt so tired in his life. It was fatigue that seemed to shroud him like a cloak: his head felt heavy and throbbed almost constantly; his eyes stung and he found it hard to concentrate. Trudging back and forth between the Xara Palace, he sometimes wondered how he had the energy to lift his feet.

Both at dispersal and in the mess, the atmosphere was like that of a morgue. No-one said much – what was there to say? Everyone was tense, edgy. It wasn't just Butch Hammond glowering about the place. They were losing; it was obvious. So much hope had been placed in the arrival of those Spitfires. That hope had been shattered, and now rumours were going round that gliders were being brought over to Sicily – the photo reconnaissance boys had taken pictures – and that meant only one thing: an airborne invasion was being prepared.

For the first time in his life, Edward began to doubt his immortality. Death was such an incomprehensible thought, and yet he knew there were only so many times he could survive these one-sided aerial battles. As it was, he'd been lucky, but he felt that luck would surely run out, and he would be hit. Despite his fatigue he began lying awake at night, staring up at the ceiling, thoughts of his body being crushed and mangled or incinerated. He wondered how he would live if he lost an arm, or a leg – or both. *I'm not even twenty,* he thought. He wanted to talk to Harry, but stopped himself – he had barely admitted such fears to himself. In any case, Harry was as dispirited as the rest of them. More so; Harry was pining for Kitty.

There were further changes in the squadron, too. Tony, the CO, recovered from his bout of Malta Dog only to be shot down and badly wounded. Squadron Leader Pip Winters arrived to take over. Michael Lindsay was wounded too – by flying shrapnel during another raid on Takali. Harry was given command of 'B' Flight and promoted to Flight Lieutenant. Edward was made a Flying Officer and switched over to 'B' Flight as well. Of the ten Spitfire pilots that had flown out in February, half were now dead or wounded.

At the beginning of May, Butch summoned the four other survivors to the Intelligence Room at the Xara Palace. He had news for them. It was evening, a hot early summer's day drawing to an end. The four of them – Lucky, Harry, Laurie and Edward – stood outside Butch's door like schoolboys summoned before the headmaster.

Lucky knocked, and Butch flung open the door. 'Come in, come in,' he said. Pip, the new CO, was already there. So too was Woody Woodhall. 'Sit anywhere,' said Butch. 'Drink?' They nodded and he went over to a sideboard and poured them all a Scotch. 'White Horse,' he muttered, 'fresh in from Cairo.' Chipped, whisky-stained tumblers were passed around. 'Cheers,' said Butch. He took a large sip himself, grimaced, then said, 'You chaps are old hands now. The original Spitfire pilots on this Island.' He paused and looked at them. 'The Originals – yes, I like that. Anyway, there's good news. It seems some of the Luftwaffe on Sicily are finally being moved out.'

'I thought they were getting ready for invasion,' said Lucky.

'Maybe, but if so, they're going to do it without all their air forces.'

'Where are they going?' asked Harry.

'God knows. Russia. North Africa. Who cares, so long as they're not bombing us. You must have noticed there have been less raids the past couple of days.'

The others nodded.

'Of course,' interjected Woody, 'they might think they've already done what they need to do. I think they could be forgiven for thinking they've neutralised our air capabilities.'

'But they'd be wrong about that,' Butch grinned, 'because we've got more Spits coming.'

'Our good friend President Roosevelt has leant us the USS *Wasp* for a second time,' Woody continued. 'Much bigger than any of our aircraft carriers. And we've got our own *Eagle*. Together that means more than sixty new Spits.'

Lucky whistled.

'Spitfires in numbers – that's what we need,' added Butch. 'It's no good bringing in penny packets of twelve here, ten there.'

'And we need to make sure we use them properly,' continued Woody. 'We made mistakes last time. Big mistakes, at both ends. Well, that's in the past – what we've got to do now is make sure we learn from them.' Woody stroked his moustache, then said, 'So Butch and I have devised a plan. First and foremost, we can't have aircraft arriving that are unfit for battle and which take our overstretched erks three days to put right. So we've talked to the bigwigs in London and they've promised that our sixty Spits will not leave those carriers without the proper paint scheme, without their guns properly harmonised at 250 yards, or without being fully equipped for immediate combat flying. There's also going to be a faster turnaround once they land. We're going to split them into three groups for landing, at Takali, Luqa and Hal Far. Each aircraft will also be clearly numbered, and on touching down will be directed by waiting erks into their corresponding pen. There, an experienced Malta pilot will be poised to hop into the cockpit. At each pen there will be a sufficient number of army and ground crew ready with cans of fuel and ammunition, as well as mechanics to make any necessary adjustments. Our aim is to have each one ready for action no more than twenty minutes after touchdown.'

The pilots glanced at each other. 'Sounds more like it, Woody,' said Lucky.

'Good. Glad you think so. But there's more. I don't know whether you've heard of the Magic Carpet Service?'

They shook their heads. Woody grinned. 'No? I'm glad. At least some things are still secret on this damned place.' He looked at Butch, who chuckled and rubbed his neck. 'The Magic Carpet Service, gentlemen,' Woody continued, 'is what has been keeping you in fuel. It consists of fast Royal Navy minelayers and minelaying submarines. They've been regularly visiting Malta in the dead of night, offloading as much fuel as they can hold, and zipping off back to Alex and Gib. So far we haven't been caught out but summer's here and with the shorter nights it's becoming increasingly difficult to do this undetected. The Spits are due in on the morning of the ninth. We've got enough fuel put by for a day or so of flying, but it is absolutely imperative that the minelayer *Welshman* successfully reaches Malta that night, 9th/10th May. We're going to cover Grand Harbour in smoke to hide her, and we're going to send up as many of our fighters as possible. If we unload *Welshman* without any problem and keep enough Spits in the air, we may yet turn the tables. Everything will hang on those twenty-four hours. The entire future of this Island.' He paused again, stood up and looked out of the window towards Takali. 'Now you're probably wondering why we're telling you all this now. Well, the reason is this: we need some experienced pilots to lead the new boys in, and we want you four to do that.' The pilots glanced at each other again. Edward shifted in his seat. 'Tomorrow night, a Hudson is going to take you back to Gib, where you'll meet the carriers and join the pilots headed for Malta. You're not to fly tomorrow. Just stay out of trouble and keep yourselves fit. Pip here is going to stay with the rest of the squadron until you get back. Clear?' They nodded. 'You'll be briefed properly once you get to Gib. Questions? No? Well then, good luck. I know you won't let us down.'

Three days in Gibraltar. Three days of lights, beer and steaks, of streets thronging with men, women, and an array of Allied servicemen. It took them a day just to get over the shock, another day to get over their exhaustion and then, just as they began to really enjoy themselves, it was time to leave. Back to business. Back onto an aircraft carrier, and back into the Mediterranean.

Compared with the *Furious,* the *Wasp* seemed enormous. This time, Edward felt little of the anxiety he'd experienced during that first flight to Malta. His confidence was well founded: the new Spitfire left the flight deck with twenty yards to spare. He was leading the third group, the last batch of sixteen to leave the carrier.

A little over three hours later, there was Malta, that tiny floating leaf upon a vast dark sea.

'Hullo Woody, this is Piper leader,' he called up over the radio. 'Permission to land.'

'Well done, Eddie,' Woody's ever-calm voice crackled through his headphones. 'You're clear to land. Watch out for little jobs. There are a few around.'

'All right, Woody.' Edward glanced around him. The aircraft in his group seemed to all be there. Away to his left he saw a number of enemy fighters circling menacingly. Some more were wheeling in a low-level dogfight with some Spitfires further inland. Edward breathed in deeply. German and Italian radio chatter suddenly filled his ears. Someone shouted 'Break!' and he turned to see several of his group peeling off to engage the 109s. *Well, I'm coming in,* he thought, and circling Hal Far, turned to land. The airfield, like Takali, was littered with wrecks and bomb damage, but a rough landing strip had been cleared, marked with painted oil cans and flags. He throttled back, lowered his undercarriage, and watched the ground hurrying to meet him. A slight bump and he was racing along the runway. Blue and orange tracer raced overhead then a 109 roared passed, guns rattling, followed moments later by a Spitfire. An erk ran up to him, jumped onto the wing and frantically pointed him towards a blast pen of sand-filled petrol tins some way beyond the main airfield. Edward taxied into position, and cut the engine. As he stiffly eased himself out of the cockpit, ground crew had already jumped up onto the wing, rocking the Spitfire from side to side. Men swarmed around. The gun ports were open before Edward could jump onto the wing, and long belts of bullets and cannon, were being passed up, their brass casings glinting in the morning sun. Soldiers carrying four-gallon petrol cans hurried over. Edward jumped onto the ground and saw a replacement pilot was already waiting.

'She's all yours,' Edward told him, running his hands through sweat-drenched hair.

'How's she flying?' the other pilot asked.

'Perfectly. Got me back here all right.' Edward smiled, patted the man on the back, and then hurried back towards dispersal. Planes were taxiing to their blast pens, while the last few still airborne came into land. The noise of the engines was deafening, the dust from the prop wash clouding the airfield in a thin haze. In the skies above, aircraft continued to wheel and turn, guns chattering. At dispersal, Edward met the Luqa station commander as the last Spitfire came in to land.

'That's the lot,' he said. 'Some of the Takali lot are already airborne again, you know.'

'Really?' said Edward. 'That's great news.' So Woody and Butch's plan was working.

Raids appeared over the Island throughout the rest of the day. Edward flew again just before six o'clock, one of thirty-three Spitfires scrambled to intercept a formation of Italian bombers and Macchi fighters. He'd never seen so many Spitfires heading into battle before, and he grinned to himself to see such a sight. He never even fired his guns, the raid dispersing before he could join the fray. Landing back at Takali, he found Butch in jubilant mood. Only four Spitfires had been lost en route to Malta, and a further four during the day, but there were still well over fifty fit and ready for battle. 'Tomorrow,' grinned Butch, 'we're going to cause merry havoc.' The others were no less buoyant; the change in confidence was overwhelming.

'This is more like it,' Harry said to him, 'don't you think?'

'Definitely.'

'For the first time since we arrived on this damn place, it seems as though we might actually be able to make a difference. If they do send over their gliders, they're not going to know what's hit them.'

They sat on a rock outside the wrecked dispersal hut, and smoked Lucky Stripes bought from American sailors on the *Wasp*. Activity hummed over the airfield. Pristine Spitfires and battered Hurricanes filled the blast pens, soldiers and erks scurried from one pen to another; the sound of banging, metal on metal, resounded across the hot dusty field. Edward even saw a group of erks laughing; there'd been a short supply of humour recently.

'I wonder what they'll fling at us tomorrow,' said Harry.

Edward flicked away his cigarette butt. 'I hate to think.'

The whole squadron was on standby from dawn – for once there were enough aircraft for both flights. Squadron markings had even been painted on the fuselages. At dispersal, mugs of tea and a chunk of hard bread. Someone had made a number of armchairs from petrol cans with rugs thrown over them. Edward and Harry sat in two of them, mugs resting on the arms. Edward watched strips of pale grey spread out across the eastern sky. The colour changed to pink, then yellow and finally burnished orange as the first rays of sunlight lifted over the hills and flooded across the Island.

'It's going to be hot,' said Edward.

'Hm,' said Harry, looking forlornly at his bread.

'Not hungry?' Edward asked.

'No – for some reason I'm not at all.' He winced, and breathed out deeply, lips pursed. 'Have my bread if you like.'

Edward took it gratefully. He'd quickly got used to the more normal daily diet Gibraltar and the *Wasp* had to offer. A day back on Malta and his stomach could not stop grinding.

By the time the sun had fully risen, Harry had disappeared to the latrines more than once and was wincing almost constantly.

'You've got the Dog, haven't you?' said Edward.

'I don't know, but it's bloody painful,' said Harry. 'My guts are agony.'

'You can't fly like that,' said Edward.

'I'll be fine.' Harry clutched his stomach.

'I'm getting the MO.'

'No, don't,' said Harry, but as Edward got up he made no further effort to stop his friend.

The Medical Officer asked him a few questions, pressed his fingers onto Harry's stomach. Then he felt Harry's brow. 'Malta Dog,' he said at length. 'You shouldn't fly.'

'I'll be all right, honestly,' Harry protested. The MO called over Pip. 'Harry here's got the Dog,' said the MO. 'He needs to get to bed.'

'Pip, I'll be fine, really,' said Harry.

'Harry, tell me honestly, what would happen if you farted at

15,000 feet?' Harry looked sheepish. 'Remember that someone else will most likely be flying the plane after you. Think about them a moment, will you?'

Harry raised a hand – *all right, you win*. Pip turned to Edward. 'Eddie, you're taking over 'B' Flight until Harry's better. All right?'

'All right, Pip.'

The MO turned back to Harry. 'Stay here for the moment, and I'll get you back up to the Xara Palace as soon as there's a bus going up.'

Pip and the MO wandered off. 'Bloody hell,' muttered Harry.

'They're right, though,' said Edward. 'Overdo it now and you'll end up at Imtarfa like Tony. Sweat it out and you'll be fine.' He got up, wandered over to the nearest blast pen and smoked another of his Lucky Stripes. He felt impatient. Everyone knew this was going to be a big day. His stomach was churning, waves of nausea rising up his throat. *Where the hell are they?* he thought. A glance at his watch. Twenty-past nine. *Soon*. He wanted to get on with it.

Twenty minutes later the field telephone rang. Bandits on their way, two squadrons from Luqa scrambled. Edward kicked the ground as a multitude of sirens rang out across the Island.

A few minutes later, the phone rang again. This time 636 Squadron were to scramble too. Large formations of bombers were heading towards the harbours where the *Welshman* had yet to leave. That familiar feeling: a tremor down the spine, a heaviness in his stomach, and Edward was dashing to his aircraft. Minutes later, in a flurry of dust and roaring engines, the two flights hurtled across the rough airfield and up to meet the attackers. There was no time to climb high into the sky. Instead, Edward led the flight straight towards the harbours to catch the bombers as they came out of their dives. A thick shroud of green-grey smoke covered Valletta and Grand Harbour; above it, countless dark puffs of ack-ack fire dotted the sky. Stukas and Ju 88s peeled off and dived through this hail of steel, some disappearing with trails of black smoke behind, others reappearing like ghosts from the smokescreen moments later. Higher still, Spitfires were wheeling and pirouetting with the escorts of 109s. For once the contest appeared to be even.

Edward called 'B' Flight into line astern then one by one, they peeled off and dived on the bombers as they flew out over Sliema and towards the north of the Island. Edward picked out a Junkers 88, dived down until he was beneath it then pulled back hard on the stick, and opened fire at its silvery grey underside. His tracer seemed to hit and he saw the aircraft shudder, but then another Junkers screamed over his head so close that he nearly collided again. He cursed, then banked hard and felt the blood drain from his head, and his vision start to cloud. As his sight returned and he felt the weight of negative gravity lift from his chest, he spotted a lone Stuka and turned towards it, only for a Hurricane – *of all things!* – to attack it head on. A puff of smoke, then flames erupted with lightning speed from the engine and the Stuka disappeared into the sea.

Edward flew out over the Mediterranean to try and gain height. All cohesion had gone in the brief and tumbling melee. He watched a parachute drift past. The man – a German, he thought – waved. Edward thought of Zulu. *I should shoot him,* he thought, but knew he wouldn't. Instead he waved back.

He climbed to twelve thousand, turned so that the sun was behind and scanned the skies. Fighting was still going on over the harbours, puffs and trails of smoke still peppering the sky. To the south, he could see a group of four 109s. Evidently they hadn't seen him, so he dived once more, the Spitfire shaking and screaming as he did so. At the last moment, they spotted him; he could hear them shouting to break over his headphones, but one was more sluggish than the others and Edward latched on to it. The Messerschmitt swayed in and out of his gunsight, gradually becoming larger. He hovered his thumb above the gun button. Allowing his target to drop slightly to allow for the fall of bullets, he hovered his thumb a moment more then pressed down. The Spitfire shook and he watched white smoke appear from the engine. Edward pressed down again. A second of fire then nothing. *Shit!* he cursed. *Out of bloody ammunition!* The 109 banked, then turned over on its back and dived. A controlled dive? Edward couldn't tell. By the time he had swooped himself and looked for the stricken Messerschmitt, it was gone.

Edward was one of the last to land, and for once he was not harried by enemy fighters, nor was the airfield littered with bomb craters. His shirt was drenched with sweat, and his eyes stung with fatigue.

And yet he felt exhilarated as he clambered out of the cockpit, past a row of Spitfires, gleaming and clicking as their engines cooled, and hurried over to dispersal where the Intelligence Officer stood with Butch. The others, he could tell, felt the same way, as they gabbled, all talking at once, some re-enacting their own personal battles, arms outstretched as they described how a Stuka or Junkers had plummeted into the sea. Lucky claimed to have seen no less than twelve enemy parachutes drifting down into the sea, while Laurie had watched two 109s crash, one near St Paul's Bay, the other at Naxxar. Nearly every pilot made claims.

'So you damaged a Junkers 88, and got a probable 109,' said the IO eventually to Edward.

'Yes – but the smoke from the 109 was white. Coolant – he wouldn't have made it back.'

'Hm,' said the Intelligence Officer, 'nevertheless, until proven otherwise . . .' He let the sentence hang.

Edward shrugged. 'Whatever.' He didn't care. A hand slapped him on the back. 'Christ, that was some scrap,' said Lucky. He whistled. 'Wasn't that something? Boy, there'll be some long faces in Sicily right now.'

Edward grinned. 'Perhaps they'll all go home.'

'Well, maybe they will.'

They did not, as it happened. They returned twice more that day, but on both occasions there were plenty of aircraft to meet them. By the time the sun set again, sixty-five enemy aircraft had been either damaged or destroyed and the defenders had won the biggest victory since the Island's war had begun. So Butch had been right all along, Edward thought to himself. It really *was* about having more Spitfires.

That night in the mess at the Xara Palace, bottles of Scotch were produced – Baggy Bagshawe announced he had kept a supply back for just such an occasion – and everyone drank, sang, and made innumerable toasts. Soon Edward was retching as much as Harry, not because he was stricken with dysentery, but because he was the drunkest he'd been since leaving England two-and-a-half very long months before.

Malta – June, 1942

St Paul's Bay in the north of the Island. The whole squadron had been stood down for two days and sent up to the rest camp there – a villa looking out to the sea, with a lawn that ran down to the rocks. There was even a small wooden jetty with a couple of brightly painted rowing boats moored alongside.

It had been a long walk there, but the moment he stepped onto the sweeping lawn and saw the shimmering sea beyond, Edward knew it had been worth the effort. The contrast with the dust and mayhem of Takali, the ugliness of the countless wrecked aircraft and piles of stone was so great that for almost the first time since he had arrived on the Island, he felt as though he had found a haven sheltered from the war.

Edward slept – on a day bed in the garden, beneath a large sweetly scented jasmine, where the shade offered protection from the sun, but not from the heat. Later, with the sun only slowly beginning to drop, Harry nudged him awake. 'Let's take a boat out,' he said. 'Cool off a bit.'

Edward rubbed his eyes, sat up and wiped the sweat from his face. 'All right,' he said. They ambled down to the jetty, the wooden boards almost burning their bare feet. Some others had already taken one of the boats out, but the other, a vivid blue with two eyes painted at the prow, was still lashed to its mooring.

'D'you know,' said Harry as he unsteadily clambered onto the boat, 'this is the first time I've been on the water since I've been here. Nearly four months it's taken me. And I've always loved the sea. All that swimming in Cornwall when we were first at Perranporth – it was fun, wasn't it?'

'A lifetime ago,' said Edward. He untied the rope, stepped aboard and pushed them gently away from the jetty. Beneath them, the water was clear. Small fish weaved languidly between the dark rocks, glinting silver in the sun. He sat back, letting his arms and feet trail in the cool water. 'These past four months feel like a lifetime,' he added.

'Yes. Yes, they do. I miss England.'

'Well, we'll probably be back soon. Then we'll get proper leave. Bliss. You'll see Kitty again.'

'If she hasn't forgotten about me.'

'Course she hasn't.'

'Nearly two months and I haven't heard a word.'

'Come on, Harry, you know what the mail is like. Next week you'll probably get twenty all at once.'

'Yes, I'm sure you're right. She *must* have been writing, mustn't she?'

'Of course.'

Harry seemed to brighten, then he said, 'D'you remember our perfect day? The one we dreamed about in Canada?'

Edward smiled. 'Of course. The Ritz, long baths and a fabulous dinner. And girls.'

'Well, when we get back I think we should finally do it, don't you? We're bound to get a decent amount of leave.'

'And we're not spending much money – at least apart from what I'm losing to those card sharks.'

'Exactly. Even Malta has some plus points.'

Edward was thoughtful for a moment, then said, 'But not many.'

'No.' Harry scooped up some water and splashed it on his face. 'You're right, you know, it does feel like we've been here for ever. Which is why we should indulge ourselves when we get home.'

'All right – it's a deal.' Edward closed his eyes for a moment and felt the heat of the sun's rays bear down upon his face. Harry might have been pining for Kitty, but Edward still envied him. 'I wish I had a girl to go back to,' he said suddenly. 'Don't laugh, but I hate the thought of something happening to me before I've had the chance to – well, you know.'

'Add that to the list of things to do when we get back,' said Harry. 'There'll be lots of willing punters in London. Think of all the men that are away. Many more girls to go round.'

Edward opened his eyes. 'I hope you're right.'

'Look, Eddie, I'm sorry,' said Harry. 'I've been banging on about Kitty and moping around. Thoughtless of me.'

'Don't be ridiculous.'

'No, I mean it. I've been a bore and rather self-centred of late. And I'm sorry.'

'Don't be. Anyway, what are friends for?' Edward suddenly clasped each side of the boat and began to rock it from side to side.

'Hey, stop that!' said Harry, but as he did so he lost his balance and fell into the water. Edward lost sight of him, and as the water settled again, peered over the edge. He could not see him. Seconds passed. For just a moment, he began to worry, but then the boat lurched, Edward fell backwards, and Harry, from the other side, was pulling him into the water too.

'Christ!' said Edward as he cleared the surface once more, 'you had me worried for a moment.'

'Well, it's a good job I'm such a wonderful swimmer. That'll teach you to push me overboard. Mind you, it's beautiful once you're in.' He turned onto his back, and paddled lazily around the boat. 'Look at that sky, not a cloud, not a single aeroplane. How on earth can we be at war?'

A few days later, the mail arrived with a large bundle for Harry, most of which was from Kitty. 'Look,' he said to Edward pointing out the postmarks on each, 'she's been writing since she got back.'

'I told you you shouldn't have worried.'

Harry grinned. 'I know. You were right.'

Edward had some post too – his first since arriving on Malta. His letters had also been held up; the first was postmarked February. He read his letters alone, in a quiet corner of the mess, clutching the light blue paper that his mother always used. He could picture her writing them at her small bureau in the corner of the drawing room. The writing was so familiar – the same handwriting he had read throughout his schooldays and beyond: careful, legible, with always a word misspelt somewhere. Her news was about village life, of the garden, and the increased rationing. News about the local Spitfire Fund having raised enough money for its second aircraft. Her worries for him, of course. '*I hope you are taking good care of yourself and not taking any more risks than you have to.*' There were letters from his father, too, full of equally inconsequential news. The annual grudge cricket match between Chilton and a neighbouring village had been held as normal, the teams made up from old men and a few younger ones home on leave. '*We could have done with you, though,*' his father had written. '*We were very short of batting and I'm afraid we didn't score enough runs. I managed a magnificent seven not out, including a streaky four through gulley!'*

Reading them through again, he felt his eyes begin to water. He couldn't help it, and glanced around the room to check no-one was looking at him before raising his handkerchief to the corners of his eyes. He wished he was a child again, protected by his parents; wished he'd not been so anxious to join the war. The enthusiasm with which he'd signed up for the Air Force and headed off to fight now ashamed him. Later, he tried to write a reply, but what could he say? What *would* he say even if there was no censor? That he was brushing with death every day, that he weighed less than ten stone and that he was alive and largely unscathed only due to a twist of fate he was unable to explain?

Dear Mother and Father, he began, then stopped. For a while he tapped his pen on the table, then eventually he wrote:

Thanks so much for all your lovely letters, which arrived all in a rush together this morning. You can have no idea how avidly one devours mail of any sort in this place. I think I've read them all at least four times! As you have gathered, things are pretty hectic here, but I'm well and taking good care of myself, so there's no need to worry (although a bit more to eat would be an improvement!) Life here when not flying is pretty dreary – there's little to do, (except reread letters!) and right now it's very hot. I'm glad to hear the garden's looking so lovely. There are pretty wild flowers here, but it's very dry and dusty, not at all the green lushness you get back home. I'm very glad to have had Harry here with me. His 'girl' has just sent him a bundle of letters so he's happy as anything at the moment. Mind you, most of the others are good sorts too.

We're getting through a fair few books here. Penguin paperbacks are always welcome so do send some if you get half the chance, I'll probably be back home by the time the next mail arrives if it's anything like as slow as the last lot.

I sometimes wonder what my other friends from school are doing. Don't think there's anything more to say at the moment.

Your loving son,

Edward

PS Hopefully next year I can play in the cricket match and score an unbeaten century – that would show them!

*

He wondered whether he really would be in England next summer. Unlikely, but good to end on an upbeat note. Sealing the envelope, he scrawled the address and sat back and wiped his brow. The mess was cooler than most places – the thick stone walls and high windows ensured the sun rarely had a chance to penetrate the inner sanctum of the palace – but he still felt hot, his clothes clammy. A fly buzzed about his head then flew off and briefly he followed its flight, then glanced around the room. Quiet. The drink had all but run dry, the pilots were tired, and in this heat most simply hid out in their rooms once dinner, such as it was, had finished. *I want to go home,* he thought to himself. Just a few more weeks. Changes had been made to the length of tour for pilots serving on the Island. Only the day before, new arrangements had been announced. The intensity of the air fighting over Malta had, Baggy told them, now been 'officially recognised'. Any pilots who had been on the Island for six months or more would be leaving on the first plane flying out, while henceforth three months would be considered a full tour. Well, Edward and the other so-called 'originals' had already been there for nearly five. Lucky reckoned they'd be expected to do six. 'We'll be out of here in July,' he told Edward. 'They won't want all the old hands leaving at once.' And then what? Instructing, most likely – it was seen as a break, a chance for tired and battle-worn pilots to take it easy for a while. Most probably England; at any rate, he hoped so. He wondered whether he and Harry would stick together. Unlikely. Rather, they and the others would be split up and posted all over the place. New friendships would have to be made, and yet he could not believe he would ever find such good friends again. This lot, this squadron, they were the one good thing to have come out of this posting to Malta.

Edward sighed and heaved himself up out of his seat. Although he felt drained, he knew would be unable to get to sleep – not yet at any rate. Outside, the heat was still oppressive, so he went to his room instead. Harry was there already, lying on his bed. He looked up when Edward entered. 'Eddie – what's the matter?'

'This place,' muttered Edward. 'There's nowhere to go, nothing to see and nothing to do even if you went there. And it's too bloody hot.'

*

15th June, 1942. A day spent on convoy patrol. A double convoy had been mounted, one from Gibraltar, one from Alexandria. It was the first to be attempted since the failed convoy in March, and at his pep talk the previous evening Hugh Pughe Lloyd had made it clear that, once again, the future of the Island depended on the successful arrival of these two convoys; it was critical, a matter of life and death, that one or more of the ships made it to port. Without them, the Island faced starvation and the defenders a drastic shortage of fuel and ammunition. It was as simple as that. And while there was now no shortage of Spitfires – more had arrived during the last month – without petrol and bullets they might just as well still be in England, for all the good they could do. 'We're all depending on you,' Lloyd told them. 'It's up to you to make sure you bring these ships safely into port.'

Not until his third flight of the day, did Edward finally spot the enemy: two cruisers and a dozen destroyers glinting brightly in the late evening sun. He watched amazed as the Albacores – flimsy navy biplanes – wobbled uncertainly and gently dived down towards the ships, the sky around them busy with puffs of flak and tracer. Most of the torpedoes ran wide as the Italian ships dodged and swerved to avoid them. But one of the cruisers seemed to have been hit: a huge explosion of water and smoke suddenly pitched into the sky. From the narrow confines of his cockpit, Edward cheered to see such a sight.

16th June, 1942. News of the convoys reached Takali by mid-morning. Just two ships had made it into Grand Harbour. Two out of seventeen. The previous evening, as the Albacores had been attacking the Italian fleet, the decision had been made to send the entire eastern convoy back to Alexandria. 'We lost sixteen fucking pilots trying to protect that lot,' grumbled Butch. 'What a fucking waste of time.'

Later, in the mess, they were all there to hear the Governor, Lord Gort, make a broadcast to the island. The convoy had largely failed, he admitted. It was a blow, but every effort would be made to send another at the earliest opportunity. In the meantime, it was up to every man, woman and child to do their bit and make the most of what little was left. 'We have our conviction that our cause is just,'

Gort told them, his clipped, grainy voice crackling across the mess, 'we have trust in ourselves and we have a still greater belief – our faith, in Almighty God. Strong in that faith, let us go forward together to victory.'

Baggy Bagshawe stood up and turned off the radio. The room was silent, except for the sound of the adjutant's footsteps on the wooden floor. 'Well,' he said as he sat down again, 'my wife always said I could do with shedding a few pounds.' There were a few laughs but not many. Their aerial victory of May 10 seemed little more than a distant memory.

21st June, 1942, and a messed-up attack on some Cants – lumbering Italian bombers that should have been a gift. Harry had led the flight perfectly. They'd had the advantage of height, surprise, and even the sun behind them as well. Red section had successfully drawn off the fighter escort leaving Edward's Blue Section to attack the bombers. They'd been sitting ducks, a gift if ever there was one.

'What happened?' said Harry once they had landed back down at Takali. 'I got one, the others missed,' said Edward as he jumped off the wing of his aircraft. He ached all over and winced as he stretched his legs. 'I'm sorry, Harry. We cocked it up.'

Harry shook his head. 'God, it's not your fault. No bloody petrol, no bloody ammo, so no bloody chance to practise.' He sighed and ran his hands through his hair. 'But you're right, we should have done better than that.' The sun bore down. They'd been high up there – some 28,000 feet waiting for those bombers to turn up – and now, with the sudden change of temperature, Edward's fingers throbbed and streaks of pain shot down his arms. He grimaced and clutched his hands under his arms. 'You all right?' Harry asked him.

'Burnt my fingers getting in, then they froze, now they hurt like hell.'

'You idiot. Well, make sure you see the MO.'

'Yes, sir,' said Edward.

Harry cuffed him lightly on the head. 'At least you got another one. Shouldn't be any problem getting it confirmed.'

'No, I don't suppose so,' Edward replied.

'One more and you'll be an ace.'

Edward nodded.

'I thought that's what you always wanted.'

'I suppose I did. Doesn't seem so important now, though, does it? Who shot down what – we still missed the other four.' He looked down at the dust on his flying boots, on his knees and arms. 'Christ, I'm sick of this dust and heat. I'm sick of Malta. After the war, remind me never to come back.'

Harry laughed and put an arm on his shoulder. 'Not long now,' he said. 'We'll be out of here soon.'

'B' Flight was scrambled again later in the afternoon – just one section. 'I'll take Red Section,' Harry told Edward. 'You rest that hand of yours.'

Edward acquiesced. From dispersal he watched the four Spitfires roar down the runway and head off amidst clouds of swirling dust. He ambled over to the maintenance units. In a long pit, erks were busy at work hammering at damaged sections of wing or fuselage. Two Merlin engines sat hoisted on blocks. The smell of dry earth and oil was strong on the air. Edward looked down watching – *they never stop*, he thought.

'Well done on your Cant this morning, sir,' said a voice beside him.

Edward looked round and saw Pete Summersby.

'Thanks.'

'Several of us were over there at Luqa trying to get one of the Wellingtons back in the air and we saw it come down. Smashed into a wall – otherwise I reckon he'd have made it. We thought it must have been someone from Takali that got it.'

Edward said, 'We should have had more.'

'Actually, we went over to have a look,' said Pete. 'Well – it was so close. Right old mess and burning away. Could see the pilot slumped in his seat, but then the cockpit went up in flames too. Funny thing was that as he burned his muscles must have contracted or something, because his arm came up in a kind of Nazi salute. I know they're Allies, but we thought that was taking things a bit far.' He chuckled and looked at Edward to see if he was enjoying the joke. Edward stared at him. 'It was pretty funny,' Pete added.

'I'd better get back,' said Edward, turning away.

'Keep up the good work, sir.'

Edward wandered back to dispersal trying to get the image of the Italian pilot's arm out of his mind. The other pilots sat outside quietly; some, as ever, playing cards, others reading, others asleep. Edward sat down on a rock next to Mike Lindsay. 'Want this?' Mike asked, passing him a newspaper.

'Thanks,' said Edward. A *Daily Express* sent over from home. Out of date, but better than nothing.

The Spitfires began returning twenty minutes later, a faint hum at first, then suddenly two were circling Takali and coming in to land. A third joined them. Edward watched them roll across the field and taxi towards their blast pens.

The first two pilots arrived back at dispersal. They were two new boys, on the Island less than three weeks: Bryan Hilditch and Simon Ferguson. Their hair was damp, their shirts stained dark with sweat.

'Who's not back?' the Intelligence Officer asked.

'Harry,' said Bryan.

Edward stood up immediately. 'Where is he?'

'I'm not sure exactly,' said Bryan. 'We ran into a few 109s. We chased around for a while but then they went off.'

'We both got in a few squirts,' said Simon, 'but I don't think we hit them. I didn't, anyway.'

'Simon and I were still together, so we headed home,' continued Bryan.

'I'm sure he'll be back in a minute,' said Edward.

The third pilot, an Australian called Keith Roberts, joined them. Pip had now come over as well. 'Where's Harry?' the CO asked.

Tony shrugged. 'He was on the tail of a 109 last time I saw him. Then I was busy keeping two off my arse. I dived and lost them, but I don't know what happened to Harry. I'm sure he's all right, though. He was right on that 109.'

The pilots chattered about the flight, taking off their mae wests and lighting cigarettes. Edward stood next to Pip and scanned the sky. Nothing.

'He'll be back in a minute,' said Edward.

Minutes passed. A faint whirr of an engine, but not Harry – perhaps an aircraft over Luqa. The other pilots were now sitting up, also searching the sky, straining their ears. Twenty minutes passed.

'He'll be getting short of fuel,' said Pip. He marched over to the field telephone, Edward following. 'Get Woody on the phone, will you?' he barked at the duty orderly, then snatched the receiver. 'Hello, Woody? We're missing Harry . . . No . . . No . . . Right. OK.'

Edward watched the CO, trying to guess what his expression could mean. *Come on, Harry,* he thought. *Where the hell are you?*

'Come on,' said Pip. 'Mike, you come too.'

'What did Woody say?' asked Edward as they grabbed their mae wests, helmets and goggles.

'Harry told him he was going after the 109, but now can't get through to him. Says he no longer has a plot but it could just mean he's followed this Jerry out to sea and is under radar.' They hurried towards the aircraft. 'Come on, you lot!' yelled Pip at the erks, 'Get a bloody move on!'

A dull, nauseous sensation overtook Edward as they took off a few minutes later. One moment he feared the worst; the next he thought, *No, Harry will be fine.* 'Please, Harry,' he said out loud, 'please be out there.'

'OK, we'll be White Section for this flight,' said Pip. 'Hello, Woody, White Leader here. We're airborne.'

'Hello, Pip, all right I've got you. Head out on a bearing of 355, north of St Paul's. Look out north of Gozo. You're clear at the moment, but keep a watchout for the little jobs.'

They headed out, Pip and Mike at a thousand feet, Edward at just three hundred. The Mediterranean twinkled benignly, invitingly, a deep soft blue. *It's so big,* thought Edward. *A needle in a haystack.* He'd done a few of these searches – just two days before a 601 pilot had come down. They'd found him, and had covered the air-sea rescue launch as it had ploughed across the sea to pick him up. Pilots were often baling out into the sea; an occupational hazard over Malta.

Over an hour they searched. Edward's eyes ached. The sky was empty, the sea was empty. He thought of what Harry had said in the boat at St Paul's Bay – about how strange it seemed that they should be in the middle of a war when the sky and sea seemed so peaceful. It was like that now; the war seemed to have vanished, taking Harry with it.

'Come on,' said Pip eventually. 'Home.'

'Ten more minutes,' said Edward. 'Please, Pip.'

They circled again. *What if he's still out there,* thought Edward. *What if he can see us and we can't see him?* He strained his eyes, blinked, stared again. A flash of white in the corner of his eye. He turned, but nothing; *a wave breaking.*

'Woody, this is White Leader,' Pip's voice crackled in his headset. 'Returning to base.'

No, thought Edward, *this can't be happening.* 'Harry, where are you? Where are you? Help me,' he mumbled.

'White Two, come on. We're returning to base. Now. That's an order.'

For a moment, Edward took his hand from the stick and clutched his head, crouching in the cockpit. *No,* he thought, *I can't do this. I can't leave Harry here.* 'Oh, God,' he said out loud, 'please don't let this happen.' He wanted to scream, to shout out, and tell the world of the anguish he felt. *If only I hadn't burnt my hand. Harry would still be at Takali.* His left hand found the throttle, rammed it forward, while his right turned the stick to the right. This was the moment, the moment hope was lost, the moment he was deserting his friend. Banking, he climbed to join the others, the vast expanse of sea slipping behind him. He knew then that his life would never be quite the same again.

Malta – June, 1995

There was nothing left of Takali, except for rows of post-war Nissen huts. The airfield had ceased to exist; at one end, where dispersal had stood, a football stadium had been built instead. They stopped, looked around, trying to remember where the pens and maintenance pits had once been, but the place had changed too much. Edward was glad it had gone, but it made him feel old.

'Come on,' said Lucky. 'Let's go to Mdina.'

Lucky was talking as they drove up the road towards Rabat, but Edward was not listening. It was now, more than at any point since his return to Malta, that the passage of time seemed to have melted. Gazing out of the window, the warm air buffeting his face, he looked up at the imposing bastions of Mdina, dominated by the dome of its cathedral, bleached and stark against the deep blue sky. And – yes – there was the Xara Palace; he could actually see the balcony, that place where they spent so many hours; where they watched the battles raging over Takali. This road, too – he sighed. How many times had he trod this route, up and down, back and forth? How many dawns had spread over the Island as they trudged sleepily down towards the airfield? How many evenings had he seen the lengthening shadows across the road stretch and disappear entirely at the end of another long day? It was such a small passage of his life – six months only – and yet now he could recall so much so very clearly. Even sitting in Lucky's car, the wind in his face, took him back to that first time in the bus, that hopeless, rickety old bus, with its blown windows and grinding gears. Edward smiled to himself.

Lucky turned the car up a short, steep incline, past the Pointe de Vue – *ah, yes, there were pilots housed there too* – and into the main square of Rabat.

'OK,' said Lucky. 'Let's go. Only residents or tradesmen are allowed to drive into Mdina. It's not quite the Silent City it used to be, but it's still a damn sight quieter than most places.' They ambled slowly over the bridge and through the city gate. The narrow streets were cool where dark shadows protected them from the glare of the sun.

'It hasn't changed at all,' said Edward, staring up at the high walls and stone windows, and baskets of vibrant bougainvillaea. 'It really is exactly as I remember.' He grinned at Lucky, glad to have somebody to share this moment with. They turned down a side street and emerged into a courtyard. Workmen's trucks and building materials filled one side of the square, but facing them, unmistakably, were the columns, ornate cornicing and elegant windows of the Xara Palace.

'Do you think we can see inside?' Edward asked.

'I'm sure we can.'

A workman told them to speak to the foreman. 'He's inside somewhere,' he said, then looking at them said, 'OK, I'll show you.'

They followed him into the hall and inner courtyard. *That smell,* thought Edward – stone dust, cool and musty; it was so familiar to him. A man appeared – small, dark skinned, and a four-day growth of beard. 'Yes?' he said. 'Can I help?'

'Sure you can,' said Lucky. 'We used to live here during the war. We were pilots with the RAF. Any chance we could have a little look around? For old times' sake?'

The foreman eyed them a moment, then said, 'Of course.' He spread out his hand. 'Have a good look. Just excuse the mess.'

'Oh, we're not worried about that.'

The foreman led them to the stairs. 'Up there,' he said. 'All the rooms and the balcony.'

'Much obliged to you,' said Lucky. 'We won't be long.'

The foreman waved another hand. 'Take your time.'

They found their old room easily. It had yet to be touched. Paint peeled from the ceiling, the thick floorboards were covered in dust and it was completely bare, but Edward had no difficulty envisaging how it had once been. He closed his eyes and opened them again, half expecting to see Harry lying on his bed in the far corner, one arm behind his head, the other holding aloft a folded-back battered old paperback. He could almost hear Harry's voice: '*Eddie, there you are.*' He smiled, remembering. *I still miss him so much,* he thought, then turning to Lucky, said, 'Your bed was here, beneath the window.'

'Yeah, it was, and yours was over there.'

Edward looked at the width of the walls next to the windows. 'No wonder we felt quite safe here. Few bombs would have got through these.'

'We were still pretty cavalier, though, don't you think? I don't ever recall taking shelter. Maybe we hit the deck a few times, but that was about it. I think a bomb did hit the place once, but didn't explode.'

'There were a lot of those.'

Lucky smiled. 'I reckon we owe those Polish factory workers, don't you?'

'I think we do.'

'Mind you,' he added, 'they got the Pointe de Vue, of course. How many were killed then? Quite a few.'

Edward shrugged. 'Half a dozen?'

Up another flight of stone stairs, through the old mess and the intelligence room, past several workmen, and out onto the balcony. Half the Island lay spread out before them. Edward stared, scanning the sweep of fields, villages and towns, shimmering in the late morning heat.

'Do you remember the time Butch shot down that 109 from up here?' said Lucky.

'Yes,' chuckled Edward. 'He was mad with rage.'

'He grabbed the Lewis gun and started firing away, shouting, "You fucking bastards!" Butch could get real mad when he wanted to.'

'Quite incredible that he hit him. I know that 109 was close, but I don't think I ever saw anyone else shoot down a plane with a Lewis.'

'I don't suppose that pilot could believe he'd been hit either. He went down just over there, at the foot of the hill beneath Imtarfa.' He pointed, then said, 'Remember Imtarfa?'

'Of course.'

'You used to visit me when I'd been wounded.'

'Apart from Laurie Bowles, you were the only one left. The only one of the Originals.'

'The Originals,' repeated Lucky. He savoured the word. 'I was secretly pretty proud about that. He was a cunning man, was Butch. Knew how to get the best from people.'

'I wonder what became of him.'

'Butch? He survived. And stayed in too, I think. Passed away, oh, four or five years ago now. Cancer. You see, Eddie, if you'd been in the Squadron Association, you'd know that.'

Edward shook his head. *I've been a fool,* he thought. *I've left it too late.*

They left the Xara Palace and wandered through the city. At the far end was a garden café, with seats on the old ramparts overlooking Imtarfa and the north of the Island.

'A drink, I think,' said Lucky. 'You grab a seat, Eddie, and I'll go and order.'

Edward found a table and looked out at Imtarfa's clock tower and the cluster of buildings below. His memory was less sure about those final weeks on the Island. For a while after Harry had gone missing he had been in something of a daze, refusing to accept that his friend had gone. When Pip and Lucky had suggested it was time to pack up Harry's things, Edward had angrily refused. Not until two weeks had passed did he finally acquiesce. There wasn't much: a change of clothes, shaving kit, a silver cigarette box, hair brush, fountain pen. A few books. Lots of handkerchiefs. Edward smiled, remembering – Harry *always* carried a clean handkerchief. 'It's so much more than something with which to blow one's nose,' he had said. 'A hand towel, a mop for one's brow, a neckerchief, a reminder if you tie knots in it.' Ever since then, Edward had made sure he always carried one too; he'd often echoed Harry's reasoning as well.

Edward turned the ring on his finger, then rubbed his chin. *Difficult days,* he thought to himself. He'd felt so disorientated. He kept walking into the mess, or waking up in the morning and expecting to see Harry there – and then he'd remember. But he'd carried on – flown whenever he was told to, tried to help the new boys acclimatise. He'd been promoted again – to Flight Lieutenant, his second ring. But taking command of a flight only because his greatest friend had gone brought no comfort.

As new pilots arrived, others had died or been wounded. Alex McLeish had been killed: two 109s had got him, and he crashed into a wall and was flung twenty-five yards. He survived a day or so. Lucky, Laurie and Edward had all gone up to Imtarfa to see him; they'd watched the life drain from him.

Edward wondered what had become of Alex's wife. Had she remarried? Did she still think about him? Edward could picture Alex now, sitting at dispersal or in the Mess writing endless letters to his wife. The bundle of letters that had arrived on the mail plane had thrilled Alex every bit as much as Kitty's letters had cheered Harry.

Edward had helped the new boys, but had put a distance between him and them; he'd not wanted their friendship. Only Laurie and Lucky would do. They were the only ones who really understood. Perhaps if there had been more drink, things might have been different, but they'd all been far too sober. There'd been no escape. Then Lucky had been shot down, and so he'd trooped up to Imtarfa whenever he could, sometimes with Laurie, more often on his own. *By God,* he thought, *I'd felt alone.*

Lucky reappeared with two beers, but there was a waft of something stronger on his breath. *Spirits,* thought Edward. *He's just downed a shot of something.*

'Cheers,' said Lucky, chinking their glasses.

'Cheers, Lucky.'

Lucky wiped his mouth and sighed appreciatively. 'That's better,' then eyeing Edward said, 'What's going through that head of yours?'

'I was just thinking about visiting you in Imtarfa.'

'And much appreciated it was, too.'

'I can't remember where you were hit. I just know you were lucky. Very lucky, Lucky.'

Lucky smiled, and clutched the back his shoulder. 'Cannon shell straight through there,' he said. 'A Macchi of all things. Attacked me from slightly above and at an angle, and wham! It was like being punched by Mohammed Ali or someone. The funny thing was that it didn't really hurt, not then anyway. I was mad, of course. Mad with him, but really mad with myself for not keeping a better watchout.'

'So was your plane hit too?'

'No – my Spit was fine.' He narrowed his eyes. 'And I remember thinking, 'To hell with this, I'm going to get this son of a bitch if it's the last thing I do. And here's the thing: when I'd first been in England, my instructor had been this big-shot Battle of Britain ace and he taught me a trick. You pull back the throttle and kick hard on the rudder and the Spit practically stops mid-air. So I do this, and the Eyetie screams over my head – he's got no choice or else he's going to collide, so then I've got the perfect shot 'cos this joker's now right in front of me. I couldn't miss and I didn't. Fifty yards in front and he went straight down.' He plunged his arm. 'I guess he's still down there somewhere.'

Edward said, 'I've never heard that being done before.'

'Honest to God,' said Lucky. 'Anyway, then I realise I'm in trouble. I've got a hole punched through my shoulder, my shirt's covered in the red stuff and I'm still at eighteen thousand or something. But the Spit seems to be OK – the cannon shell that hit me missed anything serious. About an inch from hitting the central petrol tank. So I'm diving down, when this fucking 109 hops onto my tail. Well, I've seen him this time and I try to out-circle him, but he's good and although I eventually manage to shake him, it's not before he's hit me in the engine and I'm spewing a ton of white coolant. I tried to bale out, but couldn't unbuckle my harness. Just couldn't get the damn thing to unclip. Maybe my fingers weren't working properly or something. Anyway, it's now too late to bale out. The last thing I remember is flying over this field and thinking my time was well and truly up. Turns out it wasn't, though.' He shook his head. 'I crash-landed, was flung out of the cockpit and ended up in a field. Broken shoulder, broken arm, and a coupla ribs. So yeah, I was all right, but poor old Alex – well, I don't know why these things happen. I don't know why I was spared. Many better men than me weren't given that chance.'

'Many better people than me too. I left Malta without a scratch. Well, perhaps a few and a few bruises too, but that was about it. I didn't even get the Dog. Where's the justice in that?'

'Ah, it's all baloney. There's no meaning to any of it. But you know what still gets me?' Edward shrugged. 'I'll tell you: that after struggling against all those goddam Jerries, and actually coming out on top – hell, I shot down five of the sons of bitches – it was a lousy Eyetie that got me in the end. An Eyetie – Jesus!'

Edward laughed. 'You know, Lucky, some of those Italian pilots were incredible. I'll tell you something,' he said. 'After Harry had gone, I had a strange experience with one. It was one of my last flights on Malta. We'd been in some dogfight or other. We'd intercepted a raid and I'd got a Ju 88 – actually, that was *my* fifth on

Malta – but then we got tangled up with a number of Macchis. Anyway, I got off a few squirts, but then ran out of ammunition and I was about to make a hasty dive for the deck when I saw an Italian on my tail. He fired a burst at me and it actually knocked off my mirror – missed my head by not very much. So I flung my Spit into a tight turn, but still this ruddy Macchi stuck on my tail. I weaved about, twisting, turning, getting lower and lower until I was right on the deck. But *still* this Italian was behind me. I kept thinking, well, come on then, if you're going to shoot me, shoot me. I was absolutely exhausted, and I had this strange moment where I just gave up. I levelled out, flew straight and waited for the bullets to come. But they never did. Instead, he did the most extraordinary thing. He flew alongside, fired his guns into the air and with a wave, turned away.'

'Son of a gun,' said Lucky.

'I swear it's true. Anyway, the next day – or almost the next day, I can't quite remember – an Italian was shot down. He managed to bale out over the Island but landed on a fountain in Sliema and was impaled on the top of it. A horrible way to go, but later some of the others were recounting this story in the mess. They told it with such relish, they thought it a great hoot. I was still feeling very cut up about Harry, and I'm afraid I rather lost my rag, telling them they were all inhuman so-and-sos and hadn't they a heart and so on. "But Eddie," one of them said – actually, I think it was Mike Lindsay – "But Eddie, it's only an Italian. It's nothing less than the lily-livered bastards deserve." So I told him about my experience the day before. "They don't want to kill us," I told him, "they're just pretending to do so, firing their guns so it looks as though they're shooting us down. They don't want to be in this war any more than we do." And this I do remember, Mike looked at me and he said, "Eddie, this is total war. We're way past the point of feeling sorry for the enemy." And he was probably right.' He took a sip of his beer. 'I think you were in hospital then. Laurie and I were sent home a few days later, so you must have been.'

'It *was* brutal, Eddie. You know, I think we all toughened up a whole load. War does that. It's dehumanising.'

'And yet I saw amazing things too – amazing human kindness. Later, in Italy – well, I met a lot of wonderful Italians.' He shook his head and looked out over the bastions wistfully. 'Sometimes it's hard to believe we saw such terrible things. Such terrible, terrible things.'

Twice before they finished lunch, Lucky got up 'to take a leak', disappearing into the bar beneath them. Both times when he returned, a noticeably stronger smell of alcohol pervaded their table, so that for the second time, when they finally left, Edward felt a little uneasy about getting back into Lucky's car with him. He wondered whether he should say something. Then he thought, *Oh, to hell with it.* Lucky seemed clear-headed enough. And anyway, nothing he could say would change him or make any difference. Lucky was an alcoholic; it was how he was now.

And as it happened, they reached the ferry in the north of the Island without any alarms. A short trip across the sea and an even shorter car ride the other side and they reached Lucky's house, a restored farmhouse on the south of the island that stood near a cluster of houses overlooking the sea, and which was surrounded by small fields of golden corn and orchards of olives and figs.

'What a place, Lucky,' said Edward as they stood on the stone terrace and gazed out at the twinkling Mediterranean, soft and blue and as inviting as it had been that June day when Harry had gone missing.

'I'm glad you like it,' he said. 'Come on, let me show you around.'

Lucky was an attentive host. He had told Edward he rarely had people to stay, but had clearly made an effort to make his guest feel welcome: there were books about Malta placed on the bedside cabinet, several fresh towels on the bed, new soap, bath salts, and shampoo in the guest bathroom, and he had stocked up the fridge and his larder. 'Help yourself to anything,' he told Edward. 'My house is your house. And if there's something I haven't got in that you'd like, just say. We can go and get it in Victoria.'

'Honestly, this is perfect,' Edward assured him.

'Well, I know you've given up your hotel room.' They were in the kitchen and Lucky opened the door of the fridge. 'I got in various kinds of fruit juice because I wasn't sure which ones you liked. And tea,' he said, producing two packets from a cupboard. 'I met an English lady in the shop and she suggested English Breakfast and Earl Grey – does that sound right?'

*

That afternoon they talked less of the war and more about other things: the slow pace of life on Gozo; Maltese politics; America; sport – baseball and cricket. They walked along the coast and down to the tiny fishing village of Xlendi. They took their time; after all, there was no rush, and the sun was high and hot. They passed two farmers, neighbours of Lucky's, and waved. Even the scent in the air – ripe corn and wild flowers – felt dry and hot. The rocky path crunched rhythmically underfoot. Edward was impressed by the beauty of the place: an island of soft earthen colours, surrounded by the deep blue sea. He'd never thought of Malta in such a way.

In Xlendi they bought some fish, took it back to Lucky's house and barbecued it for their supper. They talked some more. Conversation came easily. Edward wondered why he could never talk in such a way with Simon; why he could rarely talk in such a way with anyone. He and Lucky were poles apart in so many ways, and yet with him he felt a sense of the camaraderie that had been missing from his life for so long. And then he thought, *it's because of the war. The war has linked us. We're like blood brothers.*

The next morning, Edward woke with a dull, throbbing headache. 'You're probably not used to the wine,' said Lucky as he fried them some breakfast. 'Maltese red is a bit heavy, and I admit it doesn't mix that well with whisky.'

'It's not the wine, it's the amount of alcohol. I woke up in the middle of the night still sitting in an armchair in the lounge with the light on.'

Lucky looked sheepish. 'I'm sorry. I didn't like to wake you. But we had a good evening, didn't we?' For a moment he looked almost childlike.

'Yes, we did,' said Edward. 'And if I've a headache, it's my own stupid fault.'

Lucky grinned. 'Some breakfast will sort that out.' He stood by the cooker, striped apron covering his front, frying bacon, eggs and fried bread. 'And afterwards,' he added, 'I thought I'd show you my photographs.'

'I hoped you might. I've been looking forward to seeing them.'

'You should have reminded me. I'd have got them out yesterday.'

Edward shrugged. 'I was stringing out the anticipation.'

Lucky's study was a small room down two steps at one end of the house. The old stone walls had been kept, but carefully built bookcases had been added. Underneath the window stood a wooden desk, clear except for a word processor and several models of aircraft. A few photographs stood on the bookshelves: Lucky during the various phases of his life. One showed him in middle age, arm round another man, with mountains behind. Edward guessed it must be Alaska. Another was of Lucky taken during the war with flying helmet and goggles, sitting in the cockpit of a Spitfire. 'Me and my Spit' he'd written across the bottom.

Lucky pulled up another chair to the desk, then stretched up to one of the bookshelves and brought down a dog-eared photo album. 'Here,' he said, laying it on the desk. 'Have a look through this.'

Edward opened it and the first page nearly fell away in his hand. 'Don't worry,' said Lucky. 'The paper's completely crumbling.' Gingerly, Edward turned the pages. There were pictures of pilots training in Canada, then in England, and of the Eagle Squadron – Spitfires, groups of smiling pilots. Snapshots of his friends.

'Skip these ones,' said Lucky. 'Malta's coming up.'

Edward turned the pages slowly, carefully. Then there they were: Edward, Laurie, Alex and Harry, grinning at Lucky's camera up on the balcony at the Xara Palace. Alex with his cap on the back of his head, the others bare headed, hair roughly swept back. They looked so young, so unafraid of what lay in store. His first feeling was of relief: that his memory of Harry had been right.

'My God,' said Edward. 'Can that really be us?'

Lucky laughed. 'Hits you hard, doesn't it, when you realise how we've aged. Such baby-faces we all were then.'

Edward stared at it. He brought a hand to his mouth, biting firmly on a knuckle. 'I – I just can't believe it,' he said at last. 'After all these years. I can't believe it's us. That – that it's Harry. That I'm seeing Harry again.' His legs felt weak and he dropped back on the chair, then felt Lucky place a hand on his shoulder.

'You ready for some more?' said Lucky.

Edward nodded.

The pictures were small, black-and-white, each carefully tucked into tiny black corner mounts. There were photographs of aircraft, both intact and burning, of Takali under clouds of smoke. Blurred pictures of them all outside dispersal and on the balcony of the Xara Palace. A picture of Butch scowling and Baggy Bagshawe behind, smoking his pipe.

'The gharrie race,' exclaimed Edward, as he turned another page. 'I don't believe it. Look, there's Zulu!' Another picture showed Zulu, Harry and Lucky grinning and flexing their arms.

'I don't know who took that one,' said Lucky. 'Boy, that *was* a funny day.'

There was a picture, too, of Harry and Edward together, their hair wet and dishevelled, mooring the boat at St Paul's Bay.

'Tell me, how *did* you get hold of all this film?' Edward asked. 'You were always very guarded about it.'

Lucky chuckled. 'From a guy I knew in the photo reconnaissance squadron over at Luqa. He made me swear not to tell anyone. Guess he didn't want lots of other people asking him for it. Then the word would get out and he would be in the pan.'

Edward laughed. 'Well, they're just wonderful, Lucky, really wonderful.'

'I'll get you copies of some of the good ones if you like.'

'Would you? Really? I'd absolutely love that. I'll reimburse you, of course.'

Lucky waved a hand. 'Don't be ridiculous. I'll get them done and mail them to you. Anyway, I've got a few other bits and pieces,' he said, producing a large old envelope. 'Here, look at this,' he said, carefully extracting a frail and yellowed sheet of folded paper. 'An old copy of the *Times of Malta.*'

'It's so thin!'

'Four pages of joyous morale-boosting propaganda. I read somewhere that the islanders used it to wipe their backsides.'

Edward laughed, then spread out the paper on the desk. 'May 11, 1942,' he said then read out the headline, '"Battle of Malta: Axis Heavy Losses. Spitfires slaughter Stukas."'

'That was us,' said Lucky. 'I got one that day.'

'Listen to this: "It has always been known that man for man, and machine for machine, the RAF were infinitely superior to the Hun."'

'Amen to that.'

'Amazing. Pure Hugh Pughe. It could have been written by him.'

'Probably was. I can see him now, strutting up and down his office in the Hole, clutching a tumbler of gin in one hand, cigarette in the other, dictating to some WAAF or other. "Take this down will you, Marjorie."'

'I'm sure you're right,' Edward laughed.

Lucky also produced a small wooden box, in which he kept his hand-stitched wings badge and his medals. 'I had the medals mounted a while back. I'm proud of what I did, and I'm damn glad they gave me a DFC and an Air Force Cross. I reckon I deserved 'em.'

Edward looked at them, fingering the heavy metal of each in turn. He was conscious of Lucky watching him, so he turned and smiled. 'They're heavy, aren't they?'

'You haven't got yours, have you?' said Lucky.

Edward shook his head. 'No. That is, well – I wore the ribbons when I was still in, but after the war, no. I never did get the real things.'

'You got a DFC for Malta, right?'

Edward nodded.

'You should be damn proud of what you did, Eddie. Who else in the RAF had to go through what we did on Malta? Tell me that. If you ask me, they should have given every goddam one of us a DSO at least.'

'Well, I suppose that's partly the problem. Why did I get one and, say, Alex didn't? He gave his life, after all.'

'Doesn't mean you should feel bad about yours. I tell you, Eddie, we did a hell of a thing back then. I know we were young and pretty clueless half the time, but you know, we played our part. We helped save Malta and that was a big deal. We might not have done much since, but we did something with our lives back then. Something worthwhile. Listen, do me a favour: when you get back, order them up will you? You should have them, and what's more you should be damn proud to have them, too.'

Edward looked at him and smiled. 'All right, Lucky.'

They ate out that night, Lucky driving them into Victoria. But first, drinks – at a bar in the main square. 'Negronis,' I think, said Lucky.

'No, really, Lucky, I don't think I will,' Edward told him.

'Oh come on, Eddie. It's your last night. You can dry out again when you get home. Just keep an old drunk company for one more night.'

Edward smiled. *What the hell?* he thought. 'All right, then. You've twisted my arm.'

'That's the spirit!'

When the drinks arrived, Lucky chinked their glasses and said, 'Cheers, Eddie. You know, it's been really great to see you again.'

'It's been wonderful,' agreed Edward, and lifting his glass said, 'To old friends.'

'I'll drink to that. And to absent friends as well.'

'Yes – to absent friends.'

Lucky took a sip of his drink, smacked his lips with satisfaction, then said, 'Incidentally, did you know the Americans built an airfield here on Gozo? Knocked the whole thing into shape in about two weeks. Amazing.'

'Actually, I did know that. I came back to Malta, you know, in June and July 1943.'

'Really?' said Lucky. 'Goddam, I never knew that. Why didn't you say?'

Edward shrugged. 'It was only a couple of weeks. The place was so different by then that it hardly felt like the same island at all. I can't really remember that much about it, to be honest. I was posted back here as a supernumerary flight lieutenant just before the invasion of Sicily. I was based at Qrendi. That had been built specially too – south of Takali. Honestly, the change in a year was staggering. Heaving with aircraft and ships. And there was food and drink on the Island, too.'

'So you took part in the invasion?'

Edward nodded. 'Went on to Sicily, then took over command of a squadron at Termoli in southern Italy.'

'Squadron Leader?'

'Well, you know how it was. If you survived you could hardly fail to be promoted.'

'And you stayed in Italy until the end of the war?'

'Yes.' He wondered whether he should say more. He took a sip of his drink and fingered his earlobe.

'And what was that like? I knew a guy back in the States who flew P-51s in Italy. Said it was pretty tough.'

'Really?'

Lucky eyed him. 'Why are you being such a closed book about this? C'mon, Eddie, I never went to Italy. You know, it's interesting for me: we fought against them, then suddenly we're over there, flying from their bases and so on.'

'I'm not being a closed book,' Edward lied. 'It's just that there's not much to say.' He sighed. 'It was mainly low-level stuff, ground-strafing and escorting medium bombers – that sort of thing. It was pretty hairy at times, but of course there was almost no Luftwaffe left by then.'

'And that's it?'

Edward sighed again. *I'm not ready for this.* 'I got shot down and spent about six months with the partisans. Terribly dull, really. We didn't achieve very much.' He sighed again. 'And then I eventually got back to the Allies and served at Group Headquarters before being given another squadron just before the final push. Then back home.'

Lucky looked at him suspiciously. 'All right, Eddie. Well, perhaps you can tell me a bit more about it another time.'

'Really,' said Edward, a snap of irritation entering his voice, 'there's nothing much more to tell.'

It was just before six o'clock that evening that Lucky poured them the first of several whiskies; a little over an hour later and Edward was already beginning to feel slightly light-headed. The sun was beginning to lower, but the sky was still bright, and the sea twinkling benignly beyond the cliffs.

'D'you know what I think?' said Lucky as he sunk back into his chair. His voice had begun to slur. 'I think you and I are more alike than we think. The war – it's made us unhappy, hasn't it? I know I've not had a particularly happy life, and I'm not so sure you've been that happy either.'

'Why do you say that?'

'I dunno. You haven't told me much about it. You tell me it's been dull and a bit boring. You haven't mentioned your family very much.'

'You're right. No, I can't really say I have had a "happy" life.'

'You've never got over the losses, have you? Harry, the others. You probably lost good friends in Italy too.'

'Yes.'

'Christ, I know how close you and Harry were. Jesus, you were like brothers.' They were silent for a moment, then Lucky said, 'You think you should have gone instead of Harry, don't you?'

Edward sighed. 'Yes. Yes, I do. Harry was a brilliant person: charming, funny, talented. The sort of person who would have made a great success of life. I haven't made a great success of it, Lucky. All right, so I've never been a drunk or fooled around with other women, but I've achieved very little. I've hidden away in some tiny boarding school all my life, I married a woman I loved but was never in love with, and I have a son I barely know – a son who tends to get into a temper whenever he sees me. And I don't really blame him. I've few friends, and when my time does come there won't be many at my funeral.'

'There'll be even less at mine. It's just the war, Eddie, it's the fucking war. It messed up all our lives. I sometimes think the lucky ones were the ones who died. But then, you know, these past few days – I've enjoyed myself, Eddie. I've had a good time.' He took another gulp of whisky. 'You know, if you and I had met for the first time ever a few days ago, we'd probably scarcely have looked at each other. I'm a washed-up drunk, and you're such a closed book it hurts – not about Malta, but everything else. But we've got *this* place, haven't we? A shared experience. We're blood brothers, Eddie. The survivors of a great and terrible thing. I'm rambling, I know, but I can't tell you what it's meant to me to see you again these past days. You were a great pal back then, and as far as I'm concerned you always will be. You come and see me again, Eddie. Will you do that? Keep in touch. We must keep in touch.'

'Of course, Lucky,' said Edward, meaning it. 'And I'd like you to visit me in England, too.'

Lucky slowly lifted his glass, and grinned. 'You try and keep me away.'

On the way to the airport, they stopped outside Valletta, at the RAF memorial they had seen on Edward's first evening on the Island. It had been Edward's suggestion. They parked outside the church of St Publius then walked over towards the Phoenicia Hotel, crossed the road and slowly stepped up the narrow path to the foot of the column. Brass plaques were pinned to the curved stone, the names of every member of the RAF who had gone missing during the battle for Malta and Sicily. They found Zulu's name first, and then Harry's. Flight Lieutenant H.W. Barclay, 21.6.1942.

Edward gazed at it, ran a finger over the embossed lettering and felt his throat tighten and his eyes begin to fill with tears. He stood back, stumbled a step, and tried to surreptitiously dab his eyes, but Lucky said, 'It's all right, Eddie,' and suddenly he knew he could keep it in no longer and that his self-control had momentarily deserted him. Crouching to the ground, he clutched his hands to his eyes and wept, his whole body convulsing as fifty years of grief poured out of him in an unstoppable stream.

Somerset – June, 1995

When he opened the front door of his house in Brampton Cary and stepped inside, everything looked exactly the same as it had done a week before when he had set off for the airport. And yet it wasn't, because in the intervening six days, so much had happened that Edward now viewed everything differently. He was struck by the pristine starkness of his sitting room. Three photographs – that was all! The one of Cynthia, another of Simon as a baby, and one of his grandchildren. It was, he realised, a room devoid of any personality.

A pile of post was waiting for him, mostly bills, but there were two letters that immediately caught his eye. The first was a typed envelope with Pete Summersby's address stamped on the reverse. Inside were details of the Squadron Association and the latest newsletter. There was also a note from Pete, telling him about the next meeting, which would be at Biggin Hill on 15th August. '*Hope to see you there,*' he'd added. '*There'll be a few faces you'll know.*'

The other letter was handwritten. Neatly slitting open the envelope with his paper knife, he carefully took out the page of light blue paper and saw it was from Andrew Fisher. His heart quickening, he sat down, then began reading. '*Dear Squadron Leader Enderby,*' it began, '*I hope you will forgive me for writing to you out of the blue, but Pete Summersby got in touch with me about my uncle, Harry Barclay, and mentioned he'd seen you recently and suggested I write to you. I was very pleased as I have been trying to trace you for years, as I know you were close friends. I have a wealth of my uncle's letters and other effects of his. I am trying to learn more about him, and feel sure there is much you could tell me. Would you consider allowing me to visit you? I would be happy to come and see you wherever you are and at a time that suits you. I also have some things of his that might interest you. I look forward to hearing from you. Yours sincerely, Andrew Fisher.*'

Edward read the letter through several times. He felt annoyed that Harry's nephew had beaten him to it – and silently cursed Pete – but was also surprised to find that, having prevaricated and put off contacting Andrew Fisher for so long, he now felt excited and suddenly impatient to meet him.

He decided to reply almost immediately, so having unpacked and made himself some tea, Edward sat at his bureau and finally began the letter he had promised himself he would write several weeks before. *I would be very happy to meet you whenever you like,* he wrote. *Why don't you telephone me at your convenience, and then we can arrange a rendezvous?* Having completed that task, Edward then filled out the Squadron Association membership form, wrote out a cheque for five pounds, and added a brief note to Pete thanking him for putting him in touch with Lucky.

Two weeks passed and he heard nothing from Andrew Fisher. He did, however get a call from Simon. He had not told his son about his visits to Cornwall or Malta, and it had crossed his mind that Simon might have tried to call him while he had been away and then, not getting a reply, become worried. But there had been no such calls; that soon became clear enough when they did finally speak – for the first time, Edward realised, in nearly a month.

They began with the usual stilted pleasantries before Simon cut to the point. He was calling about the air show. 'Dad, do you remember you promised to go with Nicky to Duxford?'

'Yes I do,' Edward told him. 'When is it?'

'Two weekends' time, just after the schools break up. The only problem is, we're on holiday then.'

'Ah. Anywhere nice?'

'Only France, Dad. Where we usually go – but, listen, there's an air show at Biggin Hill the first week of September. Would you come along to that instead? It seems they've still got plenty of Spitfires due to be flying.'

'Of course – makes no odds to me. Actually, if anything that would be better – Biggin's much closer than Duxford. So, shall I put that in the diary?'

'That would be great. You sure you don't mind?'

'Course not. A promise is a promise.'

And by then, he thought, *I should have finished.*

When Andrew Fisher did eventually call, he apologised profusely. He'd been away, he explained, but was thrilled to have got Edward's letter. His voice was soft, rather gentle; not unlike Harry's, Edward thought. He lived in Oxford – not so very far away; he'd happily drive to Somerset. How was Edward fixed this Saturday? Or Sunday? Sunday would be better, Edward told him – *no cricket*. Well, it *was* the last Saturday of term.

Andrew told him he would be with him by around eleven, and so Edward spent an impatient morning waiting. He was too agitated to concentrate on the paper or his book, and the hours passed slowly. He filled the kettle, plumped up the cushions on the sofa again, went out and bought biscuits to go with the coffee, and agonised over which pub he should take him to should Andrew wish to stay for lunch. He then decided he should fetch his logbook, so went upstairs and took it out of its metal tin. Glancing through it again took up a few more minutes.

Eleven o'clock came and went. Edward looked at his watch, then the carriage clock above the fireplace, repeatedly. 'Where the hell are you?' he muttered. Nevertheless, when the doorbell did finally ring, just after a quarter past eleven, the sudden shrill noise made Edward jump.

He hurried to the front door and opened it to see a middle-aged man with greying hair and a warm, pleasant face that reminded him immediately of Harry. 'Andrew,' he said. 'How nice to meet you.'

'I'm sorry I'm so late,' said Andrew, shaking his hand. 'It took a little longer than I'd expected. I thought I'd left plenty of time, but there were a lot of slow and winding roads.'

'Doesn't matter at all,' said Edward. 'I wasn't doing anything. Anyway, come on through.' He led him into the sitting room, then offered him coffee. 'Why don't you have a look at this while I make it?' he said, handing Andrew his logbook.

As Edward made the coffee, he hoped he would be able to keep his composure. *Now, don't go getting emotional,* he told himself. When he walked back into the sitting room with a tray of coffee and biscuits, he saw Andrew had the logbook open on his lap.

'I've got Harry's logbook in the car,' he said. 'It's amazing how similar they are. Canada and Cornwall and Malta. You were even on the same OTU.'

'Yes. I think we were pretty unusual, actually.'

'Harry perhaps wrote a few more notes in his.'

'Well, everyone was different. I noted down things occasionally –

when I'd hit something, or if anything particularly important happened.'

'I notice on 21st June, 1942, you've written, "HARRY MISSING."'

'Yes.' He cleared his throat. 'Do you take milk and sugar?'

'Milk, please.' Andrew shifted in his seat, then said, 'I really am very grateful to you. I've been hoping for some time that I might find you, but it was quite difficult.'

'I'm afraid that once I'd left the RAF, I never really kept up with anyone. Like everyone else, I simply got on with my life.'

'I can't say my parents ever talked about it much, either. My dad was in the navy and mum worked in the ATS. No, to be honest, it's only in the last couple of years that I've become so interested. My father passed away and then my mother decided to move. It was when we were clearing out the house that I found a trunk full of Harry's things. Of course, I knew all about him – we had a couple of pictures of him in the house. In fact, we had one of the two of you. I'm guessing it was taken in Cornwall sometime. You're both in shirt sleeves, sitting on the edge of a cliff, it looks like. So I've known about you most of my life.'

Edward looked down at his coffee and pinched his leg. *Come on, take a hold of yourself,* he said. He coughed, and said, 'I think I remember the one. It was taken at Perranporth. I had a copy once.'

'Well, I've brought you another.'

'Have you?' He felt his spirits rise. 'How wonderful. Thank you.'

'Not at all. And I recognised you immediately when you opened the door. From the photograph.'

'I don't suppose you ever knew him – Harry, I mean.'

'No. My parents were married before the war, but I was born afterwards. My mother has never talked that much about Harry – to be honest, I think she knew very little about his life in the RAF apart from the letters she got from him – and of course the censors stopped him from saying too much. But for me he's always been this rather romantic figure – the dashing fighter pilot uncle. When I found the box of his things he started to come to life, so to speak. And I wanted to know more.'

Andrew did not leave until after four o'clock. Edward had discovered that talking about Harry had been easier than he had imagined; he'd been stunned by how quickly time had flown. They had lunched in one of the pubs in the high street, (an easy decision in the end); had argued over who would pay (Edward insisted), and then had gone back to the house, where Andrew had shown him his box of Harry's letters and other belongings. It was strange seeing Harry's handwriting once more; to look at them and think, *he wrote this when he was still alive.* And Edward felt as though he were somehow intruding, too: these letters had not been written to him. It unsettled him, and yet his desire to make that link with the past was stronger than his sense of impropriety. There were other things: old school reports, mostly commenting on Harry's sporting prowess and cheerful disposition; the telegram warning Harry's parents that he'd gone missing; an official inventory of Harry's belongings – the very belongings that Edward had so reluctantly packed up during those terrible days on Malta. And there were the photographs too. Not many, but enough to remind Edward that his memory had not deceived him. Harry *had* been the person locked away in his memory.

Andrew had asked about his death, and Edward had struggled to keep his voice steady. He wondered whether Andrew had noticed.

'He must have gone down in the sea somewhere,' Edward told him. 'But whether he was shot down, or something went wrong with the aircraft, we will never know. Going "missing" is a terrible thing. At least if we'd found him, there'd be a grave or something.' He wanted to say more, to tell Andrew that barely a day had gone by when he hadn't thought of Harry, that Harry had been the best friend he'd ever had. But he just couldn't.

When he'd gone, Edward sat back down in his wing-backed armchair and looked again at the photograph Andrew had given him. He would have it framed, he decided, and then put it next to the picture of his wife. *I'm not going to shut you out any more,* he thought.

His thoughts turned to Kitty. There'd been mention of her in the letters. '*She's an absolute cracker,*' Harry had written to his sister, '*and I'm sure we're going to get married after the war.*' But although Andrew had asked him about her, Edward had told him only part of the story: the gharrie race, the brief romance, and the pining for her after she'd gone. He'd not mentioned what Harry had told him: that Kitty had been the love of his life.

Edward closed his eyes, remembering a wet night in London – must have been early August; while he was still on leave after returning home from Malta. He'd found Kitty's address amongst Harry's belongings and had written to her from Malta, but had heard nothing back; he had no idea whether his letter had even reached her. Had no idea whether she even knew. So he'd been determined to visit her, to explain in person; to see if she was all right. He felt he owed it to Harry.

When she'd opened the door of her flat, she had been surprised to see him; a moment had passed before she'd recognised him. 'You're Harry's friend,' she'd said.

'Yes – Eddie. Eddie Enderby.'

She looked as though she were about to go out: wearing a dress, pearls and brightly coloured lips. Her appearance flustered him.

'Well, come in,' she said. She glanced anxiously behind her. Another girl poked her head round a door at the far end of the corridor. 'That's Annie,' said Kitty. 'Don't mind her.' She led him into a large high-ceilinged drawing room. 'Can I get you anything? I don't think I can offer you much, though.'

'No, no thank you. Kitty, it's about Harry.'

'Is he all right?'

Edward's heart sank. 'No. No, Kitty, I'm afraid he's not. He went missing in June.'

Her eyes widened and then she put her hands to her face. 'Oh no, poor Harry.'

'I'm sorry,' he said. 'I wrote to you, but you obviously haven't received it.'

'No,' she said. 'I haven't heard from him for a while, but then I thought, well – I didn't blame him.'

Edward looked at her. A tear ran down her face. 'The mail was terrible from Malta, but I promise he wrote every day. Here,' he said, handing her a handkerchief.

'Thank you. Oh God, poor Harry. I feel so responsible.'

'Why would you feel that? No, Kitty you mustn't. Really, it's just one of those terrible things. Hardly any of us made it back from Malta.'

'But don't you see, if I hadn't written . . .' She stopped, froze, as the doorbell rang again. She looked at him and then glanced at the door. 'I really must get the door,' she said.

Edward sat there, confused. Voices in the corridor – a male voice. He heard them kiss on each cheek, then muffled conversation. Moments later she reappeared, with a man in army uniform. She introduced them, then said, 'Eddie, we're going out to supper. Would you like to come too?'

'Supper?' said Edward. He couldn't understand; he felt himself redden.

'Only if you'd like to.'

'No – thank you. No, I must get going. I just thought . . .' He looked at her, then at the man beside her – a young man, about Harry's age, good-looking, impeccable in his uniform. The ribbon of an MC above his tunic pocket. Edward stood up. Suddenly it was all so clear. He felt hot in the face and angry – real rage coursed through him. 'Christ – to think Harry loved you,' he said. 'How could you be so bloody heartless?' He stormed past her, without a glance.

'Eddie, wait,' she said after him, 'I'd already broken up with him. I'd sent him a letter . . .'

Edward opened his eyes. *Ah, the betrayal,* he thought. He could still recall the sense of hurt he'd felt; the humiliation. Somehow, she had belittled Harry, denigrated him. He had walked for miles, cursing Kitty, cursing Malta, cursing himself for surviving. Eventually he had stumbled into a pub, and drunk until his brain became so addled he no longer knew what he was thinking.

At the time he'd wondered whether Harry *had* received her letter, but then had dismissed the idea. There had been no post in the few days before, he was certain. And anyway, Harry would have told him. No, whatever the reasons Harry disappeared, it was not because of Kitty. Of that he was sure – sure now, as he had been then.

He thought about those months that followed his return from Malta. It had taken him a long time to adjust to life back in England. During that first leave he had been sullen, withdrawn. His parents must have been shocked by the change in him. *It can't have been easy for them,* he thought. He tried to remember those days, but his mind was hazy. Home had been frozen in time; his mother and father still treating him like a precious child. But he was not a boy any more. Far from it. He was still twenty years old when he came home, but felt twenty years older.

A memory came back to him – of a dinner his parents had given. It must have been soon after his return from Malta, while he had still been on leave. His mother had done her best, managing a vegetable soup, vegetable and rabbit stew and even baked apples; his father had been hard at work in the garden since the start of rationing. The guests had been friends of his parents whom Edward had not met before, but they had lived on Malta some years before. He was a retired naval commander. *What were their names? Lively, Linley – Commander Linney, that was it.*

'We thought you might like to talk to someone who knew Malta before the war,' his mother had told him, and then had apologised for not being able to invite anyone his own age. Talking about Malta was, of course, the last thing he'd wanted to do, but his mother had already arranged it, and he had not wanted to upset her.

But of course, that's exactly what he had done. Commander Linney had barely drawn breath. Was such-and-such still there, he'd asked Edward? No, well it used to be quite the place. Do you remember, darling? Yes, when old so-and-so stood up and danced on the table . . . Anecdote followed anecdote. The Gut, the Snakepit, the parties, races at Marsa – an endless whirl of social engagements, a gay time had by all. If Edward had tried to explain something, the commander invariably cut him off. 'Have much to do with the Maltese?' the Commander asked him.

'A little.'

The Commander smiled and shook his head. 'They're a lazy bunch, you know. The niggers of the Mediterranean, we used to call them. Couldn't believe they were given the George Cross, although I suppose we needed to do something to keep them on side.'

'They were very brave, the ones I met,' said Edward. 'They deserved that award, if you ask me. They've been bombed to smithereens. Whenever we were bombed at the Xara Palace they barely flinched.'

'Yes, I remember the Xara Palace,' said the Commander. 'Baron Chapelle's place. You know, there's the most fantastic balcony there overlooking the Island.'

'Yes, I know,' said Edward, 'I lived there.'

'You can see everything from there: that wonderful dome of Mostar church, the Dingli cliffs? Did you ever go down there? Swim at the Blue Grotto?'

'Well, I flew over them enough times, but swimming, no, I –'

'Oh, you really should have done! The Blue Grotto is marvellous.' He turned to Edward's parents. 'One of the most beautiful swimming spots I know. I can't believe you never swam there,' he said, turning back to Edward. 'We had many happy times there, didn't we, darling.'

'Yes, it was lovely,' agreed his wife.

'I think Edward was quite busy flying,' said his father.

'And being bombed and shot at.'

This last comment was ignored. Instead, the Commander launched into a story about a review of the Mediterranean Fleet and how the ships in Grand Harbour had dazzled in the summer sun.

'Oh, for God's sake,' Edward had said at last.

'Edward!' said his mother.

'Well, I'm sorry, but I'm sick to death of hearing about this. There were no ships in Malta, only half-sunken crates. There are no bars, no restaurants, no parties or race days at Marsa. And how dare you bad-mouth the Maltese. They never asked to be attacked and they've put up with it all heroically – and they're still there, with no food and living in squalid caves under the ground. So think about that before you tell the next person how dreadful they are. And Malta's not some island paradise. It's a hellhole, a stinking pile of rubble, the most God-awful place on earth.'

For a moment no-one said a word; they just looked at him aghast. Edward felt himself redden, and then, defiantly slamming his napkin on the table, pushed back his chair and stormed out.

He winced, just thinking about it now. His poor parents; they had deserved better. Later, after the Linneys had gone, his father had come into his room and sat down on his bed beside him. 'I know you've been through a lot,' he said, 'but that was unfair of you, you know.'

Edward had said nothing.

'Get some rest,' his father told him.

Edward nodded then turned his face to the wall. He felt his

father's hand on his shoulder then heard him stand up and leave the room. It was a strange paradox: he was no longer their boy, but a battle-scarred man of twenty-one, and yet at that moment it was as though he were ten again, having been sent to his room in disgrace.

He had apologised – profusely – and had written to the Linneys as well, but his relationship with his parents had changed after that; it was as though his mother, in particular, was wary of him. The difference in him had been so marked, he now recognised, they must have felt as though they hardly knew him any more, nor what to say.

Perhaps, he wondered now, that had had something to do with his desire to be posted abroad again. That sense of shame; he remembered that keenly. Far better to get away, and then he could not disappoint them; then they would not have to see what was happening to him.

First, however, there had been nine long months instructing in Gloucestershire, passing on his considerable experience to eager young pups – boys really, just like he'd been. He'd hated it – the lack of camaraderie, the isolation; the loneliness. Time and again he'd asked for a transfer, but he'd always been refused. But then the Allies began preparing for another invasion – Sicily, southern Europe at long last. Experienced men were needed; men who knew Malta, who knew the Mediterranean. And so in May, 1943, when he asked yet again for a transfer, his request was granted.

21st June, 1943 – that was the day he'd touched back down on Malta. One year to the day since Harry had gone missing. When he'd left the Island the previous July, he'd looked out of the window of the Dakota that was taking him and Laurie Bowles back to Gibraltar and had watched the Island shrink until it was nothing more than a dot on the wide expanse of sea. He'd sworn to himself he would never return. *And now I've broken that promise for a second time,* Edward thought to himself.

He rubbed his eyes, and looked at the picture of Cynthia. 'You never knew any of this,' he said softly.

He had told Lucky that Malta had become a very different place by the summer of 1943, and it had. The rubble had not gone – the Island still looked utterly wrecked. But it was now heaving with men and equipment and, particularly, aircraft. Six hundred fighters crammed onto both Malta and Gozo. Six hundred! The fuel shortages were a thing of the past – the only hindrance to movement now was the amount of traffic. Edward's squadron even had the use of a couple of American army jeeps. Nor were there any more food shortages; the siege for which so many had given so much had been lifted the previous December; the tide in the Mediterranean had turned. And there was drink, too, and nights out in Valletta where pilots and sailors could once more make their way from one bar to another – not that Edward joined in very often. A couple of whiskies in the mess was all he wanted.

In August they moved off again – this time to Sicily. It had come as a relief; for all the changes, Edward was glad to get off the Island a second time. After the surrender of the Italians at the beginning of September, the Allies moved once more, this time to southern Italy. The Italians might have been their allies now, but there were still plenty of Germans to fight in Italy. Edward's wing followed the advancing armies to the Salerno beachhead and then, as winter set in, they moved to Capodichino on the edge of Naples.

Naples. In October, 1943, it was just another city ruined by the ravages of war. Too many houses lay in ruins; the streets were wet and windswept, the gutters full of rubbish and filth, and swarming with wretched, threadbare Italians, starving and scavenging off the sudden influx of Allied forces. The pilots moved into requisitioned buildings in the city. Most people became ill – jaundice, typhus, and, of course, dysentery. Once again, Edward was untouched by disease, the one person whose intestines appeared to be made of steel; and so he continued flying, escorting Baltimore bombers as they pounded the front line forty miles to the north.

No-one was happy. The Allies were not doing as well as had been hoped, the flying conditions were atrocious, and the cold and rain infected every man in the wing, so Edward was relieved to be posted to Cairo in the first week of the New Year of 1944. More instructing, but this time in the sun. He felt as though he were finally emerging from a very dark cloud, but it was only a brief respite. At the beginning of March he was promoted again and sent back to Italy – to Termoli this time, on the east coast. And there he took command of his own squadron – 629 Squadron, equipped with Spitfires.

*

It was funny, Edward reflected, how the memory worked. Some things were so vivid, imprinted with crystal clarity on his mind; while others were a complete blur. He really had to think hard to recall much about those first few months in Italy. But maybe, he wondered, that was because nothing very significant had happened to him. That changed the moment he arrived at Termoli. The events that followed were seared into his memory; they'd been haunting him ever since, intensely so recently.

The moment he'd stopped in the churchyard at Chilton on that Monday two months before, he knew he had subconsciously embarked on a journey that he would have to follow to the bitter end. He had dreaded going to Malta, and yet now he was glad he had done so. It had been the cathartic experience he'd hoped for.

And now he knew he had to go back to Italy. He felt exhausted. His week on Malta, the time with Lucky, meeting Andrew Fisher. It had drained him, both mentally and physically. *I'm not ready for Italy yet,* he told himself. A couple of weeks; he'd rest and recharge his batteries and then he'd go. He wondered whether this time he should tell Simon, but then dismissed the idea. He had to stick to his rules: he would tell Simon when he got back. And then he'd tell him everything.

But just the thought of it filled him with a terrible sense of foreboding. For too long, dark memories had been held safe in the recesses of his mind. 'I'm scared,' he admitted to Cynthia's photograph one night. 'I'm scared of what I'm going to find.'

PART III

Italy

Italy – April, 1944

Edward sat at his desk looking out of the window. Rain streamed down the glass, while waves crashed against the shoreline, white against the grey of the sea and sky. It looked more like Southend than the east coast of Italy.

His room was cold too, and he turned up the collar of his battle-blouse. A gust of wind shook the window and it rattled loudly. Outside, a jeep rolled past, hitting a puddle and sending a fountain of spray across the road. Edward turned back to the blank piece of paper on his desk, and tapped his pen thoughtfully. *Dear Mr and Mrs Tomlinson,* he began then stopped again. *Dammit,* he thought, leaning back in his chair, his hands behind his head.

It was evening. Two hurricane lamps already lit the room, while on the chest of drawers on the far side of the room, a candle flickered. As squadron leader, Edward had been given his own room in this requisitioned house on the seafront – and on the first floor, too, with views over the sea and a small balcony. He had never really imagined having his own squadron, but although still a few months short of his twenty-third birthday, he was not the youngest squadron leader in Italy by any means. Experience was what counted, and, he supposed, leadership. In the six weeks since he'd taken over, he seemed to have done all right; he'd had no complaints from above, at any rate. In truth, he didn't feel there was much difference between being squadron commander and a flight commander: there was just more admin now.

Nor had he had much opportunity to make the most of the perks of his position. His room, while large, was cold, and since arriving back in Italy after his stint instructing in Egypt, the weather had been consistently dreadful. He'd not been out on his balcony once. After a few days of bright sunshine at the end of March, it had managed to rain almost every day, although this had made little impact on the amount of flying. At the airfield, just over a mile away on the edge of town, a temporary runway had been laid with pierced steel planking – or PSP as everyone called it – an American invention and a panacea for all conditions. And since most of their operations were low-level stuff, there was less dependence on weather conditions; cloud base had to be at almost zero feet to stop them flying.

Sometimes, Edward couldn't help but marvel at the change since those days on Malta at the height of the siege. The Allies had almost complete air superiority now – the roles had been spectacularly reversed. He'd barely seen an enemy plane since arriving back – just a pair of Focke-Wulf fighters a week before – and so this meant that the old Desert Air Force, still supporting Eighth Army as it had done all across North Africa, was able to keep an almost constant stream of fighters in the air. They operated in wings these days, whole squadrons at a time flying over the front line, waiting to be told to attack an enemy gun position, or strafe a column of enemy trucks, or shoot up a farmhouse where a German sniper was causing particular trouble. The 'cab rank' as it was known; there were even ground controllers scuttling along the front in armoured cars co-ordinating between the troops and the pilots in the air.

For Edward, the novelty of this massive show of strength had long since worn off. Perhaps the cab-rank system was effective, but it was also extremely dangerous. Flying at low altitude meant there was little chance to bale out, and while there were now few 109s hovering about waiting to pounce, the Germans had highly efficient anti-aircraft gunners. No matter how experienced the pilot, a shard of shrapnel or a stray bullet could end his life in a trice. Mortality rates were higher even than on Malta, but they were also flying so much more. Squadron Leaders were not expected to fly as much as the rest of the squadron, but even so, Edward had flown almost every day. He'd lost four pilots in his first month: three killed and one so badly wounded he would never fly again. And another one today – Edward had seen him come down himself as they'd tried to bomb German tanks near Ortona. Pilot Officer Stan Tomlinson, who had joined the squadron just a few days after Edward. A good pilot and an eager, likeable, fellow. Flak had got him, blasted a hole through his rudder and elevators, and he'd lost control and hurtled into the ground.

A knock on his door.

'Yes?' called out Edward.

Danny, the Adjutant, came in, holding up a bottle of wine. 'We've just got hold of new booze supplies,' he said. 'Care for a bottle?'

'Thanks,' said Edward, gesturing to Danny to sit down in the armchair the other side of his desk. It was certainly the most comfortable room he'd been in since joining the RAF. The house had come fully furnished, complete with beds, tables, chairs, and even the ornate leather-topped desk he was using now. He'd often wondered who owned it; who the family were and what had become of them. Italy seemed to be seething with displaced persons.

'Stan's parents?' Danny asked, pouring two beakers of wine.

Edward nodded. 'The worst job in the world. Anyway, where did the wine come from?'

Danny shrugged. 'Didn't like to ask. It's jolly good stuff, though. Nothing like as rough as the last lot.'

'Hm,' said Edward. 'Not bad. Thanks, Danny.'

The Adjutant stood up. 'I'll leave you to it – you're sure you won't let me do it for you?'

'No – thanks, but I feel I should, really.'

When Danny had gone, Edward looked back down at the letter. *I'm so sorry to have to be writing this to you. Stan was a wonderful chap and extremely popular within the squadron – the life and soul of the Mess. We will all miss his singing in the bar and his enthusiasm and constant cheeriness. It has been a hard few weeks with poor weather, and he did much to keep up spirits.*

He was also a gifted pilot and in the short time he'd been with the squadron had become a much relied-upon member of 'A' Flight. I was nearby when he died, and hope I can assure you that he would not have suffered in any way. He will be greatly missed, but he died doing important and valiant work, and you can feel very proud of his achievements.

Yours sincerely,

Squadron Leader Edward Enderby

He took a large drink of wine, then read it through again. Slightly patronising? And was it personal enough? He sighed, then folded the paper and wrote out the envelope. *It will have to do,* he thought, then looked out his window once more. Soon it would be summer. Just a few more weeks; everything would seem better then.

The next day, 9th April, the squadron was given a different task.

They would be escorting some bombers on an attack on Bologna, a task usually left to the American fighter groups. But there was more.

'We'd like you to have a look at something for us, Eddie,' Wing Commander Templeton had told him at the morning briefing. 'Come and have a squint at this map.' Edward had stood up and followed him to the large map of Italy hanging on the Operations Tent wall. 'So here's Bologna,' Templeton pointed out, 'and here's the River Reno running south.' He was tall and thin as a rake, with a dark moustache that made him look older than his twenty-five years. Not as dominant a character as Butch had been, but no less effective for that. Edward liked him; there was no side to Dick Templeton. He was fair, listened to what others had to say, and treated all the squadron leaders on equal terms, regardless of age or experience.

Dick ran a finger down the map. 'And here it forks. The Reno continues to the south-west, while the River Setta carries on almost due south. And as you can see, there's a whole load of bloody huge great mountains in between.'

'So the two river valleys are the main arteries to the north,' said Edward.

'Exactly. There are major roads running alongside them, both completely metalled, and the one running along the Reno is one of the few major routes through the Apennines. Of course, north of Bologna you've got the open plains. Flat as a board, so no major difficulties for the enemy there. But there are not many roads through the mountains, so if Jerry wants to move trucks and tanks and what have you south to the front, he's almost certainly going to be using these roads.'

'I see.'

'Once the Baltimores have done their stuff over Bologna, I want you to leave one section with the bombers and take the other two down to have a peek at these valley roads. One section can sweep down the Setta Valley, the other down the Reno. And if you see any movement, give them merry hell.'

Edward had briefed the squadron before the flight. Green section was going to continue escorting the bombers, while he would take Blue section along the Reno Valley and Red section would sweep along the Setta. 'You know the form,' he had told them. 'Hit the deck and shoot anything that moves. One sweep down the valley – in and out. And if there's a lot of cloud about, make sure you keep within sight of each other.'

'All right,' said Edward.

Dick patted him on the back. 'Thanks, Eddie. And you never know, you might see some sun up there above the clouds.'

Five hours later the squadron was circling at 22,000 feet above Bologna. Edward looked down over the front of the huge elliptical wing of his Spitfire and saw the forty-odd South African Baltimores a few thousand feet below spread like a grid over the city as they began their bomb run. Puffs of flak dotted the sky, but the bombers kept their line and unwaveringly droned on over the city. Moments later he watched the first clouds of smoke silently burst four miles below.

It was over in just a few minutes. They'd been lucky – low cloud had covered the ground much of the way, but there had been a gap just south of Bologna that had extended right up to the city. Edward watched the Baltimores plough on north of the city, then wheel for the return journey to Foggia. Edward led the squadron around in another wide circle. Above them the sky was wide and clear, as Dick had promised, the sun glinting across his canopy and along the wing as he gently banked. *Ah yes,* thought Edward, *this is better.*

Now, as Edward turned the squadron west of Bologna, he fumbled in his boot for his map. The cloud was thickening again, the city disappearing from view.

'This is Barley Leader,' he called over his radio. 'Green and Red sections follow me down to the deck.' He dived down, out of the clear and into cloud, so that his Spitfire was enveloped by a white nothingness. His altimeter told him how quickly he was losing height, but it always made him nervous, flying blind in an area full of mountains, so he tried to maintain a westerly course as they dived, keeping north of the foothills. *Where the hell is that cloud ceiling?* His ears clicked and popped as they continued to lose height. Either side of him he could see his wingman and Blue Three, flitting through the cloud like spectres. Six thousand, five thousand, four thousand. *Come on,* he thought.

They cleared it at just over two thousand feet. Edward looked at his map again, lying awkwardly with its creases ruffled on his lap, his mind racing as he tried to latch onto a recognisable landmark. He spotted a road that led back east towards Bologna and followed it until he saw a large river snaking ahead of him. *Ah, good,* he thought. *Must be the Reno.* Banking gently, he led them south. He guessed the fork was less than ten miles away, and in just under two minutes there it was, green mountains rising either side.

'This is Barley Leader,' he called again over the R/T. 'OK, Red One, have you got the Setta?'

'I've got it, Barley Leader.'

'Right, then let's split.'

He led his section down, so that the hills and mountains either side of the valley loomed above them. Just two hundred feet above the river and flying at three hundred and fifty miles an hour. The road hugged the river and Edward spotted a small town. A glance at the map – *must be Mazzola* – then he saw traffic just a short way beyond: a column, dark, grey trucks and transporters – *yes,* there were two tanks. In moments they were over them, men scurrying from the vehicles and diving off the road. Edward lined himself above, inched forward the stick and pressed down on his firing buttons. Bullets, cannons, and tracer from both hurtled from his gun ports, tearing into the column. His Spitfire roared over them at fifty feet, then he heard a noise from the engine – just a light knock – and the plane immediately began to splutter and groan. *Shit, shit,* he thought. 'This is Barley Leader, I've been hit,' he said, as he eased the stick into his stomach and tried to lift himself out of the valley. The enemy column was already way behind. His headphones crackled. Chatter in his ears from the others. How bad? What was it? 'It's the engine,' he told them. No chance of nursing it back to Termoli: had they been twenty-five miles away, the normal range they were operating in, well, perhaps; but they were now more than two hundred and fifty miles north. 'You head on back,' he told them. 'I'm going to try and get some height then bale out. Over.' He hoped he had sounded calm. 'Jesus Christ, oh Jesus bloody Christ,' he said as he switched off the R/T and looked at the dials in front of him. Oil pressure falling, manifold pressure dropping too: confirmation of what he already knew – a dying aircraft. A deep, grinding sound was coming from the engine, and he was losing power – but he was climbing, up out of the valley and into the hills and mountains between the two rivers. How high did he need to be to bale out? For a moment his mind was blank. He couldn't think. He couldn't think what he was supposed to do at all. His heart was pounding in his chest, his whole body trembling. He looked out, down below at the mountains and thought how inhospitable they looked. *I don't want to go there,* he thought. The cockpit of his plane felt safe, familiar; yet he knew he had to leave it and plunge headfirst into an unknown sky.

The engine spluttered again and he watched the speed drop off further. Any moment the engine would seize and the aircraft fall out of the sky. *I haven't long,* he thought, and glanced at his altimeter. Fifteen hundred feet. *Try and get to two thousand.* The needle inched higher, then a puff of smoke belched from the cowling in front of him. 'You've got to do it,' he told himself. Trembling fingers. He tried to fold away the map, but couldn't, so stuffed it into his boot scrunched up like a ball of waste paper. Radio plugs, oxygen leads. He lifted his hand to the rubber knob inside the top of the canopy, then held it there for a moment. *Do it!* he told himself. Edward closed his eyes, felt his hand tighten around the knob and then he pulled. Instantly, the canopy flew off, crashing into the radio mast behind his head and tumbling behind. He unclipped his harness, pushed the stick over and felt himself lift out of the seat, but as he began to slide out of the aircraft his parachute caught on something. Now the Spitfire had begun to dive, falling almost vertically. Frantically, Edward felt behind him, heard something tear and he was tumbling free, the ground hurtling towards him. Far away, he heard an explosion, a flash of light in the corner of his eye. *The ripcord, the ripcord.* He grabbed it with his gloved hand, yanked, and closed his eyes. *Please,* he prayed.

The wind was knocked out of him and his arms almost pulled from their sockets as the parachute opened. *Thank God,* he thought. A few seconds later he was winded again as he hit the ground. Searing pain coursed through his back and down one arm.

Grimacing, he lay prostrate on the ground, gasping for air as he tried to get his breath back. He knew he had to try and keep calm. *Breathe slowly, breathe slowly,* he told himself, then as he felt his lungs begin to work properly again, he hoisted himself onto his good arm, and managed to get onto his knees. *Get the parachute in.* With one arm he begun tugging at the cords and trying to gather up the silk canopy that was now being ruffled by the wind. Another stab of pain, and he cried out, then paused, his breathing laboured once more. He looked around him. He had landed on some low mountains, in a semicircular clearing. Ahead of him were thick woods climbing up to the summit of one of the peaks – he supposed – that he had seen from his plane. Behind were more woods, chestnuts and oaks, and thick with dense undergrowth.

The field he was in was damp and full of a green-stalked crop of some kind – wheat? oats? – he had no idea. No idea what he should do. Through clenched teeth, he began trying to gather in his parachute once more.

Movement caught his eye, and he turned to see two women running towards him, from over the crest of a ridge at one end of the field. Edward froze, and watched them slow as they realised he had seen them. All he could think was: *thank God they're not Germans,* then realised that was no guarantee of safety. Perhaps they would turn him in; perhaps they were fascist in these parts.

Twenty yards from him they stopped and stared. One was older than the other, and slightly taller too. She had fair, shoulder-length hair, and a narrow face and wide eyes, while the other had the same-shaped face, but was dark. They wore simple cotton dresses, the blonde girl with a man's jacket over the top, while the younger one wore an old woollen cardigan. Both wore socks and mud-caked boots.

'Buongiorno,' Edward called out, and forced himself unsteadily onto his feet. 'Sono un pilota inglese. RAF. Mio aeroplano, um –' He lifted his good arm and made a diving motion. 'It crashed, er, fracassarsi.'

The two girls looked at each other and began talking rapidly, then the fair-haired one strode towards him. She was shorter than he had first appreciated – a little over five foot, he guessed, but slender and well proportioned. Her eyes were pale, but her eyebrows quite dark, surprisingly so with such straw-like hair. Edward thought her the most beautiful woman he had ever seen. She spoke to him, but Edward barely understood a word. He'd thought his Italian was reasonable – his first Wing Commander in Sicily had underlined the value of learning something of the language – but this tongue was very different to the patois in the south.

'Scusi,' he said, 'non lo so. Piu lento, piacere.' *More slowly, please.*

She smiled, and apologised, then beckoned over the younger girl. Between them they silently collected the rest of his parachute, then the fair-haired girl spoke again. 'Mi chiamo Carla,' she said.

'Carla,' Edward repeated.

'E la mia sorella Christina.'

'Ah, sisters,' said Edward nodding – *I understand.*

Carla spoke again, this time more slowly. Edward managed to catch certain words as she pointed and gesticulated. Zio – *uncle,* podere – *farm.* Grenaio – *barn.* He was sure they wanted to help him. Beyond the end of the field, out of sight around the edge of the mountain. Carla then asked him something. He shook his head, and grimaced as another wave of pain coursed through him. 'Ferite alla spalla?' she said holding her hand up to his shoulder.

'Si, si,' said Edward. 'But I can walk. Io cammino.'

'Bene,' she said. 'Fa presto.' *Quickly. Yes,* thought Edward, looking around him. There was no-one about. The girls were talking to each other quickly, urgently, hurriedly gathering the silk parachute. 'Velocemente,' said Carla, looking round anxiously. Edward unbuckled the harness and tried to take the straps off his shoulders, but the pain was too great. Seeing his discomfort, Carla hurried over to him and eased the canvas straps off him as gently as she could. She looked at him, her eyes scanning his face, then grimaced sympathetically.

'Grazie,' said Edward, his breathing laboured, 'grazie tante.'

She smiled briefly, then said, 'Affretiamo.' *Let's hurry.*

They walked briskly by the edge of the field, alongside the undergrowth beneath the mountain's summit. The narrow strip of young corn narrowed, and began sloping downwards, and soon Edward could glimpse the Reno Valley beyond. He wondered how far it was to their uncle's house and what reception he would get. The girls spoke rarely; mostly they walked in silence. Edward's shoulder throbbed and he cradled his right arm with his left.

They left the field and continued down a track, already bursting with the growth of spring. It began raining, a light drizzle, and Carla turned and spoke to him again. *The weather?* He wasn't quite sure.

He smiled and nodded. The track came to an end and Edward realised they were now underneath the far side of the mountain. There was a clearing and a series of small terraced fields. Below, behind some chestnut trees and an orchard, was an old farmhouse. Carla pointed. 'Il podere di nostro zio.' *At last,* thought Edward. It couldn't have been much more than a mile from where he had landed, but he felt exhausted.

A sand-coloured dog on a chain barked and snarled as they entered a yard thick with mud and dung. A few chickens scampered across their path. The girls led him into the main house and called out. 'Zietta! Zietta!' Edward was still adjusting to the sudden darkness when Carla turned to a figure sitting on an old chair in the corner.

'Eh, nonno, dove zietta?'

The old man mumbled something and pointed outside. Edward looked around: a kitchen living room, with a stone floor, large fireplace at one end, the fire smouldering gently; next to it was a cast-iron stove. At the other side of the room stood a long wooden table with chairs and benches. By the window, next to the doorway, was a large stone basin. The fire was barely drawing; the room was hazy with woodsmoke and the smell of damp animals and food. The old man sat in the corner, large, knuckly hands clutching a stick. His face was creased like brown paper. On his head he wore a wide cap; a white moustache covered his top lip, and stubble his chin. He mumbled something again, just as a middle-aged woman came in from outside. Looking at Edward, she put her hands to her mouth and began talking rapidly. Carla and Christina began speaking too. An animated discussion began, each occasionally glancing at Edward. He stood there feeling bewildered by his predicament, watching and wondering exactly what they were saying. A sense of helplessness overwhelmed him. His shoulder was agony; he needed their help, yet was unsure whether he should trust them – well, he would have to. He had no choice. *If only,* he thought. If he'd flown over that enemy column a fraction of a second later, then he would have been back at Termoli by now.

The conversation stopped. The women looked at him again, then the middle-aged woman beckoned him to follow. Accompanied by the girls, she led him back across the yard to a barn on the far side.

Running up the outside were a set of stone steps leading to a second floor storeroom. The woman climbed the steps and again motioned to him to follow. The door was low and riddled with woodworm. It creaked open and Edward ducked as he stepped inside. The room was dusty but dry, save for one corner where the rain dripped through a hole in the roof. At one end were fat sacks of grain, in the other, stacks of hay and straw. The woman motioned him towards the hay and spoke to him. He looked at her. 'Lui ripsoa,' she beckoned. 'Ecco.'

'OK, grazie,' said Edward. He was to lie down and rest and so did as he was bidden. Carla smiled at him and spoke to him gently. Again, Edward could only pick out a few words: food, doctor. 'Il dottore,' she said slowly. 'Stasera. Sta-sera.' *Tonight.*

'Grazie, Carla, molto grazie.'

She smiled at him again, then the three of them left. Edward looked at his watch – nearly two o'clock. *Only.* He shut his eyes – there was a lot of the day left; it would be a long wait until the doctor arrived. He wasn't sure what he had done to his shoulder, only that it hurt like hell. Outside, the rain became heavier. He could hear it drumming against the tiles of the barn, and dripping into a wooden pail on the far side of the room. Below him, oxen stirred. A warm smell of dung and urine wafted up through the gaps in the floorboards. He wondered what would become of him. The fighter pilot's existence may have been a fragile one, but at least there had been innumerable constancies in his life at Termoli: the familiar faces, the mess, his camp bed, the daily routine. Now, he had nothing. He could speak less of the language than he'd thought, and was at the mercy of people he knew nothing about. He had no more clothes, no razor to shave with, nor a toothbrush. The farm appeared to have neither electricity nor running water, while it seemed likely that the Germans were now scouring the area looking for him. Then what lay in store? Imprisonment, torture? He had no idea.

A long afternoon of boredom, pain and mounting anxiety. Time in which fear began to plague him. Carla visited him with a plate of warm bread, hard cheese and red wine, coming over and kneeling beside him.

'Mangia, mangia,' she said. 'Ne hai bisogno.' *Eat up, you need it.*

She watched him intently as he tore off some bread and bit into the cheese. It had a sharp and cloying taste, and he drank gingerly from the half-full bottle of wine, but still could not help an involuntary tremble as the strong, rasping liquid went down his throat.

'Bene,' he said, smiling, and she laughed.

'La signora,' he said, 'er, tua zia?' He tried to think. 'Um, come lei chiamo?' *What is your aunt's name?*

Carla laughed again. 'Eleva Casalini. E il mio zio chiamo, Orfeo, e mio nonno, Arturo.'

'Mi chiamo, Edward,' he said. 'Edward Enderby.' He supposed he probably shouldn't have told her his name, but it seemed rude not to.

'Ed-ward,' she repeated. 'Eduardo.'

'Lei e molto gentile. Loro sono molto gentile. Grazie.'

Once he'd finished his meal, she left him. Back to work, it sounded like. He tried to sleep, but the pain in his shoulder was too great, even after the wine. It was hard not to think about his predicament – he thought about the others returning to Termoli, about the telegram that would be sent to his parents. He wished he could tell them that he was all right, and that he was thinking of them. He wondered what tomorrow would bring, and about how these Italians – these Casalinis – must be feeling, worrying, with an English airman lying wounded in their barn. And he thought about Carla: her gentle face and soft voice, the callused hands, chipped and blackened nails and worn clothes. Scratches on her slender arms, mud on the men's boots she wore, the fair hairs on her legs. Of course, he thought, she would not have the sophistication of a city-dweller; these were country people, mountain people. Yet, despite her appearance, there was a soft femininity about her, and as she'd crouched beside him, watching him eat, he'd been overcome by a desire to kiss her. He chastised himself, then smiled. Perhaps it didn't hurt to think about her just a little.

It was dusk by the time the doctor arrived, but almost completely dark in the barn. Edward had been lying awake listening to the oxen moving in their stalls, and to mice – or maybe they were rats – scurrying somewhere over the wooden floorboards, when he'd heard voices outside, making him flinch with another wave of fear.

But it was OK. Four men had come in to see him, and Carla was also with them.

'Buena sera,' said the first man, then added, 'Good evening. I am Salvatore Gandolfi – the doctor.'

'You speak English,' said Edward.

'Not so well. A little.'

'Well, thank you for coming.'

'OK,' said the doctor. 'Let's see.'

The others gathered around, staring at Edward. There was an older, middle-aged man – *Orfeo?* – but the other two were younger, in their twenties. Edward looked up at them, feeling increasingly vulnerable. One was lean, long dark hair swept back off his forehead; the other was shorter, stockier, and with a rifle over his shoulder.

The doctor crouched beside him and asked them to hold up the lamps above him. Edward looked at them again, dark shadows across their faces. The doctor carefully felt his shoulder, prompting another stab of pain. Edward clenched his teeth as the doctor moved his hands around his collarbone. 'Does this hurt?' he asked.

'No.'

'Here?' he said, pressing his shoulder blade.

Edward shook his head.

'Hm,' he nodded. 'You have, um, dislocated your shoulder. Yes? The arm, it is hanging free. Very painful, but not so serious. OK. Now this will hurt.' The doctor suddenly grabbed his right arm, yanked then pushed it firmly. Edward cried out as the joint clicked back into place, then fell back on the straw, gasping.

'There,' said the doctor. 'Mended.'

'Thank you,' mumbled Edward. The men were grinning at him, as the doctor looked in his bag. The older man handed Edward some more wine.

'Thank you, grazie,' he said, taking the bottle in his left hand.

'Here,' said the doctor. 'La benda al collo. What is the word?' He held up some cloth, which he began tying around Edward's neck.

'A sling?' said Edward.

'Yes! A sling, thank you. Wear this for two weeks, maybe three, and you will be fine. Try and sleep tonight. You will feel much better domani – tomorrow.'

'Thank you,' said Edward again.

The doctor felt his brow and pulse. 'Good. You're strong and fit. You will be OK. And now,' he said, 'let me explain.'

Edward nodded.

'This is Orfeo Casalini. He will let you stay here. These other two are anti-fascisti – *partigiani* – you understand? This is La Volpe – the Fox,' he said, pointing to the taller, dark-haired man, 'and this is Giorgio. They want to help you.'

Thank God, thought Edward.

Orfeo looked at him and grinned, then muttered something Edward didn't quite understand and the others all laughed.

'What did he say?' Edward asked the doctor.

'He said he's been waiting patiently for the Allies to arrive ever since the armistice, but hadn't realised they'd be just one lone pilot.'

Edward smiled. 'Advance guard,' he said. The doctor translated, prompting more guffaws.

'You don't need to worry about the Tedeschi, the Germans,' the doctor continued. 'Your plane exploded into the ground and they think you died too – some *contadini* watched the Germans examining the hole in the ground where it went in. Only a few people saw your parachute. You were lucky. Carla says it only just opened in time.'

I was, thought Edward, remembering the brief seconds between the parachute opening and landing on the ground.

The doctor continued. Edward had a choice: the partisans would try to get him back to the Allies, or he could stay here and help them until the Allies arrived. Their *banda* was new – just a couple of hundred recruits, but they knew they could do a great deal to disrupt German transports going up and down the Reno and Setta Valleys.

'That's what I was doing this morning,' Edward told him. 'Tell them I shot up a column of trucks and tanks.'

Dr Gandolfi told them and they grinned and nodded. 'They would like you to stay with them. You would be useful to them – an officer, and English-speaking. They are trying to make contact with the British secret service. You would be most valuable to them.'

'I see,' said Edward. 'And getting back to the Allies?'

'Possible. But difficult – there are many Tedeschi now in Italy, and around here the Black Brigades – fascisti militia. But do not worry yourself – you do not need to decide now, although I suggest you stay where you are for the moment.'

Edward nodded. Carla spoke to the doctor, but as she did so, kept her eyes on Edward.

'Carla says she will teach you Italian,' he said. 'She lives down in the valley with her family, but is working here on the farm for her uncle. She will come here and teach you while your shoulder heals.'

'Grazie,' said Edward again, turning to her.

She smiled. 'Prego,' she said.

'And here,' said the doctor, delving into his bag again. 'This might help.' He handed Edward a book.

'An Italian dictionary,' said Edward.

'Yes. I had a friend – an American doctor in the last war. Sadly, he died. But this was his. It might help, I hope. Now,' he said. 'We will leave you. They are good people here. Good simple people and they will look after you. We will try and keep your presence here a secret, as much for the Casalinis' sake as yours. Not many people come down here, but there have been more Blackshirts and even Germans poking around, demanding food and wine and making a nuisance of themselves. You won't see them at night – they wouldn't be stupid enough to stay up here after dark. The only other person to keep a watchout for is the *postein* – er, the postman – who comes by. He's no fascist but has a big mouth, so try and keep out of his way if you can. I will come and see you again in a day or two.'

'And Volpe and Giorgio?'

'In a few days. And Carla tomorrow. Now get some rest.'

Italy – April, 1944

Edward slept fitfully that first night in the hayloft: the pain of his shoulder, the noise of the oxen below and the mice scurrying nearby, as well as the discomfort of lying on straw on a hard wooden floor, ensured that the hours passed slowly.

For much of the night it was pitch black and he was unable to see anything at all – not even his hand in front of his face. The farm and the mountains lay in utter darkness, and he couldn't help imagining things – that there was someone else in the loft, that rats would soon start nibbling his feet; even that the place was haunted. Eventually he dozed off, only to wake again, disorientated, until a dull sense of dread descended on him as he remembered where he was and how his fortunes had so dramatically changed. Staring wide-eyed into the inky blackness, he thought about the squadron and the house on the seafront at Termoli. News of him being shot down would have been quickly digested and then that would have been it. One of the flight commanders would be given temporary command of the squadron and they would all have drunk as much as usual – if not more – in the mess. By morning, Edward would rarely be mentioned again until he reappeared. It wasn't callousness, it was just the way everyone coped. Out of sight, out of mind.

Until I reappear, he thought, then reconsidered: *rather, if I reappear*. It dawned on him that he could not have been much further from friendly lines if he had planned it. The front was several hundred miles to the south, while Switzerland was probably the same again to the north. How was he ever going to manage to reach either? The doctor had spoken as though he had a choice, but really, it didn't seem that way to him; not lying there in the darkness of that barn. The Allied offensive would be launched soon – the moment the rain stopped and the ground hardened. With any luck they would advance swiftly, either as far north as he was now or at least close the gap. Waiting for a while, he reasoned to himself, was the best course of action. And yet, what of these people, these mountain folk in whose barn he was now lying? Would they let him stay? For a week or two, it seemed – after all, Carla had promised to teach him

Italian. That was something worth waiting around for too. Her simple beauty, the kindness she had already shown him; she was bewitching.

Round and round went these thoughts, over and over, never progressing further until at last he must have drifted back to sleep.

It was raining when he awoke once more – he could hear the rain drumming hard on the tiles above him, dripping in places and running off the roof onto the yard below. The first grey light of dawn cast a faint light across the barn. For a while he watched the loft lighten further until he was jolted to his senses by the sound of a door opening and voices out in the yard. It was just after six and the farm was wakening.

With his good arm he hoisted himself onto his feet and, crouching, walked over to a narrow slit in the wall, from where he could watch the yard and the comings and goings of the house. The rain had stopped, but it was overcast and looked as though it might start again at any minute. A girl he'd not seen the previous day crossed the yard. She looked, he guessed, about twenty or so, clearly the daughter of the middle-aged woman he had met in the kitchen: the same small features and narrow face, long black hair loosely gathered behind. Like Carla and Christina, she wore work clothes: an old and tatty dress, woollen cardigan and men's boots.

Just below him she suddenly looked up directly at him and said, 'Buongiorno, Signore Pilote.' Edward immediately shrunk back, but then leaning his face back to the slit, lifted a hand and said, 'Buongiorno,' in turn.

Below him, he heard the girl feeding the oxen and the cow. She hummed softly between words of encouragement to the beasts. Occasionally, one or other of them lowed gently and Edward could hear their hooves moving on the hard floor. When eventually the girl walked back across the yard, she looked up at him again and smiling asked, 'Ha dormito bene?' *Did you sleep well?*

'Er, si, si, grazie.'

The smell of woodsmoke now wafted across the yard and Edward watched the smoke drift out of the chimney, and heard the faint chatter coming from the kitchen: the farmer, Orfeo, his wife, and at least two girls, who often seemed to talk at the same time. Edward wondered what they thought about having an escaped Allied airman in their hayloft, and whether, after a night's sleep, they had changed their mind about letting him stay with them. He also wondered whether they might bring him some food; he was beginning to feel hungry.

Edward looked at the farm. Both the main house and its buildings were clearly old, but to him the place seemed to be on the verge of collapse. Where it had been rendered, the plasterwork was crumbling. Underneath, the cement between the brick and stonework also looked as though it needed urgent attention. The terracotta roof tiles were a mismatch of different hues, and there were heavy stones dotted over the roof, which, he later discovered, were acting as weights to keep the tiles in place. The walls of the barn were also beginning to spread outwards, while the amount of woodworm made him wonder how the place was still standing at all.

He wondered what lay beyond. Hurrying there the previous afternoon, he had been so concerned about being caught and about doing as the girls had bidden, that he now realised he had taken in little of the surrounding countryside. He was unsure if he would even be able to retrace his steps on his own. Miraculously, his maps had stayed stuffed in his boots during his brief time baling out of his Spitfire, and so he shuffled back to the pile of hay where he had slept and took them from underneath his flying jacket, and spread them out on the dusty wooden floor. Following the line of his journey south of Bologna, he found the fork in the river: the Reno snaking south on one side, the Setta on the other. In between was a triangle of mountains; this, he realised, was where he was now. He remembered seeing these mountains rising from the river valley where he had been hit. The high ground climbed steeply to begin with, then levelled off on a kind of high plain; it was on this plain that he had landed, but he could recall seeing several mountain peaks bursting up through the undulating high ground, standing sentinel over this hidden countryside. They were not enormous peaks: rather like the mountains in Wales he remembered from a boyhood camp with the Scouts. On his map were marked Monte Luna, Monte Torrone and Monte Amato, and further south, a dozen more.

Footsteps in the yard made him stop and hurry back over to the window slit. It was Carla and Christina. Glancing at his watch he saw it was now nearly eight o'clock in the morning. To his disappointment, both girls disappeared straight into the farmhouse without even a glance in his direction, but then a few minutes later, Carla reappeared with a bowl and some bread and crossed the yard to the hayloft.

The door creaked as she pushed it open. 'Buongiorno, Eduardo,' she smiled. 'Ecco a la prima calzione per lui.'

Edward thanked her, gratefully drinking the hot dark liquid in the bowl. 'Caffe,' she told him, 'di ghianda.' Edward nodded but was unsure of the word. 'Lei guarda mia carta,' he said, showing her his maps. 'Er, dove il podere?' he asked. 'Dove sto?' *Where am I?*

He watched her as she leant over and looked at the maps intently. Her brow furrowed; Edward stared at the smooth skin of her face, so close to his. 'Bologna,' she said at last to herself, placing a finger lightly on the city. 'Ah, Monte Luna!' she said, then pointing to the high ground rising above the farm, explained that the farm was on the slopes beneath the mountain. *The mountain of the moon.* 'Qui,' she said, eyeing him and then the map. 'Qui. Pian del Castagna. Il podere chiama Pian del Castagna.' *So that's the name of the farm,* thought Edward.

She left him again soon after, and he examined his map once more. The farm was nestled on a small narrow plain on the western slope of the mountain. There were villages nearby – further below, overlooking the Reno River, where he had been hit the day before, and to the east, the far side of Monte Luna; but Pian del Castagna was, he now realised, an ideal place to hide. Hidden from the Reno Valley below and from the other mountain villages to the east of Monte Luna, it was isolated and, it seemed, reached only by the narrow path on which he had arrived the day before. Moreover, its isolated nature was enhanced by another mountain rising from the high plain directly to the south – this, he now saw, was Monte Torrone. Where he'd come down had been a narrow strip of the high plain between these two mountains. He'd been fortunate, very fortunate indeed.

Edward lay back down on the hay, and wondered what lay in store. There was much to think about; and many questions that remained unanswered. There was, though, little he could do. Chance had delivered him safely into the hands of these people, and it seemed they were willing to help him; he would have to put his trust in them, hope for the best, and above all, be patient.

A week passed, then two. It rained most days, which pleased Edward because it meant Carla would visit him for longer. She was a patient teacher, but once he became more accustomed to the local dialect, he discovered he knew a lot more of the language than he had first realised. He learnt quickly and could soon understand what was being said to him, even if he struggled harder to speak much himself. This surprised him; he'd never been much good at French at school, but then, he reasoned, he had had no incentive. As a schoolboy, it had seemed incomprehensible to him that he would ever want to speak the language. Nor had his teachers been exactly inspirational. Now, however, he realised his very survival could depend on his ability to speak Italian; moreover, he wanted to be able to talk to the people he was living with – it frustrated him terribly to begin with, as a stranger in unfamiliar surroundings, when he was unable to understand what was being said. But most of all, he wished he could talk properly to Carla, to know everything about her.

During the long nights in the barn, he found himself thinking about her, yearning for her next visit. He sometimes wondered why: he barely knew her, after all. But sitting in the barn together, her laughing and smiling when he said something right, or remembered a particularly difficult phrase, filled him with a joy he'd forgotten could exist. They were moments of intimacy, it seemed to him; moments when he once again could forget about the war. The world shrunk. There were just the two of them sitting there in the dusty barn; there were no Germans, or fascist militia, or partisans.

Even when Carla was not with him – and that was much of the time – he worked hard learning words and verbs and testing himself over and over. Anyway, apart from the doctor – who visited him one more time – there was no-one with whom he could speak English. If he wished to communicate, he *had* to do so in Italian. At mealtimes, he joined the rest of the family and listened carefully to the frenetic gabble that flowed around the table, and sure enough, with every passing day he found he could understand more. Gradually, he began to learn more about the place and the people who lived there.

During his first few days there, Carla had taken him all around the farm. At one end of the barn, above the chicken house, was a stone oven. Later, he asked her what this was for.

'To keep the chickens warm in winter,' she told him. 'Then they lay more eggs. More eggs to eat and more to hatch.' In the yard were two water troughs hacked out of an old tree trunk. Behind the house, in the orchard, there was also a well, the only water supply. At mealtimes, food was limited, with barely enough to go around. There was almost no sugar, and no salt: both were severely rationed and prohibitively expensive on the black market, and although the Casalinis lived on a farm with animals and crops, so small were the profits, and so irregular the harvest on this high, mountainous, clay soil, careful planning had to be maintained all the year round to ensure they never ran out of food altogether.

The day started early. Edward was always awoken at first light by voices in the yard. Inside the main house, the stove and fire were lit, while outside the animals were fed and the cow milked. An hour or more later, the household sat down for a breakfast of acorn coffee – the *caffe di ghianda* Carla had brought him that first morning – and warm milk. Lunch was usually eaten in the fields and tended to be bread, cheese and wine. There was scarcely more at supper, when everyone once again sat around the table: sausage, perhaps, maybe some chicken and potatoes or a dish of pasta.

And they all worked hard, from dawn until dusk. There were the oxen and the cow to milk, the sheep to tend, constant repairs, washing, cooking, cleaning, collecting wood, chopping wood, building fires, keeping the stove alight. As soon as he was able, Edward began to help too: small chores that did not require too much physical effort; and he enjoyed it, chopping kindling as he recited his verbs, or feeding the animals.

There was no electricity, and no running water: all water had to be drawn from the well behind the farmhouse. There was an outside toilet, but this was just a bucket, to be slopped out twice a day. Edward had a bowl with him in the loft of the barn – a *vaso da notte* – which he would bring down every morning. The farm depended entirely on the household and the two oxen for labour. There was no machinery, nor even carthorses.

The way of life up there seemed to Edward to belong to a bygone age. Almost everything about the lives of the Casalini family was different from the family life Edward had known as a boy. Theirs was an existence that had barely changed in a thousand years: they were part of a rural peasant community, isolated from the modern world, and one that had never been exposed to the revolutions in land and machinery that had so changed the way of farming life in Britain two centuries before. It amazed him; Edward had simply had no idea people still lived in such a way. The difference with the farms in Surrey, or even Cornwall, was marked. When he had been there nearly a week, Orfeo began making a new plough in the barn below. The single blade was still all right, he explained to Edward, but the wooden frame was not. The only way Orfeo could get a new one was to make it himself.

With his good arm, Edward helped as much he could, steadying pieces of wood as Orfeo sawed and passing him tools, glad to be able to do something of use, however small.

'You're a good carpenter,' Edward told him; that much was obvious, but he was keen to talk and practise his Italian.

Orfeo grinned. 'I have to be. Farmers up here have to do everything, not just plough the land and cut the corn.' He paused, wiping his brow with the back of his sleeve. Some inches shorter than Edward, he was lean, but with strong, muscular forearms. His dark hair was thinning, and his face, lined from long months out of doors, was nut brown. Like his father, the old man Arturo, Orfeo had a moustache, black but flecked with grey. Tufts of hair already sprouted from his ears and his chin was blackened with several days' growth of beard. Despite this rough appearance, his eyes were kindly and he was quick to smile, revealing darkened, widely spaced teeth. His voice, too, was soft – quite gentle. 'With luck,' he added, 'this plough will last ten years at least.'

Edward watched the process, fascinated. It would take a while to finish, Orfeo explained – such things took several days' work – but Edward could see the form the plough was taking. It reminded him of pictures of Iron Age ploughs he had seen in his history books at school.

The farm was called Pian del Castagna – *the chestnut plain* – and the family had worked the land there for many generations. Orfeo's father, Arturo, had lived and worked there all his life, so had his father and his father's father. They were *contadini*, sharecroppers, part of a centuries-old feudal system. The landowner, Edward discovered – the *padrone* – owned nearly every farm around the mountain, and there were many. Orfeo never saw the *padrone*. 'He lives in some castle near Florence,' he told Edward, but most weeks the agent came by on horseback. Half of everything they grew and produced at Pian del Castagna, half of every *lire* they made, was handed over to the agent. Most of the *contadini* in the area could neither read nor write, but Orfeo proudly told Edward that he had made sure he could do both, and had ensured his family were the same. 'Otherwise, those agents will have you every time,' he said. 'If you can't read or write, you'll always end up owing more than you think. But not me – they can't pull that trick on me.'

Everyone in the household was expected to work on the farm or in the house, or both. Orfeo and Eleva, his wife, had a son, Franco, but he was in Russia. They had not heard from him for over six months. There was a photograph of him in the kitchen, on the dark oak dresser. A good-looking boy, a split of both parents and taking the best of their features. He was rarely mentioned, but Edward often saw them glance wistfully at his picture.

Instead, Orfeo depended on the women in his family; he and Eleva had only managed the one son. As Edward discovered, the women of the house had always been expected to work, but not in the fields in the way that they did now. 'It's the war,' Orfeo shrugged. There was just one daughter, Nella – the girl Edward had seen cross the yard on his first morning. Twenty-one, she lived in the house with her parents and grandfather, as did another girl of the same age called Rosa. A round-faced girl, with thick, light brown hair, Rosa was one of Eleva's nieces, the daughter of her sister, who lived in Bologna. Rosa's mother had sent her to Pian del Castagna once the Allies began bombing Bologna. Rosa was a shy, diffident girl. She spoke little at mealtimes. Nella told Edward that Rosa missed the city. 'She wants to go back. She likes having soft hands, not hands covered in dirt and scratches.' Nella, on the other hand, had inherited her mother's looks, but her father's character: like Orfeo, she was always affable and quick to laugh. Everyone called him 'Eduardo,' except Nella; to her, Edward was always 'Il Pilote,' or 'Signor Spitfire.' He did not mind; he rather liked it.

Nella was engaged to be married, to a man from Saragano, the village that lay below them on the lower slopes overlooking the Reno. He was older than her and still away at war. He'd been in Greece and she worried about him and why he had not returned. Every time the postman arrived on his bicycle and ringing his bell, she rushed out to him, but on the three occasions there had been any mail since Edward's arrival, there had been nothing for her. 'One day he'll be back,' Nella told him. 'One day. And then we will be married at last.'

Orfeo also had the help of his two nieces, Carla and Christina, who walked up to the farm and back most days from their home, some three miles away in the Setta Valley, the far side of the mountain plain. Most days, they reached the farm by around eight in the morning, but occasionally, if their mother needed help at home, they would be later, as they had been the day Edward came down.

Carla had been born at Pian del Castagna. 'Upstairs, where Nella and Rosa sleep,' she told him one day, nearly two weeks after his arrival. The rain had stopped and Carla was teaching him by the well behind the house.

Orfeo, she explained, was one of two brothers and for a while they had lived and worked on the farm together, helping their father. But first Orfeo had married Eleva, then his brother Federico – Carla's father – had also married. Children had followed, and there was no longer the space or enough food to go round. So Federico had moved down into the valley taking his wife, Isabella, and two daughters – four-year-old Carla and baby Christina. That had been fifteen years ago.

'Didn't your father mind?' Edward asked Carla.

Carla shrugged. 'No. He was the younger brother. He'd always known it would happen at some point. It's just the way it was.'

Federico had got a job working for the railway. There was a line that ran along the Setta Valley, and he became a maintenance man and moved his family into a small house in the village of Montalbano. Another child followed: a boy, Gino. Life was hard and money short but they never went hungry. And Carla never lost her love of the mountains. In the school holidays she used to go up to Pian del Castagna whenever she could, to help her uncle and aunt. She was close to her cousin Nella, as well. 'She's only two years older than me,' Carla told Edward. 'I've always thought of her as more an older sister than a cousin.'

She had only recently come back to Monte Luna. 'Just a month ago,' she told him. 'Before that I was in Bologna.' She had first gone to the city on a school outing with their teacher, Sister Anna, when she was thirteen. It was Christmastime and she had never seen so many lights before, nor shop windows. 'I thought it was amazing,' she said, 'and so beautiful. When I came home I asked my father whether we could move there.' She laughed. 'But I did go and work there.' At fourteen she left school and through Eleva's sister, managed to get an apprenticeship as a dressmaker. Every day, she took the train to Bologna. 'Because my father worked for the railway, I got free travel,' she explained. Then when war came, she moved there permanently, living with Eleva's sister's family. 'Like Rosa, I came back when they started bombing Bologna. My father wouldn't let me stay.'

'Did you mind?' Edward asked.

'No – I wanted to come back. I've enjoyed being back here – working on the farm. Seeing my family.'

'You're close, aren't you? All of you?'

'Yes. My family are everything to me. I don't know how you can bear it, being away from yours for so long.'

Edward looked down at the well; he could just see a tiny glimmer of water caught in a fraction of sunlight. 'I do miss them, but –' He stopped, trying to think how to say what he wanted. Carla looked at him, her eyes watching his. 'I went away to school. I have no brothers or sisters.' He shrugged. 'It's different in England. Friends are also very important.'

'And your friends are also away with the war?'

'Yes. And some won't be coming back. My greatest friend – Harry – he was killed nearly two years ago.'

'Was he a pilot too?'

Edward nodded. 'We trained together and flew together. Then he disappeared into the sea one day. I keep hoping to discover he's a prisoner of war somewhere, but I know he's gone, really.'

'I'm sorry.' She looked at him intently. 'So many people missing:

Franco, Nella's man, Enzo. Half the men from these mountains. It's the same all over.' She sighed. 'So far, we have not seen much of the war here. Blackshirts come round occasionally and life is harder, but we're lucky to live in a corner of Italy that the rest of the world seems to have forgotten.'

'Long may it last,' said Edward.

'Yes,' Carla smiled, 'otherwise life could become very difficult.'

If any of the household resented Edward's presence, they never said, nor gave any indication of feeling so – perhaps it was because of this feeling of isolation, of being forgotten, that Carla had spoken of. After her initial shock at seeing him, Eleva seemed to treat him just like any other member of the household. She was a quiet woman, thin and lined, and with grey streaks in her dark hair; but she was kind, and while the men, Arturo and Orfeo, may have been the masters of the house, Edward soon realised that it was Eleva who kept the place together and who managed to the day-to-day running. Neither she nor Orfeo seemed much interested in politics or the war – they just wanted their life to continue as normal, for their son to come home, and for the Germans to leave Italy, and the Blackshirts to be swallowed into the ground. 'Thieves, the lot of them,' Orfeo told Edward one night, banging his fists on the table. Like most people, he'd had his fascist card, but so what? That didn't mean he was a fascist; it meant he'd wanted his children to be able to go to school. For many years, he had accepted Mussolini – he didn't much care for him, but he didn't much care for any politicians. But the war had changed everything. 'That stupid bastard brought ruin on Italy,' he told Edward. 'I was glad when they kicked him out, but now he's back and it's even worse than it was before.'

Yet such outbursts were rare. The conversation rarely turned to war. Instead they talked about what they had done that day, what needed to be done tomorrow, or laughed at some incident recalled.

There was music, too. Orfeo was also an accomplished pianist, and after supper, his head full of wine, he would take himself over to the upright piano and play delicate songs from his favourite operas. The girls would often hum along; sometimes, Eleva stood next to him, an arm on his shoulder, singing softly and swaying gently from foot to foot, while the old man, rooted in his chair, tapped his stick.

Italy – April, 1944

Edward began to believe that Pian del Castagno was a forgotten community all on its own. It was so insular, each person – Carla and Christina included – so wedded to the daily fabric of the place, that it was hard to think of it in any other way; and yet they had accepted Edward into their fold so willingly, apparently without question.

Only very occasionally did the outside world penetrate this haven. When Edward had been there just over a fortnight, some Blackshirts suddenly turned up at the farm, and the precariousness of his situation – and even more so that of the Casalinis – was starkly demonstrated. Like a slap around the face, Edward realised he had been foolish to believe their existence there was anything but fragile.

It was afternoon and he was in the loft when he heard the dog in the yard barking furiously and then voices entering the yard. Carefully, through the slit window, he watched them bang loudly on the door of the house. Eleva and Nella came out. He could see that they were frightened. Two of the men groped at Nella, who slapped one of them across the face. The other men laughed. Edward felt anger surge through him. Then one of the men began pointing at the chickens. Edward couldn't quite make out what they were saying, but they seemed to be accusing Eleva of having too many. Then they turned towards the barn. Edward hurried as quietly as he could to the straw and hid himself. They were talking directly below him, quizzing Eleva about how many cows and oxen they had, then asking what was in the loft. One of the men banged the floor with a stick. Underneath the straw, Edward held his breath, not daring to move an inch. Straw and dust tickled his nose, and he knew he would sneeze. Slowly, as quietly as he could, he lifted a finger to his top lip and pressed hard. He prayed the movement would not send straw drifting down through a crack in the floorboards and give him away. *Thank God,* he thought as the desire to sneeze passed.

The men went out into the yard again then climbed the stone steps to the loft and the door creaked open. 'There's nothing in here,' Eleva told them, 'just straw and the remains of last year's hay.'

Seconds passed. Sweat trickled down the side of his face. He could feel their eyes boring into him. *Any moment now,* he thought, *they'll come over and shoot me and then shoot Eleva and Nella.* He closed his eyes. He couldn't remember if he'd put away his razor and mirror that morning. One of the men was walking around the far end of the loft – slow, steady steps.

'All right,' said the man eventually. 'Now give us some wine.' Edward remained where he was, rigid and not daring to move as he heard the door close and the man noisily walk back across the yard to the house. They remained there about an hour, and when they left, took four chickens with them. As they wandered back down the lane, Edward heard Eleva crying from inside the kitchen.

'I'm sorry,' he said, when he eventually crossed the yard.

'It's not your fault,' she said, her eyes red with tears.

'But my being here is putting you all at risk.'

She suddenly sat up and stared at him. 'You're not leaving on their account. I won't let you. I am not going to let them bully and intimidate us. One day soon this will all be over and then they will pay. In the name of the Holy Father, they must pay.'

Edward felt torn. By staying there he risked putting people he had begun to care for in extreme danger. Carla, especially; he couldn't bear to think of her being harmed, and yet all of them could be shot for what they were doing. But by leaving he would almost certainly be caught, becoming a prisoner, or possibly executed as well. There were no shortage of horror stories – at Termoli, a pilot who had successfully made it back to Allied lines had witnessed exactly that, when a solider he'd been travelling with was captured and gunned down just yards from where he had been hiding.

The alternative was to join the partisans in the mountains. As his shoulder began to heal he'd started to think more about the offer he'd been made that first evening when La Volpe had visited him. He wondered what use he would be, however. He was a fighter pilot, not an infantryman. What did he know of such things? He'd barely lifted a rifle in his life; once he'd fired off a round of the Lewis gun on the balcony of the Xara Palace, but that hardly counted.

Later that evening, however, Orfeo seemed to be of the same mind as his wife. 'This is what we have to put up with,' he muttered at supper. 'They make everyone's life a misery. They're taxing us so much now we can barely feed ourselves.'

'I really should leave,' said Edward.

'No, no,' said Orfeo. 'No, we want to help you. This is not your fault. And fortunately, they don't bother us much – not up here. It's the farms on the lower slopes who get regularly pestered by these creatures. But you must always be on your guard. Use your eyes and ears at all times.' He tapped his eyes. 'We all must.'

Even so, by the next morning, he had made up his mind. He would join the partisans. When they next came to see him, he would tell them.

The prospect depressed him. He liked being at Pian del Castagna. Despite the lurking danger, he had enjoyed the long days he had spent there, cocooned with the Casalinis. It had been a time to rest, a time to think. And his time with Carla was something he had come to treasure; more than treasure: he craved her company. His Italian was now sufficiently proficient for them to talk quite freely together, and he was doing everything he could to spend as much time with her as he possibly could. He found her easy to talk to, and was happy hearing her stories about growing up on the farm and in the valley, and about her life in Bologna before the bombing began. She was an attentive listener, too. He had talked more about Harry to her than he had to anyone since his friend had gone missing; he instinctively felt he could trust her. The others seemed to be aware of the friendship that had developed between them; and Orfeo and Eleva let them work together much of the time. 'You must keep up the Italian,' Orfeo told him with a wink.

And so it was that later that afternoon, Edward was helping Carla to clean out the cattle stalls. April was now nearly over. Summer was coming. The first leaves were on the trees and the rain had begun to lessen. It was warmer, too. Before the war, the onset of summer had always lifted his spirits; there was always so much to look forward to. But now, all he could think about was the prospect of leaving Carla and the farm.

For a while Edward hardly spoke; any proximity to her was now a kind of torture. He yearned to be with her so much yet he desperately wanted more: to be able to hold her and kiss her and tell her how much she meant to him. But friendship was better than nothing; soon, he would hardly see her at all. He felt desolate.

'You're quiet today,' said Carla. 'What's the matter?'

'Nothing.' He smiled.

'Your shoulder is much better,' she said. 'You can use both your arms.'

'Yes,' said Edward. 'The doctor did a good job.'

'So what will you do? You're not going to stay, are you?'

He stopped, and leant against a post. 'I can't. I've already stayed longer than I should. The other day those Blackshirts could so easily have found me. Imagine what would have happened then.'

Carla stopped too, leaning against the stall opposite from him. 'Uncle likes having you here. We all do.'

'But my being here is making life even more dangerous for you. I'd never forgive myself if anything happened.'

Carla looked away, then said, 'So will you join Volpe?'

Edward nodded. 'I don't think I've much chance of reaching Allied lines. They're too far to the south at the moment, but hopefully not for long. With summer nearly here, they'll be on the march again in the next few weeks.' He looked out; large white clouds drifted across an otherwise clear blue sky.

'Well, I think you should stay.'

Edward picked up his fork again and continued shifting the hay, his heart dancing: *she minds me going,* he thought, but at the same time he felt miserable. 'I'll wait until they come for me, though,' he said.

'You have to still be here on Sunday,' said Carla. 'My family are coming up for the day. They want to meet you.'

'All right, Carla,' he smiled, 'you have my word.'

As he leant down again, he caught his jacket on an old nail, and cursed.

'Here, let me see,' said Carla. She frowned and looked at the shoulder of his jacket. Then she lifted her hand and touched him. As Edward's heart began thumping in his chest, she said, 'I can mend that for you.'

'Thank you,' he said.

'Wait here. I'll get a needle and thread.'

It was an old jacket of Orfeo's, part of a suit they had given him.

It was dark, charcoal grey, and ill-fitting, although Carla had done her best to lower the trousers and arms; without turn-ups, the trousers were just about the right length.

She reappeared soon after and sat next to him on the edge of the wooden trough outside the barn. She was so close to him; one of her arms was touching his, while her face, her brow knotted in concentration, was just inches away. He felt quite overwhelmed by his desire to kiss her. He could barely stand it. She liked him, he knew that, but he was an English pilot, from a different country, with a different religion. Religion seemed to infuse every part of their lives: the crucifix on the wall outside the house and in the kitchen, the pictures of the Virgin Mary and the baby Jesus; the talk about Sister Anna, or Father Umberto, the priest at Capriglia, the village the other side of the mountain. It all meant one thing: she would never be able to love him. It was impossible. And soon he would have to leave. A few days. A week at most. That was all he had. He wished time could slow down.

'There, done!' said Carla. She looked at him and smiled.

Sunday, 30th April. After Mass in the church at Capriglia, a mountain village the other side of Monte Luna, the entire Casalini family returned to Pian del Castagna. Edward was reading in the hayloft when he heard them coming down the path into the yard, and so putting down his book, went outside to join them.

On seeing him, Carla hurried towards him, took his hand and led him to her parents.

'This is Eduardo,' she smiled as Edward held out his hand to Federico and Isabella.

'We've heard much about you,' said Federico. He looked much like Orfeo, but a few years younger; his hair was fuller and his face less craggy. His wife was much like Carla: Isabella's hair was greying, but she had been flaxen once too, and her face was the same oval shape as her elder daughter's. Like Carla, she seemed gentle, but was softer spoken.

A boy ran over and wrapped his arms around his mother's waist, grinning at Edward as he did so. 'And this is Gino,' Isabella smiled.

'Are you really a pilot?' Gino asked him.

'Yes. At least I was, before I was shot down.'

'I want to be a pilot,' said Gino.

'He's always been crazy about aeroplanes,' said Isabella. 'Ever since he was little.'

'It's a wonderful thing – to be able to fly,' said Edward. 'The world looks very different from up there.' He pointed to the sky, now deep blue without a cloud to be seen.

'I can't imagine,' said Isabella, and shuddered. 'I wouldn't go up in a plane if I was paid to do so. They seem terrifying to me.'

'Well, when the war's over, perhaps I can take you up in one – see if I can change your mind.'

'Can I come?' asked Gino.

Isabella laughed, and ruffled his hair. 'We'll see, darling.'

There was roasted chicken for lunch – two of them. 'Don't go getting ideas, brother,' Orfeo told Federico, as he carved the two birds. 'I'm not doing this every time your family pays a visit. I love you all, but not that much.' Everyone laughed. 'We had a visit from the Blackshirts,' he explained. 'I'm damned if my birds are going to fill the stomachs of those thugs. Better we eat them now, even if it means less later.'

The chickens were delicious, served with bread and some of last year's oil crop. Edward made the most of every mouthful, all too aware that he might not taste such food again for some time. In between mouthfuls, he was asked a barrage of questions from Gino. What aircraft had he flown? How many planes had he shot down? What did he think of the German and Italian planes? Had he always wanted to be a fighter pilot? Edward tried to answer the questions as best he could, although struggled with some more technical words. But he did tell Gino about his first flight in a Spitfire: about the immense power, the lightness of the controls, and the sense of joy and exhilaration of flying at such speeds and dancing through the sky. 'It was like touching heaven,' he said, 'I felt like a God up there.' He suddenly realised the whole table had been listening too, and felt himself redden. 'Well, not a God – I didn't mean to be disrespectful – to take His name in vain – but it was certainly a wonderful feeling.'

Orfeo raised a hand. 'You're not being disrespectful. I'm sure I would have felt the same.'

After lunch, the party began moving outside. It was warm and the sun high in the sky. They took their wine and settled beneath some apple trees a short distance from the well. Within minutes, Orfeo was snoring gently.

'Reminds me of the old days,' Eleva smiled. 'Enough food to eat, the worries of the world forgotten for a day.' She sighed. 'Ah, well.'

'Those days will come again,' said Federico. He turned to Edward. 'Let me show you something.' He got to his feet. 'Come with me.'

Edward followed him as they climbed the terraces and went up through the orchard away from the others. 'Look here,' he said pointing to a tree. There, etched into the bark were three initials and a date: FGC, 12.x.01. 'We have a tradition here,' he said. 'We plant a new tree every time a new member of the family is born. When the tree is big enough, the initials and the date of birth are carved into the bark. Eventually, of course, the trees grow so big that it becomes hard to read, but we all know whose tree is whose.'

'What a good idea,' said Edward. 'I hadn't noticed the carvings before.'

'Here's Carla's, just here,' he said, walking further on. 'Smaller than mine, but coming on. Bears lovely apples, this one.' He stopped and sighed. 'Tell me,' he said, 'when do you think the Allies will come?'

Edward thought carefully for a moment and then said, 'There'll be a new offensive soon. It's been a bad winter. We have material advantage, but that's not much use in deep mud. But now that it's getting drier – well, events should start moving pretty quickly. I don't think anyone believes Germany can win the war now. Perhaps the Allies will get here this summer. I hope so – I'd like to think we can. But honestly, I don't know. I couldn't say for sure.'

Federico nodded thoughtfully. 'What about landings? There's been talk of the Allies landing somewhere north of Rome.'

Edward shrugged. 'I don't know. I haven't heard of any such plans. But nor would I. Most of these things are kept secret.'

Federico was quiet again, then said, 'We had such hopes after the armistice. Mussolini gone, the King and Badoglio ending the war. We thought the nightmare was over. But in fact it had only just begun. We've eaten well today – Orfeo jokes about it, but things are getting really bad, you know. There's almost nothing in the shops.

People are going to starve. The rationing –' He raised his hands to the sky. 'It's terrible.' He turned to Edward, and patted his back. 'Anyway, thank you. You've given me some cause for hope.'

Who would be a father now? Edward wondered, then his thoughts turned to his life just a few weeks before, when he'd still been at Termoli. His world had been so much smaller then: the RAF, his squadron, where they would be flying that day. He'd barely thought about the millions of Italians caught up in this increasingly brutal war; had never even considered there were men like Federico and Orfeo: good, honest men, trying to do their best for their family, when all around them the life they had always known was gradually crumbling before their very eyes. Some time this summer, he had told Federico, the Allies might be here. He prayed he had not given him false hope.

Italy – May, 1944

The first day of a new month; the first day of summer. Morning, and Edward was sitting on a three-legged stool clutching a hand-held mirror and shaving, wearing only his trousers and a vest. It had become something of a morning ritual before joining the others for the ersatz coffee. The soap, made from animal fat, had been given to him by Eleva, the razor and mirror by Carla. He took his time. Perhaps it would be his last morning in the hayloft: the previous evening, word had reached him that Volpe and Giorgio would be visiting him that night. His time at Pian del Castagna was all but over.

A light knocking on the door. 'Come in,' he called.

'Eduardo – good morning.'

'Carla,' he turned. 'Sorry, I didn't –' He looked frantically for his shirt and she laughed.

'Do you think I've never seen a man in his vest before? I see my father almost every day.'

He relaxed. 'Well, I've nearly finished. You're here very early.'

'Don't you want me to be?'

'No, no – I mean yes, of course. It's unusual, that's all.'

'I woke up early. It's the beginning of summer, and a beautiful day. So Christina and I both walked up right away. Anyway,' she said, sitting down on an old box next to him. 'There's somewhere I'd like to show you after breakfast.'

The ground was still damp with heavy dew when they walked through the orchard and out up the lane. Cobwebs twinkled in the sunlight, insects hovered and bees crawled over the wild flowers growing abundantly either side of the path.

'Where are we going?' Edward asked.

'Wait and see.'

She suddenly parted two newly leafed branches to the side of the track. 'Here,' she said, 'follow me.' Beyond was a hidden path through the undergrowth and trees that headed up the mountain. Edward heard scurrying away to his right. It made him start. He looked round to see a wild boar hurrying away.

Carla laughed. 'There are still quite a few in these woods. They hide themselves pretty well most of the time – the partisans have been learning from them.' It was cool in amongst the trees, but the climb was quite steep and muddy underfoot and Edward soon felt himself begin to sweat. He felt slightly disorientated, but guessed they were heading back on themselves, on the side of Monte Luna that overlooked the Pian del Castagna.

'Look,' she said, pointing through a narrow clearing in the trees. 'There's Monte Torrone. It's hidden from Pian del Castagna, but we can see it when we walk up and down the mountain. The top is clear – that means it's going to be sunny all day. If there's cloud covering the summit, it's going to rain. There's a saying: when Torrone's got his hat on, take your umbrella. If he's got his hat off, you can leave it at home.'

Edward breathed in deeply. The wood smelled damp and comforting; like the smell of damp woodland at home. He leant his arm against a chestnut tree and felt the moss growing around its trunk. A mass of muddied, russet leaves covered the ground and he looked up to see a jay hurry past and disappear amongst the branches.

They continued on and a short while later came to a larger clearing, where there was a crevice in the rock. The ground beneath was quite flat, and behind two small oaks and an underhang on one side of rock, stood a small wooden hut with a door and a tin chimney.

'Here,' said Carla triumphantly.

'What is it?' asked Edward.

'It used to belong to an old charcoal burner, but no-one's been here for years. They know about it at the farm, but I don't think the partisans do. There're lots of hidden paths and caves in these mountains and Volpe's men are using a number of them, but this place is still a secret.'

Edward looked at it and shook his head in amazement. 'You can't even really see it from the path.'

'No. You'd walk right past if you didn't know.' She opened the door and beckoned him to follow. Inside it was dark and simple: a chair and a small table, a cot at the far end and a shelf with candles and two old tins. Once again, Edward felt his heart begin to pound.

They were alone, no-one knew where the were; it would be so easy to reach down and kiss her. The stillness in the room was total.

She sat on the cot. 'I brought you here because I want you to know there's somewhere you can hide. Your shoulder's much better. Volpe and Giorgio are coming to see you later and you'll have to go.'

He looked down; his desire was so intense, he could hardly bear to look at her.

'I want you to know that if things get difficult, you'll have this place, somewhere safe where you can hide for a while.'

'Thank you,' said Edward. 'You've all been so good to me. More than I can ever repay.'

She smiled. 'Everyone's liked having another man about the place. There are not many around here any more – not young ones, anyway.'

'I know about Franco.'

'Well, he's in Russia. We all pray daily that he's still alive. But most of the men have simply fled to the mountains. After the armistice, lots of the men around here came home. But then they announced that all former soldiers and anyone born in the years between 1922 and 1925 had to sign up immediately and fight for the fascist army. No-one did, so they said there would be an amnesty, but after that anyone who still had not reported for duty would be considered a traitor and shot. Everyone's in hiding. It's why Volpe's suddenly had all these people flocking to him in the last couple of months. God only knows how many of them there are at the moment, but they're all hiding in barns and caves all over the mountains.'

'I had no idea,' said Edward. 'What sort of people decide these things?'

'Evil people,' said Carla. She looked down and picked at her nails.

'Carla, please be careful,' said Edward.

'I was scared at first, when we found you. I know the fascists wouldn't have liked that. But when the doctor told us the Germans thought you were dead I relaxed. But it's the young men they're after – they don't seem so bothered about the women.'

'Are there many fascists around here?'

Carla shook her head. 'No. Most who used to be pro-Mussolini in the old days realise now that he's just a puppet for the Nazis.

There's a fascist shopkeeper in Montalbano, but I don't know of any others. The *carabinieri* are supposed to be fascists, but I don't think many of them are now. Not really. There was a fascist in Veggio who denounced a few people, but although the *carabinieri* arrested a number, they were soon let go again. No-one wants war around here, but the Blackshirts pester everyone. So do the Germans. Not many come up here into the mountains, but some do and then they make a nuisance of themselves, frightening and threatening people. Well, you've seen it first-hand. One girl in Sant'Angelo was raped. It's terrifying.' She sighed and Edward watched her chest rise and fall. 'Volpe and his men haven't done anything much – they only have a few old rifles. But if that changes . . .' She let the sentence trail, then turned to look at him once more. 'If you join the partisans and they catch you, they'll try and shoot you too.'

'I have to help them.'

'I know.'

'But, you know, I've been in this war a while. Every time I used to fly I might have been shot down and killed. I'm probably safer now than when I was still flying.'

'Perhaps, Eduardo.'

For a moment they said nothing. The silence in the hut overwhelmed him; he felt sure she would be able to hear the hammering in his chest. His desire to hold her, to kiss her – to tell her that he loved her and had done so from the moment he set eyes on her – was so overpowering, he thought he would burst. In the coolness of the room he could feel the warmth of her body next to him. Her face, her hands – they were so close and yet so completely out of reach. He stood and walked away towards the door, the knot in his stomach tightening so that his legs felt as though they might give. But Carla stood up too, and walked towards him. For a brief moment he rested his left arm against the doorway then turned and said, 'Carla.' She looked at him, her eyes searching his face, and he lifted a hand to her cheek. She did not flinch, or recoil, but closed her eyes, and lifted a hand to his. As he leaned down towards her, and felt his lips brush hers, a lightness enveloped him, so that the pain inside vanished in a trice and his spirits began to soar so rapidly he wondered whether he might faint from the giddiness of this ecstasy.

'Eduardo,' she said, 'I love you.'

He kissed her again and this time felt her lips part. He could taste the soft heat of her mouth, feel her hands on his cheeks, around his neck, running through his hair. He pulled away and began kissing her cheek and her eyes, her forehead and underneath her jawline, down onto her neck, and she preened and sighed and laughed all at once; and when he kissed her eyes again he tasted tears. Only then did he stop kissing her.

'Why are you crying?' he asked softly.

'Because I'm so happy and because I'm so sad.'

'Carla,' he said. 'I've been in pain these past weeks, not from my shoulder, but because all I've wanted to do is hold you and kiss you.'

She laughed again. 'Me too.'

'I never thought you could possibly love me too.'

'But my darling Eduardo, why ever not?'

'I don't know. Because I'm English, because I'm not Catholic. Because.'

'I don't care where you are from or what you believe. I love you – I can't help it. I loved you almost the moment I saw you. You looked so young, so helpless. And you looked so kind. You have kind eyes. Gentle eyes.'

He leant down and kissed her again, then she ran a hand over his chest. 'Eduardo, what are we going to do? I can't let you go now.'

He sighed, and a stab of melancholic dread came over him; the joy he had felt just moments before seemed to wither. 'I'm never going to let you go,' he said. 'Never.' He wondered whether he was telling the truth; he hoped so. *Please God,* he thought, *let it be so.*

'The war can't go on forever,' said Carla.

'No.'

'I wish we had longer. I wish Volpe and Giorgio weren't coming tonight.'

'Maybe I can stay a while longer in the barn,' he said.

She laid her head against his chest and linked her hands around his neck. 'I'm never going to forget this,' she said. 'Never. Not as long as I live.' She kissed him again then said, 'We must go back to the farm.'

Edward pushed open the door and there was the world again. It seemed to him as though a spell had been broken. Outside, the birds were singing, the woods were alive with sound. Through the trees, he saw a pair of buzzards circling. Carla gripped his hand.

'Eduardo, never tell a soul about this place. It must be our secret.'

'I promise.' He stopped and held her tightly to him once more. 'Carla, I'll never let you down. Never. I promise you that.'

Over supper, he did not listen to the others' conversation. He could not stop thinking about the momentous events of that morning. Since she had left for home an hour before, he had felt delirium one moment and anguish the next. He longed for the next time he would see her, and wondered whether she was thinking about him too. 'Will you tell your parents about us?' he had asked her as they'd walked back down to the farm.

'I think they've already guessed what you mean to me,' she had told him. 'I haven't been known to spend so much time with a man before.' That had relieved him, too. 'But anyway,' she had added, smiling coyly, 'it's none of their business.'

He was surprised no-one else seemed to have noticed the sea change in his life; but neither Eleva, Orfeo, nor the girls looked at him differently or said anything that would suggest they knew what had happened between him and Carla, and so he said nothing.

'You're quiet tonight,' said Eleva eventually, as Edward helped her clear the plates. 'Are you all right?'

Edward nodded. 'Yes – sorry.'

'There's much to think about these days,' she said, smiling kindly.

'There is,' he agreed.

Outside in the yard the dog suddenly began barking furiously. 'They're here,' said Orfeo, and banging his fist on the table, told the girls to go upstairs. 'We have things to talk about,' he said, waving them away. 'Eleva, get some more wine, will you?'

Volpe and Giorgio came in and Orfeo gestured to them to sit at the table.

'We've left a guard outside on the lane,' said Volpe. 'I hope you don't mind.'

Orfeo shook his head. 'No, of course not, although we have the best guard in the world in that stupid hound of ours.'

The two men chuckled.

'How's the shoulder?' Volpe asked Edward.

'Not so bad. Pretty good, really.'

'Good enough to fire a rifle?'

'I haven't tried. Good enough for my pistol, though.'

'Good – you still have it?'

Edward nodded.

Eleva brought the wine, and placed some chipped tumblers on the table.

'So, how many are there of you now?' Orfeo asked them as he poured out four glasses.

'More and more,' said Volpe. 'Since March people have been coming daily. A few old soldiers, but mostly men from the class of 1922–25. The problem is the lack of arms. There are a few fascist barracks around here, so we can raid those, but really we need help from the Allies. A few air drops, before the Germans work out what we're doing up here.'

Edward nodded. 'I want to help, but what do you think I can do?'

'A lot. You're an officer, to start with. That gives you authority, and you have military training.'

'I'm a pilot. I've no infantry training.'

'Listen, you're a squadron leader. I know you are – I could see that on your battle blouse. You know how to organise men.' Edward wondered about that, but Volpe continued. 'And you speak English. That will be helpful when we try and make contact with the Allies, and when the armies in the south finally reach us. Tell me, Eduardo, how much do you know about what is going on here?'

'Not much. I know that most men are supposed to be fighting with the fascist army, that the Germans occupy all of the country north of the front line, and that Mussolini's government is a sham.'

Volpe smiled. He was a good-looking man, his face delicate, almost feminine. Unlike Giorgio, there was nothing swarthy or tough about him; he barely needed to shave. He spoke quietly too, but Edward was aware that Volpe possessed both intellect and iron-willed determination. It was clear that the others at Pian del Castagna held him in nothing less than awe: the way they spoke about him, the hushed tones and throwaway comments. 'There's fire in him,' Orfeo had told Edward. Even Eleva mentioned Volpe's intelligence. 'He always was a bright one,' she had said, 'even as a boy. Ran rings around the others.' Earlier in the day, Nella had said to him, 'So Volpe's coming to see you tonight, then?' as though Volpe were the *padrone* rather than a twenty-seven-year-old resistance fighter.

'Listen,' said Volpe now, 'I was always anti-fascist. Always. I hated Mussolini even as a boy, but before the war they were nothing to what they are now – Nazi stooges. They want to destroy Italy, to make it a vassal state of the Third Reich. They want to bleed us dry: take our money, use our young men as cannon fodder and the older ones as slaves. There is no Fascist Republic – republic! Ha! It's a joke. The whole system of government has collapsed. We are submerged in a wave of chaos, of anarchy. Everyone fears for the future. Nothing is certain any more. Even here, on Monte Luna, a place by-passed by war for centuries, our way of life is threatened. Everyone is being taxed to the point of starvation – money that goes straight back to Berlin!' Edward thought of what Federico had told him. 'In the valleys below,' Volpe continued, 'we have Germans and troops of the Fascist Army rolling up and down, we have the fascist militia, evil men who want to make their bed with the Nazis and profit from the misery of others, and we have old diehard fascists who don't know which way to turn.' He paused, drank from his glass, then said, 'Most people round here signed up to the Fascist Party in the old days. They had to, or else you couldn't work, your children couldn't go to school, you couldn't buy food. And most people could live with that. But now, it's very different. Do you know what the SS did in Rome? Did you hear what they did? They rounded up three hundred and thirty-five innocent men and shot them.' He fired an imaginary pistol. 'Just like that. For every German that is killed by an Italian, they have promised to murder ten civilians.'

'My God,' said Edward. 'I didn't know.'

'It is a reign of terror. Even Mussolini's fascism was not that. Everyone wants their old way of life back. They want to be left alone, but that will never happen until the Nazis are defeated. We have no choice but to fight, and to help the Allies. The more we can hinder the Germans and the Republican Army, the sooner the Allies will be here and the sooner we will be free.'

'We're about to make contact with the British,' said Giorgio. 'We're now in contact with an agent of the CLN in Bologna.'

'CLN?' asked Edward.

'Comitato di Liberazione Nationale, Committee of National Liberation,' said Giorgio.

'It's national now,' said Volpe. 'Politicians, men of influence. The CLN started in Rome after the armistice but has spread to all the main cities. It's the unofficial government, the political wing of resistance. The communists are also growing in strength but we're not communist here. We're not anything. We're just anti-Nazi and pro-freedom.'

'The agent is coming to see us tomorrow,' Giorgio continued. 'We want you to come with us. Your presence will give us credibility.'

'You think that if the British know I'm here with you, they'll be more likely to help.'

'Yes,' said Volpe. 'Exactly.'

'All right,' said Edward. 'By the way, who knows I'm here?'

'More than you'd think,' said Orfeo. 'News travels fast, but most of the farms and villages on the mountain are full of partisans now. Where else do you think all these men are living?'

'We all have to be careful,' said Volpe. 'There are already bounties on our heads.' He pointed at himself and Giorgio, 'And there's a bounty for Allied troops as well. Times are hard: who knows who might be tempted?'

Orfeo snorted. 'Up here? You must be joking.'

'You never know,' said Volpe, 'and especially down in the valleys.'

The old man, Arturo, suddenly tapped his stick. 'The Germans,' he hissed. 'Bastards the lot of them. I fought them in the last war. We should never have become their friend. Get rid of them. Get them out, I say!'

Volpe and Giorgio grinned. 'We will, Mr Casalini,' said Giorgio.

The two men left soon after. Edward bade Orfeo and Arturo goodnight, then walked across the yard to the barn. *So, another night here.* But sleep did not come easily. As Eleva had said, there was much to think about. Not for the first time, he wished the war would go away, and wondered how he had ever once thought it romantic and glorious. That person he used to be, that naive eighteen-year-old; he hardly recognised himself at all. The people back in England – they had no idea what was going on here in Italy. The war was brutal and ugly and ruined far too many lives. But while it brought out the worst in human nature, it also brought out the best, too. That much he could see: the kindness of the Casalinis, the bravery of these mountain people. The growing respect he had felt for the Italians when he'd been on Malta had been justified after all. Not for the first time, he realised how ignorant they had all been. What was it Mike Lindsay had said about that pilot who'd been impaled? 'But he's only an Italian, Eddie.' Edward cringed at the thought; he wished Mike and even Laurie could witness this.

Carla, he thought, and closed his eyes, tracing the contours of her face in his mind. Without the war, he would have never known her – that much was true. Yet perhaps it would have been better for both of them if they had never met. He sighed and smelled the sweet smell of straw and hay and oxen dung. *No,* he thought. *She's right. The war can't last forever.*

2nd May, 1944. Around eight o'clock in the evening. Giorgio arrived at the Pian del Castagna, where Edward was ready waiting for him. It had been another clear day of white cloud and blue skies, the birdsong loud and constant and the mountains rich with the promise of summer. Edward had debated about whether to take his pistol – a revolver he had never once fired – but in the end decided to leave it in the barn.

He felt apprehensive as they walked up the lane and conspicuous too; as they walked into the field of young corn where he had landed, he was conscious he had not been so far from the farm since his arrival. Now, as he walked beside an armed partisan to meet an agent of the CLN, the reality of his precarious situation began to sink in once more. He felt rather as he had done on reaching Malta, a place so different from what he had expected. He'd felt then as though he were being carried along by events over which he had no control.

They talked as they walked. Giorgio was reluctant to tell Edward much about himself but he did admit he'd lived in the area most of his life. He'd known Volpe since he was a boy – and the Casalinis too. A good family, he told Edward.

Giorgio was several inches shorter than Edward, with a square, solid face and frame. His hair was light brown and thin, combed back off his wide forehead. He walked with a certain swagger, his arms wide. He looked tough, Edward thought. Suddenly, Giorgio said, 'You like Carla, don't you?'

'Yes,' admitted Edward. 'Yes, I do.'

'She's a beauty, all right.'

'Beautiful? Yes she is.'

Giorgio suddenly nudged him and grinned. 'And I think she likes you too.'

Edward smiled.

'A-ha!' said Giorgio. 'Don't worry,' he winked, 'your secret's safe with me.'

They reached the end of the cornfield and crested a brow.

Suddenly the mountains were spread before them, ridge after ridge of woods and tiny green fields. Dropping in front of them lay a long winding white track that led to the valley below.

'That's the Setta, down there,' said Giorgio, pointing to a narrow silvery sliver of river. 'Montalbano is directly below us. Keep on this track and that's where you'll get to.'

Edward nodded and gazed at the wide and unexpected view in front of him. All across the mountains, at various different heights, were small settlements, a cluster of pale stone houses with their terracotta roofs, nestling between the oaks and chestnuts and silver poplars.

'Over there,' he said pointing to a hamlet away to their left, 'out on that small ridge there. That's Cortino.'

'And where are we going now?'

'To Capriglia. It's along this track and through the trees. You can't see it now, but it's not far.' He grinned again. 'I used to go to church in Capriglia every Sunday when I was a boy. You see, everyone knows everyone around here. Everyone has family who are *contadini* up in the mountains. It's the people we don't know that we need to be careful about. Strangers.'

'Like myself.'

'Exactly, Eduardo. But we don't think you are a fascist spy.' Edward could not tell whether Giorgio was joking. 'Anyway,' Giorgio grinned again, 'now you have Carla to think of, eh?'

Edward smiled, but a renewed sense of apprehension welled within him. He decided to change the subject. 'I can see why this is a good place for partisans to base themselves.'

'We thought so. We didn't know what we were doing when we started. It was last September, just after the armistice. I'd been in the navy, but when the armistice was signed everyone just walked off the ship. The officers, the crew – everyone. It was amazing. No-one said, "Go home," or anything, but that's what everyone did. I was on a train full of troops all heading back to their homes.' Somehow – he didn't explain how – he'd met up with Volpe, who suggested they raid the newly empty army barracks in Bologna and steal as many arms as possible. 'We just walked in there and took what we could,' Giorgio told him. 'There was no-one about. There were storerooms full of rifles – you never saw anything like it.' Loading them onto a waiting cart, they later managed to borrow a truck and drive them to Montalbano. Moving to the mountains had also been Volpe's idea. 'We both knew Monte Luna like the back of our hands, and we knew the mountain people would help us. The towns attract the fascists. That's where the *carabinieri* are, where the Blackshirts lurk. Anyway,' he added, 'this is an easy place to hide, and if any stranger comes up here it's not too hard to spot them. And of course, it's not easy for vehicles. There are tracks and paths but no roads like they have in the valley. I don't think a car has ever been up here. Perhaps a tank could get up here.' He shrugged. 'I don't know. I tell you, Eduardo, the Nazis might run the country at the moment, but Volpe's king of Monte Luna right now.'

A faint rumble of engines in the sky and they both looked up. High above them – just pinpricks – a formation of bombers hummed over, white contrails vivid in the fading sky.

'The Allies off to bomb Bologna or Milan,' said Giorgio.

'Yes,' said Edward, and wondered whether he would ever fly again.

More oaks and poplars lined the track, providing a cool, dark avenue as they approached the village. Although Capriglia had its church, the place was made up of just a cluster of houses, barns and other outbuildings, although, Giorgio told him, there was also a larger property owned by the *padrone* known as the Palazzo, and a cemetery a few hundred yards along the track towards Cortino. 'My grandparents are buried there,' he added.

Giorgio took them off the main track and down a narrow driveway to another tired-looking farmhouse, a ramshackle collection of stone walls and cracked plaster the colour of faded umber. Giorgio tapped lightly and the door opened almost immediately. Another *contadino* with wild grey hair and a large dark moustache looked at them and nodded.

Edward followed Giorgio past the man into another stone-floored kitchen. Volpe was there, as was a priest and another man, sleek with dark hair and clean-shaven, and wearing a suit that looked too clean for the mountains. Tallow candles lit the room dimly. Shadows fell across the room and across the faces of the men gathered there. There was the same smell of the kitchen at Pian del Castagna: animal fat, herbs and a distinct mustiness.

'Eduardo – some introductions,' said Volpe, taking his hand and clasping him on the shoulder. He turned to the man who had opened the door. 'Sergio Panni – a good friend of ours. Three sons, all with us. Sergio is good enough to allow a number of our men to sleep in his barns. He hates the fascists – he's been particularly singled out by the Blackshirts. They keep turning up and pestering him, raiding his stores and supplies and claiming them as part of the new taxes he owes.'

They shook hands and Sergio muttered, 'Next time they come I'll kill them myself.'

'And this is Father Umberto,' said Volpe. 'He is the priest here in Capriglia.'

'The famous pilot,' beamed the priest, taking both of Edward's hands in his. 'I've heard so much about you.'

'Really?' said Edward, glancing at Volpe and Giorgio.

The priest laughed. 'But of course! News travels fast around these parts.'

'The postman,' said Giorgio.

Edward was quite taken aback.

'Don't look so shocked,' said Father Umberto. 'Nothing escapes him. Perhaps someone saw you land, they told Luigi Balieri and then he gets talking. He can't help himself. He's the biggest gossip in the whole of Monte Luna, that postman.'

'And this,' said Volpe, turning to the man in the suit, 'is Colonel Bianco.'

'Good evening,' he said. 'Pleased to meet you.'

'Colonel Bianco is also a pilot,' Volpe smiled. 'He flew fighters for the Regia Aeronautica before the armistice.'

Edward nodded. 'Where?'

'North Africa and Malta.'

'Malta? When were you there?'

'In the summer of 1941 and again in 1942.'

'Me too,' said Edward, shaking his hand vigorously. 'I was there February to July, 1942.' He grinned, feeling a spontaneous sense of fellowship.

'Incredible,' said Colonel Bianco. 'Hurricanes or Spitfires?'

'Spitfires.'

'Ah!' he exclaimed. 'Hurricanes were no problem, but those

Spitfires – well, they're beautiful aircraft. They should have been built by an Italian. Anyway, Eduardo, I am glad we're friends now.'

'Yes,' said Edward. 'Me too.'

'We must compare stories one of these days, but right now we have other things to discuss.' He looked at Volpe, and they all sat down at the table. Sergio poured them all wine, then left. When he was gone, Colonel Bianco leant towards them, his fingers together. 'The Allies are about to launch their offensive in the south. The winter has been long and hard, but now summer is almost here. They've been building strength and the drier weather will play to their strengths. They're confident that this time they will break the Germans and take Rome. We must believe they will.'

'I'll drink to that,' said Father Umberto.

'If that happens, the Germans will probably carry out a fighting withdrawal, hoping to delay the Allies as long as possible, while the bulk of their forces retreat to their next line of defence.'

'The Pisa-Rimini Line,' said Edward, remembering a lunch he'd gone to at Group Headquarters where some senior army staff officers had been present and had been talking about it. It had been just a few days before he'd been shot down.

'Exactly,' said Colonel Bianco. He looked impressed. 'Although the Allies have now renamed it the "Gothic" Line. We don't know quite what defences have been prepared there, but we do know the Germans have been busy. It crosses the Apennines about twenty miles south of here.' He looked around the table. 'This obviously has huge implications for you here. First, you can expect many, many, more German and Republican Army troops in the area. Second, these mountains here overlook two very important routes to the Gothic Line.'

'With the proper arms we could make life very difficult for them,' said Volpe.

'Yes, and the Allies understand that. The British understand that. They want to help. I should tell you that I am now working not only for the CLN but also for the British. Let me talk frankly. Volpe, you have done a good job here, gathering men to your banner. But you need to organise yourselves. Eduardo, I know you are an RAF man, but you must help Volpe and Giorgio shape these men.'

'But I have no more experience as a soldier than Volpe and Giorgio,' said Edward.

'But you have experience of leadership.' He turned to Volpe. 'You must dominate this area. This must be your kingdom.' Edward glanced at Giorgio, who winked. Colonel Bianco continued, 'And spread your net wider. Move onto Monte Torrone and beyond.' They were to remember where their strength lay. Hit-and-run tactics were the key. 'Then disappear back to the mountains. Do not be fooled into operating in large forces. You know this area and the Germans don't. You must always guard that advantage. Split your band up into companies, with specialists in each company. These can then operate individually under your instruction. And keep everyone on the move. Never, ever confront the enemy directly. Sneak up behind him, hit him in the arse then slip away back into the mountains.'

'All right,' said Volpe.

'And give yourself a name.'

'Like what?' asked Volpe.

The Colonel shrugged. 'What's your favourite colour?'

'Blue.'

'What about the Blue Brigade? You can wear blue scarves. Easy to get hold of and easy to identify your men with.'

'The Blue Brigade,' said Volpe. 'Yes, I like it. Giorgio?'

Giorgio nodded. 'It's simple, and it doesn't sound political.'

'Good,' said the Colonel. 'The British will not just send you arms but uniforms as well. 'Wear them. Eduardo, get rid of that old jacket and put on your battle blouse again. I know the mountain people are behind you but you must show them that you are an effective fighting force, not a rabble; that you are fighting for the freedom of Italy. Then more will follow, and when things get tough – and they will – they will be less likely to waver. Gentlemen, if you can begin to severely hinder the German lines of communication to the front, then the Allies will have a greater chance of breaking through before the winter, and your freedom will be assured.'

There was silence for a moment, then Edward said, 'What about the mountain people?'

Colonel Bianco nodded his head. A candle flickered behind him; half his face lay in shadow, while the other, a smooth cheek and defined jawline was coloured by a flickering orange glow. The atmosphere seemed tense, close. He spoke softly, his voice lowered. 'This is war, Eduardo. Innocent people will get killed wherever the fighting passes. But you have to remember that here, operating from these mountains, you can make a big difference. If, by your efforts, peace comes to this area sooner, then the hardships that have to be endured until that day comes will have been worth it.'

Edward felt sick. He wanted to stand up and leave right away, to find Carla and to tell her to come with him; they would flee and hide until this monstrous storm had passed. *Why here?* he thought. *Of all the places in the world, why does this tiny community have to get caught up in this appalling mess?* He thought about the Casalinis and the Pian del Castagna, of the generations that had peaceably lived and toiled on the land. *I must leave them,* he thought. *I must do what I can to help them keep apart from all this.*

'If we're going to do as you ask,' said Volpe, 'we are going to need a lot more arms. We have plenty of rifles, but they're old and we don't have enough ammunition. We need machine guns, grenades, mortars, and bullets – lots and lots of bullets. And soon.'

Colonel Bianco held up his hand. 'I know, I know. Don't worry. The British will make three separate drops by aeroplane this month alone. You need to prepare a drop zone.'

Giorgio and Volpe looked at each other then at the priest. 'What about where Eduardo landed?' suggested Giorgio. Edward felt his heart sink – it was too close to the Pian del Castagna. 'That cornfield – it's hidden from both valleys.'

'Sounds good,' said the Colonel. He produced a map – a pre-war military map of the area. They debated for a moment where exactly the field was until Edward said, 'May I see? I might not have much weapons training, but I do know how to navigate.'

'Yes, let Eduardo have a look,' said the Colonel. Volpe passed it over. Edward scanned it, finding '*Pde Pian del Castagna*' almost immediately. 'Here,' he said. 'This is the field, right here.'

Colonel Bianco made a note of the grid reference then said, 'Now, you have a radio, don't you?' Volpe and Giorgio nodded. 'All right, good,' he said, then outlined the drop procedure. They were to tune in nightly to the BBC. If the British were preparing a drop in the next few days, they would hear the phrase, 'Prepare yourself,

Mario, prepare yourself, Mario.' When they heard the words, 'The birds are singing,' that meant the drop would be the following evening at ten o'clock. They needed to be ready in the field. As soon as they heard the aircraft coming they were to start flashing the letter 'M' in morse, then light a series of flares in the shape of the letter 'T'. 'Those are your two code letters,' the Colonel told them. 'Get any part of them wrong and the pilot will turn around and go home. Understood?'

'Yes,' said Volpe. 'How soon, though?'

'Soon,' said the Colonel. 'Days. Make sure you're ready.' He pushed back his chair noisily and stood up. Taking his hat, he said, 'I must be off. I'll come and see you again soon, but if you need me you know what to do.' He glanced at Father Umberto, who nodded acknowledgement. 'Goodbye, and good luck,' he said as he opened the door and stepped out into the night.

Carla found him in the barn the following morning. She had discarded her jacket; now she wore a simple blue cotton dress that came down just below her knees, with her socks and men's boots on her feet. A single clip kept one side of her hair back off her face. She smiled as she walked over to him. It was cool in the barn and Edward saw the goosebumps on her arms.

'Carla,' he said, 'Darling.' He rose and kissed her then held her tightly, breathing in the smell of her hair. 'I've got to leave. I've got to join Volpe.'

She sighed. 'Now?'

He nodded. 'In a minute. I was just waiting for you.'

'It's not fair. I'm going to miss you more than you know.'

'I'll come down here whenever I can.'

'But I won't have you to myself any more.' She put a hand to his cheek. 'We can meet in the hut. Can you remember how to get there?'

'I think so.'

'How will I be able to contact you? I won't know where you'll be.'

'I'll visit you here, or leave a note for you. Or you can leave a note with Father Umberto. He'll know where I am.'

'Darling Eduardo, be careful, won't you?'

'Of course I will.' He kissed her again. *So this is what Harry felt when Kitty left,* he thought. But Carla was not Kitty; there was nothing coquettish about her. He'd told her about Kitty, and the time he had visited her on his return from Malta. 'I'd never betray you,' Carla had told him, and he'd believed her. He'd known her such a short time and yet his trust in her was complete.

It was with a heavy heart that he said goodbye to her, and left the Pian del Castagna. He wondered how he would ever repay the kindness of the Casalinis. *Not by bringing the fighting closer to their homes,* he thought bitterly. He hated himself for what he was about to do – and yet he felt he'd had no choice. *You had to join them,* he told himself as he walked up the track that led away from the farm. Colonel Bianco had been right: this was war; choices were never easy. But as a fighter pilot, the war had at least, for the most part, remained impersonal. He had rarely seen the men he was firing at – it was the machine not the man; a battle between machines, nothing more. A single stray bullet – that was all it had taken. One chance shot that had hit his engine when many thousands of rounds had missed him in the past. *I'm just me,* he thought. *I'm not strong enough for this.* The dull ache of dread, a sensation to which he had become horribly familiar, descended over him like a shroud once more.

As Colonel Bianco had promised, the first air drop came within days. Volpe had told only a few – the partisans were spread across the mountain – and had taken just twenty men with him for the drop. Edward was with him, standing to the side of the field in the darkness, looking up at a clear sky of a million twinkling stars, when they heard the faint hum of an aircraft. Volpe actually grabbed Edward's arm. 'My God,' he said. 'They're coming. They're actually coming.'

He hissed at his men and they scampered out to their flares, while Volpe clutched the lamp. The sound of the engine drew closer. 'Where is it?' he whispered to Edward.

'There!' said Edward as a dark shape loomed towards them from over the valley. 'Quick, flash the code.' Volpe did so repeatedly, then as the aircraft dropped height, he gave the signal for the flares to be lit. In moments the field glowed orange as a giant letter 'T' burned brightly up towards the sky. The aircraft banked, and turned over the field, just a few hundred feet above them. *There's an RAF pilot up there,* thought Edward. Fifteen small white parachutes fluttered open and then the plane flew on, the sound of the engine fading into the night.

The men scrambled towards the canisters as they drifted down. Two fell almost perfectly in the middle of the field; another landed in the undergrowth, one at the far end and another two in the trees the far side of the field, but despite having rapidly extinguished the flares, all fifteen were quickly found. The canisters were heavy, but two men could just about manage to carry them. There was only a sliver of moon, but it gave them just enough light to see the dark shape of the land and the almost luminous glow of the track back towards Capriglia.

Edward had been staying with Volpe and Giorgio in a large empty barn set amongst the trees overlooking the village, and it was to this barn that they now took the canisters. Volpe could barely contain his excitement. 'Come on, come on,' he said as they reached the barn. 'Let's get them open and see what there is.' He knelt down and undid the fastenings of the first of the canisters and lifted the lid. Inside were ammunition boxes, Sten guns and rifles. The others were opened. One had boxes of grenades, another more ammunition and explosives. In one there was nothing but uniforms: British khaki battle blouses, trousers and army boots. A further canister was full of half a dozen Bren guns, the heavy machine guns Volpe had so craved. He clapped his hands together and laughed. 'Bren guns! Just think what we can do now. Now we can teach those bastards a thing or two.' He passed around the Sten guns and uniforms. 'Put these on,' he said. 'Tomorrow we'll start distributing this stuff.'

Bottles were brought from a stash in the corner of the barn. 'Let's drink to this,' he said, 'and to future victories.' Edward drank the rough wine, feeling it burn and cloy his mouth, and looked round at the other men, their faces smiling and laughing in the dim light cast by a handful of candle lamps. *They think they can take on the world now,* he thought.

Later. Most of the men had settled down for the night. Edward lay on some straw in an old cattle stall along with three others: Alfredo, Bruno and Pietro. The three of them tended to stick together,

Edward had noticed, especially Alfredo and Bruno. Since his arrival, Edward had also noticed that they tended to stick close to him, too.

'It's exciting, isn't it?' said Alfredo. He was small, a boy of just eighteen.

'Yes,' said Edward, *but not the word I would have used.*

'I think it is,' said Bruno.

'But it brings it home a bit, don't you think?' said Pietro. 'I mean, it makes it suddenly seem very real. We've been hiding up here for two months and now it's time to do something. To take on the enemy.'

Edward remembered that same sense of excitement, of exhilaration, when he'd joined 324 Squadron in Cornwall. But this lot, *they're scared too,* he thought. It was interesting, watching them, talking with them. For Volpe it *was* an adventure; he could see it in the way his eyes had shone ever since the meeting with Colonel Bianco – the way he'd been that night out there in the field and back in the barn as they'd opened the canisters. Volpe's confidence, his zest for the partisan life, for leading these men, was real. And Giorgio – so calm, and cool as can be. Edward couldn't imagine anything fazing Giorgio; a good man in a crisis. And he had some experience, too – he had done his naval training, had been to sea on a battleship. That counted for a lot. Like Volpe, he was also a little older. A little more worldly.

But these boys – well, they are only boys, Edward thought. They were in awe of Volpe, he thought, of his charisma, but a bit scared of him, too. None of them had ever fired a gun in anger; none of them knew what to expect. Edward wondered how they would react when they came up against trained German troops for the first time. He wondered how he would react, too.

'Eduardo?' said Alfredo.

'Yes?'

'Did you – did you ever feel scared when you were flying?'

'Of course. But mostly before I got into the plane. Once you were in the sky there were too many others things to think about. When you are in the middle of a battle all you are thinking about is flying and shooting. There's no time to be scared.' *A half truth,* he thought.

'I expect it'll be the same for us,' said Bruno.

'Probably,' said Edward.

They were fascinated by him, he knew – by his Englishness, but mostly for being a pilot, and had peppered him with questions: about flying for the RAF, about the aircraft he had shot down; they'd asked him what it was like to fly fighter planes and to be caught up in a dogfight. Was he an ace? *Well, strictly speaking . . .* You are! Hey, everyone, Eduardo here's an ace! How about that! Kids' questions. Colonel Bianco had been right: his battle blouse had made a difference. *They're a little in awe of me too,* he thought. He hoped he wouldn't let them down.

In truth, he was just as fascinated by them. He had talked to them, asked them questions too: about joining Volpe. How had they known where to go? All three – Alfredo, Bruno and Pietro – had lived in Bologna, and all three had been obliged to report for duty at the nearest Republican Army barracks. Pietro had confessed that he'd nearly done so. 'I'm no fascist, but it makes you think twice when you know you could be shot for not doing so,' he'd said. The others had fled just before the March 8 deadline expired. Alfredo and Bruno had known each other since they'd been young. They'd gone to school together, been friends all their lives. They had planned to make a run for it together. For Bruno it had meant tearful farewells with his family. 'It was terrible,' he'd confessed. 'The moment I left my home I had to get rid of anything that linked me to my family. I haven't had any contact with them since. I don't even know whether they are alive. They might have been killed in an air raid for all I know, or arrested by the Blackshirts. Anything might have happened to them.' But he could not contact them; he could not take the risk. To do so would be to risk not only his own life, but theirs too.

Alfredo had not said goodbye to his family. He was the oldest child, with three younger brothers; they all lived in an apartment on the edge of the city. Instead he just left, one afternoon – he thought it best; otherwise they would have talked him out of it. As planned, he met up with Bruno, and they walked all night until they were out in the country, the mountains looming ahead of them. 'A *contadino* family helped us,' Alfredo told him, 'and they told us some partisans were gathering on Monte Luna. So we came here and eventually found Volpe and Giorgio.'

Edward closed his eyes.

'Eduardo,' whispered Alfredo.

'What?'

'Do think Volpe will let me be a Bren gunner?'

'Go to sleep, Alfredo. Go to sleep.'

Italy – May, 1944

Two more arms drops arrived, the third on May 20th. In between, news reached them that a battle was raging in the south. The Allies had renewed their offensive. But the Blue Brigade were now beginning their own battle. Volpe had led a small group to attack a German anti-aircraft battery at Veggio. They'd killed a handful of Germans and hurled grenades at the guns, then hurried back to the mountains in triumph. Two days later, Edward had gone with Giorgio and another group of partisans and had attacked a small column of German trucks just south of Montalbano, in the Setta Valley. Giorgio and Edward had chosen their position well: as the road climbed, slightly away from the river and the railway line. Trees and thick shrubs had lined either side, and they had hidden on the crest of the rise, looking down at a hundred yards of straight road. Behind them, through the trees, was a track that took them back to the mountains.

'Should we put men on both sides of the road?' Giorgio asked him.

'No,' said Edward. 'Let's attack from this side only. If we don't knock out the whole lot it'll be easier for us to get away. Remember what the Colonel said: hit them hard then disappear.'

Giorgio nodded. 'You're right.'

They had two of the Bren guns, a handful of Stens, grenades, and rifles. Edward crouched on the bank next to Giorgio, staring down at the road. With him were Bruno and Alfredo, manning one of the Brens.

'Now you're sure you're going to be all right carrying that thing in a hurry?' Edward asked them.

'Of course,' said Alfredo. 'It's not that heavy.'

'All right, but I'll be right with you if you need help, OK?'

They waited an age. A man was positioned down the hill at the end of the straight where he could see around the bend in the road. One whistle meant something was coming, two whistles meant it was the enemy.

There was almost no traffic. One car came past; Edward tensed when he heard the whistle, then relaxed. An hour passed, then two.

'Where are they?' asked Bruno.

Giorgio grinned. 'Patience. They'll come, don't you worry. And remember: no twitchy fingers, all right?'

It was late morning, and another fine one, with barely a cloud in the sky. Edward was warm in his jacket. He undid the buttons of his battle blouse and wiped his brow. The trees around them were alive with birdsong.

Suddenly two whistles. Edward felt himself tense again, felt his chest begin to pound. Bruno and Alfredo looked up at them anxiously. *They're terrified,* thought Edward. They heard the rumble of engines, a change of gear and then heard the driver push down on the accelerator. He looked at Giorgio, who winked. *Christ, how can he be so calm?*

'Hold it,' said Giorgio, 'hold it boys.' Edward could see now: two army trucks, that was all. Fifty yards, forty yards, thirty: he could see the Germans in the front of the cab. *Good boys,* he thought, *no-one has fired too soon.*

'Now!' said Giorgio, firing his rifle into the cab of the first truck – it was just a few yards from them, crawling at a snail's pace. The windscreen shattered and the truck swerved. The Brens chattered, rifle fire cracked, sudden and deafening, the noise resounding through the trees. Acrid cordite filled the air

'Hold the grenades,' yelled Giorgio. A handful of German troops clambered from the backs of the trucks but were cut down almost immediately. Edward started as a small explosion erupted and the engine of the second truck burst into flames. He could see men scampering on the far side of the trucks, then heard someone in English shout, 'Hold your fire, we're Allies!'

'Hold fire!' Edward shouted, 'Hold fire!' then turning to Giorgio said, 'they're prisoners, they're Allied prisoners.'

The firing stopped, almost as suddenly as it had begun. Silence – even the birds had stopped singing. The attack had lasted less than half a minute. A thin haze of smoke covered the road. Edward could see the driver of the first truck slumped over the steering wheel, and the second dead against the side of the door. He swallowed and felt a small amount of vomit rise into his mouth.

'Come out slowly with your hands in the air,' he called out in English.

A head tentatively poked around the edge of the first truck, then a man emerged, hands held aloft, followed by several more.

'All the Jerries are dead,' said the man in a Scottish accent, 'but we've got two wounded.'

Edward glanced both ways along the road, then leapt out of his position. 'Where are they?' he asked the man.

'In the second truck.'

Edward beckoned for some of the partisans to come over. Half a dozen men jumped from the bank. Most wore British army battle blouses, but one – a tall man with dark wavy hair, was wearing an RAF jacket. For a moment Edward froze. 'Harry,' he muttered, and felt his heart leap. But then he saw that it wasn't Harry at all, someone quite different. He cursed. A renewed sense of grief swept over him. For a second, he'd sworn it had been Harry.

'Fucking hell,' said the Scot, 'how many are there of you?'

'Thirty,' said Edward, picking his way over the dead soldiers. A pool of thick, dark blood spread from underneath one who lay face down on the road. Edward swallowed hard again. 'But many more in the mountains,' he added.

One of the wounded men had been hit in the arm and was groaning in pain, but the other had taken several bullets, including in the stomach. His eyes were wide, his face pale. 'Let's get them out, quick,' said Edward.

'Lucky we weren't all hit,' said the Scot. He called to the man with the wounded arm. 'Hey, d'you think you can walk?'

The man nodded. 'Jesus, my fucking arm,' he cried. Two partisans jumped up into the truck and helped him down, then they lifted the other.

'Come on,' said Edward impatiently, 'we need to get off this road.'

'He's nae going to make it,' said the Scot.

'Well, we can't leave him here. Come on, get him onto the bank at least, out of the way.'

They had no stretcher; instead they had to carry him, hands under his shoulders, crutch and legs. He groaned softly as they scraped through bushes and undergrowth away from the road. On the path they laid him down. His teeth were chattering, his eyes glancing at the faces looking down at him. 'Where's Billy?' he said.

'Here,' said Billy, pushing through. He was young – early twenties, Edward guessed, like himself, with two stripes on his arm and a maroon strip on his shoulder that said, 'Rifle Brigade.'

'Don't leave me, Billy,' said the man, grabbing Billy's hand.

'I won't. You're going to be all right.'

'Someone get him some water,' said Edward. A flask was handed forward.

Edward looked down at the man, at the waxy complexion, and at the blood pumping dully from his stomach. It looked almost black against the dark khaki serge.

'Shit,' said Billy.

Edward looked again. The man's eyes were still open, but the chattering of his teeth had stopped. Billy dropped his hand, then closed the man's eyelids.

'Stupid fucking war,' he said.

'I'm sorry,' said Edward.

'Yeah, well what can you do? At least we're all free now, I suppose.'

'Eduardo, we need to get a move on,' said Giorgio. 'Tell these men they're free to do what they want, but if they'd like to come and join the Brigade we'd welcome them with open arms.'

Edward did so. 'We could do with your help,' he told them. 'Men who have some experience and training – you could make a big difference.'

To a man they agreed. 'What about Parky?' said Billy, pointing to the dead man. 'We can't just leave him here.'

'We'll take him back to the road, son,' said the Scot. 'He'll be picked up all right.' Quickly, they carried the dead man back and laid him down on the bank, then hurried back up the track to the mountains.

Volpe's headquarters were now in some barns in Sant'Angelo, a mountain village several miles further south of Capriglia. The mood was buoyant, the younger members of the band talking animatedly and gesticulating wildly, just as Edward remembered he and other young fighter pilots had done on returning from a hard-fought sortie. Volpe was also pleased to see the eleven men liberated from the German trucks. They were prisoners of war, and had been on their way to a different camp. All had been captured since being in Italy. Two were engineers: the Scot, 'Jock' McGuire, and another sergeant. Four were riflemen, including Billy. The others were all South African, except for the pilot, the man Edward had thought was Harry. The similarity seemed less close up – and he was a New Zealander. Unsurprisingly, the others called him 'Kiwi'.

Edward had mixed feelings about them, even after he'd got used to the fact that Kiwi was not Harry. They reminded him of what he had been like before he'd been shot down; they all carried a faint air of superiority and condescension towards the Italians. Nonetheless, he was glad to be able to speak to people who understood the world that he had come from. Talking to them, they all seemed willing to stay and help. Like him, they were confident the front would be moving forward soon. And there was no doubting their experience and training would make a big difference: the riflemen could teach the others much about using the new weapons that were being dropped by the British, while the expertise of the two engineers would prove invaluable.

It was late afternoon, and Edward was lying under a chestnut tree outside the barn. His head was heavy and he kept drifting in and out of sleep. The sun was warm on his face, the fresh leaves above occasionally rustling in the light breeze.

He awoke as a shadow fell across him.

'Eduardo, we're needed,' said Giorgio. Edward rubbed his eyes, yawned and stood up. 'Volpe wants to talk to us.'

Giorgio led him to a clearing in the trees overlooking the barn. Also there was Jock McGuire and one of the South Africans. Shafts of sunlight shone down on them, so that the clearing looked almost hallowed. Insects darted in the light, and Edward slapped his neck as he felt something land on his skin.

'Eduardo, there you are,' said Volpe. 'I've been thinking more about what Colonel Bianco told us. The arrival of these prisoners makes a difference.'

'I agree,' said Edward.

Volpe squatted on his haunches, his Sten gun hanging loosely at his side. 'We've got to get these companies better organised. These men can help us, but I've also just been told that there're some Italian regulars hiding out not far from here. They're looking for us, apparently. I've sent a couple of men to try and make contact.' He outlined his plans. The core of the brigade was to be the Headquarters Company. He wanted both Giorgio and Edward to stay with him. 'We're in charge – me, then Giorgio, then you,' he said. He also wanted Jock in his company. 'He's an explosives expert.'

Edward nodded. 'Yes – we were talking about it earlier. It's good news.'

'And I want Billy as well. He used to be a mortar man.' The rest would be split up in pairs and attached to the other companies.

'What about the wounded laddie?' asked Jock. 'He's a bullet hole through his arm.' Jock was older than the others – thirty at least, Edward guessed. He was missing one of his front teeth and had a broken nose that had been flattened against one side of his face. Crow's feet stretched down from the corners of his eyes. There were tattoos on his forearms. Edward was not surprised he was a sergeant: there was an air of toughness about him, of confidence too. Volpe had chosen wisely.

Edward repeated the question back to the others.

'It's a clean wound isn't it?' Edward said to Jock.

'Aye. It shouldn't take long to mend.'

'We'll get the doctor to look at it,' said Edward, 'but he can still join his company.' He turned to Volpe. 'What about language differences?'

'There's nearly three hundred of us now,' said Volpe. 'There must be enough people amongst us to act as interpreters in every company. But let's put the word around the rest of the brigade.'

'Do we know how many there are in this band of Italian regulars?' Edward asked.

Volpe shook his head. 'No, but hopefully there'll be enough to help train up the others. We want each company to have a core of people who know what they're doing.'

After Edward had explained Volpe's plans to the two sergeants, they were sent back to Sant'Angelo. 'But you, Eduardo,' said Volpe, 'stay here a moment. I need to talk to you and Giorgio alone.'

He chewed his fingers for a moment, then said, 'This is getting pretty big, isn't it? A month ago we were just a rabble. Now look at us.' He eyed them both. 'We've got to be careful. We're dependent on the *contadini*, but we all know they can barely feed themselves half the time, and especially not with bastard Blackshirts hassling them and taking their stocks. As our numbers grow this is only going to become more of a problem.'

'What do you suggest?' said Edward.

Volpe shrugged. 'I'm not sure.'

'We could make some raids. Attack some of the fascist barracks. They'll have supplies.'

'Maybe. How do we get the supplies back again?'

Giorgio shrugged.

'Perhaps we should widen the net even more,' suggested Edward. 'Operate in a larger area. It's what Colonel Bianco suggested, isn't it? How far do these mountains go?'

'Quite a way,' said Volpe. 'A lot further south than we're operating now. Maybe we could start occupying the mountains the other sides of the valleys too.'

'If we make sure there's never too many companies in any one part of the mountains at the same time, the pressure on the *contadini* will be less,' said Edward.

Volpe nodded. 'Well, we must think about it.' He smiled. 'And eat less. We can't afford to turn the *contadini* against us, especially as the Germans are bound to launch a *rastrellamento* soon.'

'They will,' nodded Giorgio. 'They won't take these attacks lying down.'

They walked back down through the trees towards the barn. Volpe put an arm around Edward's shoulder. 'Are you all right, Eduardo? You look sad.'

'Ah, don't worry about him, he's just lovesick,' said Giorgio. 'He's missing his girl.'

'Well, that's understandable,' said Volpe.

Edward smiled. 'I'm fine, Volpe. Just a bit tired.'

'You did well today, Eduardo – you and Giorgio. I'm proud of you both.'

'Thank you, sir,' Giorgio grinned.

'You know,' Volpe continued, 'for so long I've felt completely powerless. I can't tell you how frustrating it has been, to hate fascism, to loathe every aspect of it, and yet not be able to do anything about it. But now – now I feel we're really doing something, and I tell you, I've never felt more alive.'

Taking part in fire-fights and watching men die before his eyes did not invigorate Edward, however. He was pleased that he had kept his fear and apprehension under control, but the sight of the dead men had affected him more than he would have liked. Of course, the Germans were the enemy, but the sight of those men, slumped in their trucks or lying prostrate in ever-widening pools of viscous blood, had shocked him, and he thanked God he had been a fighter pilot and not an infantryman. He realised that when he had first joined the RAF, the thought of seeing anyone actually die had never occurred to him. Once more he marvelled at how he could have been so small-minded and so callow. He thought of Chuck burning to death in his Hurricane at Takali, and of the young man today: Parky, they'd called him. Watching his life drain away, and the fear in his eyes. He had been alive just a few minutes before, a man with friends, family, and people he loved and who loved him, a man with a lifetime of memories, thoughts and learning. Now he was nothing. It was horrible, and yet these were images that were now seared into his mind.

Volpe had suggested he get some rest, and so once again he had settled under the chestnut tree by the barn. He was not asleep, but he had his eyes closed when he heard someone approach, and looked up to see Father Umberto.

'Ah, you are awake, then,' said the priest. 'I was just wondering what I should do – whether to wake you or not.' He beamed.

'No, I'm wide awake,' said Edward. Father Umberto had a genial, kindly face, round, like his glasses. He was, Edward guessed, in his late thirties, and while hardly fat, was certainly more amply covered than most of the people in his flock. Priests, Giorgio had told him, never ever went hungry. 'The women all cook for them,' he'd told him. 'They feel they need to mother them. And, of course, it makes them feel closer to God.'

'I have something for you, Eduardo,' said Father Umberto.

'Really?' said Edward, sitting up.

'A letter from Carla Casalini.'

'From Carla?' He brightened immediately.

'A beautiful girl,' smiled Father Umberto.

'She is, Father.'

He held out the letter and Edward took it eagerly, then paused, not wanting to read it in front of the priest; some things, even in these strange times, needed to remain private.

But the priest continued to stand over him. 'May I speak frankly?' he asked.

'Of course,' said Edward, a touch of irritation in his voice.

'She's a lovely girl – a *kind* girl; and I don't think I'm betraying any confidences when I say that she has rather lost her heart to you.' He adjusted his hat, and glanced around furtively to check no-one was listening, then said, 'So I'm trusting you not to break it, or act in any way improperly towards her.'

Edward laughed. 'I would never do such a thing, Father, really you –'

Father Umberto raised a hand to silence him. 'I do worry for her, Eduardo. The time will come when the Allies will reach here and you will be sent back to the Royal Air Force. You'll have to leave Carla, and no doubt when the war is over and a thing of the past, you will return to England and then the differences between you will seem too great. Maybe you will remember her beauty, and her charm but you will say to yourself, "She was just a peasant girl," and you will forget her.'

'No, Father, you're quite wrong.'

'These wartime romances,' he continued, 'so easily begun and too easily ended as well.'

'No,' said Edward again. 'I swear to you. When the war is over, I'll come back and if she'll have me, I'll marry her.'

The priest looked at him, eyeing him thoughtfully, then his face softened once more. 'All right,' he said, 'I've said my piece. I think you're a good man, Eduardo; I do so hope you won't prove me wrong.'

'I won't father, I promise – not where Carla is concerned at any rate. Did she seem all right to you when you saw her?'

Father Umberto smiled. 'A little melancholy perhaps, but otherwise perfectly well.' He clasped Edward's hands. 'I'll leave you now to your letter. Keep up the good work.'

As soon as he was alone once more, Edward tore open the envelope; he was familiar with her handwriting already from the lessons she had given him: old-fashioned, florid even, yet precise. He pulled out the letter, a simple sheet of thin white paper.

My Darling Eduardo,
I've missed you these past days, and am thinking about you constantly, wondering what you are doing, and where you are. We heard the partisans held up some German trucks this morning. Mamma heard the shooting. I wonder whether you were there. I hope you are all right and that you are safe.
My darling, I long to see you. Everyone at Pian del Castagna has a rest in the afternoon now, but I will walk up the track and wait for you by the hidden path. I will be there every day, about two o'clock, and hopefully, one time, you will be able to come too.
Be careful – please be careful.
Carla

Edward read the letter over and over again, then folded it away into the right-hand breast pocket of his jacket. *Tomorrow,* he thought. All things being well, he would try to get see her tomorrow. The thought lifted his spirits.

The Italian soldiers arrived in the night; there were over a hundred of them. There were also a number of Russians, Mongolians – an entire platoon who had deserted from their German infantry division a few days before. Sant'Angelo became an army barracks for the night, swarming with men in various degrees of uniform, but all armed, and many talking and laughing loudly, excitedly. Edward wondered what the villagers made of it. Did it make them feel safer, or more vulnerable? Quite intimidated, he guessed – young men with guns, but with little military discipline *were* intimidating, regardless of what side they were on.

He slept near the three youngsters again: Bruno and Alfredo, and Pietro, another fair-haired lad like himself. They had been at his side during the ambush earlier in the day and had stuck close to him during the climb back to the mountains. They had been solemn that night. The adrenalin and initial euphoria brought on by the attack had worn off; they had become sullen, sombre.

'I keep thinking about the man driving the first truck,' Alfredo confessed as they lay in a corner of the barn. 'I saw his face. He was terrified – just for a moment. Then we killed him.'

'You have to try and put it out of your mind,' Edward told him. 'And if it makes you feel better, the first is always the worst. The shock of it, I suppose.'

They looked thoughtful. 'I hate the Germans and the fascists,' Pietro said, 'and I hate what they're doing to Italy, but I never wanted to kill anyone. I still can't believe I'm doing this.'

'Do you think they'll come after us?' Alfredo asked.

'Yes, but they'll have to find us, won't they?'

'Yes,' agreed Bruno. 'And we know this place better than them, don't we? They won't be able to get us up here, will they?'

'No, because we'll be able to see them coming and we'll be waiting for them. It'll be all right.' They seemed to accept his word on this, but Edward really had no more idea about what to expect than they did. He watched them: Alfredo re-lacing one of his boots, his tongue sticking out of his mouth as he concentrated on feeding the frayed shoelace through a narrow eye; Bruno, polishing the barrel of his rifle with a handkerchief; and Pietro, his eyes staring without focus, and absent-mindedly picking his nose. *What's he thinking?* Edward wondered. Probably much the same as he was thinking himself: fearing for the future, and scared about what the ensuing days would bring. That sense of dread again – it was consuming him: a dull and constant beat drumming in the back of his mind, making his heart pound and his fingers shake; making his stomach heavy and his throat tight. He wished he was a child again; how carefree he had been. Oh, there'd been worries and anxieties, but they had been about whether he would get any runs in the next day's cricket match, or whether he would make an ass of himself on his trumpet in the school concert. Remembering made him sad.

He thought of Carla again, picturing her sitting on the edge of the track, waiting for him. A fantasy came into his mind: he had gone to meet her and together they climbed the path to the charcoal burner's hut. But then the Germans decided to attack Monte Luna and they were trapped up there, first for a day, then for several more. Then for weeks on end. No-one knew they were there; they were stranded, their mountain hideaway like a desert island, the German troops that surrounded them as impassable as the ocean. For months they would survive, like orphans of the storm, living off nuts and wild fruits and the occasional boar. Then the Allies would finally come, Monte Luna would be free and the war all but over. They would descend from the mountain, and the Casalinis would welcome them home, ecstatically relieved to discover they had been safe all along.

Ah, well, one can always dream.

Soon after he awoke he knew, with a sense of crushing disappointment, that he would not be seeing Carla that day. Partisan scouts further down the slopes had spotted truckloads of German troops pulling into Montalbano, news that was soon after confirmed by sympathetic *contadini* living near the village.

There was no time to lose. They had to leave the villages and barns immediately and head for the woods and shrub that surrounded the peaks of the mountains.

'We're going to go to the heights above Capriglia,' Volpe told Edward. 'I'm going to leave half our force at Monte Torrone, but I want our headquarters on Monte Luna. That's our base, and that's where we'll fight.'

Quickly, they hammered on the doors of the farmsteads and houses in Sant'Angelo. 'The Germans are coming, the Germans are coming!' they shouted. 'Stay inside and keep out of the way.'

It was half-past six in the morning. Bruno, Pietro and Alfredo were once more beside Edward as they haphazardly marched along the path towards Capriglia. A low mist hung over the Setta Valley, thick and creamy. The fields either side of the path were thick with dew and silvery cobwebs. The air was fresh. Edward fretted about Carla and Christina. He hoped they had stayed put in Montalbano; they lived on the edge of the village, to the north. The Germans, it appeared, had come from the south, along the same road where the partisans had launched the ambush that day. *They should be all right,* he thought. *Please God, let them be all right,* but he was tormented by the thought of the girls already climbing the white, dusty track towards the mountains and then finding themselves caught in the crossfire. As the track from the valley came into view, Edward watched it constantly, straining his eyes trying to see if there were any figures climbing towards them out of the mist. But there was no-one.

Before they reached Capriglia, they climbed onto the slopes of Monte Luna. Edward had been walking towards the back of their column and watched as they melted into the shrub.

'Now you see 'em, now you don't,' said Billy, the young rifleman, who was standing beside him. 'That's amazing cover.'

'We've got to get the Brens in good positions,' said Edward.

'Shouldn't be too difficult,' said Billy. 'Well hidden, but with a very clean line of fire.'

They scrambled off the track and into the trees and thick undergrowth, Alfredo, Pietro and Bruno following close behind. Some thirty feet above the track they found a small outcrop of rock, almost flat. Billy stood on it, then lay down and looked ahead. 'Here,' he said. 'Here would be good. Those with rifles can stand if necessary, but the Bren can go here. Perfect place.' He stood up again, ran his hands through dirty brown hair and lit a cigarette.

'All right,' said Edward, and told Bruno and Alfredo to set up their machine gun, then he went in search of Giorgio and Volpe, struggling through thick undergrowth of brambles and ferns.

He found them with another of the riflemen, who was helping them set up the mortars. Once more, Volpe's eyes were shining with excitement. *He's enjoying this,* thought Edward.

'We must be disciplined,' said Volpe. 'We mustn't fire too soon. We've got to remember what Colonel Bianco told us: that we should only fire back when we're fired upon.'

'Billy thinks this is a brilliant defensive position,' said Edward.

Volpe grinned. 'And we'll be ready for them. The reports I've had are that they're infantry only. No field guns.'

'What's he saying?' the rifleman asked Edward.

Edward told him. 'Good,' he replied. 'It's always difficult attacking a strong defensive position, especially with like on like.'

Edward made his way back. The woods were thick with men, and not just partisans – a number of *contadini* had also left their farms and villages and had taken temporary refuge in the wooded slopes of the summit. Most of the partisans now wore blue scarves around their necks; Edward wore one himself under his RAF jacket – Volpe had given it to him. Some had on their adopted British battle blouses and trousers, others wore only cotton shirts, dark wool trousers held up by braces or thick leather belts. They looked a ramshackle bunch, Edward thought, even with British uniforms. The assurances of Billy and Kiwi had given him confidence but he still doubted whether they would be much of a match for the highly trained and disciplined Germans. *We look like boys playing soldiers in the woods,* he thought.

It was some time after nine in the morning when they saw the first of the troops. The mist in the valley was just beginning to thin under the force of the sun's rays, when small, dark figures emerged, walking up the paths and across the fields in open formation. They were spread out, flushing out the lower slopes in an unhurried fashion.

'They're nervous too, you know,' said Billy. 'They'll be on edge, waiting for that first shot.' Directly beneath them, half a mile below, stood an isolated farmhouse. They watched them encircle the place. A dog was barking furiously then a single shot rang out, resounding across the undulating slopes of the mountain, and the dog stopped barking. Edward saw Alfredo and Bruno flinch. Distant shouts – Germans yelling at the farmer; a pig began squealing – another shot and then the troops moved on, climbing the slopes, drawing ever closer. Edward thought about the Casalinis at Pian del Castagna. Where was Orfeo, he wondered – hiding in the woods or defiantly working on the farm? It seemed as though the Germans were attacking from the Setta Valley only, in which case they would be spared for the moment. He hated the idea of Germans swarming over the place, shooting oxen and chickens, violating Rosa and Nella.

'The Bren's quite a good range, but like anything, it's more effective the closer they are,' said Billy beside him. 'About four hundred yards should be about right.' He chuckled to himself. 'These blokes are goners. They've got nowhere to hide at all. I can't believe I'm seeing this.'

The troops continued to climb towards them. There were hundreds of them, well spaced, carrying rifles and light machine guns. Edward spotted several machine-gun teams. Beside him, Billy was giving a running commentary. 'Five hundred yards, that's good – don't want to get too excited yet. Good lads, good – hold your fire just a bit longer.'

'You don't think they can see us, then?' Edward asked him.

Billy shook his head. 'Nah – and look, they're just beginning to fan around towards those villages.'

Edward watched – Billy was right. They were heading for Capriglia and Cortino, on the extended spur below and away to their left.

'Any moment now,' said Billy, raising his rifle to his shoulder. 'Come on, you fucking Jerry bastards.'

A long burst of machine-gun fire chattered loudly away to their left, and a row of Germans crumpled to the ground.

'Well, that's all right,' said Billy, firing his rifle. Alfredo also began shooting, empty bullet shells clanging onto the rock beside him as Bruno fed through the ammunition belts. Cracks of rifle fire rang out sharply from all along the partisans' position. More Germans were collapsing to the ground, some because they'd been hit, others because they were desperate to flatten themselves against the sudden fusillade of fire. Edward was startled by the noise, deafening amidst the close cover of the trees. He saw a German raise himself up and try and move forward, and aimed his rifle and fired, the snap of the bolt making his ears ring. To his relief, he missed. The woods were thick with the stench of cordite. Bullets pinged into the trees above, making him involuntarily duck and crouch, branches and twigs breaking and tumbling among them. Edward could see a German machine-gun crew open fire, but their bullets were low and wide.

The enemy had stopped advancing. They were pinned down a few hundred yards below. The firing lessened; Bruno changed belts on the Bren. In between, Edward could hear shouts, Germans yelling orders to their men. Then all of a sudden they began to disappear entirely. For a short while Edward watched tensely, wondering whether they were moving into an area of cover from which they would try and outflank the partisans. A cheer from within the woods to their left told him otherwise, and then he looked again and saw what the others had seen: the Germans were retreating back down the mountain. Left behind were the bodies of more German dead and wounded than Edward could count.

'Told you,' said Billy. 'Stupid fucking Jerries.'

There was jubilation amongst the men. Alfredo stood up from his position and ran his hands through his hair. 'Look at my hands,' he said, grinning, and held them out. 'They're shaking. I can't keep them still.' They laughed; Bruno slapped Alfredo's back. 'I think it must be from the vibration of firing the Bren,' said Alfredo.

'Of course it is,' Edward laughed.

'We must have shot about fifty, don't you think?' Alfredo said to Bruno.

'If not more,' said Bruno.

'There's more than fifty lying out there,' said Edward.

'I mean Bruno and me.' The others laughed.

Edward smiled, but thought, *we're joking about killing*. It was as though they'd knocked over skittles, not young men. He wondered whether the Germans joked about killing Italians, but already knew the answer. Everyone hardened in war – even airmen, and he suddenly remembered Mike Lindsay and the Italian pilot who'd been impaled on the fountain. What a joke that had been too. He wiped his brow, then shouted along the line of men still standing, waiting in the trees. Was anyone hurt? No, came the answer. Well, that was something.

Distant firing now broke out, yet resounding across the mountains. 'The others on Monte Torrone,' said Billy. 'Those Krauts are probably getting a bellyful over there too.'

Once again the firing died down, and a while after they saw more Germans in the distance returning back down towards Montalbano. More cheering – first blood to the Blue Brigade.

Giorgio appeared.

'What now?' Edward asked.

'We'll move up a bit – in case they come back. How are you doing for ammunition?'

'All right at the moment.'

'Good. We'll stay on these slopes all day, and then move south when the sun begins to go down.' He glanced out to the open land where the Germans lay. 'First, though, lets go and scavenge that lot.'

Boots, watches, grenades, rifles and ammunition belts: all were lifted without respect or ceremony from the dead. There were few wounded; most had been taken back down the slopes as the Germans retreated. Edward sat on the track watching. He saw Billy going from man to man, kicking any he thought might be alive and occasionally firing several rounds into them, their bodies lurching as he did so. None of the others seemed to bat an eye; rather, several were copying him.

Edward looked away. *We've become hardened, all right.* Billy had been at Cassino, captured in March during the Third Battle. Before that, he'd been at Salerno. He'd told Edward something about what they'd been through. 'I wouldn't wish it on anyone,' he'd said of Cassino. 'I knew it was going to be tough the moment I saw that fucking great monastery on top of that fucking great mountain, and even bigger fucking great mountains behind. But I hadn't realised what total fucking hell it was going to be. I nearly cried with joy when I was captured.' And now here he was, fighting with the men who'd killed his friend, against the men who'd rescued him from his prolonged nightmare at Cassino, kicking and firing and plundering like a dog in a pile of rubbish; like a man who had lost all respect for humanity.

The Germans did not attempt another assault that day, and at dusk the partisans slipped out of their positions and tramped back to Sant'Angelo, where those who had been on Monte Torrone were waiting for them. They, too, were in triumphant mood. In both battles, only one partisan had been wounded; but over two hundred Germans lay dead and the Blue Brigade had further stocks of arms and ammunition.

Night fell and they continued southwards, making their way along moonlit mountain paths until they reached San Stefano, a village some eight miles south of Monte Luna.

Edward settled down in an orchard above a farm, where the hay had been newly cut and stacked in sheaves. It smelled sweet and comforting. The men were everywhere – a tired and hungry ramshackle force, billeting themselves on an unsuspecting *contadini* community: in barns and sheds and under trees; and like locusts they ate and drank whatever they could find. Pietro discovered a sausage and several bottles of wine and he came back to the orchard clutching them to his chest, a wide grin on his face. Edward took long swigs of wine as the bottles were passed around and chewed on the fatty sausage, with its strong taste of garlic and pepper. For once, the rough wine tasted delicious.

Italy – August, 1995

Despite having flown over the city and despite his proximity to the place during his time with the Blue Brigade, Edward had never been to Bologna before. He found driving into it from the airport an alarming experience, and soon realised he had made a terrible mistake. How much easier it would have been to have taken a bus or a taxi into town, and then, once he got his bearings, to have hired a car from his hotel. He cursed his stupidity. 'You damned fool,' he muttered, 'you're too old for this sort of caper.' On the motorway, cars had undertaken and overtaken, swerved in front of him and sat close on his tail, beeping their horns and making him realise what an ordered and civilised place Britain was to drive in. As he went further towards the centre of the city, the speed lessened but the number of cars and scooters – not to say amount of horn-blaring – increased. To make matters worse, his efforts at map-reading were hindered by the number of one-way streets and the standard of signposting, which to his mind was extremely poor. As a consequence, he missed turnings, got lost more than once, was blared at for trying to turn down a one-way street the wrong way, and spent much time dabbing his increasingly hot brow and cursing. When he did at last reach his hotel, he emerged from his car feeling quite shaken, and somewhat surprised that both he and the car were still in one piece. It was, he reflected, a much easier place to fly over than drive through.

A certain degree of calm was restored by a stroll into the centre of the city. His *pensione* was only a short walk from the Piazza Maggiore where he found, quite by chance, a large memorial tableau dedicated to the partisans of the area. He did not recognise any of the names, but the faces of some of those imprinted on oval-shaped discs in the stone reminded him sharply of many of the men he had served alongside: the dark eyes and black hair swept back – their youthfulness – had been a feature of many of them. He could remember few who had been fair like him: Carla, of course; perhaps a handful of others.

He wondered where Carla had lived during her time in the city, when she'd been working as a dressmaker. Fairly near the centre, he

316

remembered. And Bruno and Alfredo had both been Bolognese too. *Well, here I am at last,* he thought. He walked on, around the church of San Petronio and then down a quieter side street where he found somewhere to eat. Much of his Italian had long since been forgotten, but as he sat at his small table, turning his fork around the first bowl of pasta he'd eaten in years, and listening to the waiters and other diners, he was surprised by how much he could still understand, and how quickly it all came flooding back.

He'd told no-one he was coming to Italy – no-one apart from his next-door neighbours at home. Nor had he tried to contact anyone he'd known back then. There was no Lucky to guide him round his old haunts; nor, for that matter, did he know of anyone like Pete Summersby, who could have pointed him in the right direction. Anyway, his time in Italy – on Monte Luna – had been so very different to Malta, and his memories so especially personal, that he wanted to begin his pilgrimage alone.

Bologna was a new experience for him and so he had not felt particularly troubled to be there; even when looking at the partisan memorial, he had been able to distance himself. The following morning, however, he awoke feeling irritable and apprehensive, and not just at the prospect of driving through the city once more. Not for the first time, he wondered whether he would be able cope with what lay in store; whether coming face to face with the places that had troubled him for all this time would prompt even darker memories – things he had successfully suppressed for fifty years. Shakily, he poured the warm milk into his coffee. *You can't turn back now,* he told himself. *Not now you've come this far.* As he drank his coffee he again examined the road map of the area; it was the largest scale map he had managed to find. The Monte Luna area was now a national park: *Parco Storico di Monte Luna,* it said over a shaded area of green that ran between the Reno and Setta Valleys. Monte Luna itself was marked roughly dead centre – only 668 metres above sea level; not that high at all really, but both Monte Luna and the peaks and high ground around it had been the ideal place in which to operate as partisans, of that he was sure. Of the many mountain villages and hamlets, there was no mention, although there appeared to be several roads now crossing over the mountains.

With a biro, he jotted down his route in words on a piece of paper.

He needed to avoid the motorway altogether this time. Instead, he had to aim for Sasso Marconi and then Pistoia. He wondered whether the valley of his memory matched the reality. Would he remember the place where his plane had been hit? The trunk road he needed was the 64 – yes, it was definitely the same road, hugging the valley with the Reno on its left if he was driving south. There had been a town just before they had seen that column of Germans: they'd flown over the town, then spotted them a short distance after. *Mazzola.* He circled the place with a pencil.

He slowly made his way out of Bologna. The traffic was better, and driving less fraught, then he realised he'd arrived the day before in the middle of rush hour. *So of course it was busy. What did you expect?* he chided himself. Pistoia, especially, was well marked and he found the road easily. Almost as soon as he was clear of the city, the mountains rose from the flat plains, looming ahead of him. Ten miles south, he reached Sasso Marconi, and just as he cleared the town, he saw the river fork – an old landmark that he'd last seen just a few hundred feet off the ground.

He continued south, the traffic thinning further. That old feeling of dread settled over him once more and when he reached Mazzola, he nearly stopped – a coffee would waste a bit of time and delay the moment he climbed into the mountains once more – but instead he drove on through until he saw the mountains away to his left and a peak poking up beyond the first line of ridges, and felt a lump rise in his throat. 'My God,' he muttered to himself. 'Monte Luna.'

No sooner had he seen it than the road ahead began to weave and bend and he knew he was roughly in the place where the German column had been. The sheer side of rock into which the road had been cut – he could recall that distinctly, while across on the far side of the river, a much larger cliff of rock, too steep for any trees to grow, rose up from the narrow river valley with distinctive familiarity. He pulled over the car into a lay-by and got out. It was now mid-morning, the summer sun high and hot in the sky, so very different from that wet day of low cloud and poor visibility. He pulled an imaginary rifle to his shoulder and swung high and fast across the sky. Really, it was incredible that he'd been hit. Travelling at well over three hundred miles an hour – it was a one in a thousand chance, maybe more. He wondered who that man had been, the soldier whose bullet had lodged in the engine of his Spitfire; whether he had survived the war – whether he was still alive. Shaking his head, he ambled back to the car.

Just a few hundred yards further on, he turned off the main road and across a bridge over the Reno. The waters were shallow, but running fiercely over a multitude of small and large rocks; here and there were narrow islands of stones. A memory, long forgotten, now returned. Night time, with a sliver of moon – it had been about this time of year – and a small band of them were crossing the river by foot. He could remember struggling over the slippery stones, the sound of their splashes jarringly loud in the still night air. But no-one had heard them, and the following day they had surrounded the small fascist barracks, held everyone at gunpoint and taken all their arms and ammunition. Giorgio had shot the commandant in the knee and they'd tied and bound all the others.

Slowly the road began to climb, wiggling upwards into the mountains. His way became steeper, the hairpin bends more frequent. He drove through a thick mountain wood, and the landscape and terrain began to look increasingly familiar, until he crested a ridge and emerged onto the sweeping plain, the rolling fields once farmed by the many mountain *contadini* – the high ground above the valleys from which the peaks of the area rose. His hands tightened around the steering wheel of his car. It was as though he had walked out of a sealed kingdom and then fifty years later rediscovered the portal that allowed him back in. The shape of the peaks, the roll of the open slopes, the abundance of oaks, chestnuts and poplars and thick undergrowth, was all exactly as he remembered. And it was beautiful, truly beautiful, even after being baked dry by the harsh summer sun. The woods still looked green and lush; only the fields had turned sandy gold.

Reaching a junction, he saw a village sign that said 'Sant'Angelo' and so he turned and drove on, slowly. Besides the church, there were only a few houses; he remembered it as being bigger. Where were all the farmhouses? Nor did he see any sign of the barns that had once housed so many of them. Perhaps they had been away from the main road through the village. And of course, he reminded himself, that had been just a track then, a rough cart track and nothing more.

Edward turned around. There were two places he wanted to see above all, and they were in the opposite direction. He reached the junction again and drove straight on until the tarmac suddenly stopped and the road became the track he remembered it had been. The land was rising slightly; Monte Torrone was on his left, Monte Luna almost directly in front of him. *Where is it? Where is it?* he wondered, then as he approached another dense wood ahead of him, leading up towards the summit of Monte Luna, he stopped, pulled the car off the road, and got out.

Edward breathed in deeply. The air was fresh and clean. He squatted down and picked up a handful of dust in his fingers. He smelled it, then rubbed it between his hands. A few yards further on, a pathway turned left down an open field between Monte Luna and another wood. *Well, well,* he thought. The path was signposted to Monte Luna, and beneath it was a mounted map of the area with *Parco Storico di Monte Luna* written across the top. So it had become an official walking track. He shook his head in wonder, then set off down it, trying to keep his back straight and his legs steady, and wishing he had a stick to help him.

Glancing back, he could no longer see his car. The track and the high plain were hidden. He stepped off the path and onto the field of dried grass. *Yes,* he thought. *It was here,* and he looked up, half expecting, half hoping, to see Carla and Christina walking towards him.

How much further had it been? Half a mile? Perhaps a little more. The field seemed longer than he remembered, but eventually he reached the end and another signpost directed him along a path with high banks on either side.

He continued until he met another signpost, and this time the official pathway directed him into the woods. The sudden realisation that he had found their hidden path filled him with both excitement and an overwhelming melancholy, and for a moment he paused and leant on the post, trying to steady himself and collect his thoughts. The path, once known to only a very few people in the entire world, and used by only two, was now the main track to the summit of Monte Luna. He wondered whether he had the strength to continue. 'Come on, you old fool,' he told himself. 'This is why you're here.'

Breathing in deeply, Edward looked up at the path as it rose up through the wooded slopes, then he began to climb.

He knew he was at the right place the moment he reached it: the sudden levelling off, the slab of rock retreating into the mountain and the still dank and dark overhang looming above. The two trees in front of the hut had gone – their stumps could be seen – as had the charcoal burner's hut itself. There was no trace of it at all. Instead, there was now a long bench on which weary walkers could pause and look at the view of the Reno Valley through a clearing in the trees ahead. *Well, what did you expect?* he told himself.

Sitting down, he sighed once more. How many people had sat here since? Thousands, and yet this had once been such a secret place. *Their* place. Their refuge, where no-one had been able to reach them. Edward closed his eyes. Could he really be here again? After all these years. He felt the light pouring through gaps in the trees, flickering over his face. 'Carla,' he whispered.

That first assault by the Germans . . . He sat there, thinking, remembering. The day after that battle, when they'd been far to the south, the Germans had returned to Monte Luna and had pounded the mountain for much of the day with their field guns, shells whistling and screaming through the sky. The *contadini* had huddled in their cellars and wondered whether the end of the world was finally upon them. When the troops finally plucked up the courage to climb up the slopes once more, they found the mountain deserted. No-one fired back, not even when they gingerly probed the woods.

After that the Germans gave up, pulling out of Mantalbano and disappearing to the south, while the Blue Brigade moved back north. For Edward, the return to the Monte Luna area meant one thing: seeing Carla again. 'I need to see her,' he told Volpe. 'Carla and the Casalinis. I need to know they're all right.'

'Of course,' said Volpe. 'Go.'

It was just after one o'clock when he reached the bank by the hidden path. For the best part of an hour he agonised over whether she would come. *Please,* he prayed, *please come, Carla.* It had been a week since they had last been together – the longest time they'd been apart since his arrival on Monte Luna – and he yearned to see her. It was eating him up, occupying much of his thoughts, and now, in the knowledge that he might see her within an hour, knotting him even more. Over and over, he looked at his watch. Why was it that time slowed down the more one wanted it to speed up? And then if she did come, their brief time together would be gone in a trice.

When he finally saw her coming towards him, he stood up and ran to her. 'Carla,' he said, as he reached her and wrapped his arms around her. 'Carla, I've missed you so much. Are you all right? Let me look at you.'

She was laughing and crying at the same time as he held her face in his hands and kissed her.

'I'm all right,' she said between kisses. 'I'm so glad to see you, my darling Eduardo. Glad to see you safe – I've been worried sick. I thought being in love was supposed to bring happiness, but it just makes me miserable.' She laughed again as they reached the hidden path. Having both looked to see no-one was around, Edward parted the branches and they stepped into their secret world once more. He held her hand tightly as they climbed the path towards the charcoal burner's hut. 'Tell me,' he said. 'Tell me everything. That you've been safe, that they're all OK at the Pian del Castagna.'

'We're all fine – they haven't touched us,' she told him.

'I was so worried when the Germans first arrived that you'd already started walking up towards the farm – that you and Christina would get caught in the crossfire.'

But they hadn't. The Germans had started arriving in the night and had made a terrible noise – truck after truck and motorbikes had all rumbled into the village. Everyone had woken up. Carla's father had told them all to stay where they were: all the children had gone to their parents' bedroom and had sat huddled on the bed with their mother, while Federico Casalini had gone out to see what was going on. A German had yelled at him. Federico hadn't understood exactly, but had got the gist: stay at home, keep out of the way. Soon after, the Germans began climbing the tracks that led up to the mountain.

'All I could do was think of you,' said Carla. 'Mamma kept saying, "Don't worry, he'll be all right. They'll have been warned. Don't worry."'

'So they know about me?'

'Of course – you don't mind, do you?'

'No – no, I want them to, I just thought that maybe they wouldn't –'

'That they wouldn't approve?' She laughed. 'Eduardo, they want me to be happy. And, you know, there's a large part of everyone around here that wants to better themselves. Their daughter's dating a squadron leader in the RAF – an officer! Believe me, Mamma and Papa are delighted.'

Edward grinned. 'I'm not very rich, you know.'

She clasped his arm. 'I don't care. I just want you to be safe.'

In Montalbano they'd heard the battle. Everyone in the village had stood in the square and listened in silence as they heard the shots chatter away, but then they had quietly gone back to their homes when the Germans had come back down again. There had been a renewed sense of alarm when the guns arrived and when, the next day, they had bombarded the mountains. Carla and her family had then turned their fears to those trapped at Pian del Castagna.

'They'll be all right,' Carla's father had reassured them. 'Orfeo's no fool. He'll make sure they hide up somewhere.'

'And that's what they did,' said Carla. 'Orfeo took them all into the woods below the farm, even Grandpapa. But as it happened, not a single shell landed anywhere near. The troops searched the place and took a couple of chickens, but otherwise . . . well, they're all fine. Grandpapa is still cursing all Germans and waving his stick around. We were glad to see them, though. Glad to see them safe and sound.' She turned to him. 'I'm even more glad to see you alive and well. Tell me, Eduardo, tell me what happened.'

He did so, briefly, but sparing her the details: the blood, the dying Englishman, Parky; the scavenging after the battle.

'Did you –?'

'Did I shoot anyone? No, no I didn't. I've discovered I'm a hopeless shot, I'm glad to say. I'm all right when I've got an aeroplane, but with a rifle – well, I'm hopeless.'

They reached the ledge of rock by the hut and Edward was conscious that they had suddenly fallen silent and that Carla was leading him towards the door. It creaked as she pushed it gently open. It was dark inside, but shafts of light shone through a number of gaps in the roof and above the door; dust particles swirled idly. On the floor were several woollen blankets, laid on top of one another.

'I brought them up here,' she said. Half her face was caught in light, and it ran down her neck and across her chest. Her chest was rising and falling, her mouth slightly apart; Edward could feel his own heart beating faster in his chest, but this time not because of any fear.

'Eduardo,' she said, drawing close to him so that he could feel her breasts press against his chest, 'I love you so much. More than I ever knew was possible, and I –' She left the sentence unfinished, instead lifting her head slowly towards his, until her lips were brushing his and he felt her tongue in his mouth, and her hands around his neck and running through his hair. He kissed her back, urgently, and then he felt her take his hands in hers and pull him down. Together they dropped onto their knees. Her fingers pulled the braces off his shoulders then began undoing the buttons on his shirt, pulling the tails from out of his trousers. When his shirt was free she pushed it gently off his arms, while kissing him still, then tugged at his vest, so that for first time her hands were gliding across the smooth bare skin of his chest and back. Lifting his arms, she pulled the vest over his head and dropped it on the floor.

There were buttons on her dress, too, and as he kissed her neck and felt her hands caress his back he slowly began to undo each one. Fumbling fingers made him clumsy, but gradually the cotton parted and he kissed her chest and shoulders as he eased her arms out of the dress and let it drop to her waist. 'I've never done this before,' she breathed.

'Nor have I,' he said, and for a moment paused, and they looked at each other and laughed – a giddy, happy laugh. An old and worn brassiere covered her breasts, and she leant behind her and undid the clip, then slipped it down her arms, so that her entire top half was naked. She shifted so that a beam of light fell across her and Edward gasped. 'You're beautiful,' he said, staring at her – her bewitching face, her hair loose around her shoulders, the pale skin of her body and the round, firm breasts. They kissed again, Edward moving from her mouth to her chin, her chin to her neck, and her neck to her breasts. Her skin felt young and smooth, unblemished save for one small birthmark above her left breast. Her breathing quickened once more and she gasped and then broke away and lay down on the blanket, drawing her legs to her chest as she untied her boot laces and kicked them off. Edward did the same, frantically, not wanting to waste a moment of time. They laughed as their boots banged against the floor of the hut, then Carla was pushing off the rest of her dress and underwear as Edward did the same with his trousers. For a moment he felt overcome with embarrassment as he knelt there over her, naked in front of a woman for the first time in his life. But she grabbed his hand and pulled him towards him, entwining her legs with his so that he could feel the rough, darker hair of her crotch against his thigh. His joy was so intense he wondered how long he would be able control himself. She had wrapped herself around him, so that he felt as though they were almost one. 'Now, darling, please now,' she said, and she took him and guided him into her. Her rough nails dug into his back and she gasped, so that he briefly stopped, worried that he was hurting her.

'No, my love, don't stop,' she whispered, and so he continued, an uncontrollable yet ecstatic sensation coursing down his body. Her back arched and then he could control himself no more and he felt himself spasm and explode inside her.

For a few minutes they lay there, clutching one another and not saying anything, until Carla pushed him over and lay beside him, one leg over his and her head resting on his chest. 'I'm so glad it was you,' he said at length. 'Now I can die happy.'

She lifted herself up and looked at him. 'Don't say that.'

'But I mean it. That was the most wonderful thing that has ever happened to me.'

Her face, solemn one moment, broke into a smile and she kissed him again. Once more he felt her breasts brush across his chest as she moved.

'Now I feel I love you completely,' she said. 'I feel wedded to you now. Maybe not in the eyes of God, but in my eyes. In my mind and in my heart.'

He felt intoxicated by her words. It still seemed incredible to him that she could feel this way. Why? How was it possible? He wondered what he had done to deserve such fortune. 'I want to know everything about you,' he said. 'Everything, starting with your body.' He began to kiss her again, lightly, a mere brush of the lips.

'A thorough examination.' He kissed her eyes. 'What happened here?' he said, looking at a narrow line in her eyebrow.

'I fell down the stairs. At Pian del Castagna when I was little. There was so much blood – I cried and cried, and now I'm scarred for life.' She giggled as he ran a finger down her back and then her arms, kissed her breasts and then her belly, the hair between her legs and then her thighs, shins and feet. 'You're perfect,' he said, meaning it. 'Everything about you is perfect. Even your eyebrow.'

She laughed again and then her expression changed to one of wistfulness. 'We must go,' she said, 'but I want to stay here with you forever.' She sat up and rubbed her face. 'I could scream, really I could. It's so unfair. What is the point of this ridiculous war? Nothing. Why can't we all be left alone?'

'We will be one day. Soon,' said Edward. He sat up too, and held her to him, a hand stroking her hair. 'You know Father Umberto gave me a talking to.'

'Father Umberto? Why?'

'He wanted my word that my intentions were honourable. That after the war I wouldn't go back to England and forget about you.' He paused, feeling her head tilt upwards – *and will you?* 'And I told him that I would do no such thing, and that if you would have me we would marry as soon as the war was over.'

She looked up at him, tears in her eyes. 'My darling, of course I'll marry you.'

'I don't know what we'd do, but I want to be with you forever, Carla. I mean that. I really do. I'm going to love you 'til my dying day.'

'Buongiorno!' exclaimed two walkers in unison, waking Edward from his reverie.

'Buongiorno,' he muttered, and looked down at his feet so that they would not see the tears that were running freely down his cheeks. They said something about the summit, he nodded, and then they stopped a moment, admiring the view. They were young – a man and a woman, both wearing shorts and walking boots, and colourful T-shirts. The man took a long draw from his plastic water bottle.

'Una bella vista,' said the girl, smiling.

'Si, si,' nodded Edward. *Please go.*

They smiled at him again then said, 'Arrivederci!' and carried on up the mountain path.

'I'm going to love you until my dying day,' Edward mumbled to himself, and rubbed his forehead. He stood up and was about to leave, when he looked back one last time at the place where the hut had once stood. *Where are you?* he thought – those two young lovers for whom this place had been so secret. He looked at the ground – at the countless footprints stamped into the damp mud, then stared up the trees. The leaves rustled gently, but no, there was nothing. No trace at all.

Italy – August, 1995

Edward had gone straight back to Bologna after his visit to Monte Luna. As he had walked back down the path, feelings of grief, and regret for a life that had never been, had been so overwhelming that he had known he had seen enough for one day.

Sitting in heavy traffic, he looked around at the hundreds of cars, scooters, buses and other vehicles, and at the multitude of people, and he realised he had never felt more alone in his life. He began to wish again, not for the first time, that he had never left Monte Luna, that his life had ended there, or even earlier, on Malta. That he had died instead of Harry; instead of countless others.

He was wallowing in self-pity, he knew, but he couldn't help himself. *Go home,* he told himself. *Get on the plane tomorrow and go home.* He thought again of the imaginary funeral he had discussed with Lucky, about the few mourners that would be there. How could that be, when Carla had loved him so passionately, so completely? When he had once had so many friends? What had he become? A man who shunned others, who was barely able to communicate with the small amount of family he had left. Would the Casalinis have ever allowed that to happen to one of their own? Would any of those *contadini* families on Monte Luna? *The waste of it,* he thought. Again, he felt his throat tightening and tears welling from deep within him. 'Bloody hell, man!' he told himself. 'You don't seem to be able to stop bloody blubbing these days.' He sighed, as if to scold himself, then added, 'Get a bloody grip of yourself.' He breathed out deeply several times, then switched on the car radio. *Good to improve your Italian,* he thought to himself. *Keep your mind off things.*

The next morning, he felt better. He had been dreading going to sleep, fearing nightmares and long hours brooding on the past, but the day had exhausted him and the wine he had drunk at supper had ensured he slept deeply and without interruption. He had woken with stiff legs, however. *You are nearly seventy-three,* he reminded himself. *Not the sprightly young man you once were.*

Over breakfast at a café in the city centre, he thought about the Casalinis – about what a close family they had been. Of course they had bickered with one another, but family life had been at the very heart of their existence. How different from his own family! A pang of remorse swept over him. Cynthia had been a good wife, but he'd been a difficult husband: taciturn, more irritable than he should have been, and, if he was honest, emotionally cold. They'd not made love once in the twenty years before she'd died. And she'd put up with him, being the constant friend and companion that had helped make his life bearable, and getting so little in return.

Simon, on the other hand, had created a much closer family: he adored Katie and the children and their house was an untidy mishmash of colour and mess, but a happy, family environment. The Casalinis would have approved of Simon's home; they wouldn't have sat there stiffly staring with distaste. Edward cringed to himself. He wished he could furl back the years. Make amends. 'I've made a terrible mistake with Simon,' he mumbled to himself. 'A terrible, terrible mistake.'

When I get back, he told himself, *I must try and atone.* But first there was this journey to finish – a journey, he realised, he had begun in many ways because of Simon. He now wanted to tell everything to Simon – to offer an explanation – but not until his task was complete. It had to be that way.

It was mid-morning by the time he was leaving Bologna behind. He was about to turn off the main valley road and cross the river, when he noticed a signpost for Tolé. He'd not noticed it the day before – he'd been thinking too much about seeing Monte Luna again – but it now reminded him again of the raid they had made on the fascist barracks there – a trip to the far side of the valley that had been more successful than any of them had ever at first imagined.

On a whim, Edward turned right towards Tolé. The road followed a narrow valley beside a small river that fed into the Reno, rising gradually as the stream climbed into the mountains of its source. He stopped at one point, looked at his map, then smiling to himself drove on, until he reached a convergence of five roads. Instead of turning to Tolé he turned right, following a signpost to Bologna. *Ah, yes,* he thought, *this is right.* 'There should be a church along here somewhere,' he mumbled to himself, and sure enough a church soon appeared. He smiled to himself again, slowing as he came to a bend in the road. *Somewhere here,* he thought. Yes, there was Monte Vignola, looming above him to his right, thick woods of chestnuts and pine covering its slopes. Spotting a track running down on his left, he turned into it and parked the car, then walked back a short way and crossed over the road. *I'm sure this is it,* he thought, as he stiffly clambered up the bank to the edge of the trees . . .

It was as they'd been returning from the raid on the fascist barracks at Tolé – one morning in the summer of 1944 – and had been Giorgio's idea. They had noticed that the Germans were using the valley roads less and less, particularly the one along the Reno Valley, presumably for fear of partisan attack. But Giorgio knew there was another lesser road – a *strada bianca* – that wound its way through the mountains roughly parallel to the Reno. 'Let's set up an ambush along here,' he'd suggested. 'You never know what might come along.'

'It's got to be worth a try,' Edward had agreed.

There were just six of them: Edward and Giorgio, Jock and Billy, Pietro, and another Italian from the headquarters company known as Toro. They'd heard the car coming long before it turned the bend, slowly climbing through the gears as the road rose. Then there it was, a German kübelwagen, with a driver in the front and two officers in the back. It was travelling slowly – not more than twenty miles an hour – and before Edward had properly taken aim, all three had been shot dead and the vehicle had careered off the road and down the bank on the far side.

Scrambling out of their positions, they had scurried over to the wrecked car. One of the officers had been a doctor, the other a colonel in intelligence. He had been carrying a briefcase with him, which Giorgio took and gave to Billy – the only one amongst them who could read any German.

'Christ,' said Billy as he rifled through the papers inside. 'We've struck gold.' He scanned the pages, again, his eyes darting across them.

'What are they?' Edward asked. 'What have you got there?'

'Well, I'm not a hundred per cent sure, but I think these are details of all the fortifications along the Gothic Line.'

They whistled, and congratulated one another. 'The Allies'll be happy with us,' said Giorgio.

'We need to get them to Colonel Bianco right away,' Edward said to Giorgio.

Giorgio nodded. 'But first we should hide this car.' He looked around. 'We need the help of some *contadini* round here. Then we'll bury it.'

And that was exactly what they had done, rolling the car further down the hill, out of sight, then digging as deep a pit as they could manage and covering the remains with bits of wood and other vegetation. In the end, Giorgio had shrugged and said, 'That'll have to do,' and then they had set off back towards Monte Luna, crossing the Reno again that night.

Fifty years on, Edward now crossed back over the road, and peered down the densely covered slopes, wondering whether the car and those three Germans were still under there somewhere. He hoped the men had been dug up and given a proper burial; that their families had been given a chance to grieve properly. He paused a moment, looking at the silent wood, then walked slowly back to his car.

Colonel Bianco had been delighted, Edward remembered, as he drove back down towards the Reno Valley; the Colonel had managed to ensure the documents safely reached Allied hands. This had been confirmed a few weeks later, when during another arms drop they had discovered a note of thanks. Their achievement, they were told, in capturing such important information would considerably help the Allies in their efforts to liberate Italy.

Edward tried to remember when exactly they'd captured those documents. June some time? Or had it been July? Rome had definitely been liberated by then – of that he was sure – and the Allies had been closing towards Florence. *Ah, well, no matter,* he thought, as he reached the Reno once more and crossed the bridge towards Monte Luna.

Another warm day, yet up in the mountains the air was fresh and today, at any rate, there was a cooling breeze. Edward parked the car in the same place as he had the day before, and retraced his route of the previous afternoon, the crickets loudly chirruping in the long grass. He had a stick with him this time – a simple, tall, hazel walking stick he'd spotted in the window of a shop in Bologna. Even so, he took his time. His legs were still stiff and it took him time to feel them loosen up. Still, he didn't have far to go – a mile at most, and then back again. He could manage that all right. *You might be getting old,* he told himself, *but you're not* that *old.* He passed some more walkers – a group of them this time – and wondered whether any of them knew that such scenes of violence had once occurred on the mountain. Probably not – and that was just as well.

This time, when he reached the path to the summit of the mountain, he took a deep breath and continued on as the track gently descended through the trees. He passed no-one, but then began to think he had gone too far; he didn't remember the distance between the farm and the hidden path being more than a few hundred yards. Perhaps he was wrong, though, he told himself, and so he walked on. But then the path joined a small mountain stream; that had been away below the farm, leading to the nearest village, Saragano, a mile or two further down on the lower slopes of the mountains, overlooking the Reno River. 'Damn,' he said to himself, pausing. For a moment he felt confused, doubting his memory.

Turning back, he soon discovered where he'd gone wrong: the path now forked, but the right-hand fork was so overgrown he'd not noticed it initially. Picking up a stick, he swished at the ferns and nettles that blocked his way and stumbled through the undergrowth until the trees thickened and the path at last began to clear.

The trees stopped abruptly and Edward stepped out onto the Pian del Castagna. Immediately, he felt a lump building in his throat, and for a moment he paused, his hand over his mouth. 'What's become of you?' he asked out loud, and wiped his eyes and face where tears were once more running.

Standing on an old terraced field, he looked down at the orchard and the remains of the farm. His legs suddenly felt weak and shaky, he picked his way down into the yard. Grass and weeds sprouted up through the stone. The roof of the old house had partially collapsed, while the barn had completely done so. *The woodworm got the better of you at last,* thought Edward. All that remained of the hayloft where he had spent so many nights were the stone steps on the outside, now leading to nothing but the sky.

He crossed the yard. The main door that led to the kitchen stood haphazardly closed, held there by one screw on one hinge. He pushed it open, disturbing a number of pigeons as he did so, which made him jump back in alarm. Having recovered his composure, he gingerly stepped inside. There was nothing left. The room was empty: no table, no Arturo waving his stick in the corner; no picture of the long-lost son, Franco, on the dresser. The air smelled dank and musty. Bird droppings and mud covered the flagstones. The stairs still climbed to the next floor, but he'd never been up there, not even when he'd been living with them; the three bedrooms had already been spoken for.

Edward went outside again and walked round the back of the house to the well, now surrounded by overgrown grasses and nettles. With his stick, he cut them down and sat on the edge as he had done the day Carla had sewn the slit in his jacket. He picked up a stone and dropped it down the well. 'One, two, three,' he counted softly, then heard the gentle splash forty feet below.

It occurred to him that there were few more depressing sights than a derelict and deserted house; a place where there had once been such life and vitality. He wondered who owned the place now. The *mezzadria* system of farming, the feudal sharecropping to which all the *contadini* had been tied, had, Edward guessed, vanished long ago both on Monte Luna and throughout Italy. Was there still a *padrone,* an old family, who owned much of this land? It had to belong to someone, he reasoned. Perhaps even a member of the Casalini family.

But it was irrelevant. The fact of the matter was clear: no-one lived here now and no-one farmed this side of Monte Luna any longer. There had been scarce little money to be made from it fifty years and more ago, and clearly no-one believed a living of any sorts could be made here now. Instead, it had been left to nature, crumbling and decaying further with each passing year, so that now it was entirely forgotten about, hidden even from the main track. Edward suspected he was the first person to have walked around it in years.

What had you expected? he asked himself. *Ah, well.* He wiped his face again: *more tears,* then stood up. 'Pian del Castagna,' he mouthed. Perhaps one day someone would rebuild it, live in it again, and banish the weeds once more. But what a sorry sight it was now, fading as the imprint of the Casalinis was fading. All too soon enough, there would be no-one left who remembered anything about them at all. He closed his eyes, imagining the sound of the animals, of Orfeo yelling at the dog; the sound of laughter coming from the kitchen and the soft sound of the piano with Eleva humming gently along to the tune. He could remember it all so vividly; the image, the sound – they were so clear, that it seemed impossible to think these things belonged to half a century before. Sometimes fifty years seemed so little time – almost yesterday. And yet as he looked at the decrepit remains of the farm now, those long years seemed more like a century. Edward wiped his face and eyes again, then, with a heavy heart, began picking his way back to the main path.

Italy – August, 1944

By the middle of June there were over a thousand partisans in the Blue Brigade. Word of the exploits of Volpe and his men had spread wide, a magnet for every roaming prisoner of war for miles around, for every frightened young Italian, disenchanted *carabinieri*, ex-convict, Russian deserter, and escaped *Todt* labourer – slaves brought into Italy by the Germans. Volpe had split them into four working battalions, all answerable to his headquarters company. In practice, however, they were largely operating independently of one another, in different parts of the mountains and across both sides of the two main river valleys. Roads were blown up and repaired, then blown up again. The same happened to the railway. A bridge near Veggio was bombed by the Allies, and the central brick structure collapsed into the River Setta. Within days, the Germans had repaired it with a temporary span of steel. A few days later, after another visit to Volpe's headquarters from Colonel Bianco, the partisans destroyed it again.

For the most part, Volpe insisted they stick to the kind of guerrilla warfare that the Colonel had advised: hitting hard and fast, then disappearing into the mountains, constantly on the move. There were few large-scale clashes with either the Germans or the fascist militia after that first battle on the mountain, although the Red Battalion, led by the Russians, had found themselves involved in an all-day fire-fight in Grazoldino, a mountain town some miles to the south of Monte Luna. Men had been killed on both sides. Afterwards the Germans had taken a dozen of the townsmen hostage – innocent men who had had nothing to do with the partisans. Most were later released, but three, evidently chosen at random, had been hanged in the town square, and left there for all to see.

Soon after, two German soldiers were attacked by partisans as they walked in woods near the town of Roggio, a few miles south of Montalbano – their bodies were nailed to trees. In response, the Germans rounded up eleven men from the town and shot them. A few days after that, two Germans were trying to buy eggs in Saragano when they were seized by a small band of partisans led by a former thief known as Balbi. One of the soldiers was shot and killed almost immediately, while the other was dragged to a partisan encampment in the wooded slopes above the Reno. There he begged for his life, showing them photographs of his wife and two small children. His pleas for mercy were ignored: Balbi told his men to find a clearing and to pin the German to the ground with knives through his wrists. He was then left to die in the sun.

Edward heard about this from Balbi himself during a visit to Volpe's headquarters, at that time a *contadino*'s hayloft in the mountains north of Monte Luna. He was small and sinewy, with short hair and several day's growth of beard. When he spoke, it was with a lisp; half his teeth were missing, the rest stained and crooked. Edward disliked him intensely.

'If you had to kill him, couldn't you just have shot him in the head?' Volpe asked him.

'No,' said Balbi. 'We've got to make them fear us. They've got to know that if they shoot innocent Italians a fate worse than mere death awaits them.'

'We're not animals, Balbi,' said Volpe.

Balbi looked incredulous. 'What do you care about the feelings of Germans? They're scum. They're raping Italy. If we can put the fear of God into them, maybe they'll think twice next time they're rounding up our people for the firing squad.'

'It doesn't work like that, Balbi. Reprisals are one thing – crucifying people is another. I don't want to hear of this again.'

'Yes, yes,' said Balbi, waving his hand nonchalantly in the air.

'For the love of God,' muttered Volpe when Balbi had gone.

'The man's a maniac,' said Edward.

'He's a thief and a murderer,' said Giorgio.

Volpe sighed. 'Come on,' he said. 'I need some air. Let's take a walk.' They ambled into the olive grove behind the barn and, pausing to sit on a collapsed stone wall, rolled cigarettes. Tobacco of sorts; the smoke was thick and pungent, the taste sweet but sharp.

'It was easier when there were just a few hundred of us,' said Volpe, 'but we mustn't lose sight of what we've achieved.'

'Where we've been successful has been in virtually stopping all traffic along the two valleys,' said Edward. 'Random butchering of Germans will not help the Allies.'

'All right, Eduardo, enough. Look, I feel the same way as you do, but we have to be careful here. At the moment my authority is undisputed, but we are only partisans. We're not a proper military outfit. We have no official rules and laws of war. There are people among us now I hope I never have to speak to again once the war is over – Balbi and half the other criminals, or those Mongols. They're vicious, with no respect for God or man. But I can't lean on them too heavily. This is war; terrible things happen, but we need these men on our side, working with us, helping us to clear the way for the Allies.'

'As long as they do work with us,' said Giorgio, 'and don't become more of a hindrance than a help.'

'Well,' said Volpe, 'let's hope we hear no more stories like this.'

His hopes were to prove misplaced.

August arrived. The *contadini* did their best to carry on farming their fields, but it was difficult with partisans swarming over the place one minute, and bands of German and fascist patrols the next. Many of the men spent their days hiding in the woods on the highest slopes of the mountains. The women did what they could, but when the corn ripened, too many fields remained unharvested. The wheat went from glowing crisply gold in July, to dusty brown by August. For weeks, the sun had continued to shine day after day, bearing down and scorching the land and people of Monte Luna. And yet a menacing cloud of violence continued to hang over the mountains and valleys.

Saragano – a small village on the lower slopes of Monte Luna. At its heart was a small square with a water pump and a memorial to those lost in the Great War of 1914–18. There was a store bearing empty shelves, a small church, a large house, and a handful of smaller buildings, farms and barns. Saragano was also home to Dr Gandolfi, the man who had reset Edward's dislocated shoulder and who had become unofficial doctor to the partisans.

With the help of Alfredo and Bruno, Edward had brought another partisan to see the doctor. The young Italian, a fresh-faced youth known as Vito, had been hit in the leg during an attack on the militia headquarters in Veggio. The bullet had gone clean through his thigh but needed to be properly cleaned and dressed.

'I'll keep him here a few days,' the doctor told Edward as he treated the boy. 'There are signs of infection, so I want to keep an eye on him.'

Edward nodded. 'Whatever you say, doctor.'

'Now help me lift him upstairs. I've a cot in the attic he can have. He'll be safe and comfortable enough there.'

The staircase was not wide, and there was only a ladder leading from the first floor into the attic, so it was with some difficulty that they carried and hoisted Vito up to his hideaway. But after much grimacing and yells of pain from Vito, they set him down on the cot.

Vito lay back and closed his eyes. 'Remind me not to get shot again,' he gasped.

Dr Gandolfi felt his brow. 'You've a slight temperature. Get some rest and I'll be up again shortly.'

'You take care of yourself, Vito,' Alfredo called out as he began climbing back down the ladder. Vito waved his hand.

Back downstairs again in the hallway, Dr Gandolfi turned to Alfredo and Bruno and said, 'Now would you mind leaving us for a few minutes? I'd like a word with Eduardo.'

'Sure,' said Bruno.

'Wait for me on the track,' said Edward, 'I won't be long.'

Once they were alone, the doctor said, 'So. How are things?' He spoke in Italian.

'All right,' said Edward. 'Tense.' The doctor led Edward into his kitchen and offered him some wine.

'Yes,' the doctor nodded, pouring out two tumblers, 'it feels like the spring is tightening. I must say, I'm nervous. The reprisals are getting worse. No-one is safe any more. Not even doctors. For God's sake, just for talking to you now, I could be shot.' He smiled ruefully and they sat down at the table. Behind them, a tall grandfather clocked ticked and then chimed the hour. Dust particles glinted in the air where the sun shone through the wide window. The room gave the impression of time only slowly passing, not accelerating as it had seemed to Edward these past few months.

'There're a lot of us now,' said Edward. 'Well over a thousand, and of course, the more of us there are, the harder it is for Volpe to keep a tight rein on everyone, especially as we're now well spread –

and we have to be. By covering a comparatively large area we can operate more efficiently, but also it makes it easier to feed everyone. But I fear there are some who are more interested in causing trouble and throwing their weight around than actually helping the Allies. Did you hear about the land agent of La Morazza?'

The doctor nodded. 'I heard they lynched him. What's Volpe doing about it?'

'Nothing. There's little he can do. We're pretty certain it was Balbi, but there's some communists amongst us now. It might have been them. The man was a rent collector and still kept his fascist party card. The Reds don't like people like that.'

The doctor shook his head. 'My God,' he said, 'what times we live in. Everyone's suspicious these days. You always used to be able to trust people – well, on matters that counted. Oh, I know there were always people who cheated a little, who told the odd white lie here and there, but for the most part the communities here were bound very firmly together. You've seen this, I take it?' He passed Edward a newspaper. 'Field Marshal Kesselring's latest proclamation – another warning to the partisans.'

Edward looked. 'No, I haven't,' then read aloud: '"Wherever bands of partisans gather, a percentage of the male population is to be arrested and, in cases of acts of violence, to be shot. If military personnel should be fired on from villages, the villages are to be burned."' He put the newspaper down and ran his hands through his hair. 'But the Allies are coming. They're getting nearer. Florence will be in their hands any day now. Hopefully, they'll break the Gothic Line before winter and we'll all be free again.'

'Let's hope so, but in the meantime, my English friend, you need to watch it. There's a price on your head and times are hard. If the partisans start murdering and pillaging from the mountain people, the loyalty the *contadini* have shown so far will be severely tested. You know, most of us are patriots, but for many, family will always come first. For a bag of salt and a few *lire*, some will sell their souls. There's *sixteen thousand* dollars on Volpe's head, you know.'

Shots suddenly rang out, startling both men. They looked at each other, then the doctor said, 'Quick, hide in the cellar,' and lifted a worn rug to reveal a trapdoor in the floor. 'I'll see what's going on.

I'll be back as soon as I can.' The doctor lowered the trapdoor and Edward heard him leave. Another shot – closer this time.

It was dark and damp down there, and Edward had just a single candle. The minutes passed slowly. He paced about, sat down, then stood up again, chewing his fingers and wondering what the hell was going on.

When at length the doctor opened the door, he had blood all over his shirt and a dark expression on his face. 'It's all right, you can come out again now,' he said wearily.

'What is it? What's going on?'

'Come on out and I'll tell you.' Bruno was sitting at the kitchen table, his head buried in his arms, sobbing uncontrollably.

'Bruno?' said Edward. He climbed the steps then walked over and placed a hand on his shoulder. 'What's happened? Where's Alfredo?'

'It was the Blackshirts,' said the doctor.

'Jesus, no! For God's sake,' said Edward angrily.

'We were lying on the track,' sobbed Bruno; he could barely get the words out.

'It's all right,' said Edward. 'Take your time.'

Bruno's eyes were red, and tears rolled down his cheeks. 'We were watching a kite circling overhead. Then suddenly it dived, as though it had been startled, so I looked up and saw a militia patrol walking out from behind the church towards us. I told Alfredo to run and then made a dash for the woods as fast as I could. I thought he was behind me, but then I heard shots and saw Alfredo running back towards the village. I don't know why he did that.'

'Panic, probably,' said the doctor.

'He was hit in the leg, but he staggered on. They went after him – they seemed to have forgotten about me. Then I heard another shot and I knew they must have killed him.'

'I heard it,' said Edward.

'He was in the village square,' the doctor continued. 'Apparently, he had offered to surrender. He couldn't run any more – his thigh had been shattered. But the corporal merely put the barrel in his mouth. Alfredo begged for mercy – pleaded for his life – I heard him as I was coming out of the house – but the bastard pulled the trigger. When I got there, Sylvia Moretti was cradling him in her arms and screaming abuse at the corporal – she's already lost two sons in

Russia. A number of the villagers had crowded around. Brave of them, really. "He was a traitor," the corporal told us. "Nothing but a useless rebel," then he told Sylvia that he'd shoot her too, if she didn't shut up.

'I sensed he meant it too, so I tried to get them to leave. "Look," I said to them, "this whole area is full of partisans." I told them it would be best if they cleared off right away. The crowd had grown considerably, and were beginning to press angrily around them. I think the corporal realised he was about to lose control of the situation. "He was shot because he was a rebel," he said. "Let that be a warning to you." Then the three of them pushed their way through the crowd and hurried out of the village.'

Bruno looked up, his eyes red. 'I saw them leave, so I ran down to the square. Oh God!' He began sobbing again. 'And there was Alfredo, lying there with his brains blown out. Alfredo – he was my friend. My best friend in the world.'

Edward put a hand on Bruno's shoulder: *I know how you feel.* Then he thought, *I wish Harry were here now.* 'Where is Alfredo now?' he asked Dr Gandolfi.

'In the church,' said the doctor. 'It's cool and safe there. Poor boy.'

Edward banged his fist on the table. 'When is this madness going to stop?'

The doctor patted his shoulder. 'You must get out of here. Take Bruno back to the mountains in case more militia reappear. Leave Alfredo with me. I'll make sure he's properly buried.'

As Edward led Bruno back out of the village, he passed a large patch of blood where Alfredo had lain. Small rivulets had weaved their way down between the stones and were now being enjoyed by a number of flies. Only that morning, as they'd walked cheerfully down to the village, Alfredo and Bruno had been telling him some of the escapades they had got up to as children. They had been just like any other young boys: getting up to no good, teasing the local priest; forever in trouble. Alfredo had been barely able to control his laughter as they remembered stealing Bruno's sister's clothes one time when they went swimming. *And now he is dead,* thought Edward. *Poor Alfredo.* Edward could scarcely believe it was true.

*

Two days later, word arrived that Florence had fallen and that the Germans were in retreat once more. It was news that was greeted with excitement at the headquarters of the Blue Brigade. They had moved again, this time to an old abandoned farm high on the slopes of Monte Amato, some three miles south of Sant'Angelo.

'We should celebrate,' said Volpe, as they sat outside the farmhouse in what had once been the yard. An oak grew in one corner, offering shade from the afternoon sun. Round about were old stone drinking troughs and a few logs of wood, which the partisans used as seats. 'Hey, Pepe, find some wine, will you?'

'Sure, boss,' said Pepe. He was new – he'd been with the partisans only a couple of weeks. He soon returned with a stone flagon of rough wine, and passed it to Volpe, who drank thirstily from the jar, then passed it around. 'Listen,' he said suddenly. 'There.'

'Thunder,' said Pepe.

'That's not thunder,' said Giorgio. 'Those are guns. My God, those are the guns from the front.'

Volpe raised his arm and cheered. 'Ha!' he cried, 'the front at last. To the Allies!' he grinned, 'and to freedom!'

They all drank to that.

Volpe's men were still on Monte Amato when they received a visit a few days later from Colonel Bianco and a British agent introduced as Prospero. It was evening, and sitting under the chestnut tree they could see for miles, across the Setta Valley to ridge after ridge of mountains, bathed in the last glow of sun.

'Hard to believe there's a war going on up here,' said Prospero. Giorgio and Edward had joined them, as had Jock and Pepe. 'This is a stunning view.'

'The whole area is beautiful,' said Volpe. 'The most beautiful part of Italy. We're pretty well cut off from the rest of the country up here – always have been. For centuries this part of the world has been left to its own devices, and that's how the mountain people would like it be again. They just want to be left alone, to a way of life that doesn't involve fascists and Nazis or even partisans.'

'That's as maybe, but right now this stretch of mountains are of enormous strategic importance. I'm afraid they're not going to be left alone – not until we've broken through the Gothic Line and got the Nazis on the run. Come on,' Prospero said. 'You and I and the Colonel need to talk.'

Volpe took them for a short walk away from the farm. Edward watched them from a distance. He saw Volpe gesticulate, then pace about pensively.

'I wonder what they're talking about,' said Pepe.

'We'll know soon enough,' said Giorgio.

'Hopefully they're going to drop more arms,' said Edward.

Giorgio nodded in agreement. 'Yes, let's hope so.'

They watched Volpe embrace the Colonel and clasp hands with Prospero. For a few minutes he stood still, deep in thought as the two men set off back down the mountain. Behind him, the summit of Monte Amato glowed a deep and burnished orange as the sun began to set, and Volpe appeared to be framed by a strange luminescence, momentarily giving his silhouette an almost spectral appearance. Then slowly he turned and walked back towards them.

The British had promised them two more arms drops, Volpe told them as he rejoined them by the oak tree.

'Where?' asked Giorgio.

'At the old site beneath Monte Luna.'

'Well, that's good,' said Giorgio.

'Yes – yes it is.' Volpe paused for a moment and leant forward, hands together. 'The Germans are in full retreat,' he told them, 'and the Allies are about to make an all-out effort to break the Gothic Line in the next couple of weeks. They're expecting to be through before winter – as we hoped.'

'Hope is one thing,' said Jock, 'reality another.'

Volpe raised his hand to quieten him. 'They've broken through Pistoia and are now at Porretta and Castiglione dei Pepoli. We could walk to the front in a morning. Look, I don't need to tell you this – we've been listening to the guns for the past couple of days.'

'And watching the skies,' added Edward.

'Exactly. We've seen how many planes have been flying over. Even Eduardo's old squadron have probably been buzzing about here.' He grinned at Edward, then said, 'The Allies need our help now more than ever. They want us to make sure the Monte Luna area is completely secure. They cannot afford to let the Germans capture the high ground and hinder the Allied advance through the Setta and Reno Valleys.'

'Surely Monte Luna is secure,' said Edward.

'No,' said Volpe, 'it's secure whenever we're there. Not when we move off again.' He looked at them all again, nodding his head as he did so. 'My friends, we're going to move back to Monte Luna and stay there.'

Edward's first reaction was one of relief. *Carla,* he thought. *I can see Carla again.*

Giorgio was incredulous, however. 'What?' he said. 'All of us?'

'Yes,' said Volpe. 'All of us. All four battalions.'

'Isn't that asking for trouble?' he said. 'The Germans will soon find out; we'll never be able to keep twelve hundred men hidden for long. Our strength has always been our manoeuvrability. Our ability to hide.'

Volpe shrugged. 'We've got more arms coming. There's lots of us now, and the Germans are in disarray. And anyway, those are our orders.'

'Christ, man,' said Jock, shaking his head. 'I wish I shared your optimism, but I tell you, I've heard all this before. They said this before Cassino. I tell you something, you can say what you like about the Jerries, but they know how to defend. The Gothic Line will be no easy nut to crack.'

'Orders are orders,' said Volpe again.

'Well,' said Jock, 'you're the boss.'

As promised, the two arms drops arrived. The first landed safely, but there was just one plane and only half a dozen canisters – Volpe had been promised four aircraft at least. On the second, German troops were ready and waiting and easily saw off the partisans who were there to collect the drop. Although only two men were killed, the Germans managed to capture all the canisters and escape back down the mountain before enough partisans could be roused to launch a counter-attack.

Headquarters was now a cave near the summit of Monte Torrone. They had heard the firing on the plain below – had known something must have gone wrong. The news had been confirmed soon after.

'Shit,' said Volpe, standing up and pacing by the edge of the cave. 'We've got a spy amongst us.'

'Or spies,' said Giorgio.

'Can't we get a message to Colonel Bianco?' suggested Edward. He was sitting on a rock by a small fire. Beyond, the sky was clear. Millions of stars twinkled benignly. 'We could change the drop zone.'

'Ah, maybe,' he said, his hands on his hips.

Giorgio rolled a cigarette, sucked the end then spat. 'Perhaps we could move for a few days. Ask Prospero.'

'No,' said Volpe. 'Our orders are to stay here. We don't know when the Allies might break through. We've got to be here, holding these mountains when they do. No, we must get some more arms. I want to know about any suspicious behaviour. Everyone needs to watch everyone else very carefully. We've been careless. Some treacherous little toad is tipping off the Germans, and I want to know who. No-one, and I mean no-one, is going to be allowed to join us now unless his story is absolutely watertight. All right? Any doubts, you know what to do.' He passed a finger across his throat. 'There's too much at risk now.' He ran his hands through his hair, then raised his arms to the sky in frustration.

Edward felt tired. He looked at Giorgio and Volpe. They were both unshaven and dirty, faces and hands smudged with grime, and looking worse in the flickering light of the fire. He was filthy himself. They all smelled: of sweat and piss and dirt. Moreover he was hungry; all of them were hungry. *Tomorrow,* he thought, *I'll go to the Pian del Castagna.* There he could wash and clean himself, and see the Casalinis – and Carla. She had been his solace these past months. When he was with her, everything was *tranquillo* – a word for which there was no precise translation, but which, he felt, so perfectly described the calm serenity and gentleness she possessed. Unlike him or any of the partisans, Carla was somehow pure and unsullied. She reminded him that there was a life beyond the killing and maiming, the brutality and suspicion. To many of his comrades in arms he had both a deep attachment and sense of commitment: to Giorgio, Bruno, and Pietro; to Volpe too, and Jock, and even Billy. The camaraderie was as intense as in any fighter squadron. And he grieved for Alfredo as he had for so many friends in the RAF. But

Carla was the person who occupied most of his thoughts. Time and again, he imagined the life they would live together after the war, and it filled him with hope and lifted his spirits. Everything that had happened to him, and everything that was to be endured in the weeks and even months ahead, would be worth it with that promise in mind.

He yawned, then so did Giorgio. 'You're tired,' said Volpe. 'You two get some sleep. I'll take first watch.'

'All right, thanks,' said Edward. 'Wake me in a few hours and I'll take over.'

He took a blanket and settled down next to Pepe, who looked at him drowsily. 'Night, Pepe,' he said, and pulled the rough wool over his shoulders, so that it rubbed roughly against his cheek. The cave was dry, and the air warm from the fire and smelling sweetly of woodsmoke. Edward was asleep in minutes.

He was woken by a cry. For a brief moment he lay there, eyes open, wondering what was going on, then he heard Volpe say, 'For God's sake, what are you doing?' followed by the groans and the strains of men fighting. Flinging back his blanket, he saw Volpe and another man grappling with a bayonet near the mouth of the cave, silhouetted against the starlit sky.

'For God's sake, get him off me!' yelled Volpe.

Giorgio was also now awake and lunged at the man. Volpe fell away, clutching his arm, as Giorgio and the other man rolled onto the floor of the cave. The fire was out and the cave dark. Edward couldn't see what was happening, or tell who was who, so he hastily lit a match, saw a bayonet lowering onto Giorgio's forehead, then grabbed the man's arms and yanked him backwards. As he did so, the man yelled in anger and Giorgio, blood streaming down his face, rose and punched the man first in the stomach and then the face.

The man gasped and Edward felt him collapse, unconscious. 'Jesus Christ!' said Edward, holding onto the man's arms and shoving him roughly face-first to the ground. Jumping on his back, Edward shouted, 'Someone light a candle, quickly.' Pulling off his scarf, he frantically began binding the man's hands.

Another match was struck and then a candle. In the dim,

flickering light, Edward turned the unconscious man over. 'My God,' he said, 'Pepe.'

'Pepe,' repeated Giorgio breathlessly. 'Volpe, are you all right?'

'Yes,' said Volpe weakly. 'But he got me in the arm. Giorgio, what happened to you?'

'It's nothing,' he said, dabbing at his forehead and looking at the blood on his fingers. 'Just pierced the skin.'

'We need to get Dr Gandolfi up here,' said Edward, then looked down again at Pepe. 'Pepe, I can't believe it.'

'Nor me,' said Volpe.

'We knew very little about him,' said Giorgio. 'I've always felt you've been too trusting with him.'

Pepe groaned and Giorgio grabbed him by his shirt and shoved him against the side of the wall. 'Pepe!' he shouted, 'Wake up!' Pepe rolled his head and opened his eyes. For a moment he struggled to focus then suddenly his eyes widened with fear. Volpe stood over him, clutching his arm.

'Why?' he said. 'Why, Pepe? How could you side with those people?'

'There's a lot of money on your head,' he stammered. 'My family are starving.'

Volpe turned away. 'Giorgio,' he said, 'do it.'

Giorgio lifted Pepe up onto his feet.

'No!' said Pepe, as Volpe passed Giorgio a revolver. 'No, please, don't kill me! Please, Volpe, please!'

Volpe looked at him and lifted his good hand to Pepe's face. 'Please, Volpe, please,' Pepe cried.

'I'm sorry, Pepe, I truly am. I liked you, you know. But you know I can't let you go.'

Giorgio took Pepe to the edge of the cave. Edward turned away. He felt sick, both physically and in mind. The night was still except for Pepe's whimpering and muffled pleas for mercy. Edward closed his eyes and flinched as the single shot cracked and echoed around the mountains.

A long night, even for a partisan. The bayonet had gone clean through Volpe's forearm as he'd tried to defend himself; it was only by chance that he had turned his head as Pepe was about to plunge the blade into his back. Giorgio's wound was less severe, but both were bleeding profusely and unable to stem the flow. 'I'll go and get Dr Gandolfi,' Edward had offered. Waking Pietro, the two of them had then hurried down the mountain to Saragano.

They roused the doctor, who wearily dressed, and then together they hurried back up the mountain. 'You did well to get me,' said the doctor on seeing both men. 'These wounds need stitches and dressing right away.' He gave Volpe a stick. 'Put this in your mouth,' he said. 'I'm afraid this is going to hurt.' Pietro and Edward held him down as the doctor began stitching his arm. Volpe's eyes looked wild with pain, and the veins on his neck strained and pulsed. 'Nearly done,' said the doctor, 'keep still now.'

In the early hours of the morning, Edward accompanied the doctor back down the slopes. 'I'm going to Pian del Castagna,' he had told Volpe and Giorgio.

'Give Carla a kiss from me,' Giorgio had said, winking. The first pinks of dawn were rising in the east. As they stumbled down Monte Torrone, they saw the Setta Valley shrouded in a deep mist. The first rays of sun crept over the mountain ridges, then spread slowly and soothingly across towards them, so that Monte Luna glowed and the sky turned to gold. Birds began to sing, and a deer paused then darted away from them. They tramped around the edge of the field where Carla had first found him then joined the mountain stream that led into Saragano. It bubbled gently. The air was still cold, but sweetly fresh. There was mist over the Reno Valley too.

'You can leave me here,' said the doctor. 'Go on to the Casalinis. Honestly.'

Edward thanked him and made his way back towards the main track, walking through dew-sodden grass that soaked not only his boots but his trousers as well. Thousands of cobwebs, silver with moisture, shone in the dawn sun. Looking at his watch, he realised it would still be some time before Carla arrived at the farm. He was desperate to see her. The hour or more he would have to wait suddenly seemed like an eternity.

Orfeo was standing in the yard stretching as Edward reached the farm. The dog barked and Orfeo turned and waved.

'Ah, Eduardo,' he said, grinning, 'what a pleasant surprise. How are things?'

'Not too bad. But I could do with a clean-up.'

'You look like you could do with a sleep.'

'That too.'

'Well, Carla will be pleased to see you. Come in. Have some coffee with us.'

They were all there: the old man, Eleva, Nella and Rosa. What was the news, they wanted to know. Were the Allies really coming this time? They'd heard the guns in the distance. Edward told them what he could. 'We've just got to hope for a quick breakthrough,' he told them. 'They've reached Castiglione, you know.'

'And how is Bruno?' Eleva asked. Edward had stopped at Pian del Castagna after Alfredo had been killed; Eleva had given Bruno wine and an old chestnut liqueur she had kept hidden. 'Drink it,' she had told him kindly, 'it'll calm you down.'

'Oh, he's heartbroken,' Edward told her now. 'But he's being brave. He's a good fellow. I think it's made him even more determined to carry on the fight.'

After the acorn coffee, he washed by the well, shaved using one of Orfeo's razors, and borrowed one of Orfeo's shirts. Then he went over to the hayloft to rest. The familiar smell of straw and dust, and cow dung; the warmth rising up from the bodies of the oxen beneath him, and their occasional and gentle lowing; they were comforting. *I feel at home here,* he thought, then his mind wandered to his real home, in Chilton, and he thought about his mother and father, picturing them sitting in the drawing room drinking tea; his father cross-legged in his armchair reading *The Times;* his mother perched on the edge of the sofa doing her needlepoint. Sitting in amicable silence. He wondered whether they knew he was safe, and what they would think if they could see him now. His mother was no countrywoman. 'Darling, all that mud and muck – it's just so ghastly.' The thought made him smile.

When he awoke, he saw Carla's face just inches from his, and for a moment thought he must be still dreaming.

'Hello,' she said.

'Carla. Darling.'

She kissed him. 'What were you doing last night? Uncle Orfeo said you came down here at dawn.'

'A bad night. Tell me how you've been?'

She reached over and leaned on his chest. 'No,' she said gently, 'first I want you to tell me what has happened. Please, Eduardo. How can I say the right things if I don't know what happened?'

Edward looked at her. He'd decided earlier not to speak about Pepe, but now he wanted to, as though he were at confession, whispering through the grille. He wanted to unburden himself, to talk to someone other than Giorgio and Volpe. She lay with her head on his chest as he talked. With one hand, he absent-mindedly stroked her hair. 'It was terrible. I hated to see him shot, but Volpe had no choice. I still can't believe it. I liked Pepe – we all did, I think, except maybe Giorgio.' He sighed. 'When I think of what I've seen in this war . . . do you think one can teach oneself to forget?'

'Perhaps if you have enough distractions,' she said.

He smiled. 'What have you in mind?'

'Oh, I don't know. A demanding wife, naughty children . . .'

Edward laughed. 'Yes, that ought to help.'

She kissed him again then said, 'You've gone solemn again. What is it?'

'I was just thinking that I'm nearly twenty-three. I hadn't expected to feel so old.'

She ran her hand across his cheek, then a finger along his eyebrows and over his eyelids. 'The Allies will be here soon. You'll see.'

Tuesday, 15th August. *Ferragosta,* the Feast of the Immaculate Conception. By eight o'clock in the morning, Father Umberto had reached the cave on Monte Torrone. He paused to talk with Volpe and some of the other partisans and then he led those that wanted to celebrate Mass to the very top of the mountain. There were hundreds there: nearly all those from the headquarters company, and most from the Falcon Battalion who were living on and around the mountain. Edward went too, walking with Bruno and Pietro as they picked their way through the trees.

It was another clear day with not a breath of wind. Father Umberto, small trails of sweat running down from his temples, began the makeshift service. His hands aloft, he gave thanks to God and to Jesus, and prayed for the quick arrival of the Allies and for the souls of those who had already given their lives 'in the cause of freedom'. Next to Edward, Bruno covered his eyes with his hands. His shoulders gently shook. *I know Bruno,* thought Edward, *it's a terrible thing to lose your best friend.*

Few feast days were as important as this one, Carla had explained to him. In normal years, it was like Christmas and Easter, families coming together for Mass at Capriglia followed by a huge party. No matter how hard the year had been, food and wine was always put aside for the *Ferragosta* above all others. It was also a tradition to invite friends, the priest, and anyone who had helped them out at some point during the year. Father Umberto was never so well fed as he was on 15th August, when, as the guest of every family in his parish, he staggered from one party to another. *Ferragosta,* Carla had told him, was her favourite day of the whole year.

Edward watched the men lining up to drink the wine and eat the bread. 15th August was a special day for the Maltese, too: the Feast of Santa Maria. He had still been on leave when he'd heard the news that the convoy had reached the island. The oil tanker, the ship the island needed above all, had inched its way into Grand Harbour on 15th August. He could imagine what the Maltese had said about that: a miracle, a sign from God. And yet, they'd been fighting the Italians as well as the Germans then. Could God be on both sides? He knew how Father Umberto would answer: God does not take sides; God favours the righteous. 15th August used to be a special day for Edward too. It was his birthday.

Afterwards, Father Umberto hurried back down the mountain to give his second service of the day at the church in Capriglia. Edward watched him scuttle down through the trees, looking at his watch, then thought about the Casalinis. They would be attending Mass – Carla's family too – and then afterwards they would all go back to the Pian del Castagna. 'It won't be much of a party this year,' Carla had told him, 'but a family get-together all the same.' Edward was going to join them. He'd been praying he would be able to, ever since Carla had mentioned it a week before: Monte Luna was blissfully quiet.

There had been little partisan activity at all since they had returned to Monte Luna. The Germans were preoccupied at the front, while the worrying lack of arms meant offensive operations had ground to a halt. Instead, Volpe had insisted they kept the men occupied with training, by building defence posts in the mountains, by practising their signals and keeping a lookout for any signs of trouble. 'We must keep them busy,' he had said repeatedly. 'When young men become hungry *and* bored there's trouble.'

But Edward could be excused on *Ferragosta*. 'I'm granting you a day's leave,' Volpe grinned. He put an arm around Edward's shoulder. 'I envy you,' he said. 'You're a lucky man. Now go to Carla and her family. We know where to find you if we need you. And make sure you give my regards to the Casalinis. They're good people.'

Unbeknown to anyone but Eleva, Orfeo, sensing hard times ahead, had the previous autumn dug two secret stores on the edge of the farm, lined them with brick, and placed inside them as much food and wine as he could spare. The day before, he had opened them up – with some trepidation he freely admitted – and had taken out the cured meats and fruits that had been kept there. Much of it had survived well, and the kitchen now smelled richly with the sweet aroma of hams, cheese and open bottles of wine. There might not have been the amount of food and drink of years gone by, but there was certainly more than anyone had seen in a very long time.

A makeshift table had been added in the kitchen – they did not dare eat outside. Edward was seated between Carla and her mother, Isabella. There was a tiredness in Isabella's eyes; even on a feast day, the worry about her family and the uncertain future seemed to weigh heavily. Edward could understand: they were all doing their best to forget the war, but it was impossible to do so completely – not with the guns still booming dully in the distance, not with hungry partisans roaming all around. Not when an atmosphere of menace and violence still hung so heavily over the mountains.

And yet there were many images Edward would remember from that day: Federico and Orfeo, arm in arm, grinning inanely and Federico saying, 'I've always said there's no-one cannier than my brother'; Christina telling joke after joke that had everyone doubled up with laughter; the songs they all sang later, even 'Happy Birthday' – his blushes at seeing all their eyes on him; Carla rubbing his leg under the table; the tin plane that twelve-year-old Gino had given him. *Ah, yes – that plane.* 'A Spitfire,' Gino told him, proudly handing over the model. 'Happy Birthday, Eduardo,' he said. 'I made it for you.'

'From an old tin,' added Isabella. 'It's taken him days.'

'Well, it might be tin but it looks like silver,' said Edward, turning the model over in his hands. 'It's perfect – just like my old Spit. And the wings – you've got them just right.'

'A pair of silver wings,' said Carla.

Gino smiled bashfully.

'Thank you, Gino,' said Edward. 'I think that's just about the best present I've ever had.'

He looked around the room, at the smiling faces. Even the old man grinned at him toothlessly. Carla put an arm on his shoulder and leaned up and kissed him lightly on the cheek. 'Happy Birthday, Eduardo.'

'Thank you,' said Edward. 'Thank you, all of you.' He felt a little drunk and a little overwhelmed, too. 'I will never forget this day, or the kindness you have all shown me. I hope that next August we can all celebrate again, but with the war behind us at last.'

The old man tapped his stick on the floor. 'Well said, young man. Well said.'

Italy – September, 1944

By the second week of September, South African troops had been spotted advancing towards Riovecchio in the Setta Valley, just a couple of miles south of Montalbano. They were also seen within sight of Volado in the Reno Valley. The sound of the guns was now so close that the mountains reverberated with the noise of shellfire. At times, even the whistle of the shells passing through the air could be heard. Allied bombers were seen swarming over the German front lines. Explosions of bombs and shells made the ground tremble.

Still the Blue Brigade remained around Monte Luna. Volpe had repeatedly asked the British agent, Prospero, for more ammunition and permission to resume their old tactics. The reply was always swift, but always the same: there would be no drops for the moment, and the partisans were to stay where they were.

17th September. The brigade headquarters was now an isolated farmhouse called Ca' di Maggio, a little over a mile east of Monte Luna itself in a clearing surrounded by oaks and chestnuts. The leaves on the trees were just beginning to turn, the nights gradually but perceptibly drawing in. There were around thirty partisans of the headquarters company living there alongside the *contadino* and his family. It was a large house, and for the first time since parachuting onto the mountains, Edward slept inside, in a bedroom at one end of the house. There was no bed, but nor were there rats, or mice, or the smell of cattle and animal dung.

An early visit from Colonel Bianco. There was the chill of autumn in the air and they sat around the stove on wooden stools and chairs, smoke wafting into the room.

'The answer's the same, I'm afraid,' said the Colonel. 'They want this mountain secure.'

Volpe ran his hands through his hair. 'Every German in Italy must know we're here,' he said.

'We can't afford to let them occupy these mountains,' said the Colonel. 'If they get some of their guns up here overlooking the two river valleys it could be disastrous.'

'But our strength has always been our mobility,' said Giorgio. 'And anyway, we don't have enough ammunition to fight off the enemy if they decide to attack in strength.'

'I'm sorry,' said the Colonel, patting his knees and looking apologetically at Volpe – *there's nothing more I can do.*

'All right,' said Volpe. 'Well, we'll just have to stay and hope for the best. Orders are orders, but all this inactivity is making life very difficult. There are far too many in the brigade who think the war's already been won. Discipline's beginning to go in some of the battalions. I keep getting reports of partisans swaggering about the villages on the lower slopes, brandishing their rifles and chatting up the local girls'

'Can't you do something to stop it?' said Colonel Bianco.

'What? I can't keep a watch on everyone all of the time. We're keeping them as busy as we can.'

'Listen, I know how you're feeling, but it won't be long now,' the Colonel assured them. 'Really.'

Edward was leading a small patrol of men back up along a mountain track later that same day. They had gone to retrieve the final cache of medical supplies that had been captured from a German truck some weeks before, and which had then been hidden in a dried-up well in a ruined farmhouse. The farmhouse overlooked Veggio, still largely a fascist-controlled town, but they had not been spotted; or at any rate, they had not been challenged.

'Hey, Eduardo,' said one of the men. It was Enrico, another teenager from Bologna.

'What is it?' Edward said.

'Where's Pietro?'

They looked around but there was no sign of him.

'Where the hell has he got to?' said Edward. 'Who saw him last? He was with us when we left the well.'

No-one knew.

'Bruno?'

Bruno shrugged. 'I don't know. Do you think we should turn back and look for him?'

Edward thought for a moment. He couldn't understand it. Perhaps they should retrace their steps. But then another thought crossed his mind. *What if it's a trap?* What if Pietro was being used to lure them back? 'No,' he said eventually. 'Let's keep going. He knows where to go.'

Back at Ca' di Maggio, Volpe was equally perplexed. 'Pietro?' He shook his head. 'Has he got a girl somewhere?'

'I don't think so,' said Edward. 'I've never heard him talk about one.'

'Where's his family?'

'Bologna.'

Volpe looked pensive. 'We'll have to post extra guards tonight.'

'Surely you don't suspect Pietro?'

'I didn't suspect Pepe.'

'I know, but Pietro's been with us almost from the beginning. He hates the Germans. Pietro wouldn't betray us.'

'I'm sure you're right but you know as well as I do we can't take any chances.'

Edward was woken the next morning by Bruno. Pietro had reappeared.

'I woke up and there he was,' said Bruno. Pietro was still asleep as they stood over him a few minutes later. He was breathing gently, the faint snores of a man deeply asleep. Edward squatted down and shook him awake. Pietro opened his eyes slowly, rubbed them sleepily and yawned.

'What the hell happened to you?' Edward asked him.

'Sorry, Eduardo,' said Pietro. He grinned sheepishly. 'I went to see my girl in Veggio.'

'Why didn't you tell me? We've all been worried sick.'

'I thought you wouldn't let me go. I'm sorry, really I mean it. But I think I'm in love. I had to see her.'

'For God's sake,' said Edward. 'Volpe could have you shot for this.'

'You can't think I'm a spy?' Pietro laughed, then realising Edward was serious, said, 'Surely you don't? That's ridiculous.'

'Is it, Pietro?' Edward stared at him.

'Yes, of course it is! Come on, Eduardo, you can't think that?' There was a sudden flicker of fear in his eyes.

'No,' said Edward eventually. 'No, I don't think that. But I've got to tell Volpe you're back. By God, you'd better not do anything like this again.'

'I won't, I promise. Sorry, Eduardo. I really am.'

Volpe was furious. 'And why didn't anyone spot him coming in? For God's sake, it's not good enough. Bring him to me now.'

Pietro stood before Volpe in the farmhouse kitchen. He looked scared, and, Edward thought, rather pathetic. He had a young face, and kept looking down at his feet like a disgraced schoolboy. Who was this girl, Volpe wanted to know. When did he meet her? Where did she live? How many times had he seen her? Pietro answered his questions meekly. 'I'm sorry, Volpe. Please don't think I'm a spy. I'd never betray any of you, I wouldn't, really I wouldn't.'

Volpe glared at him. 'I'm going to be watching you, Pietro. You better be telling the truth. Now get out of my sight.'

When Pietro had gone, Giorgio turned to Volpe and said, 'I hope that was a chance worth taking.'

Volpe bit his fingernails. 'He's a little fool, not a traitor.' He sighed, then forced a smile. 'Look,' he said, 'we're all just a little on edge at the moment. Pietro's all right, you'll see.'

20th September. Brigade headquarters was now back at Sergio Panni's farm on the edge of Casiglia. A messenger had brought a three-day-old Bolognese newspaper in which Field Marshal Kesselring had written another threat to the partisans. It was clear the announcement was directed at the Blue Brigade. Any 'localities' found to be supporting partisans could expect no mercy, he warned them. Villages would be destroyed and those guilty of aiding and abetting these 'delinquents' would be executed and hanged in the public square. Edward felt the hairs on the back of his neck stand up as he read it.

'The ravings of a lunatic,' said Volpe, slamming the newspaper at Edward's chest. 'The threats of a man who knows he's beaten.' His mood had brightened over the past couple of days – ever since a sack of German mail had been captured. The letters had revealed the low morale of the troops at the front. Most complained of a lack of equipment and food, and the incessant Allied air attacks. The undertone was clear: many German front-line troops believed they were facing total defeat in Italy.

But not everyone shared Volpe's optimism. Jock and Billy, for example. 'In my experience,' said Billy, 'the Germans are most dangerous when their backs are against the wall.'

Jock shook his head as they sat in a corner of the hayloft. 'Aye, I'm with you, Billy. I don't like it,' he said. 'I don't like it one little bit. All this fucking sitting around. We're sitting fucking ducks here. They've destroyed plenty of other villages, you know. That place in Czechoslovakia. I remember reading about that. Wiped the place off the fucking earth. Fucking Nazis – they might be loonies, but they're bloody efficient loonies.'

Montalbano, Edward thought. *Just the place the Nazis might attack.* Lying on the Setta, it was easy for them to reach, and would serve as an example to others. He thought of the Casalinis. It was time for them to move back to the mountains – to leave their home for a few weeks until the front had passed.

Taking his leave, Edward hurried to Pian del Castagna. Passing the hidden path, he saw the branches covering it had been pushed back, some even broken. There were footprints in the dust. He felt angry, as though something of his had been violated.

He found Eleva in the yard. 'Carla's in the orchard,' she said, 'they're picking apples.'

He met Christina as he made his way up to the orchard. 'Hello, Christina,' he said. 'How are you all?'

'All right,' she said. 'Gino's happy because there're lots of aeroplanes about. He thinks he knows all the different types.'

Edward laughed. 'Where are you off to?'

'I'm just getting some water for everyone,' she said. 'It's hot work.' They both paused and squinted at the sun. It was nearly midday and warmer again, although clouds were building to the west.

He saw Carla perched in one of the trees, pulling down the higher branches with the help of an old shepherd's crook. Underneath were several boxes of apples. Her face lit up as soon as she saw him. 'Eduardo!' she called out, and Edward hurried over to the tree and caught her as she jumped down.

'They've discovered our hidden path,' Edward whispered.

'I know.' She looked at him sadly. 'There are partisans in the hut. Can't you tell them to leave?'

'I wish I could. I'm afraid there are far too many around here at the moment. There's hardly enough barns for everyone, let alone old huts in the mountains.'

She kissed him, then said, 'Have you time to help us with the apples for a bit? Then we can go for a walk.'

'Of course,' he smiled.

Christina was right: apple picking was hot work. Orfeo immediately sent him up into the trees. 'We could do with a tall man like you about the place,' he told Edward. 'If I'd known you could be spared I'd have insisted on you being here a lot earlier.'

They stopped at one o'clock. 'Here,' said Orfeo, throwing Edward a large apple. 'For your services,' he grinned.

'Smell it,' said Carla. 'Rub it, then smell it.'

Edward did so, then bit into it. It was sweet and succulent.

'That smell always reminds me of the end of summer,' said Carla, taking his hand. She led him up through the orchard, over a stone wall and into the top field, newly ploughed after the harvest.

'Where are you taking me?' Edward asked.

'Not far.' They walked around the edge of the field until they were out of sight of the farmhouse and then onto a grassy slope of wild flowers interspersed with small oaks. Above, the thick, more densely wooded slopes of Monte Luna towered over them.

They sat down in the long grass beneath an oak tree, Carla resting her head on his shoulder.

'Carla, I think you should all leave Montalbano for a short while. Things are moving fast and the front might soon be passing through the valleys.' She was silent, so he said, 'Will you ask your father? Ask him from me? It would only be for a short while.' He had decided not to mention Kesselring's pronouncement. 'I've seen what happens to villages and towns caught up in the front line. It can be very dangerous. You'd be safe up here, out of the way.'

'When?' said Carla.

Edward said gently, 'As soon as you can. Will you talk to your father?'

Carla nodded.

'I thought I would speak to Orfeo about it too – if you don't mind?'

'No, of course.' She looked up at him. 'You do think we'll all be all right, don't you?'

'Of course,' he said, kissing her. 'And probably I'm worrying for nothing. But, just to be on the safe side . . .'

They looked out across the valley and up at Monte Torrone. 'Look,' said Carla, pointing to the cloud that now covered the summit. 'He's got his hat on. It's going to rain. We should enjoy this sun while it lasts.' She lay down and Edward leant over and kissed her again. 'Don't look so worried,' he said. 'It'll be over soon.'

They made love, there on the hillside. 'No-one will come up here,' Carla had whispered as she'd unbuttoned his shirt, and kissed and caressed his chest. Nor had they.

Afterwards, he lay back, and closed his eyes. The sun burned down on his face, warm and windless. The world seemed to be diffused by a gentle orange glow. A soothing, warm, orange glow. Carla moved beside him and a shadow passed across his face and he opened his eyes: she was looking at him, just inches away, the sun lighting the back of her head and giving her fair hair an unreal glow, like a halo. 'You look like an angel,' he said.

'An angel to watch over you always,' she smiled. He watched her moist lips move, her smiling eyes; looked at the small nick in her eyebrow where the dark hairs refused to grow; the tiny mole on the end of her left earlobe; the deep-brown eyes that searched his own face. He drew her to him, breathed in deeply, smelling the soft skin and feeling the beat of her heart pulsing through her neck; a moment he knew instinctively he would never forget.

Edward had been more specific with Orfeo. 'There's every chance there will be reprisals,' he said, 'and the villages in the valleys are the most obvious places for the Nazis to attack.'

Orfeo had nodded. 'I'll go down to Montalbano myself,' he'd said. Federico had needed little persuading; he'd seen the newspaper. The following day, they packed up, taking anything precious but otherwise praying their house would be safe, and headed up to the Pian del Castagna.

They were not the only ones to head for the mountains. Over the next couple of days word got around that German troops were moving into the valleys either side of Monte Luna – and not only Wehrmacht but SS troops. People had seen the double lightning bolt insignia. Rumours of another *rastrellamento* spread, and like the Casalinis, they took to the high ground where they would be safe.

Many headed for the mountain villages of Sant'Angelo, Capriglia, Cerreto and Cortino. In Capriglia, Father Umberto arranged for a number of families to take shelter in the Palazzo, owned by the absentee *padrone*. Many others, like the Casalinis, had family in the mountains and simply squashed themselves into the homes of their *contadini* brothers or cousins. Never before had there been so many people living there – several hundred more villagers from the valleys and over twelve hundred partisans. Most were hungry, and a little frightened too – but it wouldn't be for long, they told themselves. Several days, a week or two at most. The Allies were just a few kilometres away. Soon they would be liberated. Soon they would be free once more.

25th September. Grey skies marked the end of summer. By mid-morning it was raining. From the farmhouse at Cà Serra, a kilometre south of Sant'Angelo, Edward stood with Giorgio in the main doorway, watching the rain falling over the Setta Valley and wondering what the Germans were planning.

Perched high on a rocky outcrop, the farmhouse itself looked down upon a number of barns and outbuildings clustered around a courtyard below. Crumbling stone steps led from the courtyard to the house, behind which stood a further stone hayloft and a terraced olive grove that led to more woods. Over thirty partisans were living there, alongside forty *contadini* and their relations from the valleys. They had become quite a little community. In one of the barns beneath them, Edward could hear some of the children playing football with a number of the younger partisans. The previous evening he'd been crossing the yard when three young boys had run towards him with their arms outstretched, pretending to be aeroplanes. '*Il Pilote, il Pilote!*' they had shouted; he wasn't known only as Eduardo. Remembering this, he smiled. He supposed it must be exciting for the children, living side by side with these mountain fighters with their rifles, blue scarves and their swagger. But for the women – the mothers – it was very different. They eyed him with suspicion, fear even. *They blame us for this,* he thought. He wished he could offer them some solace, some words of comfort, but he knew it would do no good: they were hungry, they'd been uprooted from their homes; and they feared for the safety of their husbands and children. There was nothing he could say that would make them feel better. *But it will be over soon,* he thought. *Soon the Allies will be here.*

Edward ducked his head as a cold, wet, drop of rain fell down his neck. He looked out again at the cloud-shrouded mountains. The expectation of violence and menace seemed to have charged the air he breathed; he could sense it distinctly. That sense of dread – he couldn't shake it off. He tapped the edge of the doorway, looked at Giorgio as he rolled an ersatz cigarette, then retreated indoors.

Six o'clock in the evening. Outside, the rain continued to pour. The dust in the courtyard, after a long dry summer, had already turned to thick mud. Inside the house, however, it was warm and dry – the warmth coming not only from the fire, but also from the dozen men that were gathered there: the battalion commanders and the core of the brigade headquarters. They were, Edward reflected, an assorted bunch: a South African, another Englishman, a Mongolian, and a Serb; an intellectual, a thief, and a former Italian army officer. Edward stood next to Volpe and Giorgio, looking at them, while they waited for the last man to arrive. In the centre was the South African, Pat Hillmann – tall, arms folded, legs apart; in the corner on a chair sat Balbi, sharpening a stick with a flick knife. Karkov, the Mongol, leant against the wall, biting his fingers. No-one said much – just the occasional low murmur. Edward wondered what they were all thinking; whether they felt the very palpable sense of mounting tension as he did.

The latch on the door clicked open and Bossano, a former army captain, and now Eagle Battalion commander, walked in.

'Sorry to keep you,' he said, taking off his jacket.

'Don't worry,' said Volpe, 'you haven't.' He glanced around the room to check that everyone was listening, then said, 'I've called you all here because of the rumours about a new *rastrellamento*. They may or may not prove to be true, but don't forget this is not the first time we've been threatened with one. And we'll do what we've done before. We'll increase the number of lookouts – I want every possible route up the mountains covered. The rest of us will spread out around the main peaks. If there are too many of them, or if we run short of ammunition, we'll simply retreat to the emergency zones: Zone X on the summit of Monte Luna and Zone Y on top of Monte Torrone. The Germans have never stayed up here overnight and I don't suppose they're about to start, so when darkness falls we can slip away to the south – if necessary, and depending on the situation, to the Allied lines.'

'What about the mountain people?' asked Edward.

'We'll tell the men to do the same: at the first sign of trouble they're to climb to the top of Monte Luna. The women and children will probably be safe, but I suggest we tell them to head for the churches of Sant'Angelo and Capriglia. Get the word out right away.'

'I still think we need to spread ourselves wider,' said Bossano. 'We're sitting ducks here, no matter what you say.'

'There's nothing we can do about that,' said Volpe. 'The Allies have ordered us to stay here. Orders are orders.'

'But we're a partisan band. We can do what we like,' argued Bossano.

'Bossano's got a point, Volpe,' said Balbi. 'Why should we listen to them?'

'Do you think we'll get any more arms if we start going against their direct orders? And how do you think they will look upon us when they get here if we start going against their wishes? No, we must do as they say.' For a moment he stared at Balbi, daring him to speak out again. Edward saw Balbi glance at Bossano, but he kept his mouth shut. There were no more dissenting voices. *So Volpe's authority remains unchallenged,* thought Edward.

Volpe held up his hands – a conciliatory gesture. 'Look, this is a contingency plan only. Our war here is almost over. The Germans are on the run. It'll all be over for them before they ever have a chance to attack us up here. So go back to your battalions feeling confident. Victory is just around the corner.'

If the others doubted his word, no-one said. Some of the men laughed and joked as they left the farmhouse. Most seemed more concerned about the weather than any *rastrellamento*.

A few days, thought Edward as he sat down on a chair by the fire.

Could it really be so soon? *I hope you're right, Volpe,* he thought. *I hope to God you're right.*

Dawn, 26th September. Edward was woken by a man standing in the courtyard shouting, 'It's over! The Germans are on the run! The retreat has begun!' Excitement quickly rippled through Cà Serra; it was just as Volpe had promised.

Later, as they moved their headquarters back to Cà di Maggio, there was further confirmation of the retreat. Dr Gandolfi, on his rounds from Saragano, told them that he'd seen troops pouring back along the Reno Valley in what appeared to be disorganised panic. Several former fascists, working as spies for the partisans, reached Cà di Maggio with news that the Germans were retreating at every point along the front.

Volpe ordered his men to carry out small harassing attacks. 'Nothing much,' he told them, 'just snipe at them as they retreat. Make their lives even more uncomfortable.'

For a couple of days it appeared his confidence had been entirely justified.

28th September. Some time in the night, Pietro had gone. When Bruno told him, early in the morning, Edward felt stunned. He couldn't believe it. 'Maybe he's gone to be with his girlfriend,' said Bruno.

'Maybe,' said Edward, but neither of them believed it.

The news had a bad effect on everyone at the headquarters, especially as there was still no sign of the Allies. Expectations had been so high, but were now quickly deflated. Pietro's disappearance added to the rapidly lowering morale. He had been popular; few had doubted his story about the girlfriend in Veggio. But to disappear twice – it was a betrayal, a cruel betrayal. The sense of intense disappointment hurt Edward deeply.

The rain continued. In the afternoon, Edward led a small patrol down towards the Reno, through the woods near Saragano. As the rain dripped off the leaves and down the back of their necks, they watched a large column of Germans trucks, tanks and guns that were halted on the main valley road. Men were standing about, in no apparent hurry.

Crouching, Jock came alongside Edward. 'Here,' he said, passing a pair of battered field glasses, 'have a look through these.'

The column was larger than Edward had at first appreciated, and through his binoculars he now saw more men, and more equipment, down by the river. He fixed his gaze on a grey lorry. A handful of soldiers were talking and smoking together. 'They're laughing,' said Edward softly.

'Aye, it's a fucking right laugh this retreat.'

Edward passed the binoculars back. 'Doesn't look much like a retreat to me.'

'No,' said Jock. 'Looks like the best part of a whole fucking division gathering for action.'

'How many's that?'

Jock grimaced. 'Thousands, boss. Thousands. Look, they're unloading their equipment. They're preparing to fucking attack.'

'It certainly looks like it,' Edward admitted. *Jesus,* he thought. *We're done for.* What were they but a rabble of ill-equipped guerrillas? What hope did they have, concentrated as they were in the mountains above, against overwhelming numbers of trained and properly equipped German troops? Edward looked at his hands: they were shaking. He felt hollow inside, and nauseous as bile churned his stomach.

'And I'll tell you another thing,' said Jock, 'this rain's not helping. The Allies will want to break the Gothic Line before winter. Looks to me like they've left it just a tad too late.'

They tramped back up the mountain without having fired a shot. The paths had turned to mud – thick, syrupy mud that clung to their boots and made their legs heavy. Edward led them via the Pian del Castagna. 'Wait for me here a moment,' he told them, leaving them in the barn next to the oxen. He wanted to see Orfeo and Federico, to make sure they knew exactly what to do should the Germans launch a *rastrellamento*.

He found them in the kitchen – most of the family were there; in this weather there was little they could do outside. They listened to him carefully, Orfeo stroking his chin thoughtfully. The others looked worried and, Edward thought, understandably frightened. He wished he had brought better news – words of comfort, that the rumours of retreat were true, and that the Allies had broken through at last. He hated telling them to prepare for the worst; that because of the actions of the partisans, Orfeo and Federico might have to go into hiding to escape the wrath of the Germans; that Pian del Castagna might no longer be safe.

When he had finished, Carla followed him to the door. 'Be careful, my darling,' she said to him.

'You too.'

She passed a hand across his face.

As Edward and the others headed off out of the yard, he looked back and saw her standing there in the rain. He waved, and watched her step back inside. On the path, tiny rivulets of water were already hurrying down the slope. Above, the sky looked even darker.

'A storm's coming,' said Jock by his side. 'A huge great fucking storm, so help us God.'

Italy – September, 1944

29th September. The previous evening, the headquarters had moved yet again, back to Cà Serra. The storm had arrived, and the men tramped through streams of mud in a deluge of rain. Edward had stayed up late, sitting with Volpe, Giorgio and a few others, huddled round the fire, drinking rough wine and trying to dry their sodden clothes.

He slept badly. In the early hours of the morning, the temperature suddenly dropped. He hugged his blanket around him, but he could not get rid of the cold. His mouth also felt dry from too much wine. As the very first hint of dawn crept over the house he lay awake, listening to the gentle snoring of the men around him and thinking, wondering about Carla and wishing he could be lying next to her. He got up to pee, then, with his blanket still around his shoulders, he stretched and looked out of the window. The rain had stopped at last, but the mountains had become thick with low cloud. He could barely see the far side of the farm.

A shot rang out, startling him, then another. Someone ran into the yard, emerging through the mist. It was Enrico.

'Enrico!' Edward yelled, 'What's going on?'

'Germans!' he shouted back. 'Germans everywhere! Quick!'

'What's that?' said Giorgio sleepily, sitting up and scratching his head.

Christ, thought Edward. His chest pounded. 'Germans,' said Edward, then more urgently, 'Come on! Everyone, get up now!' He looked for his boots – found them, but fumbling fingers struggled with the laces. Grabbing his rifle and pistol, he hurried downstairs. Germans soldiers were entering the yard. 'Jesus Christ,' he muttered. His breathing was quickening, his chest tight. He crouched beside a window then moved into the frame briefly, fired a couple of shots and hurried to the back of the house just as Giorgio, Jock and Billy appeared. More shots rang out, pinging against the walls of the farmhouse and through the window. Plaster spattered over them and a pewter plate was hit, clattering loudly to the ground. They could smell burning from outside, and shouting – some from panicking Italians, others in German.

'Fucking hell!' muttered Jock as they headed for the back of the house.

'Where's Volpe?' asked Giorgio.

'Here,' said a voice from behind them in the kitchen.

'Come on!' said Jock. 'We've got to get out of here.' Together they stood either side of the back door, then Jock kicked it open and waited a moment. There were no shots or burst of fire, so he plunged out into the mist, the others following.

'Head for the barn!' yelled Volpe. It was just thirty yards away, but now bullets started ripping into the ground all around them. Edward felt one whistle past his ear, then heard Volpe cry out. Edward stopped, even though he knew it was madness to do so. Volpe was on the ground, but Edward grabbed his arm, heaved him up, then saw that Jock was by his side too.

They reached the barn, Edward wondering how yet again he'd remained unscathed. *Why?* he thought as they laid Volpe down on the straw. He'd been hit in the leg, and was bleeding badly. The colour had drained from his face.

Crouching and huddled around the door and windows, partisans were swinging themselves into view and firing frantically and blindly, before taking cover once more. Giorgio stood in the doorway and hurled a grenade. 'Get out,' said Volpe. 'Get out the back. Make a run for the trees.'

'We're not leaving you,' shouted Giorgio.

'Listen to me,' Billy said as he crouched next to Volpe. 'Jock and I will cover you, while Eduardo and Giorgio carry you out the back. How far is it to the woods? Forty yards? In this mist you've got a good chance.'

'There's no time for debate,' said Jock. 'They'll be here in a few minutes.' A sudden burst of light glowed through the mist as one of the haylofts caught fire. Men and women were screaming. A partisan suddenly collapsed onto the floor beside them, half his face shot away. *My God,* thought Edward, *it's Pico.*

'Go!' shouted Jock.

They lifted Volpe, his head lolling from side to side. 'Ready?' said Giorgio. Edward nodded. His mind had numbed; he could barely hear Giorgio. He felt as though he were looking down on himself, watching the scene unfold. The intense fear he had felt just moments before had left him. He was clutching Volpe's arm and they were pounding through the grass, weaving between the olive trees. At one point, Volpe's legs caught on a tuft of grass, but they dragged him onwards, the woods drawing closer and closer. He glanced at Giorgio who was mouthing words he could not hear. Suddenly Volpe's head snapped forward and a shower of blood arced in front of him. Giorgio dropped Volpe's arm, shouted at Edward, and leaving Volpe face down in the grass they sprinted the last remaining yards, diving to safety as more bullets smacked into the trees around them.

Edward clutched his head for a moment, his senses returning sharply. Gasping, he peered from behind a chestnut. Ill-defined shapes were moving towards them, faceless like spectres. *They can't see us,* he thought, then emerging into the clear he saw Billy and Jock running towards them.

'We've got to keep going,' said Giorgio beside him. 'Eduardo, we've got to head for the mountain.' Edward looked at him. Giorgio's face was spattered with blood. Jock was now beside them, panting and gasping for breath. 'They got Billy,' he said. 'Volpe?'

Giorgio shook his head.

'Shit!' cursed Jock.

Edward turned again and saw two men creep forward until their features sharpened.

'Pietro,' he said, barely believing his eyes. 'It's Pietro.'

'The bastard,' said Giorgio, but Edward had already lifted his rifle to his shoulder.

'Don't,' said Jock. 'You'll give us away.'

'Too bad,' said Edward; he knew even he could not miss from that range. He fired, three times in quick succession. At least one of his shots hit Pietro, who spun and fell to the ground as another fusillade of fire ripped into the trees around them. Then Edward was running, his face stinging as branches whipped back and hit him, and as thorns caught his hands and trousers. He could hear heavy panting and realised it was his own laboured breathing as he ran blindly up the mountainside.

As he finally cleared the trees on the high plain near Sant'Angelo, he found Giorgio and Jock pausing as they struggled for breath. The mist was beginning to disperse, the sky lightening. Grimacing with the pain across his chest, Edward glanced at his watch. It was just after six in the morning. They could see the flames and thick black smoke pitching into the sky, not only from Cà Serra, but from a number of other farms and settlements on the lower slopes.

'My God,' said Edward, 'they really are going to torch everything.' His mind suddenly turned to Carla and the Casalinis. 'I've got to warn them,' he muttered, and began running again, towards the mountain path between Sant'Angelo and Capriglia.

'Wait!' shouted Giorgio. 'Wait, Eduardo!'

Edward stopped and turned to face him. 'Go if you have to,' said Giorgio, 'but then head to the top of Monte Luna. OK?'

Edward nodded and ran on ahead of them, turning down beside the field where he had first landed, and on along the track beside the hidden path. He thought his lungs would burst, his legs seize, but he refused to stop. *Keep going,* he told himself. Panic was beginning to take over. What if the Germans had already reached the farm? What would he do? Images of Germans swarming through the yard, setting fire to the barn, filled his mind.

Relief surged over him as he reached Pian del Castagna. The yard was empty; the Germans had not reached there yet. The household was only just waking, unaware of the catastrophe unfolding.

'For the love of God,' said Eleva as he burst into the kitchen, 'whatever's happened to you?'

For a moment, Edward could not speak. He leant against the wall, his chest heaving. 'The Germans,' he said eventually, 'the Germans are here. Coming up the mountain.' Eleva put her hands to her mouth. 'Quick,' said Edward, his voice gradually recovering. 'Get everyone up. You've got to get out of here.'

Eleva gasped in horror, stumbled backwards and clutched a chair. She looked terrified.

'Now, Eleva!' said Edward, marching past her. 'Get up! Get up!' he yelled, 'Everyone up!'

Carla hurried across the yard from the hayloft where the girls were all now sleeping. 'Eduardo, what's going on?'

'The Germans are coming,' he told her. 'The *rastrellamento* has begun.'

'Oh my God,' she said, looking at the dried mixture of his own and Volpe's blood on his face. 'Are you hurt?'

'No, no, I'm fine – I promise.' He took her face in his hands. 'Darling, you must go to the church at Casiglia. Stay there, and don't move. Do you promise?'

She nodded. Her eyes were frightened, her skin pale.

In less than ten minutes they were ready. Edward led them back up the track until they reached the hidden path. 'This is where we must part,' said Edward. He turned to Orfeo and Federico, and then looked at the rest of the family. They stared at him, wide-eyed and disbelieving. Edward had seen that look before in the faces of pilots he'd known: it was fear – fear and shock. They all clasped one another, Federico and Orfeo hugging their families to them. 'It's all right,' Arturo was saying to his sons, 'I'll look after them, now go!'

Edward turned to Carla, took her hands and felt her fingers tighten around his. Her teeth chattered. 'Promise me,' he said. 'Don't leave the church. I'll come and find you.'

'I promise,' she said. 'I'd die if anything happened to you.'

He smiled. 'It won't. I love you, Carla. I love you more than you can know.'

Her hands slipped from his and he turned. 'Come on,' he said to Federico and Orfeo. 'We must go.'

As they reached the summit, the cloud suddenly lifted so that they could see the mountains and valleys below. Rising into the sky from all around the lower slopes were columns of smoke. Here and there, flickers of orange flame could be seen where farms were still or newly burning. Soldiers swarmed across the open land, and along the tracks and paths that wound their way up the mountains and through the wooded lower slopes.

There were several hundred men up there at the top, some partisans, but most *contadini*. Edward stood with Orfeo and Federico, watching in grim silence as a thousand-year-old community burned before their eyes. In the distance they could still hear shellfire from the front; closer was the hollow sound of rifles and machine guns chattering and resounding around the mountains.

He could see the church at Casiglia, and the track that led towards Cortino on the end of the spur. *They're down there*, thought Edward, and wondered what Carla was thinking. His heart yearned for her. The expression on her face: the fear and anguish – and he'd had to let her go. *Should I have brought them up here too?* he wondered. At least then he could have comforted her, protected her. He felt so helpless, standing there in a clearing on the summit, looking down at the purge unfolding below. Now he really was an observer; Monte Luna, he realised with a sickening feeling, had become the box seat for the *rastrellamento*.

'They'll be safe in the church,' said Orfeo numbly.

'Yes,' said Edward. 'They're not going to be interested in the women and children.'

8.30 a.m. Giorgio and Jock found him. They needed his help to set up defence posts along the two paths that led to the summit. Rocks and bits of wood were being used as barricades. The Brens were positioned, and ammunition boxes placed beside them. No-one said much. Their faces were taut and strained. Giorgio had washed the worst of Volpe's blood from his face, but he still looked grim and filthy.

'I'm sorry about Volpe,' said Edward.

'I know,' said Giorgio. 'We tried.' He rolled a cigarette. 'At least you got Pietro.'

Edward sighed and rubbed his face. 'Yes,' he said.

It was a little after nine when Federico suddenly appeared. He looked worried – more than worried. 'Quick,' he said to Edward. 'Something's happening.'

They hurried back to the clearing. 'There are Germans at the church,' said Orfeo. Edward looked. Women and children were being ushered outside. There were more of them than Edward had realised. More than a hundred – two hundred even. He spotted Father Umberto, ahead, pleading with the soldiers.

Edward asked Jock for his binoculars. He focussed and found Father Umberto again. He was standing with two soldiers. One looked like an officer. They were leading him away, into the trees. 'No,' said Edward, his heart hammering once more. The priest disappeared behind a tree. He could see the soldier but not the officer. Two shots, Edward felt himself jolt, and then saw Father Umberto reappear as he fell forward onto the ground.

'What?' said Federico. 'What were those shots? What's happening?'

'They've just executed Father Umberto,' said Edward. He felt his throat tighten and the taste of vomit fill his mouth. No-one spoke; they were now watching the women and children as they were led down the track towards the walled cemetery. Edward swept the binoculars further along the track, to Cortino. Buildings in the village were beginning to burn. He felt confused; panic began creeping over him. Scanning back to the line of people, he searched for Carla and the others.

'What are they doing?' Federico was saying. 'Where can they be taking them?'

Suddenly Edward spotted her. She was walking together with the others. It looked like they were holding hands. He watched Carla look around, at her mother, at the others. 'They're there,' he said, passing the binoculars to Orfeo.

'What are they doing?' said Federico again. 'What do they want with them? What has any of this got to do with the women and children?'

'I don't know!' Edward snapped.

'They're putting them in the cemetery,' said Giorgio. Edward put his hands to his head.

'Can't we do something?' said Federico. 'We've got to do something. Can't we shoot the Germans from here? For God's sake, we can't just stand and watch.'

'Mr Casalini,' said Giorgio, 'try and keep calm. We couldn't possibly hit them from here – not without even greater risk to them all.'

As the last of the women and children were ordered into the cemetery, they spotted four soldiers hurrying up the track from Casiglia. One carried a machine gun, the others several boxes. Edward felt his heart stop. He looked back to the cemetery, where the soldiers were lining the women and children up against the back wall.

'No,' he said. 'No, this can't be happening.'

Federico was now tearing at his hair. 'They're going to shoot them, they're going to shoot them all,' he said. He grabbed Giorgio by the shirt. 'Do something! Do something! You're the soldiers. You can't let this happen.'

Orfeo pulled Federico away and slapped him hard around the

face. 'What can they do? What can anyone do against this evil?' Federico collapsed on the ground, sobbing. Edward felt his legs weaken. The Germans were now assembling the machine gun by the gate of the cemetery, facing the line of women and children in front of them. He took the binoculars again and found Carla. She was further away now; it was hard to see her face. A baby began wailing. Someone else screamed hysterically. He felt paralysed; paralysed with dread, with shock, with his helplessness. With a sickening feeling that had enveloped him completely and was squeezing the life from him, a crushing weight that he was powerless to do anything about.

He saw the puff of smoke from the barrel before he heard the chatter of its fire. The line of people tumbled and collapsed. Edward buried his head in his hands. 'No!' he yelled, 'No! No! No!' His legs buckled and he fell to his knees. 'Carla,' he sobbed, 'Carla.'

No-one lived in Capriglia any more. Like Pian del Castagna, the place was a ruin. Roofless houses nestled in the trees, including the farm that had once been lived in by Sergio Panni. In the kitchen – the place where Edward had first met Colonel Bianco – there was now a large birch, its branches spilling out of the open space of the roof. Nothing stirred. There was no birdsong, no rustle of animals in the undergrowth. The place was completely still.

Edward rejoined the path. The church, too, lay in ruins. For a moment, he paused, imagining the mass of women and children huddled there, believing they were safe. Carla and the Casalinis; he wondered where they'd been standing – which end of the church – and what they'd been thinking as they'd heard the soldiers ordering them outside.

He walked on, out of the trees to the cemetery. It was mid-afternoon, the sun warm. White puffs of cloud were scattered across the sky. The scrunch of his footsteps on the stony track was the only sound. Once, he thought, these mountains would have been full of noise – a vibrant community. There'd been a shop in Cortino, just a kilometre along the track, and a bar. Now the mountains seemed deserted.

As he reached the cemetery, he was surprised by what he saw. In contrast with Capriglia, it was still clearly carefully tended. There was a floral wreath fastened to the iron gate and pots of flowers on some of the graves. It struck him as ironic that where there had once been so much life there was now nothing, but where the dead had been buried, there were freshly repaired walls and newly cut grass.

He glanced up at the mountain looming above. The summit was only a few hundred feet above this mountain spur. In places the rock was sheer, elsewhere it was as wooded as he remembered. He could see a clearing at the top. *Yes,* he thought, *that was where we had stood.* He turned his gaze towards the wall opposite the gate. The view from it was stunning: a wide, sweeping view of the mountains. A place of beauty.

Edward's thoughts turned to the last time he had been inside the cemetery. It had been evening, dusk on that most terrible of days: 29th September, nearly fifty-one years before.

Volpe had been right about one thing – the Germans had not stayed up in the mountains overnight. As dusk had fallen, so they had slipped away back to the valleys. Up on the summit, the remaining partisans had begun to melt away too – heading for the south, towards the Allies, or back to Bologna; anywhere but Monte Luna. For the *contadini* there had been harder decisions: where could they go? What should they do? Edward remembered Federico's raving. He had been uncontrollable, demented with grief. He remembered the two brothers sitting on the ground, Federico crouched in Orfeo's arms, howling, while tears ran silently down Orfeo's face. *Everyone grieves differently,* he thought. 'I'm going to take him back to Pian del Castagna,' Orfeo had told Edward. 'We can live in the woods for a few days. I've got more hidden supplies. We'll survive.' But their hearts had been broken; that had been obvious. Edward wondered now, as he had many times before, whether they had survived, as Orfeo had promised they would. Whether they had learned to live again.

Edward had spent much of that day in a stupor, his brain unable to absorb what he'd witnessed. It was all wrong: the women were supposed to have been safe. He'd thought he'd done the right thing, telling them to go to the church. Instead, he's sent them to their deaths, something he would have to live with for the rest of his life. Yet again, the wrong people had died – first Harry, now Carla, and many other friends besides. And yet again, he'd survived. It was a curse; he was damned to roam the earth, while those he had ever loved were snatched away.

He recognised now that he'd become every bit as demented as Federico, but in a different way, obsessed with the need to find her. 'She might have survived,' he'd kept saying. Jock and Giorgio had tried to reason with him, but to no avail. 'I have to see her,' he had said over and over. 'I have to see her.' And so as the light of the day began to fade, they'd climbed down the mountain and crept into the cemetery. Jock had vomited – Jock, who'd seen more death and mutilation than most. Contorted bodies had lain piled on one another. The smell of death had been overpowering, one that Edward had been unable to rid himself of for weeks after. At unexpected times or places, he would suddenly detect a whiff of it on the air. He and Giorgio had begun moving the bodies, retching as they'd done so. They had found Isabella first, with Gino still in her arms. Then Edward had seen Carla. Her entire body had been covered with blood, not just from her own wounds, but also from those bodies above which had seeped over her. Edward had lifted her and carried her to one side, where beneath a young tree he had sat and cradled her lifeless body in his arms. Her hair had been matted and stiff. Four bullets had killed her – four bullets that had torn into her chest. Ripped into her heart. 'She wouldn't have felt a thing,' Jock had said, as he'd stood over him. 'Not a thing.'

'Come on,' Giorgio had said. 'Leave her. You've said your goodbye.' But even then, it had been so hard – so difficult to accept that the moment he laid her down, he would never, ever see her again; would never again feel her kiss, or hear her voice, her laughter, or see the way her face lit up whenever she saw him. That ahead of him he faced long years without her. A lifetime of wishing it could have been so very different.

As he had stepped out of the cemetery at the end of that terrible day, he had understood that he was utterly exhausted, in mind, body and spirit. There had been no reserves left. At twenty-three, his spirit, and his heart, had been shattered.

Was this the tree? he wondered, as he stood before an ageing birch. Certainly, it was the right wall. He looked down, imagining himself sitting there that night. He rubbed his eyes. *Enough,* he told himself.

The sound of a car disturbed him and he wandered back to the gate as a small Peugeot van pulled up outside. A man with greying hair stepped out and opening the back of the van, pulled out a fresh wreath of flowers.

'Buongiorno,' said Edward.

'Buongiorno,' the man replied and then Edward asked him about the wreath. It was to commemorate the massacre, the man replied. They put up a new wreath every week.

'Every week?' said Edward.

'Every week – here and all over the mountain where the massacres took place.'

'Were you living here then?'

'Oh yes,' the man replied. 'I lived in Saragano. You know it?' Edward nodded. 'It was destroyed on the second day,' the man continued. 'I ran and hid, but I watched them execute seven members of my family.'

'I'm so sorry,' said Edward.

The man shrugged. 'Time heals everything. But I still like to pay my respects, you know?'

'Do you know what happened to the doctor?' Edward asked. 'Dr Gandolfi?'

'He was killed. All the men were taken to a barn. They machine-gunned them, then burned the place to the ground. 30th September, 1944.' He finished attaching the wreath to the gate. 'Why do you ask about Dr Gandolfi? Did you know him?'

'Yes,' Edward nodded. 'Yes, he was a friend.'

'During the war?'

'Yes.'

The man looked at him quizzically, then said, 'Do you mind me asking your name?'

'No, of course not – I'm sorry, I should have said. It's Enderby. Edward Enderby.'

'Eduardo!' The man's face lit up. 'My God, Eduardo back here after all these years. We've all wondered what had become of you!' He took Edward's hand and shook it vigorously. 'I don't believe it!' he said, shaking his head in disbelief. 'Eduardo, come back to see us!'

Edward was stunned. He laughed, embarrassed, and said, 'I'm so sorry – do I know you?'

'No, my name is Francesco Soldi,' Francesco grinned. 'I was just a boy – fifteen at the time – but we all knew who you were: you and Volpe and Giorgio Corti. The Blue Brigade. There's a street named after you in Veggio! We tried so hard to track you down for the naming ceremony, but we got nowhere.' Francesco shook his head again. 'It's incredible, after all these years.'

'Well, I –' Edward felt dumbfounded, suddenly at a loss as to what to say.

'Where are you staying?' Francesco asked.

'Er, in Bologna.'

'And you're here for a few days?'

'A week. I arrived last Saturday.'

'And it's Monday now,' said Francesco. 'Plenty of time! Have you seen the memorial at Mazzola?'

'No,' said Edward. 'No, I didn't realise there was one.'

'It's very beautiful. It's where all the victims are buried – one thousand eight hundred and eight in all. It's in the centre of the town – you can't miss it. I'll gladly take you there myself if you'd like.'

'I'm sorry – how many did you say?'

'One thousand eight hundred and eight. That's how many people they killed in the three days from 29th September to 1st October.'

'My God,' said Edward and clutched the iron gate to steady himself. 'I had no idea.' *So many,* he thought. A sense of shame washed over him. 'Francesco, I'm sorry. I haven't been here since the war. You must forgive me – this is a lot to take in, to think about.'

Francesco's face softened. 'Don't apologise – I understand.'

Edward looked at the cemetery again. 'Did anyone – were there any survivors here?'

Francesco smiled. 'Just one. Christina Casalini.'

As he heard her name spoken, he felt the gulf of half a century recede. His mind reeled – with shame, with elation, with a rush of different emotions that made him feel suddenly light-headed, and for a moment he thought he might faint. 'Christina,' he said. 'Good God.'

'She still lives in Montalbano. Christina Bonelli she is now.'

'Bonelli?' Edward breathed in deeply and put his other hand on the gate.

'Yes, Bruno Bonelli. Do you remember him? He was a partisan. He died, though. Let me see, oh it must have been five or six years ago now.' He put an arm on Edward's shoulder. 'Are you all right?'

'Yes, yes, I'm fine. I'm just a bit shocked. I never knew –' He stood up again. 'I wonder – do you have her address? I'd like to see her.'

'Of course. I'll take you there now if you like.'

'Would you? Would you, really? I'm not stopping you from doing other things?'

Francesco waved a hand. It would be a pleasure, he assured Edward. They drove on to the remains of Cortino. Francesco hung up another wreath and then they drove back to Casiglia where Edward collected his car. As he followed Francesco back down the mountain towards the Setta Valley, he realised he'd never been to Montalbano before; not once in all the time he'd been living in the mountains.

She lived in a small house in the heart of the village. At first she did not recognise him and then her face lit up and she flung her arms around him. 'My God, it's Eduardo!' she cried. 'Even with that moustache I know it's you! You've come back!' Edward tentatively put his arms around her too. She looked so different: the long, dark hair had been permed and dyed amber; she had filled out, too. Eventually she pulled away and looked at him, dabbing her eye. 'I'm sorry – I'm crying,' she said, 'but I'm so happy to see you! I can't believe it – after all these years! I thought you were dead. We all did.'

'I found him at the cemetery,' said Francesco. 'Quite by chance. He's staying here a week,' said Francesco.

'A week? Where? Here – in Montalbano? Is your family with you?'

It startled him that she should presume he had one. 'No,' he said, 'It's just me. I'm staying in Bologna.'

'Oh my God,' she said, clutching her hand to her mouth. She ushered them in with her hand, then excusing herself, rushed out of the hallway. Edward could hear her sobbing from a room at the far end of the house. He looked at Francesco, who said, 'It's the shock. Hold on – I'll talk to her.'

For several minutes, Edward stood in the hallway, wondering what to do. *Perhaps I should leave now,* he thought. For a moment he felt rooted with indecision. 'Christina,' he called out eventually, and gingerly stepped forward down the hallway until he reached her kitchen. She was sitting at the table, Francesco crouched beside her.

'I'm sorry,' Edward said. 'I didn't mean to –'

'No, I'm being silly,' said Christina. 'It's just been *so* long. After all these years. So unexpected; it's the shock.'

'I know,' said Edward.

She wiped her face, and stood up. 'This is very rude of me.'

'No, no,' said Edward. 'It's quite all right. I – I didn't know you'd survived, Christina. I never knew.'

'I was the one who got away.' She sighed. 'I'm sorry, I haven't even offered you a seat or a drink or anything. Come through here, where it's more comfortable,' she said, leading him back down the hallway and to a sitting room. 'My God, Eduardo, I still can't believe it's really you.' She lightly held his arm. 'We have so much to catch up on – I barely know where to begin. How about with a drink? Coffee? Water? Grappa?'

'A glass of water would be lovely, thank you.'

'Francesco?'

'Nothing for me, thank you,' he said. 'Look, I'm going to leave you two now, but Eduardo, will you call me? There are a few other people I think you'd like to meet. Here,' he said, handing Edward his telephone number.

'Of course.' He thanked him profusely. 'This is just wonderful. I'm so pleased I stumbled upon you like that.'

After Francesco had gone, Edward was left for a moment in Christina's sitting room while she went to fetch him his water. He scanned the photographs on the mantelpiece. There were recent family pictures: a baby, a wedding. A picture of what looked like Bruno in later life. A faded old photograph of Federico and Isabella. But none of Carla.

Christina came back in and having given him his glass of water, sat down on the sofa opposite him. She wiped her eyes again, then said, 'Why now?'

He looked at her quizzically. 'You mean why am I here in Italy?'

'Yes – after all these years. After the war we tried to contact you. We sent God knows how many letters, but we got nothing. No reply at all. It was as though you had vanished from the face of the earth. They tried again when they renamed half the streets in Veggio. You know there's a street named after you?'

'So Francesco told me.'

'And now suddenly here you are. Why?'

Edward looked at his hands, rubbed his chin, then said, 'Um, because –' He stopped, paused a moment. 'I'm sorry – truly, I am.'

Christina softened. 'All right. I know, Eduardo, tell me everything. I've got all the time in the world. Start at the beginning. Tell me about your life for the past fifty years.' She wore lipstick and a heavy layer of foundation. There were a number of rings on her fingers and a gold locket around her neck. The contrast with the girl he had known – the stick-like girl in a dirty cotton dress and men's work boots – was so great he could hardly believe it was the same person. And yet it was unmistakably her, he realised.

'All right,' he said. 'I'll try.' He told her briefly – about going back to England, eventually leaving the RAF and becoming a teacher; about marrying Cynthia and having Simon. About the quiet life he had led for fifty years.

'Just one son?' she asked.

'Yes.'

'Because you chose it that way?'

Edward nodded.

'But why?'

It was none of her business, and yet he wanted to tell her. *We're like strangers,* he thought; and yet she was a link to his former life, just as Lucky had been. 'I didn't really want another one,' he told her. 'I think Cynthia would have liked more, but – well, it was selfish of me, really.' He sighed, and looked up at the ceiling. 'But it didn't seem right, somehow.' He rubbed the corner of his eye, breathed deeply once more, then said, 'I always thought my children would have been Carla's children. I loved my wife – I loved her very much, but I don't think I was ever *in* love. It's a terrible thing to admit, and I'm not at all proud of myself, but I was in love with Carla.' He put his hand to his eye again and felt in his pocket for his handkerchief. 'I always have been. When I came back from the war, I knew I could never replace her. Cynthia offered companionship and friendship. She was very different from Carla. I thought I could forget about it – about Carla, about you all. I thought I could forget about the whole war.' It surprised him that he was confessing this to her, 'I lost a great friend over Malta, as well, you see. That had been a great blow.'

'I remember Carla telling me about it,' said Christina.

'So I just wanted to put it to one side and get on with my life. Make the best of things. But the truth is, I haven't made a very good job of it. Not a single day has gone past when I haven't thought about Carla.'

'Oh, Eduardo,' said Christina. She smiled at him kindly and touched his knee with her hand. 'It's not what Carla would have wanted, you know. You should have grieved properly, not bottled it up all these years.'

'I just feel so angry,' said Edward. 'Angry that the life I should have had – we should have had – was taken from me.'

'Well, you shouldn't be. You should be thankful for the life you do have, for the wife you married, for your son, for your grandchildren. For your friends.'

Edward rubbed his forehead. 'I am – I am. But I've always wondered what would have been – what *should* have been. My son – well, Simon and I have always had a difficult relationship, and I suppose, if I'm honest, it's because I've always felt that he should have been someone else.'

'Carla's son.'

Edward nodded. He shifted in his chair and looked down at his hands. 'Um, this is difficult,' he mumbled, suddenly ashamed at what he had said. 'I really shouldn't be bothering you with all this.'

Christina sighed. 'I think it's good to talk about these things. Not bottle them up. You know, Eduardo, it's funny, but I hate seeing people argue. If I see an argument in the street it makes me sad. There's no point being angry – none at all. I think about Carla too – and Mamma and Papa, and about Gino. About my cousins and the hundreds who were killed – I think about them every day, but I'm so grateful for what I've been given. I was blessed with a wonderful husband, four beautiful children and six grandchildren – six! Can you believe it! And really, there is much to be thankful for. I lost Bruno a few years ago and, you know, I miss him terribly. He was a lovely man, as you probably remember.'

'I do,' said Edward. 'Very well.'

'And I grieve for him, but I still have fun. I love my children; I adore my grandchildren! But life is for living. Only God knows why, but I was spared that day, and ever since then I have been determined to make the most of the life I've been given. I'm sixty-seven now and I hope I have many more years ahead of me. I'm looking forward to them. Eduardo, you should be enjoying your life too. You're still a handsome man, even with that moustache of yours.' She grinned mischievously at him. Edward found himself smiling. 'You should get yourself a wife – or a girlfriend,' Christina continued. 'Have fun. You've let what happened to you in the war become an albatross around your neck.'

Edward nodded. She was right; he could see that now. For a

moment he knew he could not speak. He looked away, and then recovering his composure, said quietly, 'I don't want to feel this way.' He looked down at his hands. 'You know, it's funny, but I've never spoken about Carla to anyone. Not once until now.'

'Why not?'

He shook his head. 'I'm not sure I can quite explain. But I suppose I thought that if I never talked about her then I wouldn't think about her either.'

'But you said you do think about her every day.'

'I know, I do. I have done all my life. It didn't work, but by then it was too late. I didn't feel I could suddenly confide in Cynthia. I thought it wouldn't be fair to tell her that I still mourned for the love of my life. And no-one but Cynthia would have understood.'

'So why now? Why are you suddenly here after all these years?'

Edward sighed once more. 'It was the fiftieth anniversary of VE Day. My nightmares started coming back – they had never gone away, not entirely, but they had begun to trouble me again. Usually they were about being with Carla, and then I'd be watching the massacre again – watching it all from the top of Monte Luna. And then my grandson wanted me to come up to London to see the celebrations. I thought it would lay matters to rest, but it just stirred old memories even more. I began visiting some of my old haunts: my childhood home, the base where I'd first flown from in England during the war. Last month I even went to Malta.'

'Italy was the last stop on your journey.'

'Yes.' He looked at his watch. 'It's getting late,' he said. 'I must get back to Bologna – I'm not very good at driving in the dark these days.'

Christina smiled.

'You're here a week, you say?'

'Yes. Until Saturday. I've a few days left.'

'Well, perhaps we could meet up again. Let me give you my number and then you can call me.'

Edward nodded, then said, 'Well, are you free at all tomorrow?'

'Tomorrow – yes, I think so.'

'Would you let me take you out to lunch? Only if you're free. Don't change any plans.'

'I tell you what,' said Christina. 'Let me meet you in Bologna. I need to go, so I'll catch the train up in the morning.'

'It's running again, then.' He smiled.

'Oh yes, very efficiently. Actually, the Americans repaired it before the end of the war. We can have lunch and then perhaps you could drive me back. I'd like to show you the memorial.'

'Sounds perfect.'

'But first, let me give you something. Wait here a moment.' She stood up and disappeared. He could hear her searching for something upstairs, then a couple of minutes later she came back down the stairs. 'Here,' she said, 'this belongs to you.' In her hands was the tin model Gino had made him for his birthday.

'Gino's plane!' he exclaimed. 'My God, it's Gino's plane.'

'A little rusted, but otherwise it has lasted well.'

'Where did you find it?'

'At Cà Serra. Bruno bought the place and rebuilt it after the war. We were up there walking around it one day and I suddenly spotted it by the barn behind the house. Quite by chance.'

'I must have dropped it during the battle. I had it in my pocket.' He looked at her. 'Thank you, Christina. I mean it. I can't tell you how wonderful it is to see you – to know that you're alive! It's been so good to talk to you like this.' He laughed. 'What a day it's been! And now this,' he added, turning the plane in his hands. 'I'll take better care of it this time. I won't lose it again.'

Edward slept well that night and woke the following morning feeling better than he had in weeks. Seeing Christina had lifted his spirits enormously. She was a palpable link to Carla, the one person in the world who truly understood the loss he had been harbouring all these years. Now, on this beautiful sunny August morning, he was anxious to see her again. There were so many questions he wanted to ask her, questions he had not thought of the day before when he had been struggling to think straight; too much had happened. His mind had been reeling from the shock of one revelation after another. But everything was different now. The burden of grief for what had happened on Monte Luna was no longer one he had to carry alone. The loneliness he had felt had gone.

Standing before his bathroom mirror, he decided to shave off his moustache. He couldn't really remember why he had grown it in the first place. It had been after the war, before he'd left the RAF. It had instantly made him look older, but then he'd felt a lot older than his twenty-five years. He'd felt ancient. But Christina hadn't liked it, and he'd minded about that for some reason he couldn't quite put his finger on. When he had finished and padded his face dry with a towel, he smiled. A face he had almost forgotten stared back at him.

'Eduardo, you look much better!' said Christina as she met him in the foyer of his hotel. 'I mean, of course, I recognised you yesterday, but you look much younger again now.'

He rubbed his top lip and smiled. 'It feels odd not having it any more.'

'How old are you now? Seventy-something?'

'Actually, I'll be seventy-three next week.'

'Of course! The *Ferragosta!*'

Edward smiled. 'So, you see, giving me Gino's plane was like being given a birthday present all over again.'

Christina laughed. 'Well, you look much younger than seventy-three. You look more like the person you used to be.'

Small talk as they ambled through the streets of Bologna: a discussion about where they should eat; the weather; the sights of Bologna. Edward sensed that Christina was more relaxed too; they'd both had time to get used to each other's existence again. But only once they had found a restaurant, and had sat down and ordered did Edward finally ask her about the *rastrellamento*.

'Will you tell me what happened, Christina?' Edward asked her. 'How did you survive?'

Christina sighed. 'Yes, Edward, I will. I think you should know.' She nodded gently to herself as she collected her thoughts, then eventually she said, 'Well, it was morning. A bit before nine o'clock. After we left you and Papa and Uncle Orfeo, we went to the church, as you suggested. There were already a number of others there. About a hundred and seventy of us, I think, nearly all women and children, although Nonno was with us and there were a few other old men and women. Father Umberto was trying to keep us calm and I think we were, to be honest. I suppose I was frightened, but more for what was happening outside – to Papa, and to you and the others – to our homes. I don't think I ever thought the Germans would do anything to us. I don't think any of us did.' It had been about nine o'clock in the morning when they'd heard troops banging on the door of the church with their rifle butts. There had been just three of them to start with. 'They just told us to get out of the church – they didn't say why,' said Christina. 'Father Umberto went off with some of them – more had appeared by this stage. They led him into the trees and then we heard a shot and realised they'd killed him.'

'We saw that,' said Edward. 'I was with your father and Orfeo on the top of Monte Luna. We saw it. We saw it all.'

'I think that was when we started to get really worried. And we were horrified about what they had done to Father Umberto.' They had then been ordered to walk and were led to the cemetery. Even then, Christina had had no idea what was happening. It was only when they started setting up the machine gun that they began to realise the Germans meant to kill them. 'I can't describe to you what that was like,' said Christina.

'Don't feel you have to,' said Edward. 'I mean it. Please don't feel you have to go on.'

'No, no, it's all right. I want to tell you.' She smiled at him. 'Honestly, Eduardo, I'm all right.' She carefully took a sip of wine, then said, 'Anyway, one woman panicked. She started shouting for her baby then ran towards the gates. They shot her. I think the rest of us were too shocked to scream or shout very much. I remember feeling paralysed with fear. We all held hands. Mamma clutched Gino to her, I was holding her hand and Carla's. I can't remember who Carla was standing next to – Nella, I think.' They stood there for several minutes. 'More than five, I would say,' said Christina, while the Germans got ready.

When the shooting began, the women in front and behind her were hit, as was Carla, but for some reason, the bullets missed Christina. The weight of bodies falling knocked her over. Carla also pulled her over as she fell. Christina was squashed almost flat on the ground. 'I could barely breathe.' When the firing stopped, a number of people were groaning, including her mother. 'I'm not sure she was conscious,' said Christina, who had kept completely silent. She could hear the Germans walking around, smoking and talking. Only when she was sure they had gone did she call out; but by that time, her mother must have died. Even so, she did not dare get up. Every time she thought the Germans had gone, she heard voices, sometimes close, sometimes further away. Not until nearly four o'clock did she finally begin to wriggle out of the mass of bodies. She had lain there for almost seven hours. 'I was covered in blood,' she said. 'Absolutely covered. I couldn't see a single part of clear skin.' She stood up stiffly and shakily, carefully peered around the gates, then ran into the trees behind the cemetery.'

'I wish I'd seen you,' said Edward, 'but I didn't stay looking at that sight. To be honest, I don't know how I spent that day – I was half demented, I think. But how on earth did you get away without being spotted?'

Christina shrugged. 'I cleaned myself as best I could in a mountain stream and then ran on. I saw no-one, but passed a smouldering barn where there were a number of charred bodies. Eventually I came across another settlement. Someone spotted me then – an Italian. They had a large cellar and invited me to hide with them there. I was there for three days. When I clambered out again, the world was a very different place.'

'My God, Christina.'

'Yes – it's a terrible story.' She shook her head. 'But I came to terms with it a long time ago. You know, it's a funny thing, but a few months back a film crew turned up here. They'd found one of the German officers who organised the *rastrellamento*. They asked me how I would feel about meeting him, and I told them, "I don't particularly want to meet him, but I hope he's been a good man for the rest of his life," and they were amazed. I said, "Why are you so surprised?" and they said, "How can you be so calm about it?" So I told them. I told them I'd come to accept what had happened a long time ago, that nobody could undo what had happened, and that if this man felt remorse that was enough for me. For all this, I've had a happy life, a fulfilled life. Would I have done if I'd spent my life full of anger, and bitterness and rage? No, of course not. I regret what happened, I deeply regret it. And I miss my family more than anyone will ever know. But it was a long, long time ago. Time is a great healer if you allow it to be. I'm afraid my father didn't believe that, though.'

'Did you find him, then?'

'Yes, although first I went back to our house in Montalbano. Fortunately, it was still standing. It had been ransacked for food, but otherwise it was undamaged. The Germans had gone and the people who had looked after me came and found me and told me that Sister Anna, who had taught Carla and me at school, had set up a refugee centre in Gardellano, just up the road. I went there for a bit. Then I heard that Papa and Uncle Orfeo had been seen in the woods near Pian del Castagna, so one morning – it must have been four or five days after – I went back up the mountain to try and find them.'

'And did you? Orfeo told me they would survive. I have to say, I believed him. He still had hidden stores of food, he said. He was clever – and resourceful.'

Christina took a sip of wine. Edward was staggered by her equanimity. Only once had he detected a slight catch in her voice. 'I found them, yes,' she said. 'Poor Papa. He had lost his mind, I think. It was extraordinary, but in a week he had aged twenty years. Do you know, I think seeing him like that was almost the worst thing of all. Orfeo was not in a good way either, but he was strong. Anyway, the Germans had slaughtered the animals and burned the barn, but they'd left the house for some reason. We lived there together until, one day, Papa wandered off. We searched for him, but then someone told us he'd been picked up by the Germans. The mountains were still occupied. They carted him off and he became a labourer for them – a slave labourer. It must have been in January some time that I got a letter from the Red Cross saying he'd died. Pneumonia was the official reason, but really he died on 29th September, like everyone else.' Now she wiped her eyes. 'I'm sorry,' she said. 'It was terrible seeing how much a man could fall apart. He'd always been so gentle, so kind. He was a wonderful father to us. I pray for him every day.'

Orfeo sent her to Bologna soon after, to stay with Rosa's mother. She was still there when the war ended. 'Everyone was shouting and laughing and celebrating, but for me it was one of the worst days of my life.'

Edward nodded. 'Mine too,' he said.

'I thought: if it's over, why did it start in the first place? What was the point?'

'I remember thinking exactly the same thing,' said Edward. 'Everyone kept telling me to cheer up. "You've survived!" they kept saying. But for what? I felt I'd lost everything: my best friends, the girl I'd thought I was going marry. And about a month after I'd made it back to Allied lines I got a letter from my mother – I'd written to them, I think, within a day of making it to safety – and she told me my father had died back in March. For six months I'd not even known.' He sighed. 'It turned out they'd received a telegram that I was missing, presumed dead, and a few days later he'd had a stroke and died of it. A week or so after that, my mother received another telegram saying I was very probably still alive after all.'

'I'm sorry, Eduardo.'

'Well – at least he wasn't executed. At least we didn't have storm troopers ravaging their way across Britain.' He paused, then said, 'But tell me, what became of Orfeo?'

'Oh, he lived a long time. He never remarried, but he continued to farm at Pian del Castagna. He rebuilt the lower part of the barn and used part of the house for the animals. He was about the only person still farming up there. The old community died during those days of the *rastrellamento,* but it wasn't just the war. Afterwards the *mezzadria* system died out too. There was huge migration to the cities. No-one wanted to live and work up in the mountains, toiling away on poor soil, barely scraping a living. There had never been any running water or electricity up there – few people wanted to live like that any more.'

'Except Orfeo.'

'Well, of course, he'd never had any of those things. He worked right up until the end. I used to go and see him quite a lot, but Bruno and I were living in Bologna by then. He died – let me see – eighteen years ago.'

'I wish I could have seen Bruno again,' said Edward. 'I've never seen any of my partisan friends since Giorgio, Jock and I made it to Allied Lines. We were debriefed and then we were sent our separate ways. I think Giorgio joined an Italian unit and Jock was probably sent home. But I don't really know.'

'Well, Giorgio still lives around here.'

Edward brightened. 'Giorgio? Really? Incredible! I never thought –'

'He and Bruno worked together for many years. They were both mechanics, although Bruno did up a few houses from time to time as well. Like Cà Serra. Anyway, they had a garage here in Bologna and then they set up another one in Veggio. Giorgio left Bologna to run it. He's still there.'

'I'd love to see him.'

'I'm sure he'd want to see you too. We'll call him later.'

But first there was the memorial at Mazzola. Lying in the centre of the town, it was a large marble mausoleum, which, Edward realised, he had seen without realising its significance, as he had driven through the town his first morning three days before. *Il Sacrario*, Christina called it: the memorial Chapel. In the hallway, on one of the walls, stood a collection of photographs of every single person killed in the massacre. Edward spotted Volpe immediately, then Christina pointed out Carla.

'It's not a good picture,' said Christina, and yet Carla looked exactly as Edward remembered: the wide eyes and full lips, the narrow shape of her face; the fair hair. He stared at the other faces too: the Casalinis, Enrico, even Balbi. Dr Gandolfi was there. *A good man*, Edward thought to himself. Father Umberto too.

It was a stark but peaceful place, laid in the shape of a cross. In each wing, embedded in the walls, were caskets with the remains of every victim, a square slab engraved with each name stacked floor to ceiling.

'They're over here,' whispered Christina, leading him away from the centre of the chapel. Edward looked at the names: Isabella, Eleva, Nella, Gino, Arturo, Rosa – and Carla. He lifted his hand and brushed it across the slab, feeling the hard, cold granite on his palm. *So this is where you are,* he thought. *But you're not, are you?* No, this was just a marker – a *memorial,* nothing more.

He watched Christina, her eyes tightly closed, make a sign of the cross, then they stepped backwards and walked back out into bright sunshine.

As they drove out of the town, Christina said, 'Eduardo, do you really think you would have married Carla after the war?'

'Yes – if she'd have had me.'

'But what would you have done? Where would you have lived?'

'I don't know. I'd have gladly come back to Italy. There was little for me back in England. But I'd have gone anywhere she wished. I wanted to spend my life with her – I'd have made any number of sacrifices to do that.'

Christina looked thoughtful for a moment then she said, 'Yes, I think you would. I'm sorry, Eduardo. I've often wondered – often doubted whether your love affair would have survived the war. But I believe you – you've put my mind at rest. You know, I hope that one day you find each other again. In heaven, or wherever she is now.' She patted his thigh gently and smiled.

She took him to see Giorgio, who pumped Edward's hand and embraced him tightly. 'My dear friend Eduardo!' he said. 'It's been far too long. Have you seen your street?'

'No, but I've been told about it.'

'Pretty good, eh? I've got a bigger one than you, though,' he grinned.

'Volpe's got a square,' said Christina.

'The benefit of being a martyr to the cause,' said Giorgio, winking at Eduardo.

He was now almost entirely bald and with a large protruding

stomach, but the quick, intelligent eyes and sardonic smirk were the same. There was still a faint, bleached line in the middle of his forehead.

'I remember that night very well,' said Edward, pointing to the scar.

'This? Yes – stupid fool. Not the greatest assassin the world has ever seen.'

For more than two hours they sat and talked, reminiscing while Giorgio smoked one cigarette after another, and while his television rumbled constantly in the background.

As Edward and Christina were about to leave, Giorgio said to Edward, 'You should see the top,' said Giorgio. 'The summit of Monte Luna. There's a marker up there to the Blue Brigade.'

'You boys go,' said Christina. 'I'm not walking up that – not at my age.'

'All right, you and I will climb it,' said Giorgio. 'How about tomorrow? How about tomorrow morning?'

'Tomorrow morning suits me,' agreed Edward. 'Shall I come here?'

'Yes – about ten o'clock. We'll have a coffee then head on up into the mountains.'

Edward grinned. 'I'll look forward to that, Giorgio.'

As Edward drove Christina back to Montalbano he said, 'Giorgio is much as I remember him. It's amazing.'

'It's good for you boys to talk together like that.'

'I'd forgotten many of those things. He's reminded me that there were some good times during those days – between all the violence.'

'Bruno always used to say so. He and Giorgio and some of the other partisans stayed friends all their lives. And I don't mean just friends. They were like brothers. They would have done anything for each other – absolutely anything.' She patted his leg. 'So you see what you've missed out on by burying yourself away all this time?'

Edward made no reply.

He and Giorgio took their time climbing the summit. The path was rarely very steep and wound its way gently through the wooded slopes, but although Edward found the climb hard work, he did not struggle as much as Giorgio, who wheezed and coughed and repeatedly demanded they stop for rests. 'We used to run up this,' he grinned. 'Can you believe it?'

It was a cloudy day, but bright, the sun never far away. As they passed where the charcoal burner's hut had been, Edward said, 'That was where Carla and I often used to meet.'

'Ah, Carla,' said Giorgio. 'I think we were all a little jealous of you. She was a very beautiful girl. I'm sorry you had to see her like you did that evening.'

'It was my choice, remember.'

'Yes,' said Giorgio, 'but even so. It's haunted me ever since. I still have dreams about it occasionally – seeing all those bodies covered in blood. A terrible thing.'

'You? I always thought you were so tough. Nothing ever seemed to shake you.'

Giorgio grinned. 'Well, I did say only the *occasional* dream.'

Something scurried in the undergrowth up ahead, and then a wild boar ran across the path twenty yards in front of them, snorting as it went.

'Plenty of those up here again,' said Giorgio. 'The mountains have become wilder again. Nature's taken over once more.'

They reached the summit, short of breath and hot. A stone plinth stood in the clearing. '*To the eternal glory of the partisans who sacrificed their lives for the liberty and independence of Italy,*' was inscribed upon it, but underneath someone had roughly carved the words, 'Volpe lives' – *Volpe vive.*

Edward smiled.

'He's still quite a hero around here,' said Giorgio. 'We all are.'

'Nice to be appreciated.'

Giorgio nodded. 'I think so. It's helped me out of a few tight spots in the past. Financially, and in other ways. I mean, Bruno and I used to play on it a bit. We definitely got more customers because of what we'd done. And quite right too – we risked everything.'

'Did you ever believe the Allies would reach here before the onset of winter?' Edward asked him.

Giorgio smiled, and thought for a moment. 'Let's just say I wasn't ever quite the optimist that Volpe was. I don't think he ever doubted the Allies for a moment. But I remember talking to Jock and Billy and they didn't think the breakthrough was very likely. And they were usually right about military matters.

'There was a lot of fighting round here later. It was the South Africans who took it in the end. In March, 1945. The Germans stayed up here, with their guns, just as the British had feared they would. I didn't even get to Bologna until a week before the end of the war. Still, I think we played our part. I'd like to think it was all worth it.'

'It was,' said Edward. 'We have to believe it was.'

Giorgio turned and looked out over the sweep of the mountains. 'It always makes me feel a little sad, being up here. The shadow of death still hangs over this place. No-one lives here any more, the houses are left as ruins. I'd like to see some of these old farms rebuilt. See some life injected back into the place. It shouldn't be a shrine to the dead. It should be a place for the living.'

'Maybe it will be again one day,' said Edward.

'Maybe,' said Giorgio. He slapped Edward on the back. 'Still,' he added, 'it's good to able to walk up here without a gun, isn't it? Without having to worry about Blackshirts and Nazis, and who might be about to stab you in the head.' He laughed. 'Come on, Eduardo, let's get going.'

On his last night, they held a dinner in his honour – in a *trattoria* in Veggio owned by another former Blue Brigade partisan. There were over twenty of them: former partisans and survivors of the *rastrellamento* like Francesco and Christina. Course after course appeared. Edward thought it the most delicious meal he had ever tasted. The mood was joyful and celebratory, the endless stream of stories and anecdotes all light-hearted and humorous. At times, Edward laughed so much his sides ached. And he got drunk – not drunk to escape in the way that Lucky did – but because he was having a good time. They sang songs – old partisan songs he'd forgotten all about – and gave toasts: to Volpe, to lost comrades, to innocent victims, to their glorious Allies.

They insisted he make a speech, and so he pushed back his chair and shakily got to his feet. A blur of faces, smiling, cheering him on. He thanked them, honoured them, insisted he would be back again soon, and that he had been wrong not to have returned before. 'You all taught me so much during the war, and you've taught me much this week, too,' he told them, 'about courage and magnanimity. You've shown me that life is precious and is to be celebrated and enjoyed.' Steadying himself, he said, 'Thank you for this dinner and for so much, much more.' He raised his glass to them. 'I salute you all.'

As he collapsed back into his chair, he glanced at Giorgio, then Christina. They were clapping along with everyone else, then Giorgio put his fingers in his mouth and blew a wolf whistle. Edward laughed. He felt a lightness in his head and in his soul. He was happier than he had been in a very, very long time.

England – August, 1995

On his journey back to Somerset, Edward spent much time thinking about his son, Simon. 'Next time you come out here,' Christina had told him, 'bring your family. I want to meet them.' He genuinely hoped that might be possible. Much, though, depended on his ability to build bridges with his son. He was now desperate to tell Simon everything, to unburden himself entirely, but after all this time was not sure how he should go about it. He was nervous, too, about how Simon would react. It was bound to make his son think of him in a very different light; he would be revealing a part of himself that Simon had simply never known. It required careful thought.

On arriving back at his house in Brampton Cary, he unpacked and took out the tin model Gino had made him and also the photograph of Carla that Christina had given him. It was of her sitting on the steps outside the hayloft at Pian del Castagna. 'Carla – summer 1943' had been written on the back. 'I think it was taken at the *Ferragosta* the year before the *rastrellamento*,' Christina had told him. In the picture, Carla was smiling, her bare arms hugging her legs. A wisp of hair had blown across her face, but the image was surprisingly clear. He had wept when Christina had given it to him, but now he smiled as he placed it on the side table by his armchair, next to the photograph of his wife, Cynthia, and the picture of him and Harry. He put the plane beside them.

He sat in the chair for a moment, thinking. Rubbing his face, he felt the smooth top lip. Christina had said he looked more like the person he used to be without his moustache. *And I feel more like the person I used to be,* he thought to himself.

That evening, he finally phoned his son.

'Dad!' said Simon. 'I rang you last night. Where were you?'

'Actually, I've been in Italy,' said Edward. He couldn't help smiling to himself.

'Italy! My God! What were you doing there? Why didn't you tell me?'

'I will tell you, I promise. I'll tell you all about it. But listen,

Simon, I was wondering, do you think we could meet up – soon, before Biggin Hill. Just the two of us? Would you come down here for a day or two?'

'Er, ye-es. Of course. Dad, is everything all right?'

'Perfectly all right. I'll explain everything when I see you. Everything, I promise.'

It was the end of August, the end of a hot summer. The playing fields of the school had been scorched a pale beige by the heatwave. In the countryside around Brampton Cary, the harvest had been cut and collected. Stacks of straw bales cast lengthening shadows across stubble fields.

Edward and Simon walked along a track that led out of the town. Midges swarmed under the trees. The leaves were just beginning to turn: still green but with a hint of the russet they would become before long. Underfoot, the earth in the tractor grooves was cracked and dusty. The heat of the day had gone, but the evening was still warm.

He spared his son nothing. He told him about his first attack off the Cornish coast, of the deaths he had seen on Malta – that erk's ginger scalp, Chuck Cartwright burning to death in his Hurricane. He told him of the appalling conditions on Malta, of losing Harry; of his time with the partisans – Giorgio, Volpe, the death of Alfredo, Pepe's attack in the cave. And he told him about Carla. He told him she had been the love of his life, and that not a day had gone by since when he had not thought of her. He spoke of the massacre – watching the Germans execute Carla and her family, and clasping her blood-soaked body.

And he told Simon of his journey: how it had begun in the churchyard of Chilton; the trip to Cornwall and to Malta; his time with Lucky. He talked to him about Italy, about finding the place where the charcoal burner's hut had been, revisiting the cemetery, his reunion with Christina and Giorgio.

Christina had likened his grief to an albatross around his neck, and she had been right. As he talked, he felt the weight of his memories lift from him. *Why?* he thought. *Why did I not do this earlier?*

When he had finished, they were sitting under a large horse

chestnut, overlooking the town. The sun had almost set; the light was fading and the fresh smell of dew was heavy on the air. For a while Simon did not speak and Edward was happy not to goad him; it was, he knew, a lot for his son to digest.

'I really had no idea – no idea at all,' said Simon at last.

'No, well, I never talked about it.'

'And Carla, my God, Dad, I'm so sorry.'

'Yes, but if she'd survived then I would never have married your mother. I'd never have had you.'

'That might not have been such a bad thing.'

'Now who's feeling sorry for themselves?' He smiled. 'Look, you must never think that. I know I've probably never said it, Simon, but I love you very much, you know. And I'm tremendously proud of you, too – for what you've achieved: the wonderful family you've created, the success you've made of your career.'

'No, you haven't ever said it. Not once.'

'I'm so sorry.'

'Did you ever love Mum?'

'Very much – you must believe that.'

'But not with much passion.'

'No – but Simon, this is what I'm trying to explain. Any passion I had was spent by the time I met your mother. But we had a good marriage. I loved her, and I miss her terribly. I mean that.'

Simon was silent again, then said, 'I don't know, Dad. I don't know what you want me to say. I mean, this is a lot to take in.'

'I know. I'm sorry.'

'But why did you never share this with us before?'

'I've been asking myself the same question. I've been a fool. But Simon, you must understand, I came back from the war a broken man. What I saw – what I lost – it had a profound effect on me. I wish it had been otherwise, but it's taken fifty years for me to mend the pieces. I'm sorry. I'm sorry I've not been the father I should have been.' They were silent again and then Edward said, 'I want to make amends.' He coughed. 'I'm afraid I'm not very good at this sort of thing. But I've realised I've still got a lot to be thankful for; a lot to live for. I'm determined to make the most of what I've got left. The war has haunted me for so long, but it's not going to any longer.'

'Dad – I don't know what to say. It's just so –'

'You don't need to say anything. Look, I don't expect this to suddenly put everything right between us, but I hope you'll let me try – in time.'

Simon nodded.

'Perhaps one day you'll let me take you to some of these places. To Malta and to Italy. With the family, of course. I'd love you to meet Lucky and Christina. And Giorgio.'

'One step at a time, eh Dad?'

'Yes, of course.' Edward smiled. 'Come on. Let's go back home. There are some things I'd like to show you.'

Simon turned to him and smiled. 'All right, Dad. Let's do that.'

A Spitfire roared past, just fifty feet from the ground, then climbed and rolled, the pitch of the Merlin engine changing as it did so. Another hurtled past and then the two joined, one flying slightly behind the other. They climbed into the sky so that their wide elliptical wings were silhouetted against the sky, then they both peeled off and dived.

'Absolutely wonderful,' said Simon. 'Don't you think, Nicky?'

Nicky nodded. 'I think they're amazing!' He turned to Edward. 'Grandad, I still can't believe you flew those.'

Edward smiled. 'They are rather beautiful, I admit,' he said. He briefly closed his eyes, listening to the whirr of the engines as they thundered over Biggin Hill. It was a sound so familiar, so distinct, reaching out to him once more from across the lost years of his life. He opened his eyes again, and watched the two aircraft as they danced and tumbled high above them. *Are you up there?* he wondered, staring at an infinite sky. They'd stopped haunting him – Carla, Harry, the many others; he'd not had a single bad dream since his return to England. Perhaps he would see them again one day, as Christina had suggested. *One day,* he thought, smiling to himself, *but not just yet.*

Historical Note and Acknowledgements

Although this is a work of fiction, the wartime parts of the book are based around real events, while the experiences of Edward later in life came about through conversations with a large number of Second World War veterans. The inspiration for the friendship between Edward and Harry came from when I was working on a history of the Siege of Malta. Raoul Daddo-Longlais and 'Laddie' Lucas were two young fighter pilots who became great friends. Laddie was older than Raoul, a brilliant amateur golfer and a sports writer for the *Daily Express*. They met at their Initial Training Wing at Cambridge, were sent to do their air training in Canada, then went to their Operational Training Unit together, and were finally both sent to join 66 Squadron at Perranporth in Cornwall. It was very unusual for two friends to stick together in such a way, though, as they proved, not impossible.

Raoul's logbook and part of a diary he kept are held at the RAF Museum at Hendon, but all his papers – the many letters, old school reports and other jottings – are owned by his niece, Zoë Thomas, who very kindly allowed me to use her uncle's experiences as the template for Edward's early flying career. In the interest of authenticity, I used Raoul's logbook almost to the letter. Like Edward, Raoul was idealistic and impatient during the early days with the RAF, and he had a very low boredom threshold. Like Edward, he made an unauthorised flight over France, (although on his own), but rather than being hit by flak, was flying so low that he clipped a wing against a telegraph pole. How he survived, I have no idea. His Squadron Leader, Hubert 'Dizzy' Allen, was just twenty-two at the time, had newly taken over command of 66 Squadron (on which 324 Squadron is based) from Squadron Leader Athol Forbes, and was under huge pressure. Like Jimmy in the novel, 'Dizzy' Allen was not best pleased with the escapade.

Perranporth remains as it is described in the book. It is one of the best-preserved RAF Fighter Command airfields in the country, with blast pens and a control tower (built later in the war) that are still there for all to see. Its position, perched high on the cliffs, is also extremely dramatic. The Droskyn Castle is also still there, as is the Tregenna Castle Hotel in St Ives.

Like Edward and Harry, the real Raoul and Laddie volunteered for overseas service to escape the boredom of endless convoy patrols. They thought they were going to India but at the last minute were posted to Malta instead, which, at the time, had become the most bombed place on earth. One pilot newly arriving on the Island said that Malta made the Battle of Britain look like child's play. It was the toughest posting in the world at the time for an RAF fighter pilot, and much of what is described in the book revolves around real events. 634 Squadron is loosely based on 249 Squadron, although the others mentioned were real enough. The statistics about the Hurricane 229 Squadron are true, as are the details about the various convoys, the bombing of Takali on 20th/21st March, 1942, and the details of the Spitfire arrivals. It is also true that within forty-eight hours of the arrival of the April Spitfires, only seven were left. The plan put into effect for the consignment arriving on May 10 – and the subsequent air battle – is also described pretty much as it happened. Wing Commander 'Butch' Hammond is based very loosely on Wing Commander 'Jumbo' Gracie. Air Vice Marshal Hugh Pughe Lloyd and Group Captain 'Woody' Woodhall, were, however, real people. Woodhall was brilliant, and there is no doubt that he and Gracie were the architects behind the great aerial victory of May 1942.

Tragically, Raoul Daddo-Langlois was killed during the invasion of Sicily, while, unlike Harry Barclay, Laddie Lucas survived the war and went on to have a rich and varied career in sport, politics and as a writer. But at the time of his death, Raoul was certainly feeling pretty depressed, his youthful vitality crushed by the stress and strain of being a fighter pilot in one of the most intense theatres of the war. He was twenty-one when he died, and like Harry, his body was never recovered, although his fate is known. He is remembered on the RAF memorial outside Valletta, but a number of the people I have spoken to about the war comment on how difficult it is to grieve when the fate of a loved one is not known. 'Missing, presumed dead,' is the worst epitaph possible.

The events in Italy also occurred pretty much as described. The Blue Brigade is based on the *Stella Rossa*, a partisan brigade operating very successfully in the mountains south of Bologna during the spring and summer of 1944. I have changed all the names because a number of the partisans are still alive, including Gianni Rossi, the second-in-command of the brigade; also I wanted to make it clear that while the book closely follows real events, it is fiction rather than fact. Not that I have been subtle: the real Monte Luna is called Monte Sole; Capriglia is Casaglia; Veggio is Vado; Mazzola is Marzabotto; Sant'Angelo is San Martino. The leader of the *Stella Rossa* was not La Volpe, but *Il Lupo*, although the real *Lupo* was just as charismatic. The problems faced by the *contadini* and the partisans were largely as described, as were many of the battles and incidents. For example, Gianni Rossi still has a scar on his forehead from where he was attacked by the spy Amedeo Arcioni (on which the attack by Pepe was based), and he was involved with capturing the details of the German fortifications along the Gothic Line. There was also a Scottish ex-POW who fought with the *Stella Rossa* – he was madly in love with Volpe's sister.

Tragically, the *rastrellamento* is also based on a real event. The description of the massacre at the cemetery came from an interview I had with Cornelia Paselli, who lost her mother and brother and sister in the attack. She survived because she was knocked unconscious from the blast of a grenade thrown before the machine-gunning began. Like Christina, she waited under a pile of bodies for over seven hours before making her escape. Like Christina, her magnanimity was truly astounding. Another person I interviewed, who had watched nine members of his family be executed, showed astonishing forgiveness. Francesco Pirini had been a teenager at the time, but a few years ago a film crew tried to arrange a meeting between him and one of the officers from the 16th SS Panzer Grenadier Division, which carried out the massacre. It came to nothing, but he assured me that had they met, he would have shaken his hand willingly. Not all survivors were quite so generous, but their reactions showed that there were different ways of coping and coming to terms with such an appalling tragedy.

Eighteen hundred people were killed during three days, and the shadow of death does still hang over the ruined mountain villages of Monte Sole. Today, it is a beautiful but eerie place. Wreaths are also regularly placed in the cemetery and at other sites where the massacre took place.

Unfortunately, these terrible events were played out elsewhere in Italy: in Rome, in Sant'Anna, in Varreggio; there were over 700 separate civilian massacres carried out on Field Marshal Kesselring's direct orders, many more than in France. (There were also many more partisans operating in Italy than there were *maquis* in France.) The worst, like those on Monte Sole, were carried out under the direction of SS Major Walter Reder. After the war he was tried for war crimes and imprisoned for life by the Italians. Some years later he appealed, but the survivors overwhelmingly rejected his appeal.

Field Marshal Kesselring was tried as a war criminal at Nuremberg. He was sentenced to death but this was commuted to life imprisonment. He was, however, released in 1952 and died eight years later. In other words, he got off.

I have drawn on interviews and conversations with a number of people for this book, but would particularly like to thank the following: Ken Neill, DFC; Wing Commander Tom Neil, DFC and Bar, AFC, AE; Squadron Leader Geoff Wellum, DFC; Captain Tommy Thompson, DFC; Captain Tubby Crawford, DSC; Art Roscoe, DFC; Ray Ellis; Hector Benassi; Cornelia Paselli; Gianni Rossi; Gastone Sgargi; Carlo Venturi; and Francesco Pirini. In Malta the advice and knowledge of Frederick Galea, John Agius and Ray Polidano in particular, have been much appreciated. In Italy, I am also grateful to Anna Salerno at the Consorzio Di Gestione Parco Storico Di Monte Sole in Marzabotto. I have relied on a number of books but should give especially credit to the following: *Fighter Squadron* by Wing Commander Dizzy Allen, *Silence on Monte Sole* by Jack Olsen, *Carlino* by Stuart Hood, *Rossano* by Gordon Lett, and *Love and War in the Apennines* by Eric Newby.

I would also like to especially thank Zoë Thomas for allowing me to draw on her uncle's letters and papers.

Grateful thanks to the following: Giles Bourne; Lalla Hitchings; Julia Waley; David Walsh; Patrick Walsh and everyone at Conville & Walsh; Susan Sandon, Georgina Hawtrey-Woore, Ron Beard, Emily Cullum and everyone at Heinemann and Arrow; my father, Martin Holland; and, most especially, to Rachel and Ned.

ALSO AVAILABLE IN ARROW

The Burning Blue

James Holland

Joss Lambert has always been a loner, constrained by a secret from his past, until he finds friendship and solace firstly with Guy Liddell, a friend from school, and then with Guy's family, who welcome him into their farmhouse home. Joss increasingly comes to depend upon the Liddells and treats Alvesdon Farm as the one place where he feels not only appreciated but also truly happy.

The idyll cannot last. With war looming, Joss is forced to confront the past. He escapes through flying, becoming a fighter pilot in the RAF. But with the onset of war, even the Liddells's world is crumbling. As Joss is fighting for his life in the Battle of Britain, so he begins to fall madly in love with Stella – Guy's twin – but with tragic consequences.

Leaving England and the Liddells far behind, he continues to fly amid the sand and heat of North Africa, until his hopes and dreams are seemingly shattered for good . . .

'Holland skilfully turns the screw of tension as the last months of peace slip away . . . He has joined the few who can bring history to life' *Guardian*

'This beautifully written book is a work of exceptional authenticity' Geoffrey Wellum, former Battle of Britain pilot and author of *First Light*

arrow books